S0-AAI-267

The

Splendor

of Light

A Novel

Vernon Sanders

Author of *When a Sparrow Falls*

iUniverse, Inc.
Bloomington

The Splendor of Light
A Novel

Copyright © 2011 Vernon Sanders

All rights reserved. No part of this book may be used or reproduced by any means, graphic, electronic, or mechanical, including photocopying, recording, taping or by any information storage retrieval system without the written permission of the publisher except in the case of brief quotations embodied in critical articles and reviews.

This is a work of fiction. All of the characters, names, incidents, organizations, and dialogue in this novel are either the products of the author's imagination or are used fictitiously.

iUniverse books may be ordered through booksellers or by contacting:

iUniverse
1663 Liberty Drive
Bloomington, IN 47403
www.iuniverse.com
1-800-Authors (1-800-288-4677)

Because of the dynamic nature of the Internet, any Web addresses or links contained in this book may have changed since publication and may no longer be valid. The views expressed in this work are solely those of the author and do not necessarily reflect the views of the publisher, and the publisher hereby disclaims any responsibility for them.

Any people depicted in stock imagery provided by Thinkstock are models, and such images are being used for illustrative purposes only.

Certain stock imagery © Thinkstock.

ISBN: 978-1-4502-8114-0 (DJ)
ISBN: 978-1-4502-8112-6 (SC)
ISBN: 978-1-4502-8113-3 (ebook)

Printed in the United States of America

iUniverse rev. date: 3/1/2011

Other Books by Vernon Sanders

Poetry: This Small Ship, This Great Sea
        Beyond the Mist and the Mountains
        The Shadow of a Passing Cloud
        Whispers in the Wind
        The Glow of Ashes

Biography: To Chase the Sun

Fiction: When a Sparrow Falls

DEDICATED

To my Mother and Father

My bright and shining lights

The good man walks along in the ever-brightening light of God's favor; the dawn gives way to morning splendor, while the evil man gropes and stumbles in the dark.

King Solomon

ACKNOWLEDGEMENTS

I wish to thank the following for their
meaningful contributions:

Betty Mullenix and Betty Jane Robinson, who read the first draft
and offered their support and helpful suggestions.

Ralph Roughton, a psychoanalysis and Duke classmate, who
remains my literary sounding board.

Thomas L. Jones, whose treatise on Carlos Marcello, head of the
Louisiana Mafia, served as the primary resource for the life and
times of Tony Caruso.

George Pierce, Bill Floyd and Tom Elliot, men of faith and Christian
commitment, inspired the life of Hal Brady.

Dale Thompson, whose computer savvy, salvaged lost chapters.

A special thanks to Sally Brady, my esteemed editor (and mentor),
whose sharp eye and constructive comments were invaluable. I am
deeply grateful for her skillful guidance.

FOREWORD

Mid-century. A time of transition. Man had reeled for more than a decade beneath the devastating weight of war. A terrible sadness was etched indelibly like a birthmark upon countless shattered spirits. The memories, some of nightmarish proportions, remained and lingered like the haunting strains of a requiem. And in the silent, groping darkness, there was the gnawing fear of history replicating itself even amid man's frantic search for his own redemption. At the same time, an ecumenical cry for deliverance was heard around the world. Altruism reappeared; a fervent period of readjustment and restoration; a bold commitment to human dignity and the universal ideal. Days of glad relief, born of hope, stained by grief and bittersweet tears, buoyed by dreams of grandeur.

Prologue

The beach was tempting. Lots of girls in bikinis, soaking up the sun, partying late into the night. But Dick Frey and Andy Lebauer, pre-med students at Tulane, drove home for spring break. Graduation, with honors, two months away. On the drive to Conway, they talked about medical school and the uncertainty that awaited them. The boys wondered where their career-choice would lead them. Friends since the first grade, would their paths divide? Would one or both of them return to Conway? Dick and Andy could only shrug; they had no crystal ball. But of this they were sure, their most cherished boyhood dreams would soon come true.

Dick had just finished supper when he heard the horn out front. "Gotta go, Mom." He pushed the chair away from the table.

"Where're you boys off to this time?" his mother asked.

"Ruston, to catch a movie. Andy's got a hot date, and I get her best friend. Probably a string bean with a face that only a mother could love."

"Now Richard, be nice." (His mother always used his Christian name when issuing a reprimand or giving him advice.) "And be careful. Sometimes Andy forgets that a two lane highway is not the Indy 500."

Dick kissed her on the cheek and headed out the door. He heard the music blaring from the Chevy speakers before he cleared the porch.

Andy's left arm rested on the open window, his cigarette glowing in the dark. "What kept you?" he shouted, turning the volume down.

Dick looked at the clock on the dashboard. "You're ten minutes early. What's the rush?"

Andy tossed his cigarette and turned the ignition. "Always arrive a little early. It makes a good impression."

"Says who?"

"Says me." Andy elbowed his friend and laughed. "Of course, the girls won't be ready so they'll apologize and presto—we already have an advantage."

"I'm honored to ride with the authority on the art of dating," Dick snickered. "By the way, what's the name of Jenny's friend?"

"Katie—and according to my sources, a knockout."

"Unlike your last set up," Dick reminded him. "You still owe me for that one."

The boys crossed the Ouachita River into West Conway as twilight settled softly over the town. Gunmetal clouds billowed in from the west and a stiff March wind lashed the barren trees, carrying with it the scent of a looming storm. Both rolled up their windows.

Just beyond the bridge stood three taverns, popular with truckers and the local mill workers: The Shamrock Bar and Grill, Arnie's Alehouse, and across the road, Mario's, nestled in a stand of short-leaf pine. Their garish neon signs flashed eerie reflections on the surface of the river.

To Andy and Dick, the bars were part of the landscape, but some of the locals, especially those who wanted a dry parish, thought they were a blight on the town.

Even at Tulane, the boys had heard the gossip; a police car with its spinning light bars parked in front of the Shamrock or Arnie's on any given night, resulting in an arrest for disorderly conduct, even assault and battery. Rumors of illegal activity, including bookmaking and prostitution, floated down Main Street, into quiet tree-lined neighborhoods.

The boys crossed the bridge, when a Ford pickup, without lights, pulled out of the parking lot in front of the Shamrock, made a wide right hand turn, and looped into the far lane. Andy veered fast, but too late. The cab of the truck slammed the Malibu across the pavement and down a grassy slope, rolling over and landing on its roof in a shallow swale.

People ran from the taverns when they heard the collision and a crowd had gathered by the time an ambulance from Nabors' Funeral Home arrived. A Sheriff's Deputy, his siren blaring, skidded to a stop in the loose gravel on the shoulder of the road. The Deputy ran down the embankment; Dick had been thrown from the car. He was unconscious but his pulse was strong and regular. Not so Andy, pinned in the driver's seat, compressed by the dented roof. The door had jammed and no one could free him until a wrecker righted the car. While the Deputy called for help, Johnny Nabors knelt down next to Andy's window. Lightning streaked overhead and a cold rain began to fall. He reached through the broken glass and checked the pulse in the boy's neck. Fearful, he checked again. There was none. Johnny stood up and leaned on the overturned car, letting his tears mingle with the rain.

Chapter 1

Friday, March 10th

A flock of crows, black as soot, sailed ghost-like through a graying sky. The sun had slipped behind a distant tree line, casting long shadows across fields of fledgling plants. A chorus of crickets welcomed the darkness with evensong and cicadas chirped in shrill counterpoint.

Ben leaned against a large column and looked wistfully at the vast expanse of farmland; rich black soil, germinating the seed. Even as a child, he'd known that Madison Parish was cotton country and ten thousand acres belonged to Jacob Hamilton and his father before him. The elder Hamilton had left the Eastern shore of North Carolina before the Civil War, survived the hardships and dangers of an arduous journey, and dug his roots into the rank earth of the Delta.

Later, Ben learned the real reason his grandfather settled in Conway, once an old fort and trading post. He valued the river that flowed past the town; for its barges laden with cotton and produce and lumber, steaming south to the port in New Orleans; for the riverboats trailing black steam, paddle wheels churning the murky waters, bringing news and mail and passengers from distant places.

Ben turned to admire his stately antebellum house with its high ceilings and solid oak floors; walls of solid brick, stuccoed to give the appearance of stone and painted a pale yellow. The slate roof with dormer windows was crowned with a glass belvedere, a reminder of the Carolina coast.

Surrounded by giant magnolias and ancient oaks, the house sat majestically on a rise between Willow Road and the river. Ben could smell the sweet fragrance of jasmine and flowering quince rising from the early spring gardens.

He crossed the circular driveway and headed for his favorite tree, a towering sycamore, where as a boy he'd spent long hours among its sturdy branches. A bifurcation, halfway up, became his sanctuary following his mother's death. Ben was only twelve years old when Martha Hamilton developed lobar pneumonia with complications. He had vivid memories of those last days; the flush of fever, her racking cough, old Dr. Stafford nervously mopping his brow, an elixir that smelled of wintergreen. Her death left Ben despairing, and for weeks he cried himself to sleep.

Ben still believed it was his mother's illness that shaped his future; a decision made near the top of the sycamore tree. He shuddered when he remembered his father's heated reaction; an only child—the last in the Hamilton line—abrogating his sacred birthright. Despite the bitter protests, Ben kept the promise he'd made to his mother...and to himself.

He was grateful she had encouraged him to be a good Samaritan, imbuing concern for the less fortunate; giving something back were the words she used—matters of no moment to his father. Ben could still recite the Browning poem his mother framed and hung above his desk.

> Round the cape of a sudden came the sea,
> And the sun look'd over the mountain's rim:
> And straight was the path of gold for him,
> And the need of a world of men for me.

Nostalgia swept over him as if carried by the brisk March wind. He conjured her image out of the darkness; soft-hands, easy smile; her eyes the color of turquoise, ash-blond hair which fell below her shoulders. His shaving mirror was a reminder: he had inherited the symmetry of her face, the blond hair and fair complexion of her Swedish ancestry. While he looked nothing like his father, he possessed the rough edges and mulishness of a Hamilton. How often he'd wished for his mother's affectionate nature and her gentle ways. Even as a teenager, he had measured his parents—so different—and wondered about the forces that had drawn them together.

"Ben! Ben, are you there?"

He saw Knox in the lighted doorway. "I'm here..."

"The guests will be arriving soon."

Ben tossed his cigarette and walked slowly toward the house. Over his shoulder he caught headlights turning into the driveway. In the distance, a barn owl screeched his defiance, an unsettling cry that pierced the darkness.

☙

Adam, detained at the hospital, was late for the party. Knox greeted him in the foyer and brushed his cheek with a kiss.

She took his hand and led him to the edge of the crowd. Adam surveyed the living room. "Looks like half the town is here. Guess I'd better put on my party face and join in."

He felt her gently nudge.

Maude Harrington, shoulders bent, stood near the marble fireplace nursing a glass of wine. She was one of Adam's favorite people, full of sparkling wit and southern charm.

They had met during his first week in Conway. Maude had come to his office with a minor complaint which he believed was pretense for a get-acquainted visit. There he learned she had lived alone since the death of Ed Harrington ended a childless marriage. Looking for a constructive interest, she began the local newsletter, which later expanded, at the insistence of the business community, into a weekly newspaper with parish-wide appeal.

Adam chuckled at her admission: the weekly was more gossip than news. Marriage announcements, obituaries, and the weekly calendar of the local churches were front page material. The political climate in the nation's capital and important international events were relegated to an inside page under a column entitled, "Other News, Other Places."

He had read Maude's editorials, highlighting the back page... subjects ranging from regional politics to church picnics. Adam admired her candor, speaking straight from the heart. In his opinion, *The Review* reflected her wholesome sense of humor and the transparency of her Protestant conscience.

She greeted him with a hug, then pushed him away while still holding his hands, and looked him over as a mother might inspect a son who had just returned from a long journey. "You look tired," she said.

"Well, there've been some long hours..." Adam explained: The town was full of the flu. Some folks were real sick. Others were just running scared. A cough or a sneeze had them calling for a prescription or coming into the office for reassurance.

She understood and patted his hand. "Have you considered adding on?"

"You mean another doctor?"

"It would free up some time for your family." Maude picked up her glass which she had placed on the mantelpiece. "You and Allison could spend a few days in the mountains. I have a cottage with a glorious view and the dogwood and rhododendron will soon be in full bloom. You're welcome anytime." She hesitated, her shoulders sagged. "The vicissitudes of old age prevent me from using the cottage. Probably should sell the damn place."

Maude's salty tongue made Adam smile. "Thanks for the offer. I'd love to find the time."

She took a sip of wine and winked. "The nectar of the gods."

"Sorry I can't join you. But being on-call, well..."

"You should have gone to law school or sold real estate like the dubious Mr. Warren standing over by the piano chewing on that disgusting cigar. You could have made some real money and had the time to go deep-sea fishing in the Gulf or cruise the Caribbean during our wretched winter weather. And...you could share a glass of vino with me." Maude held up her glass which sparkled with light from the crystal chandelier. "But I guess it's too late for a career change," she said with a smile that stretched the wrinkles across her wizened face.

"'fraid so. But no regrets...at least not so far."

Maude tugged at his coat sleeve with her free hand. "Before you get away, tell me about the Frey boy? Is he gonna survive?"

Adam rocked his hand. "We're hopeful."

"My cross-the-street neighbor, a nurse in ICU, told me the poor child is paralyzed."

"When Dick was thrown from the car, he fractured two cervical vertebrae." Adam stopped and pointed to the back of his neck. "The spinal cord was compressed and will require surgery. You know Elmo Thornton, the neurosurgeon?"

Maude nodded.

"Well, he's pretty much running the show."

"He's got the personality of a toadstool but I hear he's very good at what he does."

"One of the best," Adam said. "He'll go in and decompress the cervical spine. May need a bone graft to stabilize the segment. Recovery depends on the amount of damage that the cord has sustained and the regenerative potential of the patient. At best, it will be a very long and difficult period of rehabilitation...with no guarantees."

"Such a shame," she lamented. "Two young men with the world by the tail; now one lies in repose at Nabors' funeral home and the other may be a cripple for life." Maude's chin quivered as she looked toward the ceiling. "Dammit, why not me, dear God? Or some other old buzzard?" She sighed deeply. "But I learned a long time ago there are no easy answers...life's simply not fair."

Adam took his handkerchief and gently wiped the tears that trickled down Maude's cheeks. "I went by and spoke to Andy's mother this morning."

"She must be devastated."

"And she has to handle her grief alone." Adam stuffed the handkerchief in his coat pocket. "You may remember her husband, Clarence...died two years ago."

"Heart trouble if my memory hasn't completely failed."

Adam nodded agreement. "Died in his sleep."

"The poor woman...I hope someone called the preacher."

"Hal Brady went by this afternoon. And her daughter who lives up East—somewhere in New Jersey—will be here in the morning."

During their first meeting, Adam also learned Maude had experienced her own share of adversity, not the least of which was the loss of Ed Harrington after twenty years of marriage—the only man she ever loved. Then there was the successful battle with breast cancer and adjusting to the disfigurement of a radical mastectomy. He knew she had come to terms with pain and suffering, those jet-black threads woven inextricably into the vital fabric of Everyman's life.

Maude and Adam agreed the recent tragedy was not bad karma or the fatalism of John Calvin. And certainly not, as the Baptist preacher insisted, God's will. They also agreed the accident, involving Andy Lebauer and Dick Frey, had nothing to do with luck or the "turn of a card." Rather everyone was bound to a world of natural laws...laws that were unassailable, immutable.

Maude took a sip of wine and dabbed her lips with the napkin. "You know Adam, Conway would be a better place if we could ride Markham and Dempsey and that Italian...what's his name?... out of town and close those saloons. I really mean it. They're contaminating the whole parish like the plague. And two young men named Dick Frey and Andy Lebauer would still be whole were it not for those sleazy dives."

"You have my vote, but..."

"But what?"

"How do you shut them down?" he asked. "It may be impossible."

Maude's eyes narrowed. "Nothing is impossible."

"What about the newspaper?"

"Not enough ammunition. I could rattle their cages but it would only be an irritant, not a solution."

Adam looked around and then pointed toward the Steinway in the far corner of the room. "Maybe you should start with him. He holds the lease on all that property."

"Fred Warren," she sneered. "You gotta be kidding. I'd get more satisfaction by talking to that painting." She pointed to the Monet print in a gold frame above the fireplace.

"If you decide to pursue this further, I'll listen."

Maude drained her glass of wine. "Stop by for coffee and let's talk more about how to legally move those hell-holes out of the parish."

"If you'll sweeten the invitation with a slice of homemade pound cake," Adam said with a boyish grin.

Maude crossed her heart. "It's a deal."

Adam surveyed the smoke-filled room. "I better find Allison. She's here somewhere."

"Just look for the most beautiful woman in the house." Maude patted his cheek lightly. "You're a lucky guy."

"I am...I'm a lucky guy."

"Stop by for that pound cake...soon."

Adam gave her a hug and disappeared into the chattering crowd.

გუ

Adam spotted Allison across the room talking with the Mayor's wife. He changed his mind and headed for the stairs. The door to Jake's bedroom was open. His eyes swept the room, dim-lit by a table lamp next to a vacant recliner. A hospital bed lined a side wall, its covers unruffled.

Adam decided Jake must be on the porch and retraced his steps down the hall to the French doors that opened onto the upstairs gallery. Jake sat in his wheelchair staring impassively into the darkness. The night sky was star-flecked; moonlight shimmered on the surface of the river.

"Hi, Jake." Adam leaned against the cypress railing. He could see the old man's silhouette back-lighted through the bedroom window.

Adam had examined Jake Hamilton a few days ago. At the time, nothing had changed. While Jake had recovered some use of his left side, the stroke left other impairments, as if a monstrous wave of debility washed over him, leaving him forgetful and in a general state of regression. In Adams eyes, Jake had aged greatly since the embolic event ten months ago. A once vigorous Jacob Hamilton, the wealthiest man in Madison Parish, had withered into a shell of a man, flesh sagging from his arms and beneath his chin. And Adam was sure that without Knox's constant care and vigilance, Jake would not have survived.

"You're a hard man to find. Hope nothing's wrong."

The old man rubbed a bony hand across a few strands of gray hair. "Not up to partying," he said, almost a whisper. "At my age, I'll settle for a little brandy, a cool breeze and this old wheelchair."

He banged the arm of the chair with his fist. "A real hell-raising evening."

Adam laughed, half-amused, half obligatory. "How much land is out there?" he asked, pointing toward the river.

"More'n ten thousand acres."

Adam whistled softly. "That's a lot of cotton." He looked at Jake and thought a faint smile had gathered at the sunken corners of his mouth. "Tell me about Ezra."

Jake shuffled his feet and moved the wheelchair closer as though energized by his father's name. "He was a good soldier."

"I've heard stories..."

"One of the few survivors of the Battle of Franklin. After the war, he came home to North Carolina and married Anna Boswell, his childhood sweetheart. Together, they traveled south, settled here, built this house."

Adam knew that remote memory often survived the ravages of dementia. Still, the clarity of Jake's report surprised him.

"A legacy to be proud of," Adam said.

The old man nodded. "Ezra gave me the land and it's been a blessing. But Ben had other ideas...broke my heart." His head dropped against his chest.

"Well, I'd better go find Allison."

The old man did not answer. He had retreated into his own silent world.

Adam took Jake's hand; it was stiff and skeletal and had lost its strength. He looked at the cadaverous old man, doubtful he could survive another insult. Adam patted Jake's shoulder and turned to leave.

He found Allison waiting at the foot of the stairs. "How's Jake?"

Adam took her arm and led her outside. "He has some lucid moments..."

"But it's only a matter of time?"

"Afraid so." Adam opened her car door. "I'll follow you home."

Chapter 2

Like other towns scattered across North Louisiana, most of Conway's population came from sturdy Protestant stock. Some of Irish descent were proselytized by persuasive Evangelical voices, others by marriage. A remnant remained; vibrant enough to build a small Catholic Church and parochial school next to the post office.

The town's politics, inured by long years of an oppressive family dynasty, were conservative and provincial; in a sense, a microcosm of the Deep South. However, a fervent spirit of patriotism, rekindled by World War II, permeated the region even though it was far removed geographically from the national centers of commerce and political power.

The radio and the Sunday edition of the New Orleans' *Times Picayune* were its major links to the world beyond the parish line. Although news traveled slowly in and out of Conway, a sense of apprehension had settled over the town like ominous storm clouds, as the thunder of guns rumbled out of the Far East and the country trembled once more on the threshold of another turbulent conflict.

The parish, its population shrinking, had felt the impact of the South in transition as scores of young people left for college, joined the military or moved to urban areas in search of better jobs and "bright light" excitement. Despite the shift in demographics, Conway hummed with activity; busy river and rail traffic; the center for banking and commerce, serving Madison and adjoining parishes.

℘

Adam, born and raised in New Orleans, was an exception. After completing a year's residence at Tulane's Medical Center, he spent the war years at Walter Reed Hospital in the nation's capital. Before discharge, he received a call from Ben Hamilton, a Tulane classmate, with an invitation to join his family practice in Conway. It had been a difficult decision, he remembered, as he drove slowly home along the town's deserted streets. Although he had hoped to complete his training program, Ben's offer was too attractive to refuse. After all, he had the responsibilities of a family and Allison had sacrificed enough.

It also provided Adam with an important insight: timing and circumstance could alter some of life's most pivotal decisions. The journey was not a straight line from point A to point B, rather there were crossroads and frequent divides. Adam knew a decision could lead in an unexpected direction; a course, which in his case, dramatically changed his life and that of his family. He had hoped for a suburban practice near a metropolitan center like New Orleans or Houston which afforded the cultural and medical amenities of a large city. Adam, even in moments of whimsy, never considered a town the size of Conway (population: 22,000) where the most popular restaurants featured fried catfish, hush puppies and black-eyed peas. After days of deliberation and with Allison's approval, he made the decision.

It was after eight o'clock when he pulled his car into the detached garage, connected to the main house by a latticed archway covered with ivy. Adam shivered in the night's chill and dug his hands into the warm pockets of his coat as he hurried along the brick walkway to the side-entrance of his two-story Colonial.

As he opened the door, a gleeful voice greeted him. "Daddy, Daddy." And two small arms reached up and encircled his neck as he bent down to lift her up. "Daddy, I've got something to show you. I thought you'd never get home."

"Well, it must be special to rate such a big hug," he said, bouncing her playfully in his arms.

"It is," she squealed with excitement. "Let me down so I can show you."

He dropped Robin lightly to the floor and she scurried away, her blond ponytail bobbing with each step. Adam watched her disappear up the stairs, filled with poignancy, an exceptional love for her, uniquely paternal.

In the kitchen, he found Allison in front of the stove, stirring an iron pot of homemade vegetable soup. "Something sure smells good," he said, pulling her hair aside so his lips could explore the back of her neck. "Guess what...I made the right decision when I married you."

"Well, I'm glad you haven't changed your mind." She glanced over her shoulder and smiled demurely. "Would you like a drink?"

"No thanks. I'm on call."

"But you took call last night," she protested.

"Yeah, I know, but Ben and Knox got a last minute invitation from some old friends in Pine Grove. They're having dinner together at Hank's Steak House...a new restaurant on the river."

There was a stirring in the family room. "Close your eyes, Daddy. Here we come."

"What's all the mystery?"

"Wait and see," Allison said sheepishly.

Robin came through the swinging door backwards with her "surprise" cuddled in her arms. "Now open your eyes." She looked up, her face shining with angelic delight. "Isn't he beautiful?"

In her outstretched arms, was a black ball of fur with sad, umber eyes, only half-open. Adam took the puppy and held him quivering against his chest. "What's his name?"

"Do you know one?"

"Well, let's see." He squinted at the ceiling and pondered the question. "What about Charlie? I once had a dog with that name."

Robin giggled. "Charlie—I like that. But I'd better put him to bed." She took the pup, cuddling him, and backed out through the kitchen door.

"Where did Charlie come from?"

"Charlotte Payne."

"The Mayor's wife?" Adam showed mock surprise.

"We ran into Charlotte at Safeway. She mentioned her dachshund had had a litter of pups. And would we like one? Well, Robin was so excited I couldn't say no." Allison hesitated for a second and gave him the look of a supplicant. "It's all right with you...isn't it?"

"Sure, but spare me the housebreaking chores."

"If it gives Robin pleasure, it's worth the trouble." She poured the iced tea and dropped in a fresh sprig of green mint. "You'd better wash up. Dinner is almost ready."

ↄ

While Allison cleared the table, Adam leaned back in his recliner, the medical journal in his lap. The evening meal had lulled him into a pleasant reverie and his mind spooled back through the years to their first meeting.

A fourth year medical student, he wandered into the pediatric ward to see the Christmas decorations. She, in her pink smock, was a volunteer from Sophie Newcomb who on Friday afternoons spent time with the children. Adam stopped at the nurse's station and stared at this beautiful young woman with the violet-blue eyes. She looked up from the play table and gave him a cordial smile. Those magical moments emboldened him to ask her name, and then invite her for coffee. From that cold gray December afternoon, they became inseparable. Even though the chance meeting had occurred ten years ago, the memories of those halcyon days were still acute and filled him with recurring pleasure.

Allison poured two cups of coffee and carried them into the den. "You look tired. Why don't you go to bed?" She knew that fatigue always settled first in dark circles around his eyes.

Adam moved up to the front of his recliner, held his cup in one hand and wearily rubbed his eyes with the other. "I want to do the right thing."

"About?" She placed her mug on the broad arm of her chair and pulled her legs beneath her.

He related his conversation with Maude Harrington the night of Ben's party. "Maude can become quixotic if she feels strongly about a worthy cause. In this case, it's the taverns across the river."

"What about them?"

"Maude believes they are a scourge on the parish and the tragic accident last week was the catalyst that got her wheels turning."

"Why does that trouble you?"

Their eyes met. "She wants me to join her crusade, come by and talk."

"Once there, she'll give you a dozen reasons to enlist." Allison leaned across the chair and mimicked Maude's appeal. 'Here's your commitment card...please sign right here.' Lo and behold... you're a charter member."

"That's why I'm reticent." His face clouded, a troubled look. "Should I get involved? Do I have time to tilt at windmills? What are the risks of taking on a potentially dangerous opponent? Those are the questions I'm wrestling with."

She reached over and took his hand. "It's your decision, but I'm in your corner, either way."

"I guess there're lots of reasons to stand on the sidelines, rationalizations really, but how often do we have a chance to make Conway a better place? After all, we have a daughter to consider. What kind of town do we want for Robin?" He gently squeezed her hand. "Maybe one shouldn't pass up the chance to make a difference."

"Would you like my advice?" she asked.

"Sure."

"Talk to Maude; hear her out. Is she serious or is it just an emotional response to Andy Lebauer's death. Find out what she has in mind for you. Who else does she want to enlist...that sorta thing? Then you can make a more informed decision."

"Thanks." Adam stood up and lifted Allison out of the chair. He held her close and kissed her tenderly.

She slipped out of his arms and went into the kitchen to answer the phone. Adam moved over to the window and stared at the night shadows; the pecan tree, a dim silhouette beneath the light of a yellow moon.

Adam's Family Practice allowed him to make a difference, but at a very personal level—one on one. Maude's idea, if it were more than a whim, could literally change a panoramic landscape, one that affected the lives of everyone in Madison Parish and beyond.

He turned from the window when he heard Allison come back in.

"That was Charlotte," she said.

"I hope she doesn't want Charlie back."

"No, she just called to thank me for taking him off her hands." Allison threw out her chest and lowered her voice in imitation. "I'm so pleased that he's found a good home."

"Then we should be honored to have Charlie?"

"Something like that." Her smile was irrepressible.

Allison replaced the coffee pot on the stove and returned to her chair. But her expression had changed, worry lines around her eyes. "Did you say that Knox and Ben went to dinner with the Carltons?"

Adam nodded. "He's a surgeon in Pine Grove. Why'd you ask?"

"Oh, just a little surprised. I'm sure Knox is in seventh heaven, spending one whole evening with Ben."

"What's that suppose to mean?"

She looked down at the floor, a little embarrassed. "You know how I hate gossipy women—but I wonder about those two."

"Is there a problem?"

"I'm not sure. But Ben works long hours, almost never home, while Knox cares for Jake and keeps that big house in order. He spends his free time hunting and fishing while she stays with that cantankerous old man. I just wonder how a marriage can thrive under those conditions."

Adam heard her sigh. "There's something else, something you're holding back."

She lowered her eyes again, her cheeks colored like a bashful schoolgirl.

"C'mon, tell me."

"It's probably nothing," she said diffidently. "Last night at the party, I sneaked out on the deck...to get some fresh air. They were standing in the shadows of the arbor."

"Who was standing in..."

"Knox and Brett Shelly." She spit it out like a dose of bad medicine.

"Aah!" he exclaimed lightly. "And what were they doing?"

"Talking, I guess. And you can tease if you like, but it gave me a very strange feeling...call it a woman's intuition."

"Knox may have taken him some refreshments. Brett's a first-rate foreman and 'a loner.'"

"You're probably right," she said, slipping out of her chair. "But—she added for emphasis—Brett Shelly is an attractive man."

Adam stretched his arms above his shoulders and yawned. "Sleepy..."

"I'll check on Robin and turn our bed down."

"Don't worry. Ben still cares about his marriage."

The hollow words trailed her up the stairs.

Chapter 3

Saturday, March 25ᵗʰ

The Shamrock was rectangular-shaped with a high ceiling and exposed wooden beams. Easy-to-clean, non-descript linoleum covered the floor of pine-planks. A western-style bar ran the width of the far wall and small tables and straight-back chairs crowded the raucous, smoke-filled room. Someone dropped a quarter in the jukebox but the noise level and the poor acoustics smothered the smooth country sound of Red Foley's "Chattanoogie Shoeshine Boy."

Frank Markham stood behind the bar and surveyed the room. It was a typical Saturday night at the Shamrock. The room rocked with boisterous laughter, glass breaking, chairs scraping linoleum. Beer and bourbon flowed. Every bar stool was taken and an empty table was hard to find. The waitresses were young and friendly—a signature of The Shamrock—moving around the room like sirens, taking orders with ingratiating smiles. Cut-off jeans—very short, high on the thigh—and skin-tight T-shirts with a bright green shamrock imprinted on the front had tantalizing appeal for most of the customers: hot-blooded, blue collar, white males. A tease or a touch or a whisper in the ear by one of Markham's maidens was good for business and expanded the "tip pool."

Markham owned the most popular beer joint on Highway 23, a paved two-lane that stretched from Memphis to Grand Isle, south of New Orleans. Unlike Arnie's Ale House, he never watered down the booze and managed to hire the best short-order cook in the parish. And the Shamrock was the only tavern without a bouncer; Markham handled that role himself and with relish.

Frank Markham knew Conway like the back of his hand. He was born and raised on the south side of town, a section populated by white, low income families. He was only twelve when his father died of a stroke—a ruptured berry aneurysm. Markham almost choked on resentment when his mother married Roy Hardeman, a supervisor at the mill and a lay preacher in the Baptist Church. Shortly after Mr. Hardeman moved in, his home was filled with religious artifacts; grace, which sounded more like a sermonette, was said before every meal and there were lengthy lectures on the "wages of sin" and "the fires of eternal damnation." A strict curfew was imposed. A code of conduct was spelled out and posted on the door of the fridge and on the corkboard above Frank's desk. Like most teenagers, he resented harsh rules, especially imposed by a stranger who had invaded his space. Rebellious by nature, Frank resisted his stepfather's changes which made for an uneasy, even hostile environment. His mother always seemed to side with her husband and Frank grew increasingly angry. One spring day, after his eleventh grade history class, he went home, packed a bag, and took a Greyhound to New Orleans. Before leaving, he pinned a note to his pillow: *Hardeman: take your fucking rules and sanctimonious blabbering and "stuff it." Mother: While we were never close, I hope that without me, you'll find peace and will smile again. Don't worry; I can take care of myself...Frank*

Fifteen years later another Greyhound bus rolled into Conway. Markham stepped onto the familiar sidewalk with a duffel bag, a dishonorable discharge from the Army and a pocketful of money. No one in town had the details, nor did they dare ask. Only speculation, sheltered in shadows.

Shortly after arriving in Conway, he negotiated a lease with Fred Warren, funded new construction with his own resources and in less than a year The Shamrock was up and running. The first order of business was a letter of understanding signed by Arnie Waters and Mario Gambelli. While the three men were fierce competitors, they shared a dormant but formidable adversary: the churches of Conway, and some do-gooders with considerable clout. Therefore, it was in the mutual interest of the tavern owners to maintain an open and civil line of communication.

જી

Markham had gotten his mother's letter. Hardeman retired at the end of the war and the two of them moved to South Florida. They had bought a small, stucco house two blocks from the beach. Easy walking distance. And from the screened front porch they could sit in their high-back rockers and hear the rhythmic sounds of the ocean. They had painted the house a pale green and placed pink flamingos in the front lawn. Frank was sure they had settled in the arms of boredom and languished in their confinement like prison inmates. Markham wondered if he would ever see his mother again.

He put on a clean shirt, tied a white apron around his waist and worked the congested bar. There was always a rowdy crowd on Saturday night, more business than Tex Hawkins, the regular bartender could handle. Markham checked his watch...a little after eight and the place was already bustling.

"Hey, Tex, who's the woman?" Markham asked during a breather.

"Which one?"

He pointed in the direction of the juke box. "That table...over there. She's sitting with that deadbeat, Ed Bagley."

"Oh, yeah. I've got 'em spotted. Her name is Jamie Patterson. She's the switchboard operator at the mill."

"What's she doing with a slug like Bagley? He looks like a fucking scarecrow."

"Free drinks." Tex shrugged. "What else?"

"She must be desperate...I mean the slacker is just a bag of bones. Turn him sideways and he'd disappear."

Before Tex could reply, there was a disturbance near the front of the tavern, loud enough to be heard above the noise of the crowd. Tom Dolan, a man of considerable size, stumbled through the room, bumping into tables and rattling glasses before he reached the bar and wedged himself between two disgruntled patrons.

"Gimme a bourbon and water...make it a double." His words were slurred but urgent, and he waved a twenty like a distress signal. "Make it quick. I ain't got all night."

Markham sat the drink down and leaned across the counter—almost in Dolan's face. "Settle down or I'll kick your sorry ass out of here. Is that clear?"

"Yeah, sure Frank, whatever." He finished off his drink and picked up his change. "Jamie been 'round?"

Tex pointed to the table near the jukebox.

Dolan turned in a flash and with arms flailing, headed straight for her. Bagley saw him coming and was half-standing when a huge fist caught his jaw and sent him sprawling against the wall like a man-sized rag doll. Jamie backed away frightened, screaming. Bagley struggled to his knees and swiped at the blood streaming from his nose. Before he looked up, Dolan grabbed a chair and sent it crashing against his skull, once, and then again, before Markham and Tex could wrestle him to the floor.

Markham looked at Bagley, sprawled unconscious on the linoleum floor in a pool of blood and noted the shallow breathing. He glanced at Tex and shook his head. "Gotta make a phone call."

Tex straddled Dolan, two truckers pinned his arms.

"You fellas hold him down until the Sheriff arrives."

℀

Adam had just fallen asleep when Allison called from the foot of the stairs. "It's for you. And the operator says it's urgent."

He knocked the small clock off the bedside table as he reached for the phone. "This is Dr. Swift."

"Doc, Frank Markham over at the Shamrock. You'd better get here fast 'cause we've got a helluva problem. There's a fella here that's hurt real bad. Lots of blood."

"Where's it coming from?" Adam asked as he struggled out of bed.

"It's pouring from his nose."

"Don't move him. I'm on my way."

It was a clear night. The chill felt good against Adam's face, washing away the final residue of sleep. Overhead, a March moon, full and luminous, lighted his path beneath the latticed archway. Somewhere down the street, a dog bayed, reminding him of Robin's radiant smile as she held Charlie in her arms.

Adam turned onto Main Street and passed the darkened storefronts as he drove toward the river. From the bridge, he could see the reflection of neon on the water and the revolving light atop Johnny Nabor's ambulance. The night scene was surreal, like something out of Rod Serling. He turned into the lot and parked behind the ambulance.

Sam Gentry, who worked for the funeral home, was there to greet Adam in his usual officious way. He was a big heavyset man who motioned to the crowd outside the entryway. "All right folks, open up and let the doctor through." He spoke with self-appointed authority and used his two hundred and eighty pounds as leverage to get Adam inside the tavern.

The lights were turned up and the crowd, stunned and curious, had backed away from Bagley's body which lay motionless beside the wall. Markham appeared from behind the bar with a stack of white towels. "He's still breathing but he's lost a lot of blood."

Adam knelt down beside the body and observed the steady stream of blood that flowed from the nose and oozed from the right ear, forming a sanguine pool around the man's head. "What's his name?"

"Ed Bagley," said Markham.

"Who?" Adam waved toward the jukebox.

"Tex, shut off that goddamn music." Markham, on one knee, leaned toward Adam. "It's Ed Bagley."

"What happened?"

"Tom Dolan, works at the mill. Went plum crazy when he spotted Bagley with an old girl friend. Busted one of my chairs over Bagley's head before Tex and me could put him down and call the Sheriff."

"Where's Dolan now?" Adam asked.

"Down at the jail."

Adam looked despairingly at the broken body of Ed Bagley, briefly thought of his conversation with Maude Harrington. He did a cursory exam, checking the blood pressure and carotid pulses. He noted the shallow respirations as he pulled a small pin light from his bag and flashed the beam at both pupils. Sluggish, at best. He turned to Sam. "Get him to the E.R. as quick as you can. Tell the nurse to start a bottle of saline with an ampule of Levophed."

"Oxygen?"

"It won't help with all the bleeding from his nose." Adam took one of the towels and draped it beneath Bagley's chin. He closed his black bag and stood up. "And Sam, have them x-ray his skull and type and cross-match six units of blood. Now, get going."

Ed Bagley was lifted onto a stretcher and rolled quickly into the waiting ambulance. "All right, folks," Frank shouted. "The place is closed for the night. There's been 'nough excitement round here already. But ya'll come back Monday night." He looked at Adam and softened his tone. "There's a room in the back if you wanta wash up."

"And I'd like to use your phone."

♥

"I'm sorry, Dr. Swift's not here," she said, half-asleep.

"Allison, wake up. It's Adam and I need your help."

She sat up and turned on the table lamp. "Are you all right?"

"I'm okay, but there was a brawl at the Shamrock, a fella name Ed Bagley...looks critical."

"Who?" She was now fully awake.

"Bagley. His wife's my patient. I need a favor."

"Sure, anything."

"Drive out to the Settlement, break the news to Mrs. Bagley and bring her to the hospital." He took a deep breath and let it out. "I hate to ask but the poor woman has no phone."

"Just give me the address."

He gave her the directions. "And lock your doors."

"I'll bundle up Robin and we'll be there in fifteen minutes... twenty, at most."

♥

The waiting room was austere; furnished with a few straight chairs, a small table littered with magazines, and a faded watercolor of a ship at sea. Edith Bagley was waiting anxiously when Adam walked in.

Slender, just closing in on thirty, she looked much older. Adam saw her tired eyes and shopworn face, lank hair tied loosely in the back with a piece of blue wrapping ribbon. The seams that creased her skin were premature, drawn irreparably, he was sure, by broken dreams and cold despair. The sad expression spoke more loudly than words as tears gathered in her dull gray eyes. "How's he doing, Doc? Is he gonna be all right?"

Adam walked over and placed his arm around her frail shoulders. He considered this a doctor's most difficult assignment and he felt awkward and inadequate in the role of "comforter." He often wondered why a subject of such magnitude had been omitted from his professional training. Was it because those who plan and teach the medical curriculum are, in a sense, far removed from primary patient care, forgetting their oath to support and console the distraught and dying? Or were these skills one cannot acquire in a classroom? Or was it simply an intangible, intrinsic to the human heart? It was a question he'd pondered on more than one occasion.

"It wasn't Ed's fault, Edith. Just at the wrong place at the wrong time." Adam held her hand and let her cry. When the tears stopped, he led her to a straight-back chair.

For a few minutes she sat transfixed, staring at the tile floor; then she looked up with hollow eyes and asked hopefully, "What's his chances, Doc?"

"Not good, I'm afraid." He hesitated and brought his eyes to hers. "You want the truth, don't you?"

Edith nodded.

Adam told her about the fight and the x-rays that showed a skull fracture and bleeding into the brain. "We're giving him medicine in a vein to maintain his blood pressure and stimulate breathing, but he hasn't regained consciousness and, to be truthful, his outlook isn't good."

Her eyes brimmed.

Adam put his hand on her shoulder. "You love him despite all the heartache?"

She dried her eyes with the backs of her hands. "I'm not sure why. But he's the kids' ole man. And sometimes Ed didn't remember he belonged to me." She glanced up and added ruefully, "Who am I trying to fool? He slept with every whore in West Conway. And the whole town knowd it. But, no matter his faults, I still got feeling for him. Do what you can."

A nurse appeared at the door and summoned Adam. He came back with a solemn look and again put an arm around her narrow shoulders. Those moments of silence filled her with its harsh reality. Through her tears she looked up at Adam and knew, drunk or sober, Ed Bagley would never come home again.

Chapter 4

Sunday, March 26th

Adam slept only a few hours. A heavy rain hammered the bedroom windows and awakened him. He dragged himself into the bathroom and splashed his face with cold water. It brought some relief. A shave and a warm shower washed out more of last night's fatigue. He dressed and strolled into the breakfast room taking his place at the table.

"Good morning, Mattie," he said. "Another dreary day." Thunder rumbled in the distance.

"Mawnin'. The Missus gone to fetch some coffee."

Adam counted Mattie among his many blessings. Allison had met her through a neighbor's housekeeper; a stroke of luck. It's amazing, he thought, in four short years she had become indispensable. He watched her pull a red bandana snugly around her neck to catch the sweat that rolled down her several chins.

"I hear ya'll had some 'citement last night," she said with a syncopated drawl. "Ain't nothin' good come out of them places. All that drinkin' and loose livin'…ain't nothin' but the Devil's playground."

"I guess Allison told you about the brawl at the Shamrock last night."

"Sho' did, and one of these days real soon, the Lawd will catch up with them folks. A day of reckonin' gonna come...sho 'nough," she proclaimed, her big eyes flashing with evangelistic fervor.

Adam conceded that Mattie was one of the most outspoken and ardent opponents of sin in the whole town. As far as she was concerned, those saloons were the closest thing to Hell in Madison Parish and the death of Ed Bagley was ammunition for more fiery denouncements.

She laid a plate of fried eggs and sizzling bacon in front of him. "Have you some toast in a minute."

"But that's not all the excitement we've had." Adam caught the vexation out of the corner of his eye. "You've seen the new member of the family?"

Mattie placed both hands on her portly hips and protested loudly. "You'd think I didn't have 'nough to do 'round here, trying to keep this place clean, without trailing after some little hound dog."

Allison came through the back door and placed a small sack on the kitchen counter. "Good morning, everyone. Sorry about the coffee."

Adam stood and kissed her lightly on the cheek as she slipped into a chair and rested her elbows wearily on the table. "Just coffee for me, Mattie. I can't face an egg this morning. I'm afraid the Settlement took my appetite."

Adam spread a thick layer of grape jelly over a piece of crisp toast. "Thanks for your help."

She forced a smile.

"I'm sorry, but you were my only option."

"Well, it worked out okay."

The Settlement's river-shanties, were homes for the homeless; most living on parish welfare, and even though The Mayor of Conway and the City Council had tried to improve the standard of living, their efforts were wasted on indolence and neglect. Adam wondered why the Settlement dwellers languished at the bottom of the food chain. As children, had they been abandoned, uneducated, abused or genetically flawed? Whatever the reason for their poverty, they relied on local government and benevolent charities for support.

Allison kneaded the tight muscles in her neck. "Couldn't the Bagley's have done better?"

"She has a job, a dishwasher at the mill." Adam shook his head grimly. "But she only makes minimum wage, seventy-five cents an hour and Ed worked odd jobs, here and there. Spent most of that on whiskey. It may sound cruel, but she's better off without him."

"Amen." Mattie mumbled under her breath as she poured them both a cup of steaming black coffee.

A little dog with shaky legs wobbled into the kitchen, Robin close behind. "Look, Mattie, he walked all the way by himself."

Mattie turned and managed a tolerant smile. "Yeah, honey, ain't that just wonderful."

"Charlie woke me up. He made a mess by my bed."

"Don't move, Missus, I'll get it." She glared at the dog with utter distain as she waddled out of the room.

Robin climbed into her mother's lap with Charlie yapping for attention.

"I'd better get going," Adam said. "The hospital's waiting."

"Hope it's a quiet day," Allison said.

"Me too." He kissed them both and took the last swallow of coffee.

"Don't forget Charlie, Daddy."

"Goodbye, Charlie," he called out, heading for the door.

୧୨

It was a ten minute drive to the hospital. Adam was in no mood for KMLB, an all-music station, or for the tape on Advances in the Treatment of Cardiovascular Diseases. So he drove in silence, letting his mind spin back to childhood.

Decimated by the Depression, his mother's small inheritance saved the family from State assistance. He hadn't been aware of his parent's struggle during those early years. Why should he have been? With the vegetable garden there was plenty of food for the table. Their house with its wood siding was warm in winter. Jimmy Harper, Adam's best friend, lived up the street where he remembered long hours swinging from the limbs of a pecan tree or shooting marbles in its shade or playing games of hide-and-seek with a whole slew of neighborhood children. And he remembered flying down the back roads on his second-hand bike with Charlie in hot pursuit.

Nanny had given him the bike for Christmas. His beloved aunt became ill when he was thirteen and they buried her in the family plot beside her infant daughter. The doctor said cancer riddled her body before anyone knew she was ill. The holidays were never the same; it was as if someone had punched a big, gaping hole in the middle of Christmas and left Adam with an empty feeling, an ache that lingered; attenuated by time, but rekindled by the first signs of the Christmas season.

In his mind's eye Nanny was one of those Southern matriarchs with a straight back and Victorian principles who with a firm hand watched over her brood like a mother hen. Her death profoundly affected Adam for it was the first time he had considered the subject of dying. Sure, he had heard others speak of it in an impersonal way, but like other children, he assumed if it happened at all, it was at least a hundred years away.

Nanny's death came without warning, like a searing streak of lightning. The icy wind caused his bleary eyes to sting. Adam's whole body churned as he watched the shovelfuls of dirt cover the coffin and fill the grave. Yet this was when Adam felt the first stirrings of his future path. And it was there that he took the first tentative steps across the threshold—out of a child's world— forever.

❧

Beyond the formal gardens, bounded by a cypress spit-rail fence, the east field, freshly planted with cotton seed, stretched a quarter mile to a distant row of pines. The slender trees lined the banks of the river which arose from some faraway mountain and wound, like a giant watery serpent, past rolling hills, beneath bridges and railroad trestles, into the marshy Delta, emptying itself at last into some yawning estuary.

Knox walked to the end of the porch, lifted herself onto the wooden balustrade and rested against the corner post. Dinner was ready. Jake had been cared for; he lay quietly, staring vacantly at the ceiling above his bed. A large glass of ice cold lemonade in her hand, she breathed deeply a few times, as a shimmering haze, the color of burnished gold, settled softly over the fecund earth.

She treasured these private moments, that part of the day she could call her own. So unlike her years at Christian Manor, not that she was ungrateful to the Sisters of Mercy. However, those years at the orphanage left an open wound, filled with resentment. Who were her parents? Why had they abandoned her, without an identity? Without the security of parental love? Many nights as a child, her heart ached and she sobbed herself to sleep, to dream fitfully of a faceless father, of a mother whose voice she could not recognize.

Knox needed to know. Shortly after their marriage, Ben tried to find her parents. He hired a private investigator. Yet every attempt had led to a dead end. He finally convinced her that the truth might be more difficult than not knowing. "Why not create them as you want them to be...and believe it with all your heart?" Ben asked when the last lead had been exhausted.

Knox never broached the subject again.

Now, she laid her head against the post and stared into the darkness that gathered her up in its heavy folds. Her heart leaped unexpectedly when she saw him move out of the shadows, past the arbor, and across the garden toward the garconniere, a dim figure with broad shoulders, bent slightly, work-weary. She watched him disappear around the side of the house and started to call out when a car turned into the driveway.

Whenever Knox met Brett, the meetings had seemed casual and perfunctory. But he ignited a spark. As dissatisfaction grew within her marriage, there was a quickening interest in this man of few words. And she could no longer squelch her feelings.

She left her seat and leaned over the railing, hoping Brett might reappear and speak to her. Disappointed, she stepped back into the hallway and murmured under her breath, "There'll be another time." She was certain—*there would be another time.*

Chapter 5

Arnie's Ale House sat well back from the road, fronting the river. An asphalt drive left the highway close to the Shamrock, wound through dense woods to parking lots on both sides of the building. A forest-green awning covered the flagstone walkway to a pair of heavy oak doors.

The Ale House was the first of the three taverns to open, delayed six months by the police jury who failed to approve the liquor license until enough money had passed under the table. Arnie Waters was a patient man, having played the game before as owner of a bar and pool hall on Main Street. He knew payoffs were a part of doing business in a state where corrupt politicians were embedded at all levels of government, from the Governor's mansion in Baton Rouge to the parish commissioners, aka police jury.

Inside, at one end of the room, a microphone stood on a lacquered platform. Arnie's featured live entertainment on weekends. While strip clubs were illegal in the parish, scantily clad young women cavorted on the stage to the rhythm of a three piece band. Admittedly, the performers and their costumes walked a fine line in the eyes of the Sheriff, but it was an attraction that filled the tavern with standing-room-only crowds. And Sheriff Gilstrap could always use the cash which he picked up at the end of every month.

A bar with high-back stools ran along a side wall. At one end, the waitresses served drinks to customers seated in tables clustered throughout the room. At the other, restrooms were concealed by floor-to-ceiling wood panels, open on both sides and on which hung a large Russell print...*Indian War Party on the War Path.*

A stranger, hawk-nosed and unshaven, sat alone at a corner table with his Stetson pulled down low on his forehead, sipping Pabst from a bottle. Unnoticed he wiped the bottle with his napkin and surreptitiously slipped on a pair of latex gloves. The stranger moved out of his chair and drifted behind the panel, an area bathed in shadows. A waitress in blue shorts passed with a tray of drinks. Rhonda was printed on the name plate pinned to her blue denim shirt.

He slipped into the men's room knowing the waitress would return the same way. His feral eyes had followed her during the past hour as he sipped his beer and studied her routine.

He turned off the light and cracked the door which swung out toward the bar and provided cover. Rhonda was putting tip money in her pocket when the door opened suddenly. He grabbed her around the neck and dragged her inside. In seconds, the lock clicked and a gloved hand covered her mouth. Powered to the floor, the man straddled her and put a knife to her throat.

"Listen, bitch, if you make a sound, even a peep I'll cut your goddamn throat."

Wide-eyed, she felt the point of the knife tear the skin, feeling drops of blood trickle down the side of her neck. While frightened, her senses remained on high alert. She processed her status; resistance was futile. With her heart pounding fiercely, she prayed for survival.

He tied her hands with nylon cord and shoved a small hand towel in her mouth. Rhonda felt waves of nausea roil her stomach as he cut the buttons from her shirt, one at a time; then violently ripped off her clothes. After cutting her bra straps, he raked the sharp edge of the knife across her breasts, nicking one of them. More blood oozed onto her stomach. Rhoda squirmed, screamed... the sound muted by the towel jammed in her throat.

He slapped her hard. "Shut up, you bitch. And lie still before I cut your heart out."

Terrified, Rhoda squeezed her fingers into a fist and prayed again.

The darkness hid his face but his breath was horrid, disgusting. And she would never forget the voice if he left her alive.

After he'd had his way with her, he brought the knife to her throat, hesitated, then withdrew the weapon. She heard the blade click into place and sighed silently. He stumbled around the small room, recovered his Stetson, and opened the window, dropping to the ally below. The predator crossed the road and disappeared into the heavily wooded area behind the tavern.

Rhonda managed to loosen the nylon cord and pull the towel from her mouth. She tried to scream but her throat was tight as if he were still choking her. Rhonda turned on her side and retched, wave after wave until there was nothing left. She crawled to the washbasin and hoisted herself up. With one hand she held on to the bowl while with the other, she splashed cold water on her face. The three-piece band and the country sound of Hank Snow's *I'm Movin' On* filtered from the stage though the thin restroom door. Rhonda dropped to the floor, leaned against the wall and sobbed, grateful to be alive.

Chapter 6

Wednesday, April 5th

It had been almost two weeks since the violent death at the Shamrock. Arthur White, owner of the mill, paid the bill for Ed Bagley's funeral and spared the deceased a pauper's grave. At Adam's request, Hal Brady presided over the interment and somehow cobbled together a few words of comfort for the few that gathered to say a final goodbye. Mr. White also promised the grieving widow that a marble headstone with an appropriate inscription would be placed once the ground had settled around the grave site.

こう

Adam arrived on time at Buck Shaw's café. Al Marx, the D.A. for Madison Parish had called on Monday and made the request. He promised it would be a short meeting, something he preferred to discuss in person. Adam marked two hours off the schedule since he had an agenda of his own. The Café was two blocks south of Main Street across from the post office and parochial school. It was popular with those who worked downtown...easy access...good food...reasonable prices.

When Adam arrived, the room was filled and some were waiting on benches lining the foyer. No wonder the smug look on Buck's weathered face when he motioned Adam to a booth near the back of the room.

"Thanks for coming," Al said.

"Glad to get a break."

"Hope I didn't upset your schedule."

"Maggie handled it. No problem."

"I've heard about the inimitable Maggie."

Adam laughed. "Well, she comes close."

After placing their order, Al took a sip of water and wiped his mouth with a paper napkin. "I wanted to talk about Tom Dolan. We're convening the grand jury impaneled last month. Our office is seeking an indictment."

"Should be a piece of cake. There was a room full of eye witnesses."

Al shook his head. "No one wants to get involved." He moved the water glass and rested both elbows on the table. "They have all kinds of excuses: too dark, too much to drink, happened so fast... well, you get the picture. So it may not be as easy as it seems."

"What about Markham? He must have been close to the action."

"Claims he was busy mixing drinks and didn't see anything until it was over." Al pushed his water glass aside and wiped the moisture from the tabletop with his napkin. "Besides, he wants it to just go away. A trial would be bad for business."

Adam knew Markham had lied but chose to let it go. "So why am I here?" he asked.

"I need you to testify before the grand jury."

Adam showed his surprise. He thought the District Attorney had the grand jury in his pocket.

"I'm afraid the facts will be ignored. And there's not much sympathy for Ed Bagley. Some say Dolan was drunk as if that gives him a free pass. Others are simple afraid; there're rumors of threats and intimidation."

"Maybe Dolan will surprise you with a confession."

Al shook his head. "Won't happen. He's hired Neal Jameson, a damn good lawyer who understands the mill worker, some of whom will be on the grand jury. He knows his client has a good chance to beat the indictment."

Out of the corner of his eye, Adam saw Wilma heading their way. "So, what can I do?"

"Talk about the impact of Bagley's death on his wife and kids. He may have been a loser, but he had a family."

Wilma arrived with a tray full of food. "Brought a basket of French fries. They go real good with those hamburgers. Buck says they're on the house."

"Are you sure Buck said that?" Al teased.

"Must've had a 'senior moment,'" Adam said.

Wilma grinned, smacked her gum and padded away.

While they were eating, Buck wandered over, chewing on a toothpick. "You fellas need anything?"

Adam picked up the plastic basket. "No, but thanks for the fries."

Buck was tall and slightly stooped. He leaned in as if to divulge a secret and with a wry grin tapped an index finger against his bald head. "Sometimes I wonder if I'm losing it."

"Naw," Al said. "You're just becoming more benevolent in your old age."

He gave them a dismissive wave with his gnarled fingers and trudged back to the register.

Adam pushed his plate aside. "Al, I need a favor."

"I'm listening."

"I talked to Maude at Ben's party a few weeks ago. She's deeply troubled by the death of young Andy Lebauer. And of course, the crippling of his best friend. Blames the Shamrock. Now with the Bagley killing, she'll increase her resolve to shut down the taverns...all of them."

"Go on," he urged.

"She asked me to help...said she couldn't go it alone. While the newspaper could spotlight their malfeasance and the dark shadows they cast on our town, it would serve only as an irritant but not a solution."

"It sounds like you've joined Maude's army." Al fingered a cigarette from a pack in his shirt pocket.

"I thought about her invitation and came up with a zillion reasons not to get involved. I talked to Allison and it seemed to bring clarity to Maude's proposal. Bottom line: if successful, it could make Conway a better place to live and provide a safer place for our children."

Al lit the cigarette and dropped the match on his plate. His face clouded. "If you're making a list of offenses, don't forget Rhonda Jones."

"The name rings a bell. Refresh my memory."

"She works nights at Arnie's Ale House. Needs the money since she has a small child to support. Fortunately, the mother lives a few doors down the street and keeps the kid when she's working. The husband, a worthless piece of trash, took off for parts unknown a coupla years ago." He placed the cigarette in a metal ashtray and sighed heavily. "It happened last Friday night."

Adam snapped his fingers. "Okay...the fog has lifted. The young woman who was raped at knife point?"

Al described the incident in some detail.

"How is she? I can't imagine a more traumatic experience."

"She's back at work but her life will never be the same."

"Who's leading the investigation?"

"The Sheriff's Department...but then Randy Gilstrap is not exactly Randolph Scott the intrepid lawman of the old West."

Adam ran his hand through a shock of brown hair. "Back to business."

"Yeah...the favor. What's on your mind?"

"Could someone in your office look into a legal remedy?"

Al's eyes widened. "You mean to shut down the taverns?"

Adam nodded. "I know one simple solution."

Al looked up, waiting.

"Vote the parish dry."

"Won't happen. Too much opposition from the mill workers, the country club set, and ironically, most of the business establishment. A referendum on banning alcohol would be a waste of tax payer money."

"How about the parish and its power of eminent domain?" asked Adam.

"Possible... I'll have my office do the research."

Wilma returned with the coffee and left a check on the table. She took the parting shot: "Thanks for the business boys, but next time bring your appetite." With that she put a fresh stick of Juicy Fruit in her mouth and quickly disappeared.

"I'll let you know. It'll take a week or two."

"I'll pass the news to Maude. It'll make her day."

"I prefer to stay off Maude's hit list. The woman's got more grit than T. R. and his Rough Riders."

Adam revisited the look of resolve on Maude's wintry face. "She's no shrinking violet, that's for sure."

The two men slipped out of the booth. "See you in court," Al said.

Chapter 7

Same day

On leaving the café, Adam put on sun glasses, loosened his tie and hung his blazer in the crook of an elbow. Near the office, he passed Ms. Borders' boarding house. He noticed a robin, perched on the clothesline; a trellis at either end, intertwined by wisteria, with clusters of lavender blossoms. Adam stopped for a moment to savor the arrival of spring.

At the office, he found Maggie behind the glass enclosure talking to the pharmacist at Dean's Drugstore. He leaned against the doorpost and waited. She placed the receiver in its cradle and swiveled her chair in his direction. "How'd the meeting go?"

"Like the little girl with the curl...some good, some bad."

"Translation, please?" She gave him a look of consternation.

"The good news...well, Al will try to find a legal means of closing the taverns. He thinks there's a way, but his office needs to check it out."

"And the bad..."

"He wanted to tell me in person that I'll receive a missive from his office."

"Did he explain?"

"Yep...sure did." Adam let out a deep breath of acquiescence. "A subpoena to appear before the grand jury."

"Tom Dolan?"

"Afraid so." He reached down and picked up a stack of messages.

Maggie swung her legs back around and picked up a note from beneath the appointment book. "Mrs. Bagley came by... disappointed you weren't here. Since she was late for work, she left a message."

Adam unfolded the note, barely legible, as he walked back to his office.

Dear Doc,

Thanks for everything you done for Ed. Also thank Mr. White and all the other folks who pitched in. It was a decent funeral and Preacher Brady said some mighty nice words. The Reverend sure made things a heap easier for me and the kids. It may sound strange, but do what you can for Mr. Dolan. He won't do his family no good in jail. I know in his heart, sober and all, he didn't mean to harm Ed.

Your friend,
Edith Bagley

After passing the nursing station, Adam realized the door to Ben's office door was open. Ben sat behind his desk going through the day's mail. He looked up and motioned for Adam to come in. "Arthur got tied up at the mill, but he's on his way." He tossed a journal on an over-crowded credenza. "Where's your patient?" he asked.

"Hairdresser...running late. We all know that Fran Shore has her priorities in order." He waved her message which he had picked up at Maggie's desk, crumbled it into a paper ball and sent it sailing into the wicker basket besides Ben's desk.

"Good shot. You may have missed your calling," he said with a Cheshire cat grin.

"Naw, I couldn't hit a curve ball."

Ben moved up in his chair with a worried look. "Last night was a lulu." He shook his head like a shaggy dog that had just been hosed.

44

"Give me the short version." He knew his partner was a raconteur-of-sorts and could embellish a piece of plywood.

Ben threw up his hands in a wildly animated gesture. "Got a call around two this morning. Husband says his wife was having lots of abdominal pain and would I come over. So true to my Hippocratic Oath, I drove to the house on Masonic and rang the bell. The husband opened the door, gave me a tepid welcome and pointed to the end of the hall. Then spoof...he disappeared."

"Is your malpractice paid up?" Adam chuckled.

"Funny you mention it, since that word, malpractice, kept recurring like a never-ending echo. And I felt uneasy...you know, that sixth sense...telling you something's wrong."

"So what happened?"

"I tip-toed down the hall; telling myself to get the hell out of there." Ben grimaced as he relived the harrowing experience. "I pushed the door open and there was Susan Devore, a good-looking blond lying in bed. Guess what she was wearing?"

"Nothing."

"Give the man a cigar. She was naked as the day she was born."

Adam slumped down into a chair. "What was the problem?"

"I took one step inside the door and asked that very question."

"And...?" Adam waited.

"She slurred her words big time, so I figured she'd been drinking...either drunk or almost there. Anyway, Lady Godiva said, 'I put a tampon in earlier and can't get it out. Would you please help me?'"

"You gotta be kidding." Disbelief seeped into Adam's face.

"Backing away, I said I didn't carry the necessary equipment in my little black bag but suggested she come by the office this morning. Then she started screaming like a wild Comanche; called me—and I quote— a heartless prick and managed to toss an empty bottle of Jack Daniels which shattered when it hit the wall. I turned and made a beeline for the front door where the taciturn Mr. Devore reappeared like a phantom. I gave him the same message. And you know what I thought about while driving home?"

"Relieved to be out of there?"

"Yeah, that too. But remember Dr. Lewis, our beloved Professor of Medicine and his famous maxims? 'Caring for patients will bring great rewards.' That's the one that came to mind as I blew past a couple of stop signs." Ben had already considered the possibilities. "Rewards, hell, I'll be lucky if I don't get my ass sued."

Adam smiled benignly. "I wouldn't worry. My guess is, you'll neither see nor hear from the Devores again."

"Hope you're right," Ben said without conviction.

A tap on the door jam got their attention. Mary, a matronly nurse in a crisp, white uniform stuck her head inside. "Your patients are here. I put them in your exam rooms; they know the routine and will turn on the light when ready." She took a quick look down the hall. "Mr. White's light is blinking."

Ben stood up and stretched. "Thanks Mary, I'm on my way."

⅓

Joshua White bought the Fort Miro paper mill at the turn of the century. At the time, the company was struggling to survive and the price reflected a balance sheet floating in red ink. Within two years, through hard work and innovative ideas, the mill was turning a handsome profit. It soon became the largest employer in the parish and the most successful business in North Louisiana. Joshua changed the name to the White Paper Company, became a wealthy man and weathered the depression by converting all his holdings into cash which he locked away in a 1927 American Steam Safe.

At the time of Joshua death, in the winter of 1940, signs of his philanthropy were everywhere. The Sisters of Charity received a gift of five million dollars which made a new state-of-the-art hospital possible. The parochial school became a reality because of his generous largess. However, most of his benevolence was anonymous (though secrets were hard to keep in a small town), yet everyone agreed —some reluctantly—that Joshua had a positive impact on Madison Parish and almost single-handedly transformed Conway into a thriving and prosperous community. It was a remarkable legacy bestowed by a carpetbagger from Missouri and a doctrinal Catholic in a Protestant stronghold.

After Joshua died, his son, Arthur, assumed control of the company. But Arthur was never able to gain the confidence and respect of the mill workers. He also vacillated on important decisions and compromised certain basic policies that his father had established. Sizable chunks of the business were lost and with the exception of the war years, the paper mill bled red ink. While it was unspoken, many of the locals felt that Joshua White had everything except what he wanted most—a son in his own image.

చ్ఛ

In the examining room, Arthur knew the routine. He took off everything but his shorts and put on the thin cotton gown. Ben knocked and opened the door with the same motion.

"How've you done this week?" Ben asked, opening Arthur's chart and reviewing his previous visit.

"A lot better, thank the good Lord." Arthur looked up and made the sign of the cross. "Those little pills that I put under my tongue work like magic."

"Did you remember to use them as prevention; I mean, before you have chest pain?"

Arthur nodded. "There's an incline from my parking space, then a flight of stairs to my office. I put the pill under my tongue before getting out of the car; haven't had a pain since."

"Nitroglycerin won't quit working, so don't be afraid to use it. And remember..." Ben said with his best professional smile, "... carry the vial with you. It won't help if you leave it at home."

"I understand."

Ben noted the vital signs which Mary had recorded and attached to the chart. "By the way, your blood pressure has come down nicely."

"Guess the medicine must be working."

"We'll see; it'll take a month to be sure." He lay the chart aside and reached for his stethoscope. "Now, let's check you out."

Ben listened carefully to Arthur's heart and lungs, palpated his neck and abdomen, felt for the pulses in his extremities and checked the blood pressure again in both arms. "Sit up if you like."

"Sound okay?" Arthur asked, anxiously.

"All clear." He slipped the stethoscope in his pocket. "Let's review what we talked about last week."

"I'd like that."

"Here's the problem." Ben picked up a laminated sheet with the heart's anatomy and held it up with one hand. He pointed to the coronary arteries. "These vessels feed the heart. One or more are partially obstructed and with exercise—stair climbing, for example—there's not enough blood getting to the heart muscle... and that causes the pain. Unfortunately, there's no surgical remedy, maybe in the near-future. For now, a medical regimen is the way to go." Ben held up five fingers and recounted the instructions of the previous week: diet, exercise, etc. "And get rid of those damn things," he said, pointing to the pack of cigarettes in Arthur's shirt hanging on a wall hook.

"That's the hardest part," Arthur said.

"You can do it. Just remember, it can make a difference in how this thing plays out."

Arthur took the cigarettes from his shirt pocket and handed them to Ben.

"It's a start," Ben said with reticence. "See you in a month. Set it up with Maggie on your way out."

Arthur waved as Ben picked up the chart and left the room.

Ben went into his consultation room and looked out the picture window. A solitary gray cloud covered the sun. He reminded himself that, like Arthur, he too had been a disappointment to a father who had wanted a son shaped in his own image. Out of defiance there had arisen resentments that damaged their relationship irreparably. Arthur had tried to fit the mold and failed. Ben wondered if abject feelings of failure that grew out of a father's expectations could have an injurious effect on the heart that harbored them. Conceivably in Arthur's case, it had.

Chapter 8

Wednesday, April 12th

Adam checked his watch as he entered the parish courthouse, a stately three-story building of granite, overlooking South Grand and the river beyond the levee. Built in Classical Revival style, it featured eight imposing columns, marble corridors and stairwells and a copper roof. It was the most impressive building in Madison Parish.

Inside, Adam removed the subpoena from his pocket and rechecked the room number of the grand jury. He trudged up the marble stairs and found Wade Gentry, slumped in his seat half asleep, ostensibly guarding the door to room 203 and a stack of empty folding chairs.

Like his brother, Wade was a big, barrel-chested man with the same deep-set eyes and a round mouth that seemed to pucker each time he spoke. A shiny, silver badge with the inscription "Deputy Sheriff" below a six-pointed star was pinned to his khaki shirt. He polished it with the back of his sleeve as he sat up in his chair.

"Morning, Doc."

Adam broke a generous smile. "How's it going?"

"Not bad, considering."

Adam held up the subpoena.

"Go right in, Doc." Wade pointed to the stack against the far wall. "Mr. Marx usually keeps his witnesses out here, but he said for you to sit inside."

"Thanks, Mr. Gentry. I appreciate the courtesy."

Wade puckered but decided not to speak.

Number 203 was a large room sparsely furnished. Beige carpet covered the floor, florescent lamps attached to the ceiling. At the far end, an American flag with its golden tassel, hung limp beside the time-worn portrait of Abraham Lincoln.

Adam scrutinized the jury of ten men and two women, nodded to Johnny Nabors, an unexpected member of the panel, then across the room to Albert Marx. The defendant sat behind one of the wooden tables, facing the jury and stared self-consciously at the floor. The young district attorney glanced at the wall clock, rustled a few papers on the lectern and took a sip of water.

Albert Marx was slender, well groomed and dressed in a conservative gray suit, a freshly pressed white shirt and a stripped tie. His grandfather had emigrated from Portugal around the turn of the century and Albert had inherited the square jaw, olive complexion and thick black hair of the Sephardic Jew. He had been raised by his widowed mother who owned a small dry goods story in town and later had made his way through college and law school on academic scholarships and as a part-time appliance salesman. Those who knew him agreed that he was on the fast track for a notable career in law or politics.

He stationed himself squarely in front of the jury with the thumbs of both hands buried in the pockets of his vest. When he spoke his voice was resonant, his words crisp and his syntax precise. (He had been accused of having succumbed to Yankee inveiglement, having lost his southern accent at Yale and marrying a banker's daughter from New Haven.)

"Ladies and gentlemen of the jury...you have been called to hear the State's case against one Tom Dolan who, on the night of March 25th, did willfully strike the deceased, Ed Bagley, at the Shamrock Bar and Grill...a blow that resulted in his death. I, therefore, representing the State of Louisiana, encourage you to listen carefully, hear and weigh the evidence, disregard any emotional bias, and then vote for the indictment of voluntary manslaughter as charged by this office."

After reciting the formal charge, he began again. "Many years ago, great men like Aristotle and Saint Augustine spoke of certain principles in the universe that are unaltered by the passage of time. There is permanence about them. They never change." The District Attorney moved closer to the railing that enclosed the jurors. "What's he talking about, you ask?" For the first time, Albert Marx looked up as though searching the ceiling for an answer. But in a few moments his piercing eyes were back, locked on the jury. "I'm talking about Justice. It's an iron-clad ideal which has withstood the attrition of time. You and I change. This town has changed. Our world has changed. It's not the same place I knew as a boy. The days hurry by, each different from the other. Sunshine today; rain tomorrow. But Justice is constant, unmodified..." He slapped his palms together like a clap of thunder, causing Harley Mulhern to jerk noticeably and shake the sleep from his eyes. "... and absolute."

He stopped and scanned the face of each juror, allowing his simple point to sink like an anchor into their collective minds. "You're probably wondering what these remarks have to do with the business at hand. Simply this: it is your task...no, your obligation... to meet the demands of Justice in the case before you. During the next few days, there may be those who will misread the truth, disguise it with prejudice, or even distort it for personal gain. It's your lawful duty to discern the facts, organize and evaluate them and without recourse to your own bias or yielding to the pressure of others, see that the clear, concise demands of Justice are fulfilled."

Moats floated in the sunlight that shone through the large windows. Adam felt the room's plain appearance had been burnished by the streamers of light. The flag's gold tassel seemed brighter. Even the portrait of Lincoln appeared more life-like, as though it had been brushed with fresh colors.

"The State will call its first witness. Mr. Gentry, will you ask Dr. O'Riley to come in, please?"

Desmond O'Riley came forward and raised his right hand. The foreman of the jury administered the oath: "Do you swear to tell the truth, the whole truth and nothing but the truth, so help you God?"

51

"I do," he said and without being prompted moved to the witness chair in front of the flag.

"Please state your name and occupation."

"Dr. Desmond E. O'Riley, and I am the coroner of this fair Parish," he answered with a heavy Irish brogue.

"Your qualifications, Doctor?"

Everyone in Conway knew that Des O'Riley drank too much and that the job of coroner was a position he could fill despite his faults. Long ago, he had fallen behind the rapid paces of his profession and was regarded with scant respect. Des was feckless; the Roger Dangerfield of the medical community. There was something sad about the slovenly little man in the witness chair, a silver lock of hair falling over his eyes and grazing his bulbous nose. For some odd reason Adam remembered Ms. Cain's English class and her love affair with Melinda Kendall's *The Wasted Life.* That's what Adam saw...the infinite possibilities...the lost opportunities...a wasted life.

"I am a graduate of the medical school in Dublin, spent a year in pathology at the State University, and worked as a family practitioner in Pine Grove, before assuming the role of parish coroner." He spoke diffidently; it was not a resume that one would offer with self-approbation.

"A little louder, Dr. O'Riley. The jury is anxious to hear your testimony."

"Sorry," he said, his voice contrite.

"Now, did the coroner's jury reach a verdict concerning the death of Edward Bagley?"

"We did, sir."

"And what was your conclusion?"

"An autopsy was performed the following morning. There was a large blood clot in the subdural space and hemorrhaging into the brain itself."

"Subdural...please define the term for the jury."

O'Riley moved up in his seat, elbows on the arms of his chair. "The brain is covered by tough fibrous membranes." He scratched his head searching for an analogy. "Think of a box wrapped with several layers of tissue paper. One of those layers...lining the brain is called the dura....and beneath it, the subdural space." He looked at Al Marx, expectantly. "Does that help?"

"Thank you Doctor O'Riley. I think that clarifies the term." Several members of the jury nodded.

Marx unfolded a metal chair and placed it in front of the jury box. "Is it your opinion that a heavy blow to the head with a chair—like this one—could have caused the fatal hemorrhage?" In a display of histrionics, perhaps a bit overdone, he picked up the chair and swung it wildly, driving its legs into the floor.

O'Riley was startled and it took him some time to recover. He removed a handkerchief from his coat pocket and wiped the beads of sweat that had gathered on his upper lip. "It could," he answered, finally.

"And in the case of Ed Bagley...?"

"Yes...yes sir," he stuttered. "It did."

"What is your degree of certainty?"

O'Riley shook his head. "There's not a fly speck of doubt."

"And is it reasonable to assume that death could result in a few hours from bleeding into the brain?"

"Less time, depending on the degree of trauma."

"Thank you, Dr. O'Riley that will be all for the present if there are no questions from the jury." The coroner waited for a moment, walked from the stand visible relieved that no questions were forthcoming, and bowed to Adam obsequiously as he left the room.

"Badger Wills, come forward, please."

Wade held the door open and motioned for the next witness.

Badger, a tall, ungainly man, in a red flannel shirt buttoned at the collar and baggy corduroy pants, moved with a lumbering gait past the jury box and nodded to familiar faces. He was sworn in.

"Be seated."

Albert Marx stood directly in front of Badger. "Would you give the jury your full name and occupation?"

"My name is Badger Wills and I've lived in these here parts all my life, almost sixty years." Everyone in town knew him and liked him because he was honest, and despite 'hard times' had kept his sense of humor.

"Would you tell us where you are employed?"

"All these folk know I run the express office at the railroad station. Come the 6th of November, it'll be 'xactly nineteen years and I ain't missed a day's work in all that time...'cept when Bea died...God rest her soul." For a moment, his gray eyes grew wistful and his voice trailed off to a hoarse whisper.

Al Marx waited for Badger to recover from the memory. "Are you ready to proceed?" he asked.

"I'm okay." He sniffed a few times and swiped his nose with the sleeve of his shirt.

"Mr. Wills, have you ever frequented the Shamrock?"

"I've dropped in there for a drink, a time or two...if that's what you mean."

"Were you present at the Shamrock on the night of March 25th?"

"Yessur, I shore was. Dropped by for a beer on my way home."

"And what time did you arrive?"

"Musta been around eleven or so. The westbound express dropped off the mail at 10:08—right on time. I took care of a few odd jobs 'round the office, locked her up, and went straight to the Shamrock for a nightcap."

Al Marx turned back to the jury. "Now Mr. Wills, did you see Ed Bagley, the deceased, when you arrived?"

"Yessur. He was sittin' at a table with Ms. Jamie Patterson."

"What were they doing?"

Badger rearranged himself in the chair, sitting more erect. "To tell the truth, I wasn't payin' too much attention. Seems, though, they was just sittin' and talkin' and drinkin' beer. A coupla times, Ed threwed his arm around her and pinched her shoulder—kinda playful like—but that was all he done...as far as I could see."

"Then what happened?"

"Ole Dolan here come a stompin' in drunk like he owned the place and 'cuses Ed of swippin' his woman. Before Ed could barely open his mouth, Dan put his fist right in it and sent the poor soul sprawling, slam-up against the wall. Then banged his head with a chair. Sure 'nough, as the Lawd is my witness."

"There was testimony at the arraignment to the effect that Dan Boles was done after throwing that one punch. He was finished and walked away. From that point, he was merely defending himself." Albert Marx turned toward the witness and posed the question with deliberate clarity. "Did you see it that way, Mr. Wills?"

"Can't say I did." Silas hesitated and shook his head. "Naw, that fellow started it and finished it." For the first time since the hearings began, Tom Dolan looked up and saw Badger wagging an accusing finger in his direction.

It was obvious to Adam that Albert Marx had found a witness who would corroborate the State's position, namely, that Tom Dolan was the aggressor from the moment he entered the bar; that he struck the first blow, and without provocation, picked up a chair and sent it crashing against Bagley's head. But Adam knew it would take more than the testimony of Badger Wills to get the grand jury's endorsement for "a true bill." *Justice denied.* It was only perception, but it seemed to permeate the room, an invisible part of the proceedings.

With resignation, Adam moved toward the witness chair when his name was called and took the oath. While Al had explained the reason for his subpoena, Adam felt his testimony was superfluous; the emotional slant would be neither persuasive nor even seriously considered. The coroner had established both the cause and instrument of death. Badger had verified the role of Tom Dolan as the aggressor. Maybe Al wanted, despite their earlier discussion, a vivid account of the grisly slaying in an attempt to dramatize the brutal and senseless way in which Bagley died. He was wrong; Al never asked. Instead he went right to Edith Bagley and the impact of Ed's death on her and the children.

"Dr. Swift, did you know the deceased?"

"Only by name."

"By name?"

"Yes, his wife is a patient of mine."

"Has she been ill?"

Adam shook his head. "No, but she's had her share of complaints."

Albert Marx moved closer to the witness chair and leaned forward—eye level. "Dr. Swift, without betraying the doctor-patient relationship, can you give us any insight into Mrs. Bagley's state of mind?"

"I can only tell you that the road she's traveled hasn't been easy. Misfortune has been her constant companion—more hardship than anyone deserves."

The young D.A. straightened up and again thrust his thumbs into the pockets of his vest. "Now, in your opinion, did the death of Ed Bagley free his wife from any of her problems?"

As he had promised, Al Marx was attacking an emotional facet of the case which Adam knew was hearsay and inadmissible in a court of law. But before the grand jury, Al had unlimited latitude and the prosecution needed to refute those who claimed that Bagley was an added burden and compounded the plight of his family, perhaps to the breaking point.

Adam shook his head, emphatically. "No, she was deeply saddened by his death."

"Do you think her loss will make things easier?"

"My first reaction was 'yes.' But after talking to her, I'm convinced that despite his faults, Ed will be missed by his family and life behind the levee will still be hard."

"Thank you; that'll be all." Al Marx half-turned, then in the same motion, swung back to the witness chair. "Oh, Dr. Swift, one final question. Some have suggested that Conway is better off without parasites and slackers...a lot of people thought of Ed Bagley in those terms. Do you agree with that assessment?"

From the corner of his eye, Adam caught several jurors move uneasily in their seats. "I would not judge the merits of a man's life or attempt to appraise his value to the community. I have seen men die and always a part of someone else dies with him or her. So it was with Ed Bagley." Adam turned his head and looked at the jury. "Rich-man, poor-man, beggar-man, thief...no man's death occurs in a vacuum."

A hush fell over the room and Al Marx stood quietly letting the poignant words carry their own dramatic effect. After several moments, he excused the witness with the thanks of the State.

Chapter 9

Wednesday, April 19ᵗʰ

Adam thought about Tuesday's call from Al Marx. The grand jury had voted *against* the indictment of Tom Dolan. A *prima facie* case was lost amid subjectivity and other emotional derivatives. And as Al had feared, allegedly, some jurors felt the heavy-handed pressure of sinister, self-serving interests. Adam considered it more of the miasma that arose from the taverns across the river.

He put the top down on his '48 Ford convertible and drove through Audubon Park, a divided two-lane asphalt road shaded by stately oak trees. On leaving the park, he passed the imposing statue of Joshua White, standing sentry-like on a tall pedestal of pink Georgia marble. It was a reminder of the man whose integrity and grace had redefined the meaning of community. Adam glanced at the clock on the Ford's dashboard. He had a short hospital list and since he passed Maude's house, there was time to stop for coffee.

He turned into her driveway and parked beside the brick walkway. The French Arcadian with its wide veranda, sat well off the street, its back facing the bayou, a serene body of water that meandered, serpentine, along the northern rim of the town. A giant magnolia flanked each side of the porch, providing shade during the scorching summer months.

He saw Preacher, an ageless black, mowing the back yard, the man responsible for the neatly-manicured lawn and the blue and pink hydrangea that colored the sides of the house. Adam knew Preacher had been Maude's lawn service long before he had come to Conway. And after Ed Harrington's death, Preacher had become her full-time caretaker, chauffer, and trusted friend. He was even her part-time cook when Dora, the housekeeper, was sick or on vacation. As Maude grew older, Preacher had become indispensable.

Adam followed the walkway to the front entrance. He rang the door bell and heard it resound down the hall, deep inside the house.

∽

Maude placed her book (H.A. Overstreet's The Mature Mind) on the nightstand, put on her robe and slippers, stood for a minute to ensure her balance, then padded along the carpeted hallway to the foyer. She took a quick look through one of the sidelights and unbolted the door.

"What a surprise." She took his hand and tugged gently. "Make yourself at home while I get the coffee."

"I hope you were awake."

"Been up since 4:30." She gave him a lively smile. "Thank heaven for a good book."

"Your invitation...remember...Ben's Party. Sorry for the delay."

"Just glad you're here," she said, heading for the kitchen.

"Don't forget the pound cake." Adam sank into a plush high-back and soaked up the ambiance. The living room was elegantly furnished. An Oriental rug covered the sitting area with warm tones of burgundy and olive green. A Queen Anne secretary, which Maude had found antique shopping in New Orleans, stood against the far wall, exquisite in its simplicity. Near the fireplace, a champagne velvet sofa, flanked by two wingback chairs. Jezebel, a white ball of fur was asleep on the sofa.

"Top of the morning," Maude said cheerfully, placing the server on the butler's tray table.

"So, how are you?" he asked.

"No complaints, other than waking up so damn early."

Maude stooped over, filled his cup and placed it in front of him. She watched Adam load his pipe, packing the tobacco tightly into the bowl with his left thumb and index finger. The face was finely chiseled; unlined, except for the shallow crease that ran obliquely between the cheeks and a patrician's nose.

"Oh, I almost forgot." She pulled a slice of pound cake wrapped in aluminum foil from the pocket of her robe. "Dora made this yesterday which can only mean your timing is impeccable."

They both laughed.

Adam lit the pipe and stirred his coffee pensively. "I guess you heard the verdict. The grand jury voted down the Dolan indictment."

She nodded. "How could that happen?"

"Good question. It seemed like a slam dunk."

"Weren't there eye witnesses?" she asked. "The parking lot's always full on Saturday night."

"The place was hopping, but six jurors chose to ignore the facts." Adam nestled his cup in both hands and leaned back in the cushioned chair.

"How many votes were needed for an indictment?"

"According to Al, in Louisiana, the panel is made up of twelve jurors. And endorsing a "true bill" requires at least nine votes."

"I'm sure Mr. Marx is disappointed. And it can't look good on his resume, someone as ambitious as Al Marx."

"In his defense, he was worried from the start," Adam said. "He felt a lot of emotional heat arising from an indictment."

Maude mentioned she had served on three or four juries over the years and knew the vagaries of the system. While most jurors were conscientious and took their responsibility seriously, there were exceptions—wildly imaginative, doltish, frightened or just plain weird. "So Dolan walks?"

"Yep. Kills a man in a crowded room and never makes it to trial."

Maude placed her cup on the table and sank back into the sofa beside the cat. Her gaze settled on the Drysdale, framed in polished mahogany, above the fireplace. "I smell a rat. One or two votes to kill the indictment...okay, but six! Don't think so."

"There are troubling rumors that muscle from downstate was involved."

"Well, it's no secret the Mob's been trying to gain a foothold in North Louisiana. An alliance with Markham, Dempsey and Gambelli would imperil Conway and every town within a two hundred mile radius." She stopped long enough to consider such a dangerous adversary. "It's another reason, perhaps the overriding reason, to shut down the taverns."

Adam moved up in his chair and looked straight at her solemn face. "That's why I'm here."

"Have you thought about a strategy?" she asked. "If we take on the big boys, we should have a plan in place."

Maude knew their crusade—if one chose to call it that—would be a formidable one that carried sizable risks. First, the tavern owners would have a tactical advantage. Second, the playing field is uneven when your opponent has no moral equivalents. And if Tony Caruso got involved, it would send the stakes sky high.

"I've talked to Al Marx." Adam said. "We need to find a way—a legal way—to shut down the taverns."

"And...?"

"He promised to look into the matter."

"When do you expect to hear?"

"Well, I'm glad you asked..." He shaped an indulgent smile. "Al called last night and we're meeting at Buck's...around six o'clock. Said he had news of interest."

Maude shook her fists and bit down on her lower lip. "If there's a way, we need to get busy."

Adam sat back in his chair and crossed his legs. "I'm sure you've got something in mind."

"Well, first and foremost, we need Hal Brady and Arthur White on our team."

"Hal's a gimme but Arthur may be a problem."

She refilled his cup from the silver urn and poured a dollop of cream into the coffee. A pleasing aroma filled their space. "I know Arthur is struggling, trying to get the mill running smoothly. He doesn't need more grief from the workers." She brushed back a tendril of gray hair. "But Arthur's help is critical. So we need a persuasive voice."

"If we get 'a thumb's up' from Al, I'll have Ben talk to Arthur."

"And I'll contact Roy Johns at Rotary and the other churches."

"Don't forget Father O'Brien at Saint Matthews. An old linebacker at Notre Dame might come in handy." Adam placed his cup on the tray table and kissed her lightly on the cheek. "I'm late, so I'd better get going."

"I'll arrange a meeting."

Adam waved and pocketed his pipe as he crossed the gallery and hurried to his car.

Maude stood at the window and watched him drive away. Adam would be a loyal ally, but to succeed, they needed a broad base of support. She believed most of the preachers in Conway would step up and be counted. The civic clubs...well, she was cautiously optimistic. But it was essential to send their message to the mill workers. Only Arthur White could make it happen. She hoped that Ben would talk to Arthur with his most *persuasive voice*.

Chapter 10

Same day

Adam looked at his watch; a little after 6 p.m. The bustle of the lunch crowd was missing but Buck, chewing on a toothpick, nodded toward the back of the room. Al sat in the last booth, his notes scattered over the Formica-topped table.

"Sorry I'm late."

Al waved off the apology.

Wilma popped up like a jack-in-the box. "You boys need a menu?"

"Just coffee," Al said, rearranging the papers on the table.

"Coming right up." She slipped the pencil behind her ear and disappeared.

"I have some news of interest, a way to close the taverns, but it won't be easy."

Adam's face lit up with the expectation.

"There is a mechanism under Louisiana law by which private property can be transferred to a public entity. In legalese, it's called the right of eminent domain, a subject you raised at our meeting two weeks ago. My office did the research. Then I called two of my old professors who agreed your objective is on sound legal footing. Of course, the tavern owners will be foaming at the mouth. Should be a helluva fight."

"What's involved? You know, the specifics?"

"The magic word is expropriation."

Adam shrugged. "Explain."

Al picked up a single page and began to read. "Expropriation is the right required by public exigencies, for the greater good of the people, of dispossessing the private landowner of title to his property, after indemnity was previously made, not only for the value of the property, but also when the contingency rises, for damages sustained. Tracing expropriation form the days of Rome to modern times, through certain radical developments, the court said that the private landowner is assimilated to a debtor to society. (City of Shreveport vs. Hollingsworth, 1890)." He tapped the table with his knuckles. "It's imperative that the *purpose* for the action be clearly stated, since it involves the taking of a right guaranteed by the Constitution."

After Wilma brought the coffee, Al continued, "Municipal governments are invested with the power to exercise the right of eminent domain in the laying out of recreational venues and public utilities." He put the paper aside. "In my judgment, that land across the river would be perfect for a park."

Adam nibbled absently on the stem of his cold pipe. "Take me step-wise through the process."

"Okay. First it requires a petition to pass a new city ordinance."

"How many names?"

Al Marx shuffled his papers. "The number must exceed a third of those who voted in the last mayoral election."

"We can get those numbers from the registrar's office."

Al nodded. "Then the whole process is turned over to a special council appointed by the Mayor. If either party objects to the council's conclusion, it is then submitted to a vote of the people and becomes effective with a simple majority. There is final recourse in District Court."

Adam made a quick assessment. Getting the petition signed was doable. Finding the funds to indemnify Fred Warren and the tavern owners was problematic. He knew that the Mayor and police jury would demur. Conway could not take on more debt without capsizing. And it was fantasy to think that another Joshua White would suddenly appear out of the ether. Despite his pessimistic appraisal, he knew the first step was getting the signatories, having the petition approved by the City Council. That tedious process allowed time to find some creative financing. With the help of friends, he would make it happen. Somewhere. Somehow.

"We need to talk about money."

"You must be a mind reader," Adam said.

Al searched his notes again. "Let me paraphrase the City of New Orleans versus Moeglich, 1930: 'Compensation is the true value of the land and its improvements at the time of expropriation.'"

"Determined by an independent appraiser?"

Al nodded. "Bottom line, it will cost a helluva lot of money."

"I guess the Mayor's not a viable alternative."

"Well, Conway could generate funds through the sale of municipal bonds. But the town can't handle more debt. Another tax increase and the Mayor's history."

"How about state and federal help?"

"I've already talked to Chuck Wilson, an old friend from college days who is Senator Robert Short's Administrative Assistant in D.C. He promised to discuss the matter with the Senator when he returns from Easter recess. He did mention that Short, something of an ecologist and outdoorsman, was chairman of the committee that controlled the U. S. Park Service. He inferred that funding through a federal grant was possible."

Adam leaned back against the corner of the booth. "First things first. And that's the petition."

"Oh, one other thing, shortly after the war ended, Fred Warren planned Wildwood, an upscale residential development across the river. Through some political shenanigans, he managed to get the land incorporated into the city of Conway. For some obscure reason, Warren backed off his grandiose plan and leased some of the acreage to the taverns. So you have Mr. Big Shot to thank for the legal leg on which you and your friends may stand and fight." Al gathered up his papers and stuffed them in his briefcase. "I hope I've been helpful."

"You've made my day."

"Keep me informed. I'm interested, but I need to be discreet."

As the two men slipped out of the booth and headed for the door, a voice resounded from across the room. "You boys come back now."

Adam turned and saw Wilma, waving wildly and smacking her gum.

∽

On his way home, Adam passed the annex, adjacent to St. Paul's Methodist Church. A light shone through the window of Hal's study. On impulse, he parked the car and went inside. He knocked on the door and pushed it open. Hal Brady sat behind a desk covered with commentaries, an open Bible and a large yellow legal pad, gnawing on a #2 graphite pencil. Wads of paper overflowed his waste basket. He had been wrestling with another sermon.

"Forgive the interruption but I was in the neighborhood..."

"Ah, don't apologize. I need to get away from all of this," he said, pointing to the disarray that covered the desk.

Hal Brady was slightly built, dark brown eyes beneath a broad forehead. He laughed easily, a genuine man of mirth.

Adam sat on the edge of the padded chair. "Maude Harrington has enlisted me in her crusade."

"Who's the enemy?" he asked, arching his prominent brow.

"In a word, the taverns."

Hal shook his head. "I just heard about the rape at Arnie's."

"Yeah, well, a lot of bad things are going on and the Sheriff seems to have a blind eye. So Maude decided the good citizens of Conway should take the offensive."

"Vigilantes, huh?"

Adam laughed. "No, a crusade, a Holy War."

"Seriously, can it be done?"

Adam briefly summarized his recent meetings with Al Marx. There was a legal remedy, the process was arduous and there were substantial risks.

"You mean Markham and his minions won't go away without a fight?"

"Exactly! Maude and her newspaper are the face of the crusade but we need key people on the committee. And you're one of them."

65

Hal extended both arms. "Sign me up."

"We'll talk more once the plan has been formulated."

"I may still be sitting here," he said waving a hand across the clutter.

Adam stood and turned to leave. "Thanks, see you Sunday."

Hal came out of his chair and hung over the desk. "Why are you involved?"

"Maude made a strong case, very convincing. After some serious reflection, I decided to enlist. If we succeed it will make Conway a better place to live." Adam hesitated, fumbled in his pocket for the car keys. "I believe it's a chance to make a difference."

During the drive home, Adam felt rewarded. He had known Hal since he moved to Conway four years ago, and considered him a man of courage and conviction. While self-effacing, Hal's service in the last war defined a man of heroic proportions. He had eschewed the chaplaincy and became a forward observer in the 82nd Airborne Division, jumping onto a bloody beach at Normandy, surviving the German juggernaut at Bastogne. He came home with a silver star and two purple hearts.

Adam wondered how he himself would have reacted under those deadly circumstances. In truth, he had never smelled the scent of danger, certainly, nothing life-threatening. As a boy, he had been frightened by night shadows or a Lon Chaney horror movie. But as an adult, he had never felt the spine-chilling fear of a life in peril. The clash with the tavern owners could become nasty and for the first time, test his mettle. In a way, he looked forward to the confrontation, proud to have an ally like Hal Brady.

Chapter 11

Same Day

Twilight. Knox hurried to the stable, saddled her filly, and mounted quickly. She cantered along the narrow bridle path, through the meadow and into the trees beyond. The trail cut diagonally through the piney woods, needles dripping from a late afternoon shower.

At breakfast, Ben had mentioned his weekend fishing trip, a disclosure that dampened her spirit. She needed solace and the clearing was a sanctuary.

She heard the faint sound of hoofs and looked around as the horse and rider drew near, relieved to see a familiar face.

"Hello, Knox."

"Hi Brett, you startled me."

"Sorry, hope you don't mind my company?"

She shook her head. "Missy needed exercise. We're headed for the clearing beside Saddle Creek." She slapped the horse's flank with her crop and trotted away.

When Brett arrived at the clearing, Missy had been tied to a sapling near the shallow stream. Knox sat on the trunk of a fallen tree staring into the distance. There was enough light to see her finely sculpted face and the telltale eyes that betrayed her disconsolate mood.

He slipped down beside her. "What do you see?"

She pointed to a fleck of glimmering gold.

"That's Venus, easy to see on a clear evening. Look over here." Brett turned and motioned in the opposite direction. "See the orange star, right above the tree line? That's Arcturus, one of the brightest in the heavens."

She searched the night sky. "I see it....there, over that stand of pines."

"Follow the hands of the Big Dipper and you can always find it."

"How do you know so much about..." She looked up and pointed skyward, "...all of that?"

"Flight school," he said. "At one time I knew the constellations like the back of my hand."

In the stillness that followed, Knox became aware of the encroaching darkness as it settled unevenly among the trees, creating disparate patterns of flickering lights and shadows, The sweet smell of honeysuckle, growing wild along the banks of the stream, was carried by a docile wind and filled her with a pleasant but uneasy feeling. Overhead a nighthawk circled slowly in search of food.

"What about you?" He nudged her gently. "Are you interested in Orion and Sirius and Leo?"

"I know your friends, but not by name. When one is alone most of the time, it's easy to become a stargazer, a daydreamer." She stopped and tapped her head. "Most people wouldn't understand."

Brett shrugged his shoulders. "It sounds pretty normal to me." He hesitated a moment and swallowed hard. "I have a question."

"Sure, go ahead."

He picked up a twig and snapped it in two. "You're lonely, Knox. Am I wrong?"

She tried to explain: Feelings of isolation and estrangement had lingered stubbornly from the day she first walked into Hamilton House. Perhaps it was the stark contrast to Christian Manor and the enervation of those early years. Or, it could have been the condescension and the conditional acceptance of Conway; those smug smiles which said, "Welcome, but we'll wait and see if you are worthy of the Hamilton name." Maybe it was Ben, leaving so little time for their "togetherness" and the cultivation their marriage needed. She was not sure, even now. Only that it was so.

"I stay busy caring for Jake and keeping the house in order, but sometimes the solitude consumes me and I have this feeling..." With a girlish laugh, she tossed a pebble into the stream. "I know it's crazy to think about leaving Conway. And where would I go?"

"And what would Jake do?"

Knox shook her head slowly. "I don't know. He becomes more dependent every day."

"Don't leave him, Knox," he implored. "The old man needs you more than ever."

"You're just as indispensable," she added quickly. "Were you to leave, who would operate the plantation?"

Brett looked down and scuffed the soft dirt with the toe of his boot. "Oh, Ben could find another foreman."

An awkward silence floated around them. Knox slipped to the ground and lay back against the decaying trunk. "I'm curious, Brett, where's home?"

"Oklahoma, near Enid."

"How did you land in these parts?"

"After high school, I joined the Air Force and learned to fly. Following my discharge I went back and found work on a ranch in West Texas, grew restless, joined a rodeo and made the circuit. While we were here at the fairgrounds, I met Jake Hamilton. We connected, body chemistry, I guess. He offered me a job. I accepted."

"Any regrets?"

"Nope." Brett swatted at the air as a droning mosquito darted around his head. "Crop dusting gave me a chance to fly again. And my job takes me outside where I'm most content." He extended his arms as if to say, "That's it...the story of my life."

She shivered as a cool breeze stirred the air and rustled the trees that encircled the clearing. Brett stood up, removed his flannel coat, and placed it about her shoulders, allowing his hands to rest there for a moment, then dropped down beside her.

The conversation seemed to be a prelude, drawing them closer, beneath a gibbous moon. She looked up at the star-studded sky and wondered if their meeting was mere chance or had it been foreordained. She wasn't sure but she felt the warmth in her cheeks, an intense longing from deep within.

In the darkness Knox could sense his probing stare. She shuffled her feet uneasily and moved away from the fallen tree. But the eyes were still there, at her back, following her as she strolled toward the shallow stream.

Brett stood up and moved beside her. With a finger, he tipped her chin and kissed her full lips. Knox felt ambivalent; a moment of surrender to his will, sensual and submissive, followed by a wave of impropriety which caused her to pull away. She met no resistance.

"You're lonely," Brett said. "Those were your words."

For a few brief moments, time seemed to stop. So much of the past suddenly came alive and passed before her. Knox admitted silently what she had refused to accept before: her love for Ben had diminished. When she stripped away all the excuses, and the cover of pretense, absolute truth stood before her, illuminated by moonlight.

She had talked with Ben, but he denied that the marriage was broken. With the lines of communication in disrepair, Knox knew their relationship was, at best, fragile and tenuous. But she had kept hope alive, wishing for a miracle.

Where had love gone, she wondered? It had been there, she was sure of that. Could it have withered from neglect and boredom? Knox remembered Hal Brady's last homily: "Without care and attention, love loses its luster. And like a delicate flower, without the gifts of sun and rain, its blossoms will fade and fall away."

She reached down and pulled a sprig of honeysuckle and pressed it against her face. The sweet fragrance reminded her of coming to the clearing, almost two years ago, to savor the news of her pregnancy. Three weeks later, a miscarriage. Perhaps that was when love began to slip away.

Brett spoke softly and beckoned. She dropped the flowers into the water and for a moment watched them float away in a gentle current.

He led her through the woods into an inviting glade. Near the center was a solitary fruit tree, its blossoms, released by the wind, scattered over the forest floor. Knox felt some strange enchantment, as though she had entered a primeval garden. They leaned against the tree, against each other. He stroked her cheek softly and felt the warmth in her face. Brett kissed her gently, brushed his lips beneath her neck, made her body to quiver.

Brett stepped back and unbuttoned her denim shirt. Time was suspended by the welling up of delirious pleasure. They stood in the night shadows clothed only in starlight. Together they knelt at Eden's altar, longing passionately for the forbidden fruit. Her body shuttered again, dropping limp against the damp earth.

∾

For a time, they lay in the grass, their exhilaration spent. In the distance a coyote howled at the night sky.

Knox was suddenly aware of her nakedness and Eve-like, wanted to hide herself. Ripples of remorse seeped inside her mind. Yet the yearning still lingered, expanding like eddies in the swirl of a mountain stream.

"I ought to leave," she murmured.

Brett was asleep as she gathered up her clothes and slipped away, disappearing into the darkness beyond the stream. Knox wondered if there would be other secret meetings in this Elysian glade. She couldn't be sure. It was more than she could deal with in her present state of mind. Maybe tomorrow. The thought made Knox smile...she thought of Scarlett, of whom she had read at Christian Manor. Prone to temporize. Yes, she would think of it later. Maybe tomorrow.

Chapter 12

A tire scraped the curb before the '44 Packard stopped beside the church annex. Maude checked her watch and leaned over the front seat. "We're early, as usual."

"Yessum, but better'n runnin' late."

Maude steadied herself by holding on to Preacher's hand. "May as well get moving," she said. "Looks like rain." Westerly winds chased dark billowy clouds toward Madison Parish.

The door to the pastor's study was open and both men half-stood when Maude arrived giving her a warm greeting. With the flick of her wrist she motioned them down and settled into the only padded chair in the office.

"I'll be gettin' ready for services tomorrow," Preacher said. He looked at Maude as he turned to leave. "Just call when you is done."

Hal rested both arms on the desk. "So...where do we start?"

Maude opened her purse, retrieved a sheet of paper and looked at her hand-written notes. "Let's begin with recruitment." She adjusted her glasses and glanced at the paper again. "Who's on board?"

"I called Father O'Brien," Hal said. "He likes the objective and agreed to be a loyal foot soldier."

"What about ole 'High and Mighty'?" Maude asked.

Hal laughed. "Hayden jumped at the offer. He'd lead the band if we gave him the baton. But remember, he pastors the largest church in the parish and the Baptists will probably be our most loyal supporters."

Adam spoke up. "Ben agreed to talk with Arthur. It'll be a tough sell. The poor guy doesn't need more disgruntled workers, but Arthur knows that our success will benefit him in the long run."

Hal looked out the window. It had begun to rain, chasing a sparrow into the dense foliage of an elm. "Closing the taverns won't make beer or whiskey disappear," he said. "There's the 7-Eleven or the Quick Stop package store."

Adam's mind wandered as rain pelted the glass window. He knew that courageous and committed leadership were essential for any worthy undertaking. Hal and Maude had the credentials; they had been tested by fire. Again, he wondered about his own backbone and would it withstand the force of a dangerous adversary. Or like the craven lion in the Land of Oz, would he stand at the edge of the action and pray for a "heart"? While his only bare-knuckled fight was in the fifth grade, there had been other ugly confrontations and angry encounters, but none carried him across the threshold of violence. Perhaps the pummeling he received from Harry Profit in a corner of the schoolyard inculcated a reason for restraint. Medical school and a demanding internship had been a grueling test of endurance. However, the crusade on which he was embarking challenged the will *and* the heart.

He listened as Maude laid out the plans for the Civic Improvement Coalition, a highfalutin name for a group of locals with a singular goal. Adam smiled inwardly as Maude detailed strategy and designated assignments, beginning with Hannah Hawkins, the League of Womens Voters' activist who had agreed to head up the petition drive. He was certain Maude had missed her calling; she should have been military...an Army general like Bradley or Eisenhower or Marshall, preparing for the invasion of Europe.

"I thought we'd jump start the campaign with an editorial on the front page of the Review," Maude said.

"Good idea," Hal agreed.

"Follow that with a Sunday in which all the churches announce their support of the Coalition." Maude's turned slightly, her lively eyes locked onto those of Hal Brady. "And you can preach a give 'em hell sermon. Let the black hats know the Calvary's coming."

Adam heartily approved of Hannah Hawkins to head the petition drive. She was way ahead of the curve as an advocate for women's rights, both as voters and candidates for public office. While Hannah graduated Cum Laude from Sophie Newcomb and married Charlie Bynum, a man of substantial means, she was a worker bee, fearless to a fault and willing to mud wrestle if she espoused the cause.

"How many names are needed on the petition?" Adam asked.

"I called the Registrar's Office." Maude said. "Close to twelve thousand votes were cast in the last election."

Adam made the calculation. "That means Hannah must get more than four thousand names."

"And not just anyone off the street," Maude added. "Those who sign must be residents of Conway and registered voters."

"Tough job," Hal said under his breath.

The two men gave Maude their full attention as she discussed other aspects of the crusade and suggested they may need to meet again. She closed with a caveat that made their stomachs churn; a reminder that their involvement was not without risks. She was sure that Markham and Waters would fight back. The role of Tony Caruso was problematic. But a heavy-hitter from downstate would raise the stakes enormously.

Hal grinned, trying to lighten the mood. "Well, we didn't expect them to pack their tents and disappear like gypsies."

Maude shook her head. "Won't happen, so be prepared."

Adam stood up. "On that happy note, I'll take my leave. The hospital calls."

"Before you go I have some news on Mrs. Lebauer," Hal said.

"How's the poor woman doing?" Maude asked.

"Stopped by for a visit early in the week. She's much better. Her daughter and son-in-law have insisted she move to New Jersey where they have a large house in Tom's River, near the Jersey coast."

"When you see her again, give her our best wishes," Maude said.

"Of course, I will," Hal said. "Now let me find Preacher."

☙

Preacher held the umbrella in one hand and guided Maude to the car with the other. A light rain was still falling but to the west there was a break in the clouds. A pale rainbow arced high above the shaft of light. From the car window, she watched its faint glimmering and hoped it was a good omen.

No one spoke until the car turned into the driveway on Karen Lane. "Preacher, are you registered to vote?"

He shut off the engine and turned around. "No ma' am. They make it hard for the black folks to vote."

Maude remembered that Huey Long had eliminated the poll tax but the state legislature had passed a law that required annual registration, even in a non-election year, an enactment that discouraged most black and some poor whites from voting.

"What about the Flats? Are there any registered voters in those neighborhoods?"

"Maybe a few. Don't know `actly how many." He opened the back door and helped her out of the car. "A lot of them folks Miz Maude ain't able to write."

"We need names for our petition drive. Any suggestions?"

The rain had stopped and the leaden clouds had moved along, leaving a slight chill in the April air. Preacher scratched his head while processing the question. "A coupla things comes to mind."

Maude waited.

"Talk to Reverend Johnson at the Assembly of God Tabernacle. I `pect he can tell you 'bout the black vote. Might also speak to J. R. Ridings."

"The principal at Booker T. Washington?"

"Yessum. They's come closer to knowing than anybody."

"Thank you, Preacher. I'll call them in the morning."

"'less you needs me, I'd better get movin'."

She shook her head. "See you next week."

75

Preacher pulled the collar of his flannel shirt up around his neck and quickened his pace heading for the bus stop.

Chapter 13

Adam followed the pungent aroma of fresh coffee down the stairs and into the kitchen. Golden light filled the room with the promise of warm days and scudding clouds across azure skies. He stopped at the kitchen window; grass once brown and dormant during the long winter's chill, had magically turned emerald green. While the dogwoods had shed their snowy white blossoms, the trees were thick with foliage, providing shade for the sparrows that darted among them.

"Morning, Mattie Mae."

"Mawnin', Doc Swift. Set yourself down and I'll fetch you some hotcakes and sausage." She shuttled over to the breakfast table and poured him a hot cup of black coffee.

"Guess you heard the news? We hope to put the taverns out of business."

"Praise the Lawd!" A broad smile covered her face, the color of light mocha, and her chins shook with excitement. "Praise the Lawd!" It was a bellow she could not restrain; her bulging eyes alive with anticipation. Adam knew nothing would please her more than shutting down the taverns and running the owners out of the parish.

Adam told her of the recent church meeting and the plan for the petition drive.

Mattie leaned her bulk against the porcelain sink and stared with rapt attention.

"As you know, Mattie, some terrible things have happened in the past month that were tavern-related. So we decided it's time to stop complaining and tackle the problem."

"Amen! I done told you before, it's the Devil's playground. All that whiskey and gamblin' and sinin'." Her whole body shook with delight, her voice filled with religious fervor. "Ain't nothin' good come out of them places. Shut 'em down. Praise the Lawd!" She tilted forward, with hands on large hips, a peerless pose of righteous indignation. "And it ain't gonna be soon enough."

"We need your help." Adam sipped his coffee. "In fact, we need the help of your whole community."

Mattie Mae moved to the stove and filled a plate with pancakes and covered them with melted butter. Without looking up, she asked, "How can us black folks help?"

"The petition must be signed by four thousand registered voters." Adam stopped long enough to drown the pancakes in thick maple syrup. "There are two ways you can help. First, talk to Reverend Johnson at the Tabernacle; ask him to use his influence; getting every eligible voter in his church to sign that petition." Adam knew Mattie was a deaconess and in matters of conscience, she could be very persuasive.

"Ain't many of us able."

"Maybe more than you think."

"I'll see the preacher tonight at prayer meetin'," she said, taking the red bandana from around her neck and dabbing her face.

Adam cut the soft pancakes with his fork and took the first bite, savored it for a moment, then winked at her. "I've always said you're the best cook in the parish. No, make it the whole state of Louisiana."

A sheepish smile gathered at the corners of her ample mouth. But Mattie Mae regained her composure quickly as she replaced the handkerchief around her neck and knotted it at the throat. "You say there's two ways to help." She arched her brow curiously and her eyes widened. For an instant, Adam feared they might jump right out of their sockets.

"Some of the mill workers will scream 'bloody murder' and won't take kindly to our plan. Now, the saloons are segregated, but the tavern owners will try to 'buy off' those blacks who are eligible to sign the petition. So I need Reverend Johnson to convince his flock, the mill workers in particular, that a beautiful park with picnic areas and playgrounds will make this a better place in which to live and work." Adam wiped his mouth with his napkin and his eyes latched onto hers. "If I have my way, the park will be open to everyone...kids of every class and color."

"Just be careful, Doc Swift. The Klan is still wild-eyed crazy as they ever was. Don't want you swingin' from no tree."

෭෨

He remembered Betty Ann Windom. They were both seven years old when he invited her to the movies. His mother had assigned Pansy, the Swift's housekeeper to chaperon the children. Of course, Pansy was relegated to the balcony which meant he and Betty Ann sat there as well. Even as a child, he wondered why?

When Adam got home, he found his mother in the garden. The basket beside her was full of okra and green tomatoes. She removed her gloves and pulled him to her. "How was the movie?"

"Really good. Mr. Hope is so funny and I love ole Rochester."

"And Betty Ann, did she have a good time?"

Adam stood up, his eyes downcast. "But we sat in the balcony with Pansy."

She tipped his chin up. "While your father and I don't think it's right, still, it's the law."

"Why can't they change the law so Pansy can sit with everybody else?"

His mother smiled and tousled his hair. "One day things will be different. Meanwhile, we'll continue to treat Pansy and her family with kindness and respect."

"Next time I'll ask the manager if he'll make an exception."

"Next year, you and Jimmy will be old enough to go alone."

"Yeah, that'll be great." The boy looked at the row of cabbages and shook his head. "It's still not right."

෭෨

Adam knew that segregation in the South, twenty-seven years later, was part of a culture that arose from the bitter ashes of the Civil War. Slavery had been replaced by social stigma, invidious slurs and Jim Crow laws that relegated blacks to the back of the bus. Disenfranchised...third class citizens, at best. But Adam felt the ground shifting slightly and hoped that one day soon the nation would become colorblind. In Mr. Lincoln's world, would he have been an abolitionist? Perhaps. But in his own world, he simply tried to treat—in his mother's words—everyone with kindness and respect.

Mattie poured him another cup of coffee and laid *The Review* on the breakfast table. "I'll sho talk to the preacher tonight," she said, her voice trailing off as she disappeared into the laundry room.

Adam pushed his plate aside and picked up the paper. Maude's editorial filled the front page. With a tinge of excitement, he began to read:

"A cluster of saloons sit across the river, half-hidden, by a dense forest of hardwood and pine. The taverns lie dormant most of the day. However, at night, with flashing neon lights, they come alive like some strange nocturnal creature that draws its strength from the darkness and its substance from the shadows.

Their beginning was inauspicious; one bar and gill on Main Street at the foot of the bridge. The business license was granted on January 2, 1932 to Mr. Fred Warren, whose family owned large tracts of real estate in Madison and adjoining parishes.

Recently, voices of protest have been raised. And rightly so. In the past six weeks, a series of wanton acts have occurred, culminating in unspeakable tragedy: the death of young Andy Lebauer, then Ed Bagley; Dick Frey, only twenty-one years old, a quadriplegic. And we mustn't forget the brutal assault on the waitress while working in one of those very same taverns. Her life will never be the same.

Some have argued persuasively, that the saloons are like "tainted millstones" hanging heavy around our communal neck. The inference is clear: Rid Conway of her "civic blight.

In fact, a proposal has been made by a group of responsible citizens to expropriate Wildwood (the land on which the taverns sit), after fair and equitable remunerations. A city park with recreational venues will be built in their place. THIS PAPER SUPPORTS THAT PROPOSAL WITHOUT QUALIFICATION.

Why are things the way they are? The saloon's flourish because of Conway's indifference. Some accept them as incorrigible children, displeased with their bad behavior, but tolerant because they're "kin." Others ignore the problem. "Look the other way." "Live and let live." Social concern is diminished by apathy and inaction. Euphemistically referred to as "being open-minded" or a "tolerant person."

Our assent is the seed from which acquiescence emanates. We may disapprove in principle of the taverns and find many of its activities disagreeable, even egregious, yet in all candor, we have given them our tacit approval.

What's going on over there? First, we must accept the fact that the taverns touch everyone in this community. Sometimes directly, as in the case of Ed Bagley's family. Sometimes only obliquely, which is true for most of us. There have been allegations that the taverns have been involved in unsavory activities. Gambling has been mentioned. Ties with organized crime has been conjectured. Along with inferences of pimping and prostitution. All of this breeds an unwholesome, even a sinister influence, that pervades the culture and character of Conway. In our view, when nefarious forces affect the vitality and integrity of an entire community, this paper must speak out clearly and without fear of reprisal.

Is it too late? Are we impotent and unable to act? Have we become callous and uncaring about our town? Are we unable to expiate our guilt? NO!!! The answers are categorically, NO! We have a chance to change. A reprieve. That opportunity is coming soon. A petition will be circulated among you that mandates the Mayor and his appointed committee to consider replacing the taverns with picnic areas and playgrounds. Should the Mayor fail to act, a special referendum will be held. Sign the petition!

This crusade has caused angst and anger across the river. Grumbling. Hints of intimidation. Thinly veiled threats. Conway must re-sensitize her conscience, then with courage, oppose corruption in faint disguise. Remember the words of Edmund Burke, a member of the House of Commons and friend of the American colonies: "All that is necessary for the triumph of evil is that good men do nothing." The Review encourages every citizen to join this noble cause. For the safety of the town, for the sake of the children.

Allison poured herself a cup of coffee and sat down at the table unnoticed and waited for him to finish.

Adam looked up, surprised. "I didn't hear you come in."

"That's because you were wrapped up in Maude's editorial."

The corners of his mouth turned up in a satisfied smile as he reveled in *The Review's* hard-hitting prose. "Maude came out fighting, just as she promised. Fearlessly. It's the momentum we need to get the crusade off to a rip-roaring start."

Adam folded the paper and pushed it across the table. He brushed her lips with a kiss. "Gotta go. See you tonight."

He bounded across the kitchen and out the backdoor.

Chapter 14

Ben filled his coffee mug and went outside. He found shade beneath the sycamore tree and rested against its sturdy trunk, as one figuratively, might lean on an old friend. It was his haven, stirring memories of his mother.

The sun had cleared the rooftop and the glass belvedere sparkled with prismatic light. Ben looked back and admired the imposing columns and the wide gallery that wrapped around both stories of the big house. He noted for the first time, the louvered windows and French doors had been freshly painted forest-green. Another Knox initiative. And the moss-draped live oaks, their thick trunks braided with cross-vines, cast morning shadows across a lawn redolent with azaleas and beds of multi-colored flowers.

Ben sipped his coffee as he considered the indomitable spirit of his grandfather who had traveled a thousand miles to realize his dream. But for Ben, the big house was just that, a house, not a home. He only took pride in its grand appearance as one would admire an exceptional work of art. As a child, Ben had not felt that way. But he remembered when the house grew cold and the laughter died; the day he lost his mother. As if some giant vacuum had sucked the warmth from every room, every hallway, even the *garconniere*, hexagonal structures that flanked the sides of the house. And while Knox had added a woman's touch to the plantation, for him, nothing had changed. There were days when he wished they could leave Hamilton House and live in Conway, in a comfortable home like Adam and Allison.

Ben recalled the choice he'd made in the branches of this tree. It was one that aggrieved his father, for Jake loved the land and assumed his only child would take control of Hamilton's holdings. So, Ben's decision was divisive, a sharp wedge that drove them further apart.

But the separation began at a young age. Ben remembered Jake's indifference, as if Ben, as a boy, were someone else's son. The divide was as wide as the Ouachita, and one that Martha's love could not bridge. It troubled Ben that he had been denied a father's affection, and wondered if that was why he had chosen Medicine and even now, wanted to leave Hamilton House.

Over time, father and son had formed a tenuous, unspoken truce, an uneasy accommodation between the two of them.

"Are you hungry?" Knox asked from the veranda.

"Famished."

"I'll have it ready in a few minutes." The words faded behind slatted doors.

Ben yawned and stretched himself before heading back to his father's house.

∞

Knox placed a plate of scrambled eggs, cheese grits and crisp bacon in front of him. Homemade buttered biscuits and strawberry marmalade were already on the breakfast table. She poured coffee for them both and sat down across from him.

"Is that all you're having?" he asked.

"Not hungry."

"Are you all right?"

She hesitated. "Just worried."

"About what?"

"I've got a lot on my mind." Knox's narrow shoulders sagged.

"Tell me," he insisted, his interest quickening.

She looked up. "I'm worried about us."

"Have I done something wrong?" He pushed his plate aside.

"More what you haven't done...what you haven't said."

"Go on," he urged, wanting to hear more.

"Let me explain." She shifted in her chair, her eyes intense, and disarmed him with a simple accounting. "You have your work which is all consuming, the office, the hospital; you're involved with other people; you have a sense of accomplishment. I've none of that. All I have are Jake and this big house."

"You feel neglected?"

"Lonely; my dreams are grim reminders of Christian Manor."

Ben sipped his coffee trying to find the right words.

"We have so little time together. It's been three years since our last vacation...even a long weekend...just the two of us."

"I had no idea..."

"I need you Ben."

"Then, I'll make more time for us." He reached across the table and stroked her cheek. "And that's a promise."

Knox got up, refilled her mug and stood at the kitchen window. "There's more Ben. I need you to need me. Sometimes, I think I could leave Conway and you'd never miss me."

"No...no, that's not true," he said firmly.

Suddenly, Knox felt a vague sense of uneasiness. She wondered if her conversation with Ben was the reason. Or was it the memory of her clandestine meeting with Brett in the forest glade? She looked at the kitchen clock. "Arthur should be here soon." She got up and kissed Ben on the forehead. "I need to check on Jake."

Ben slumped in his chair. Why had he not seen the signs himself? Her feelings of loneliness and neglect? This morning, they were written like the Rosetta Stone over her vacant face. He cared deeply about Knox, but had failed to convey those feelings. The last thing he wanted to do was build a wall between Knox and himself. But had he, without intention, erected a barrier, not unlike the one that had separated him from his father? Was he, Ben, insensitive to Knox as his father had been to him? He knew it was easy to rationalize his mistakes; long and arduous workweek, his passion for hunting and fishing, oversight of the plantation... leaving little time for his marriage. It was a mistake and one he needed to remedy. He had made Knox a promise and he would keep it.

❦

When Arthur arrived, Ben led him into the kitchen. He surveyed the room while Ben made a fresh pot of coffee. It was a bright, cheerful room, windows with yellow curtains brought in streamers of sunlight.

"How was Hal's sermon?"

Arthur smiled sheepishly. "Talked about money. That's a dangerous subject."

"And a delicate subject." Ben added, retrieving a mug from the kitchen cabinet.

"Hal reminded us the church has bills to pay, an outreach ministry to support and buildings to maintain." Arthur chuckled. "Stepped on a few toes but that always happens on pledge Sunday."

Ben handed Arthur his coffee. "You're probably wondering why I called."

"I am a little curious."

Ben pulled a slip of paper from his shirt pocket. "Adam asked me to talk with you."

"What about?"

"The taverns." Ben dropped the list of names on the table. "There's strong sentiment that the taverns are a breeding ground for trouble and should be shut down. I'm sure you read Maude Harrington's editorial."

"Yes, of course. And Adam is involved?"

"He talked to Al Marx, who gave him the go-ahead."

Arthur put on his glasses and picked up the slip of paper.

"You know them all. And everyone feels that you are needed for the coalition to succeed."

Arthur walked to the window and watched a butterfly flutter around an azalea bush, then come to rest amid its pink profusion. "There are some in this town who profit from the taverns. There are also those who like what the taverns provide. A lot of them work at the mill."

"That's why we need your help."

Arthur returned to his seat and ran a hand through his few remaining strands of red hair. "The tavern owners won't leave

86

without a fight. It could get ugly." He pointed to the slip of paper. "Tell Adam I'm skeptical but I'll consider it."

They ambled down the hallway to the heavy oak door. Outside, a breeze carried on its gossamer wings the scent of lilac. Arthur started the car. "Tell that wife of yours I'm still in love with her." There was a rare twinkle in his dull blue eyes as he drove away.

℧

Knox placed a barefoot in the stirrup and hoisted herself into the saddle. She tugged at the reins and Missy moved out of the barn. They took the short cut through the east field to the river. With the wind in her face she hoped the ride would clear her mind.

Her conversation with Ben earlier in the day troubled her. Can a man really change? She remembered his promise, but would he keep it? Then there was Brett; the strong attraction made her shudder. She wondered if it was only physical. Or was there something more? A rapport that drew them together, like filings to a magnet; some ill-defined chemistry.

Still, she could not shake the nagging guilt that arose from her meeting with Brett in that primeval garden. Did Ben's neglect justify her adulterous affair? She didn't need the Sisters of Mercy to answer her questions or send her scurrying across the street to The Church of the Sacred Heart with its Holy Water and confessional. Knox believed her God was one of fairness and forgiveness and with that she pushed her private polemics aside.

Would it happen again? No...no, not a second time, said her voice of conscience. But the message from the heart was ambivalent... mixed signals. She was not sure.

The evening sky was alive with celestial lights. "Arcturus? Which one is Arcturus? Perhaps it's there, Missy," she said, pointing to a gleaming star near the handle of the Big Dipper.

Knox slipped off the horse and waded ankle-deep through the warm water to a dry place on the sandbar. She lay back and allowed the stillness to cover her like a quilt of eiderdown; to sort out her problems; away from the distractions of Jake and the big house. Her eyes grew heavy with sleep while around her there arose a cacophony of sounds...the whistle of the wind through the river birches, a chorus of crickets in the underbrush.

87

Knox awoke with the mare nuzzling her face. She looked at her watch, straining to see in the failing light. "My goodness, I must have fallen asleep, Missy. We need to get home. Jake's all alone." She rode away but hoped to return, to revel in the warm shallows of the river and again smell the sweet bouquet of trumpet honeysuckle growing wild along the weedy embankment.

Chapter 15

Same Sunday

Frank Markham sat back in the swivel and laced his thick arms behind his head. He scanned the Spartan office; no pictures, no plants, no radio; only a "girlie" calendar graced one wall, paint pealing at the corners. Mario sat on the worn leather sofa and Arnie, having turned his chair around, draped his long arms over the top. Frank had chosen Sunday night for the meeting since the taverns were closed and intrusions unlikely.

He looked at the lanky Waters and remembered him from their old neighborhood; high school days together. While never friends, he had not forgotten Arnie's mercurial temper; a mean streak as wide as Conway's main drag. Frank had wondered what kept Arnie out of the Army. While he endured the insufferable heat at Camp Claiborne, south of Alexandria, Arnie opened a pool hall downtown which prospered during the war years. It was public record that Arnie sold the business in 1944 and signed a lease with Fred Warren for land across the river. When Frank arrived in Conway, Arnie's Ale House was open with high volume traffic; a favorite watering hole for truckers, mill workers, and farmers from Madison and adjacent parishes.

Frank knew very little about Mario Gambelli, sitting still as a statue, immersed in a dog-eared paperback. Frank had asked Fred Warren, but neither he nor anyone else seemed to know where Mario came from or why he had settled in Conway. It was as if he dropped from the sky like a meteorite without any apparent reason. Frank was suspicious. The thin-lipped Italian chose to sequester his secrets; answering questions with a heavy Italian accent which no one could understand...or not at all. Frank had a hunch that beneath that mild-mannered façade, with the narrow face and aquiline nose, lurked something sinister. He planned to keep an eye on Mario Gambelli.

The Shamrock was the last of the three taverns to open, but Frank had a Marine-sergeant, take-charge mentality. Maude Harrington's editorial had stirred Markham's anger. She had goaded a hornet's nest. Meanwhile, the town was abuzz with the confrontation brewing between the coalition in Conway and the tavern owners across the river. He had heard from "sources" that the District Attorney had been consulted, hoping to find a legal remedy. Frank let his anger simmer and then subside, before making a decision.

First, he called Tony Caruso who had made overtures about a loose alliance with the tavern owners, a profitable offer that allowed the Mafia a base of operations as it sought to move north, across the state line to the race track in Hot Springs and the urban area of Little Rock.

With the pressure mounting, Frank had called the meeting to formulate a strategy. Dealing with his competitors was distasteful, like a dose of castor oil, but the threat of closure made their cooperation necessary. Mario and Arnie waited like good soldiers for Frank to open the proceedings.

Frank sat up and lit a cigar, sending a plume of smoke toward the cedar beams. "I think you know why we're here," he began. "Those goddamn do-gooders in Conway have decided to shut us down. And they're looking for legal ammunition."

Arnie lifted his bald head and shook it vigorously. "No way that's gonna happen," he said.

"Mario?"

"Simple," he answered. "Frighten them and they'll back off."

"That relic at the newspaper, old 'n Methuselah, seems to be the ring leader," Frank said.

Arnie's cheeks flushed. "Kill the ole bitch."

"Whoa! Let's not stick our neck in a noose," Frank cautioned.

Arnie threw out his long arms. "No problem. Make it look like an accident. Slip O'Riley a bottle of Wild Turkey before the autopsy and we're home free."

Frank shook his head. "I don't like it. If it's necessary, we'll let Caruso handle it."

"Kill the cat," Mario said evenly.

"Yeah, I'm told she loves that cat 'bout as much as she loves that nigger," Arnie said. "Still think we should go for the ole woman."

"I prefer Mario's suggestion." Frank stared at Arnie Waters. "Can you handle it?"

"Yeah, sure." Then a dismissive wave of his hand. "Piece of cake."

Frank cautioned his conspirators that any action on their part would ratchet up the resolve of the coalition. He then recounted his conversation with Tony Caruso; the two had agreed an alliance would be mutually beneficial.

After Mario and Arnie left, Frank turned off the light and locked up. Outside, he leaned against the trunk of his car and considered the chess game about to be played out. Were Arnie and Mario assets or liabilities? He wasn't sure, Arnie was too impulsive, like a cold blooded reptile; strike first, then consider the consequences. Mario was an enigma that Frank believed had his own personal agenda. He was an x in the equation, the joker in the deck. So Frank concluded that he alone would design the game plan and make the decisions.

He stared into the coal-black night and considered the rules of engagement. (The neon signs were off; a Sunday ordinance.) Frank thought of only two: expediency would drive his defense and his tactics, no matter how malevolent, were justified. But there was a caveat: if there was dirty work to be done, he would again call Tony Caruso. He got into his car, tossed the cigar stub out the window and drove away.

∾

Maude was tired. It has been a long day. She undressed and slipped into her cotton nightgown, while Belle curled at the foot of the bed. Maude reached for her book, decided against it, and turned off the bedside lamp.

Out of habit she reviewed the events of Sunday, a nightly ritual...an inventory, a word her father often used. She spent the morning at church listening to Hal Brady's "Give unto to Caesar's sermon," a homily she could have done without. She knew the church didn't run on air like a set of tires, but she had been tithing for years and Hal's tautology was tiresome. After lunch, she spent the afternoon paying bills and answering correspondence. Before sundown, she walked around the block, soaking up the serenity of the dwindling light, ate a small bowl of cereal, and went to work on next week's editorial. Another long day; not bad for eighty-three, she concluded.

As she lay in the dark room, Maude thought about the challenge the coalition had undertaken. Was it worth the valiant effort of so many people? Was it worth the risk? Maude knew she and Adam had a fight on their hands. The tavern owners would not leave West Conway without fierce resistance. Men without conscience. And the thought of Tony Caruso sent a shiver down her spine; she knew of his ruthless Organization. The Louisiana Mafia's strong-arm tactics were legendary and those who got in their way, ended up in the reptile-infested swamps along Highway 90, east of New Orleans.

Maude remembered her father with affection. While taciturn by nature, on rare occasions, he gave her sage advice. One day, during the chaotic times of Reconstruction, he reminded her, that despite the cost, a man should always defend his home and property, just as the South had done. It was one of the few things worth fighting for. (However, her father decried the subjugation of blacks which put him in the crosshairs of the KKK and caused him to move his family, in the dead of night, from the small town of Mer Rouge to Conway. While only six years old, she could still recall vividly the wild ride; the car without lights, only the glow of a full moon.)

Her eyes grew heavy. She reached down and pulled the cat next to her, then drifted down into the mysterious land of sleep.

❧

Wednesday, May 10th

Maude looked out her kitchen window. The sun had dried the dew that earlier sparkled like tiny crystals on the blades of grass. A light breeze chased a few wispy clouds across a high sapphire sky. She could see the rose garden across the lawn and on tip toe, the hydrangea that bordered the side of the house, a palette of colors...clusters of pink and lavender and robin's-egg blue. Out of the corner of her eye, Maude saw Preacher in the shade of the red maple, resting against the hand mower.

She fixed a big glass of iced tea and carried it to the screened-in back porch. Wednesday was yard work; Preacher's day to cut the grass, trim the sidewalks and water the flowers. It was also a reminder that the weekly edition of *The Review* was in the mail and on the newsstands. Another hard-hitting editorial, a shorter version of a week ago.

Preacher replaced the rag in his back pocket and pulled the mower from beneath the shade tree.

"Morning, Preacher."

He looked over his shoulder. "Mawning, Miz Maude."

"Got you some refreshment." She held up the glass of iced tea.

"Sho can use it. Thank you, ma'am."

Maude watched him guzzle the tea, ice tinkling against the glass. "Before you finish with the grass, would you check the mail."

"Yes'um." Preacher handed her the glass and started toward the street. "Ain't no mail," he muttered. "Ollie always runnin' late on Wensdee."

When Preacher reached the front of the house, the red flag on the mailbox was upright. It didn't make sense; Miz Maude mailed everything from her office. Maybe a prank, one of the boys on the street. But the red flag made Preacher smile...Ollie had not reached Karen Lane.

The sidewalks were deserted. The children were still in school. There were no signs of Ollie walking the neighborhood. He pulled the aluminum handle, burned hot by the mid-day sun. The metal door squeaked open. Preacher tilted his head. "Lawd God hep us," he said in a subdued voice. He stood up and leaned heavily against the metal post and took a few deep breaths. Then he looked again and fought off a wave of nausea. All he could see was fur, soiled white fur and a tail that had uncoiled and dropped through the opening. He waited until he regained control, able to stand without holding onto the metal pole. He reached in and gently pulled her out, folding Belle against his chest. Another wave of nausea. And another, when he realized she was headless. He looked inside the mailbox. Empty. His eyes raked a wide circle around the mailbox. Nothing. He pulled the rag from his back pocket and covered the dead cat.

Preacher lowered the red flag and closed the mailbox. He walked slowly to the back of the house, wondering what he could say. He knew Miz Maude loved this cat with her whole heart. He tried to conjure up the words, something to comfort her. But he couldn't think of anything. Not a single phase. Not a Bible verse. As he reached the porch, he'd figured that talk wouldn't help anyway. So, he'd offer to bury the cat beneath the red maple, Miz Maude's favorite tree.

Maude was standing at the screen door. "Any mail?" she asked before seeing the legs uncovered by Preacher's rag. He tried to speak but his throat closed shut; no words would come out. Only tears, trickling down his sunken cheeks.

She stepped outside and reached for Belle. Preacher placed the cat in her arms. "They cut off her head," he whispered.

Maude winced and her face clouded; she bit down hard on her lower lip. She stood for awhile and considered the atrocity as she cuddled the headless cat against her body. "Was there a note?" she asked finally.

Preacher shook his head.

"Guess they knew I'd get the message."

"You wants me to bury her?"

"Find a shady spot beneath the maple." Maude handed Preacher the ball of fur smeared with dried blood and grease. Preacher lifted his head, her eyes surprised him. They were dry and resolute as she went back into the house.

Chapter 16

Adam closed his umbrella and placed it in the brass stand beside the door. Maggie handed him a note as he passed her station. The message was from Markham; he wanted a meeting. There was a number to call.

Turning the corner, he passed Ben at his stand-up desk.

"Got a minute?"

"Sure," said Adam.

Ben closed a patient's chart and pushed it aside. "During the night, Jake had another stroke."

"Sorry, but I'm not surprised."

"When Knox took him his breakfast tray, he couldn't speak. She was upset, of course, and called me as I was leaving. Other than for the aphasia, Jake's exam was the same. But I'd like for you to check him."

"I'll go by during lunch. Knox can use a little hand-holding."

Adam went into his office and listened to the rain tattoo the window. He thought of Jake, enfeebled by a curse of longevity. But he was sure Jake had lived a full life, none of his days wasted or wished away. The old man had had his share of disappointments but only the infirmities of aging had knocked him down. Adam

95

likened him to a tree in late autumn, leaves turn brown and fall from their twisted limbs, then scatter, only God knows where, by a swirling winter wind.

Adam returned to his desk and buzzed Maggie. She tapped on the door. He asked her to call Mr. Markham and handed her the note with the number. "Tell him I'll be at Slim's Seafood Grill on Highway 23 at 7 o'clock."

"This evening?"

"Better now than later."

Her hazel eyes narrowed and worry lines formed at the corners like crow's feet. "Will you be okay?"

Adam assayed a weak smile. "Yeah, I'll be okay."

✑

As Adam drove to the restaurant through the driving rain, he prepared himself for a verbal assault. Markham was angry; the plan to close the taverns had stuck like a fish bone in his throat and he wanted franticly to spit it out. Adam expected to be insulted, even threatened. Though ready for any contingency, he could not shake the apprehension that caused his heart to flutter. The wiper blades scraping the windshield, only heightened the "on edge" feeling. "Must be wearing out," he grumbled.

The parking lot was almost empty. Adam figured the rain had thinned the mid-week crowd. He waved to Slim guarding the register, a cigarette dangling from his lips. Adam stopped beneath the lintel; his eyes swept the dining area. On one side was a Formica counter with a dozen stools; behind it a young waitress put down her book and sipped a bottle of Coke. Booths, covered with red vinyl, lined the far wall and wooden tables and straight-back chairs filled the center of the room. The restaurant was morbidly quiet; diners occupied two of the booths.

He spotted Markham at a corner table, ambled over and without salutation, took a seat.

"What's on your mind?" Adam asked.

He watched Markham stir his coffee. The sullen eyes and prominent nose, broken sometime in the past, gave him a malevolent look. He wore Levi's and a white T-shirt; on the front, stenciled in large block letters: PABST BLUE RIBBON. A tan windbreaker and railroad engineer's hat hung on the chair beside him.

Adam waited. He tried to remember Markham from the night of the Bagley brawl. But the Shamrock was chaotic, almost surreal, and his only recollection was Markham's sleek black hair and the scar that creased his right cheek.

Markham took a cigarette from the pack of Camels, lit it by striking a match with his thumbnail, took a deep drag and blew smoke just above Adam's head. He replaced the pack in the rolled-up sleeve of his T-shirt and rested his heavy arms on the table.

He looked at Adam with contempt. "I don't like what I'm hearin'. Don't like it one goddamned bit."

Adam felt an adrenalin rush which caused his stomach to roil and the muscles tighten across his shoulders. He had planned to remain composed, but the reaction was autonomic. His voice could not hide his vexation. "Look, Markham, I'm here at your request. But not to be bullied or barked at by you or anyone else. Is that clear?"

Markham slipped back in his chair, taken aback by Adam's effrontery. With fingers yellowed from smoking, he dug his cigarette violently into the tin ashtray. "I wanta know if the rumor's true."

"What rumor?"

"That some do-gooders are trying to run me and Waters and the Wop out of town."

"That's true."

The dark eyes flashed with anger. "Why?"

"Bagley's murder, the rape at the Ale House, the death of young Andy Lebauer, playing footsy with the Sheriff's Department..." Adam hesitated. "Shall I go on?"

"What's that 'pose to mean? Some kind of goddamn riddle?" His voice grew loud and more belligerent. The waitress, stunned, looked up.

"No, it's pretty simple, the taverns cast a sinister shadow over Conway which many find offensive, even hazardous to the health of the town."

He glared at Adam and banged the table with his fist. "I have a business over there. It's all legal. Nobody forces nobody into my place. They come because they want to; so what's the problem?"

"Look, Markham, I'm not here to argue the point. You have every right to oppose the coalition as long as you fight fair."

Markham lifted his right hand and pointed his index finger in Adam's direction, waggling it as a parent might while scolding an errant child. "Lemme tell you somethin'. We're gonna fight... you damn right we're gonna fight. And it may turn into a bloody free-for-all." He pressed the finger into Adam's chest, then again, and again. "So do me a favor and tell your fucking friends to mind their own damn business."

Adam reacted instinctively. His jaw jutted, his cheeks flushed. With his right hand, he grabbed Markham's wrist and slammed it hard against the table. He locked Markham in his gaze and spoke harshly. "Don't you ever touch me again. And don't threaten me! Understand?"

Markham wrenched free and tried to stand. With his left hand, Adam forcibly pushed him back, overturning the coffee, spattering Markham's T-shirt, the cup shattering on the tile floor.

"Do we understand each other?"

Markham glanced at the diners who had become spectators. Sweat glistened on his forehead. He rubbed his wrist and stared back at Adam, his eyes glazed with rage. He picked himself up, grabbed his hat and coat, and bolted from the room past the frightened waitress.

"Dr. Swift, are you okay?" The look of alarm lingered on her face. Adam pointed to the broken cup and overturned chair.

She flipped her hand. "Don't worry 'bout that."

"Sorry Slim," he said on his way out.

The evening's acerbic encounter troubled Adam. Driving through the rain, he tried to evaluate the meeting with Markham. He would not forget the strong invective, or Markham's face, lips pinched with loathing. Trouble ahead; he was sure of it. Resistance by ruthless men.

☙

Adam took off his wet coat and hung it in the washroom. He found Allison in the kitchen, thumbing through The Saturday Evening Post. She stood and embraced him as if he had been away for a long time. He kissed her lips and moved to the stove. Adam lifted the lid of the cast-iron pot, a chuck roast simmering in a flotilla of carrots and onions and new potatoes.

"Hungry?"

"Only a bowl of cereal for breakfast," Adam said. Markham had squelched his appetite, but Allison had prepared his favorite meal. He loved her too much to risk any hurt feelings.

"Tell me about your day," she said while putting food on the table.

"Lots of news, none of it good." Adam stirred the lemon in his tea. "My first phone call this morning was from Maude. Yesterday, Preacher opened the mailbox and found her cat...beheaded."

"Oh, no!" Allison sank into a chair. "Maude loved that cat more than anything."

"The grisly death was a warning. But Maude's tough as nails and the loss of Belle only reinforces her will to win."

"I'm sure Markham and his cronies are responsible."

"A safe assumption." The roast was so tender Adam cut it with a folk.

He told her about Jake and his mid-day visit, explaining that Jake had had an ischemic event, not a stroke. But even so, it was a harbinger of a more devastating insult. "Of course, Knox is a nervous wreck, waiting for that to happen."

"Poor Knox." Allison held up both hands. "I know...I know you think Ben loves her. But neglect is written all over that marriage and Jake is just the exclamation point."

Adam speared another carrot. He chose to nibble rather than reexamine Ben's marriage.

"Mark my word, once Jake is gone, Knox will leave Hamilton House unless Ben gives her more of his time and attention."

Adam only shrugged, not wanting to go there. So they finished the meal in silence.

"There's more bad news that I've saved for last," Adam said, pushing his plate aside.

She reached across the table and took his hand. "Haven't you told me enough?"

"I had a call from Frank Markham. He wanted to meet with me. So we had our rendezvous this evening at Slim's Seafood." Adam described the encounter and a seething Markham leaving the restaurant. "We may have stepped on a bed of fire ants and Maude's cat was just their first calling card."

Allison squeezed his hand. "Please be careful."

Adam gave her an assurance before adding, "Maude thinks the coalition can handle the tavern owners. She's worried that Markham will make a deal with Tony Caruso." His brow furrowed. "It would certainly change the rules; a much more dangerous game."

Allison had heard enough. She slipped out of her chair, walked behind him and wrapped her arms around his neck. "How about some dessert? I stopped by Waldo's for peaches and made a cobbler."

"Later." He patted his stomach. "I'm stuffed."

She kissed him on the ear and turned to leave. "I'd better check on Robin."

"Let me." Adam got out of his chair and labored up the stairs. He found her door ajar, the night light on. Robin, in her mermaid pajamas, slept peacefully. Beside her was a black bundle of fur that opened his droopy eyes and wagged his tail. Adam picked him up and let him snuggle against his chest. He looked at Robin, his heart flooded by a father's love. He put Charlie on his blanket near the bed, then bent down and kissed Robin on the cheek.

Adam went to the window and opened the blind. He looked outside; the rain had stopped and a street light cast eerie shadows across the lawn. Suddenly, the rush of a despairing wind swept over him and rattled the window. Something had reminded him of Markham's menacing threat. It may have been Robin's blissful sleep.

Chapter 17

Friday, May 12^(th)

It was a gray, cheerless morning. Knox felt the fatigue stretch across her shoulders and crawl up the tight muscles of her neck. Her conscience continued to wrestle with her infidelity in the forest glade. And Jake's recent "flare-up" had taken an added emotional toll.

Wednesday night she had moved a cot into his bedroom, awakened every hour, propped on an elbow, and watched him in the half-light, listening to him breathe; then satisfied, she would lie back and drop down into a shallow sleep.

The next morning, she put on her bathrobe and padded downstairs to fix Jake a bowl of hot cereal. Every turn or tilt made her head ache. She washed two aspirin down with a glass of orange juice, put a kettle on the stove, and massaged her sore shoulders while she waited for the water to boil.

Knox thought she heard something at the back door. The second time, the knock was loud and insistent. She fastened the robe snugly with its purple sash, trudged across the kitchen and unlatched the bolt.

He stood there like an awkward adolescent, shifting his feet, waiting for an invitation inside.

"Good morning, Brett," her greeting filled with pleasant surprise.

His looked at her intently, a stare that caused her cheeks to color.

"Well, don't stand there. Come on in." Knox felt better and knew Brett's visit was the reason.

The kettle began to steam and whistle. "Coffee? Ben made a pot before leaving."

"No thanks." He sat at the breakfast table. "I came by to see how Jake's doing."

"A lot better." She poured the hissing water into a teacup.

"What happened?"

"A light stroke."

"That what I heard at the feed store."

"By the time Adam arrived, the symptoms were gone."

"Then he's gonna be okay?"

"Ben said it'll happen again. But he can't say when. And the next time it could be worse."

"Tell Jake I came by."

Knox squeezed a slice of lemon into her cup. She looked up with her engaging brown eyes and stirred her tea abstractly. "I'll tell him when I take him breakfast."

Brett searched for words as an awkward silence hung over them like river mist. "I had another reason for stopping by..." He reached across the table and took her hand. "I wanted you to know the night we spent together was special." He felt the tension as he searched for the right words. "What I'm trying to say...I care about you...I care a whole lot. And what happened was not trivial, but a night I'll never forget."

Knox reached out and placed her fingers lightly against his lips. "Shh. Don't say anymore, at least not now."

Disappointment lined his face. "I'm sorry if I've said too much."

"No, no, I'm glad you feel that way. But with Jake's illness, I just can't handle anything else."

Brett leaned over the table, his face close to hers. "Just one more thing; something is pulling us together. It wasn't planned, it's just happening."

Something was happening, Knox conceded silently.

Brett stood up and turned toward the door. "We'll talk about it some other time...after Jake gets better."

He was gone before she could answer. Her shoulders drooped under an invisible weight as the old weariness returned.

છ

During the Friday lunch hour, Ben drove out to the paper mill. It had been almost a week since he asked Arthur White to support the petition drive. He knew Arthur was ambivalent, struggling with a tough decision; wanting to support his friends in the coalition but worried about lowering morale at the mill. The taverns were a haven for the workers after long hours in the sweltering heat of the paper mill.

Ben turned on Main Street and crossed the bridge. He knew that unlike the father, vacillation and delay flawed Arthur White. Decision-making was dilatory, a fault that crippled his mill operation. Arthur had always been a foot-dragger and needed to be prodded.

Ben drove through an open, chain-link gate and parked beside Arthur's sparkling new Chrysler Imperial. He gagged on getting out of his car; the smell of "rotten eggs" permeated the parking lot. He wondered how long it took a worker to ignore the sulfuric odor caused by the separation of cellulose from other wood by-products.

Using his handkerchief as a mask, he pushed a button beside the back door. A buzz sounded and the lock clicked open. Ben took the metal steps two at a time, the clanging sound bouncing off the walls of the narrow stairwell.

The outer office was empty. Ben breathed a sigh of relief. Clara Hall who ruled the executive suite with an iron hand was missing from her perch in the outer office. Miss Clara was a spinster who dressed severely and found nothing in life amusing. Ben had heard the story many times: at a tender age she was smitten by love and compromised by a handsome traveling salesman who left Conway like a coward in the dark of night. From that day to this, so the story goes, no one had seen a smile grace her solemn face. "Thank God," Ben murmured as he past her vacant desk.

"Hello Arthur. Where's Miss Clara?"

103

"She's sick, poor thing. Touch of the grippe, I suppose. Wanted her to call your office, but you know Miss Clara, she'll suffer in silence."

"She's definitely a Stoic," Ben said with a straight face.

Miss Clara's absence was clearly evident. Arthur's large mahogany desk was disorganized, cluttered with payroll, stacks of papers, and unopened mail. A large portrait of Joshua White hung on the back wall as though peering doggedly over Arthur's shoulder. A wet bar sat between the two windows, each hidden behind louvered shutters.

Arthur pointed to a tubular chair. "What bring you across the river this time of day?"

"Just came by to check...you know...the petition drive."

Arthur squirmed in his swivel. "Care for a drink?"

Ben waved off the offer.

"I've got no quarrel with the cause, it's worthy enough. But many of the workers will express a grievance. Bad for morale. And as you know, the business is marginal. Stirring up a bee hive would only add to my growing list of problems."

Ben looked at the portrait behind the desk and knew that Joshua White, without question, would join the crusade and use it as a means to improve morale at the mill. "I know it's not easy, but the coalition is counting on you. Adam believes that success hinges on your support."

"That's nice to hear, but I'm not that important."

Ben moved to the edge of his chair. "But you are," he pressed. "White is the most revered and respected name in the parish."

"I'm flattered, of course." Arthur stood up stiffly and at the wet bar mixed a weak Scotch and soda. "Waters called this morning," he said, deftly deflecting the line of conversation.

"Waters?"

"Arnie Waters. He owns one of the saloons...Arnie's Ale House."

"And..."

"He wanted to strike a deal."

Ben slipped back into his chair.

There was a long silence as Arthur stirred the ice with his finger. "Everyone knows I'm fighting like hell to keep the unions out of the mill. Waters claims to be a good friend of Frankie

Moreno, the union organizer from Baton Rouge. He'll put in a good word with Moreno..."

"And what's the quid quo pro?"

"Neutrality."

"Neutrality?" Ben shook his head.

"Well, the inference was clear: don't join the coalition; keep their propaganda out of the mill; express no personal opinion; offer no endorsement."

"How's Water's connected?"

"I'm not sure," Arthur said. He set the glass down and walked back to his desk. "Think its family. A cousin, maybe."

"So, what did you tell him?"

"I'd think about it." Arthur squeezed a smile from his thin lips as he recalled Waters' warning. "He didn't say goodbye; only a threat. 'Don't take too long...a fire is a terrible thing...if you know what I mean.'"

"Don't let them intimidate you, Arthur. Act in the best White tradition," Ben said, stealing a glance at the portrait.

"I know what's at stake," he said meekly. "Tell Adam I'll call him Monday."

Ben thought about Water's proposal which seemed so enticing: do nothing, straddle the fence. But Ben knew that inaction was only a convenient cover for indecision. While Water's offer was a tempting trade-off, in effect, it asked Arthur to betray his friends and dilute their chances of success.

Ben stood in the doorway, a final look at the portrait of Joshua White. He wished the father were here to help Arthur make the decision. Ben knew life was full of crucial choices and for Arthur, this was one of them. Another fork in the road...and he must decide which way to go. It wouldn't be easy. Ben was sure of that.

Chapter 18

Saturday, May 13th

Johnny Pappas left New Orleans at 4 a. m. He planned the early start for two reasons: northbound traffic would be light on Highway 61 and his arrival time would take Markham by surprise. Johnny considered that a tactical advantage. The long drive gave him time to recall his close connection with Tony Caruso. They first met in Angola's steaming-hot laundry, both inmates in the infamous state prison. Caruso had received a twenty year sentence for armed robbery, but mysterious power brokers pressured the Governor, to issue a pardon. Tony Caruso spent only two years behind bars.

Johnny remembered his own release soon after, walking out the gates of Angola, relishing his freedom, cloudless skies and the flowers that grew in wild abandon along the roadside. He and Tony were reunited on the streets of Gretna, a sleazy, crime-infested suburb on the West Bank. They worked as longshoreman at the New Orleans port and saved enough money to open a bar and liquor store. They knew that in Jefferson Parish, anything could be bought or sold (even to an ex-con) for the right price or through the strong-arm of intimidation.

Johnny smiled as he thought about his marriage to Tony's youngest sister, Mary and the festive wedding reception. Johnny was a native of Hania, a quaint village on the island of Crete, an outsider who had become a bona fide member of a Sicilian family and later, Caruso's closest confidant. Johnny shook his head in disbelief, as he envisioned that stump of a man, who at the age of thirty-seven, leapfrogged the line of succession, elected head of the Louisiana Mafia.

Pappas noticed Conway wakening as he drove along Main Street toward the bridge. The sun was on the rise as a few pedestrians stood idly beneath awnings, waiting for stores and the bank to open. Across the river, he turned into the Shamrock and parked near the front of the tavern. He stepped out of the car and cautiously looked around. No one was in sight. He listened; only the rustling of the wind in the pines and slender leaf-laden elms.

He took the gun from the glove compartment and tucked it in the holster at his hip before locking the car. He walked into a large rectangular room; empty, other than for movement behind the bar, someone shuffling bottles that lined the mirrored wall.

Johnny slipped his dark glasses into the coat pocket of his grey pinstriped suit, reshaped the knot in his black knit tie and moved to the railing.

"Is Markham here?"

The bartender, startled, looked up. "Name's Tex. Can I get you a drink?"

"I'm looking for Markham." The voice, firm and insistent, ignored the offer.

Tex took a look at Pappas, for only a second, like the flash of a camera. He would not forget the mental photo: jet-black hair, an angular face with thin lips that curled down at the corners and those dark, piercing eyes that conveyed something sinister. A foreigner, he thought. Not from these parts.

"He's in the office checking receipts. Business is always good on Friday night."

The cold eyes narrowed into an arresting stare. "Tell him Johnny Pappas wants to see him...now!"

"Sure...sure," Tex stuttered. "Be right back."

He returned in a flash and pointed toward the end of the bar. "Right through that door. Frank's anxious to see you."

"I'll take that drink now...an Amaretto on the rocks with a splash of vodka," he said, leaving a ten dollar bill on the counter. "Keep the change."

"Thanks."

Markham was on the phone but motioned his visitor in. Pappas frowned as he scanned the room with its grim walls and linoleum-covered floor. The air was stale with cigarette smoke that made his eyes burn. He pulled up a chair and sat down in front of Markham's metal desk, littered with paper, an adding machine and an ashtray filled with cigarette butts.

Markham replaced the phone in its cradle. His swivel groaned as he moved up and rested his heavy arms on the desk.

"My name is Johnny Pappas and I have a message from Tony Caruso."

"How did a nice Greek boy like you get involved with all those goddamn Sicilians?" The laughter rolled out of his barrel chest in waves. But Markham stopped laughing when the stranger only stared, his expression unchanged.

"Caruso's message is short and simple," Pappas said finally.

"Let's hear it."

"The Organization wishes to expand. In a recent phone conversation, you and Mr. Caruso formed an alliance. Nothing in writing. But a man's word counts the same. The taverns will serve as a base of operation for our expansion into the northern tier of the State and in turn, we'll assist in dismantling the coalition and their petition drive." Pappas rearranged himself in the chair, crossed his legs. "The alliance is not to be confused with friendship; it's a hard-nosed business arrangement. Conway is virgin territory and the prospects for growth are promising. Mr. Caruso doesn't want the door, which has been cracked, slammed in his face. So, we need each other. Your survival is at stake. A lucrative opportunity for the Organization is in jeopardy. The threat to the taverns creates a mutual need...a connection. We're in this together, whether we like it or not." Pappas got up and went to the window, speckled with dust. "Have I made myself clear?"

Markham was fearless and aggressive by nature. He had made his way through a hostile world since leaving home a long time ago. But he knew his limitations. He and Arnie and Mario were no match for Caruso's cold-blooded organization, his pockets filled with high-level politicians and members of local and state police. Markham had heard (and believed it to be true) that those who opposed Caruso, simple vanished into thin air. He, Arnie, and Mario needed the Mafia's muscle and in addition, they would profit from the Organization's "back room" activities, all part of the verbal alliance.

"Perfectly clear," Markham said.

Pappas looked out the grimy window at the service road; whirls of dust trailed a passing delivery truck on its way to the Ale House. Pappas came back to his chair and pointed a finger at Markham. "Remember, the Organization will handle the entire operation. Don't get in the way. We'll contact you if needed. Everything will be clean, efficient and professional. That's the way we do business."

"I'd still like to kick those meddlin' bastards all the way to hell and back."

"Leave the ass-kicking to us," Pappas said with a tight smile.

Tex came in carrying a small tray and placed a liqueur and a cold bottle of beer on the corner of the desk. He stood for a moment, like a soldier waiting further instructions. Silence, only the whirr of the ceiling fan. Tex shuffled his feet indecisively. "Well, call me if you need anything." The door, ill-fitted in its frame, rattled shut behind him.

The Greek took the glass, agitated it gently between his slender hands, causing the ice to tinkle like muted chimes, lifted it close to his face and breathed deeply of its pleasant aroma. He then sipped the liqueur, closed his eyes momentarily and savored the sweet taste as it trickled down his throat.

"Remember, stay out of the way," Pappas said, placing the drink on the desk. "Your last attempt was awkward and ill-advised. And I suspect you fueled the town's resolve with an act of stupidity."

Markham leaped up with clenched teeth, his jaw jutted contentiously. He recovered control and began to scatter papers across the top of his desk. "You mean the old woman and her cat?"

Pappas nodded and let his hands slide away from the cold metal of the forty-five holstered to his belt.

"She's a fool." Markham growled.

"You're wrong. She's smarter than all three of you."

"We wanted to frighten her."

"Killing her cat?"

Markham shrugged his burly shoulders.

"You read her wrong," he said reprovingly. "She is, in fact, a woman of principle. You shove her face in the dirt or dig your boots into her side and it will only strengthen her resolve. Some are weak and frightened; they wilt under the threat of violence. Others, like Harrington, draw strength from the scent of danger; challenge begets courage. So, don't let her frail body and wrinkled face fool you. She will never relent, and death is no specter."

Markham sat back, his jaw slack. "So, where do we go from here?"

"The petition drive begins soon. We must move quickly. Fortunately, most of the voters aren't cut from the same cloth as the old lady. Fear can be an effective weapon. However, implementation must be foolproof and the plan impeccable."

"What's that mean?"

Pappas ignored the question; he had one of his own. "If we were to target someone, who would you choose?"

Markham toyed with the pack of cigarettes while he mulled over an answer.

"It must be someone involved in the park project. The town must see it as retaliation for participating in the petition drive. The intent must be clear, not simply happenstance."

"I got names, but you said we made a hero out of the old woman. What's the damn difference?"

"The difference is the degree of punishment imposed on the targeted victim. Cutting off the head of a cat is gruesome, but it would hardly frighten anyone."

"I don't want no killin' on my conscience." Markham took the last drag from his cigarette and began to cough. It came in waves, paroxysmal and violent, leaving him breathless, his face flushed and swollen. Finally the bolus of phlegm broke loose and the coughing stopped. He rolled the plug of mucous around his mouth a few times and spit indelicately into the wastebasket.

Pappas turned away. His stomach lurched but the revulsion passed. "You leave the details to us."

Markham shook his head. "I don't know if Mr. Caruso can stop a big rock rollin' down a steep hill. The newspaper's got us on the front page, the preachers are raisin' hell. The folks in

Conway are lining up to sign the petition. You'd think the taverns had infected the town with a social disease...syphilis or 'the clap.'" Markham shook the pack of Camels. "Guess you might say, we're desperate."

"Just give me some names." Pappas took out a small notebook and fountain pen from the inside pocket of his coat.

Markham found a book of matches beneath some papers and lit a cigarette. "Adam Swift. A doctor in Conway. I doubt if he's got an enemy in Madison Parish...or anywhere else."

"Family?"

"Wife and daughter."

"How old is the girl?"

"Five...maybe six."

"Wife work?"

"Don't know. Probably a volunteer of some kind."

"What's your assessment of Swift?"

"He and the ole lady are the gang leaders. And Swift's a big buddy of the D. A., who's giving them free legal advice."

Pappas looked up. "Did you say the D.A.?"

"Yep. Close friends. And Marx is a hard working Jewish lawyer who tried to get an indictment from the Dolan grand jury." Markham paused long enough to remember his encounter with Adam at Slim's Seafood Grill. "Swift is tough and won't bend easily."

"Who else?"

"I've mentioned the old biddy at the newspaper; feisty as a damned drill sergeant." He opened the top drawer and tossed *The Review* across the desk toward Pappas.

Pappas scanned the editorial, folded the paper neatly and placed it in the outside pocket of his fashionable pinstriped coat. "Anyone else?"

"The preacher."

"Got a name? There're a lot preacher's in this town."

"Harold Brady. The word's out, he's planning a sermon that'll give the taverns hell."

"Family?"

"No, he lives alone, but his mother's still alive, up east somewhere, Boston maybe. Wiry little bastard who, in a scuffle, won't give an inch. Came back from the war with a chest full of ribbons."

"This town seems to have more than its share of street fighters," Pappas said, closing the notebook.

"Hold on a minute. Add Arthur White to your list."

Pappas waited.

"He owns the paper mill and his workers are some of our best customers."

"Sounds like an ally, not the enemy."

Markham crushed his cigarette in the ashtray. "Swift and others have pressured White to go along with the petition drive. I heard yesterday he agreed to set up booths inside the plant and pass out pamphlets to influence the workers. He's not a leader but his support is crucial." Markham emptied the ashtray in the wastebasket. "There's one other thing: Arthur White's not made of strong stuff. I'm sure he'd faint dead away if someone stuck a gun in his belly and asked for his wallet."

Johnny Pappas stood up and buttoned his coat. "Don't call us. We'll contact you when the time is right. There must be no further communication. Is that understood?"

Markham started to answer but Pappas was out the door.

"This meeting never happened," Pappas said over his shoulder. "Make certain your bartender gets the message." He tilted his head toward Tex, wiping off tables in the adjoining room.

Then he was gone like a whiff of the wind.

♋

Preacher had dropped her off before the workday began. The office was quiet, just the way she liked it. Maude faced a six o'clock deadline. She sipped her coffee and went to work, two fingers pecking the old typewriter.

An hour later, she pulled the sheet of paper from the Royal. With a red pencil she made several changes. While the two previous editorials had been hard hitting and objective, she wanted a different tone. Something with an aesthetic appeal. She adjusted her glasses and read the second draft aloud:

It would be impossible for most people to believe that on a beautiful May day, beneath an azure sky, filled with powder-puff clouds, devious men, scattered across the country, meet to mock justice and plan nefarious schemes, not unlike those who operate the saloons across the river. The hillsides are adorned with wildflowers growing amid the earth's undulations and a balmy breeze coddles the fruit trees, cast in fresh green foliage. Cynicism and suspicion seems incongruous in such an enchanting setting. Will the nature of Man, with his fallibilities, ever change, or like the leopard, forever wear his spots, to carry the blemishes that diminish his spirit? On such a day, inspired by a visage of loveliness Browning declared that 'God's in his heaven/All's right with the world.' Pollyanna? Perhaps. For man seems unable to extricate himself from his own prison of selfishness and self-aggrandizement. Will he ever learn? The redolence of spring with its promise of renewal and all its expectations shouts in glorious affirmation. But the past rears its head, a reminder of man's futility and failure, and the voice of the Turtle Dove is heard throughout the land by those with ears to hear: 'God, dear God, help us all.'"

Chapter 19

Saturday, May 20th,

At first light, Ben parked his '49 Porsche coupe beside a stand of loblolly pine. He quickened his pace as he approached the boathouse. The anticipation of fishing Black Bayou always created a childlike excitement. He greeted Buster Brodnax, the garrulous proprietor, who gave him the latest weather report and the fishing "hot spots," while they sipped cups of hot chicory coffee.

"Have a seat," Buster said. "Your boat's ready to go."

Buster, a native of Grand Isle, weighed over three hundred pounds. He sat on a bar stool, which Ben was sure defied the laws of physics, and rested his massive arms and flabby breasts on a glass counter above the array of candy, cigarettes, chewing tobacco, patent medicines and fishing tackle of every description.

"Try a silver spoon," he said, his Cajon accent unmistakable. "Been hittin' 'em pretty good here lately. Yesterday, a fella caught a rainbow; a big sucker, down at Cypress Point."

Ben bought a Hershey bar and stuffed it in the pocket of his windbreaker. Outside, he felt an unseasonable chill as he walked past the bait stand and down a slight grade to the boat dock, cypress planks creaking beneath his canvas shoes.

Ben knew that each year the Department of Fish and Game stocked Black Bayou with white perch, crappie, large mouth bass and rainbow trout...a fisherman's nirvana. The boat rocked as Ben stepped inside, carrying his tackle box, the Heddon fly rod Knox had given him for Christmas, and a thermos of coffee. Buster had placed an ice chest, containing sandwiches and beer in the bow of the boat. He cranked the small Mercury engine and waited while it coughed and sputtered, then steered the boat out of the slip into the broad body of the bayou.

The Mercury droned smoothly as it cut through the water. By the time he reached Cypress Point, the sky had turned pale blue and the nebulous swirls of mist had melted away. Ben cut the engine, turned the boat with his paddle, letting it drift along the shoreline. The morning was soundless except for the splash of his silver spoon and the staccato *tat tat tat* of a woodpecker searching for food.

He thought about Knox and their Sunday conversation two weeks ago. "Why is she unhappy," he wondered aloud. She had *carte blanch*, anything for the house, for her own personal needs. Other than Jake's care, he asked for nothing more. Nor could she doubt his fidelity; there had never been another woman in his life. Perhaps her complaint of inattention was legitimate but with extra effort he could allay her concerns and reaffirm his promise... to love and to honor. "But there must be something more than my neglect," he murmured, reeling in his line to check the lure. Perhaps the miscarriage was the culprit, the real source of her discontent. She simply had not forgiven herself for losing the baby. But he had accepted her failure. Why couldn't she?

At mid-day, Ben dropped anchor in the shade, a brace of willows. He crawled to the bow and opened the ice chest. He found his lunch and settled in his fold-down seat. He finished the PoBoy and sipped the beer. But thoughts of his marriage kept nagging him. "Why the intrusion?" he asked himself. He loved Knox and losing her was unthinkable. For the first time, he tried to examine those feelings. Was it her engaging good looks and gentle manner (which reminded him of his mother)? Her devoted care of his ailing father? Overseer of house and gardens? Or was it something else, a matter of the heart? Ben chose not to play psychologist, the dynamics were too complex. He would just try harder. The glare from a high sky blinded him and he failed to notice the black head of a water snake, skimming past the boat in search of a fallen tree on which to bask in the growing heat.

Before the day was out, Ben had convinced himself that he could patch up the marriage. He started the motor and with a stringer full of fish headed back, full throttle, to Buster's boathouse.

ຄ∽

Knox called the hospital and asked the operator to page Adam. Could he come by and check on Jake? He seemed to be sleeping more than usual and at times, his breathing was irregular. Knox admitted that she worried too much about Jake, despite Ben's reminder that regression was inevitable. Any change raised her level of concern and, of course, Ben was away. She sweetened the request with an offer: a slice of Lena's custard pie.

While the purpose of her hospital page was plausible, Knox concealed the real reason for her request; Jake was only a pretext for her call; an excuse, a half-truth, even an indulgence. The words rolled off her tongue glibly, blaming the years at Christian Manor and its draconian rules.

ຄ∽

Adam tossed his coat in the backseat and looked at his watch. It was after six o'clock when he left the doctor's parking lot. He put the top up and turned on the Ford's a/c; summer seemed to arrive earlier every year. He loosened his tie and thought about his confrontation with Markham, only three days ago. He had called Maude the next morning and they agreed the coalition needed to put more pressure on the tavern owners: weekly editorials, church rallies, and vocal support from the civic clubs. While they hoped Senator Short would be receptive, they needed to search for alternative funding. They planned to meet again next week.

Adam turned off Willow Road onto the pea-gravel driveway, lined with flowering yucca plants. He noticed the light in Brett's living quarters, one of the garconniers. For some reason, perhaps Allison's comments on the night of the party, he felt a ripple of apprehension.

He parked beneath the overhang of an oak and followed the walkway to the veranda. He knocked on the heavy door with its brass hinges and listened to a mocking bird repeat its mating call while he waited.

"Adam, I'm so glad you're here." Knox wrapped her arms around him and buried her head in his chest as a frightened child might cling to her father, but just for a moment. "Let's sit on the back porch," she said, taking his hand. "Near Jake, should he need me."

Adam settled into a wicker chair. "How's he doing?" he asked.

Knox sat on the floor of the balcony and brushed back the blond hair that fell on her narrow shoulders. "Weaker every day. A lot of confusion...which comes and goes. I have to feed him and help him dress." She hesitated and shook her head wearily. "It's like caring for a two-year old."

A tear trickled down her cheek. She wiped it with the back of her hand. "He does have some lucid periods. Last week we were sitting in the garden swing, and out of the blue, he said, 'I know my problem.' I put my arm around him and asked, 'Okay, Jake, tell me what you've discovered.' With that he pointed to his head and said, 'There's nobody home upstairs.'"

Adam knew that lucid intervals occurred in some stages of dementia. The random flash; a sudden clearing as if the boarded-up window flew open and for a short time, an old man viewed a beautiful vista, snowcapped mountains sloping down to a turquoise sea; remembering Clare, lovely Clare, lying beside him, listening together, to the sounds of seabirds and the tides splashing the shore; even remembering his words of endearment. But the window slammed shut, boarded as before, and darkness covered him like a hangman's hood.

Knox closed her eyes and rested her head against the cypress railing. "I guess there's no hope?"

Adam shook his head. "I'm afraid the hourglass is almost empty."

Knox looked back at his bedroom window. "I suppose, in his chauvinistic way, he loves me."

Adam was certain Jake needed her more than ever, for his life had come full circle. He had entered that second childhood, forming a stubborn attachment to Knox whose tender care bypassed the tangle of degenerating neurons and went straight to his heart.

"How long can he go on?" she asked.

"A day, a month, even a year; no one can predict." Adam knew that Jake hung like a time-worn marionette, suspended in mid-air by tenuous strings, between living and dying, while others watched with frustration, unable to change a single thing.

The sun settled at the horizon and the river glittered in its sanguine light. Knox stood up and rubbed the tense muscles in her neck. "I'll get some tea while you check on Jake."

"Don't forget Lena's pie," he chuckled.

❧

Knox placed a silver tray on a small tile-topped table. Her hands trembled when she passed him a glass of tea. She sat on the floor, her back against the balustrade, pulled her legs up and wrapped her arms around them.

"Jake is about the same. But you have something else on your mind?" He could see in the fading light the graceful shape of her face and the fawn-like eyes which spoke of sadness.

Knox stared at the floor. "I'm worried about Ben...and me."

Adam hunched forward, placing his glass of tea on the table. "Want to tell me more?"

"I feel..." She paused, searching for the right word. "...empty."

"Ben's neglect?"

"That's part of it."

"And the rest?"

"I need to be loved and to return that love."

"And Ben has failed?"

Knox nodded. She knew that their marriage carried more baggage than most: the miscarriage, Jake's depressing illness, and the town's condescension...judgmental...unworthy of the Hamilton name. Even the night of the party, she intuited the social stigma that had marked her like a branding iron from the day she arrived in Conway.

"Have you talked to Ben?"

118

She told Adam of their breakfast conversation two weeks ago. "Ben seemed surprised I was unhappy and he promised to be more considerate."

"And...?"

"It lasted...maybe a week." She could not hide the disappointment.

Adam sat back, waiting to hear more.

"I'm only asking for some time together," she said. "Some show of affection; some sign that he cares; that I'm important to him and he, in turn, needs me. Is that unreasonable?" Her words tumbled out into a stream of silent tears.

"Maybe it would help if I talked to Ben." He gave her an avuncular pat on the knee. "I'm sure Ben loves you. And he would be devastated if you were to leave, God forbid."

"How do you communicate with someone who's not listening?"

"It's disheartening. But you've invested too much time to surrender."

She shook her head. "I'm tired of talking, tired of getting that same blank look which says, 'I don't know what this is about.'"

"Take my advice. Don't give up. Ben and your marriage are worth fighting for."

Twilight dimmed, night shadows began to form. After an unease silence, Knox stood up and walked to the end of the porch, resting her head against the corner post. Without turning around, she called to him, as though their distance apart buffered the embarrassment and allowed her to share a deep personal secret.

"Adam, you are my friend? Aren't you?"

"Sure, why?"

"I have something to tell you." She came back to the wicker settee and sat down. "Something has happened, so overwhelming, it must be shared. Otherwise, it'll drive me crazy."

"You haven't told Ben?"

"He's the one person in the whole world I can't talk to. You see, I've a confession to make."

"You have my confidence," he said.

"I've had...." She closed her eyes and struggled to get the words out. "...an affair."

Adam sat quietly and tried to absorb the full impact of her disclosure.

"Don't you want to know who my lover is?" There was mortification in her voice.

"Only if you want to tell me," Adam said evenly.

"Brett Shelly. Does that surprise you?"

He shrugged his shoulders slightly.

"Well, aren't you going to tell me what an awful person I am?"

Adam reached over, took her hand and pressed it gently against his lips. "Look Knox, I can't dispense grace and relieve guilt like some benevolent priest. But I'm your friend. Willing to listen and help, if I can."

She dropped her head, averting his eyes, even though darkness covered the porch. She described the casual meeting; Brett joining her as she took Missy for an afternoon ride. His interest in her, other than as Jake's caretaker, was a surprise. But she felt a compelling attraction and any ambivalence seems to melt like Southern snow flakes. His touch was irresistible and she followed him across the shallow stream into the forest glade, where the barriers came crashing down. "Maybe I was angry, a way to strike out at Ben. Or maybe I found Brett so appealing..." She shook her head. "Maybe I thought it would fill the emptiness..." and pointed to her heart.

"And now?"

"Guilt; I betrayed a trust." At the time, she remembered, there was an aura of excitement and release, but those feelings were ephemeral and they left the stain of remorse and, ironically, a heightened sense of disaffection within her marriage.

"Don't beat yourself up," he said. "Take off that scarlet letter."

Abashed, she bit her lower lip, her chin falling to her chest.

"It was a mistake. We all make mistakes. And often, something good comes of it. Time is your friend; the guilt will diminish." Adam stood and drained his glass of tea. "Are you going to tell Ben?"

She shook her head. "It would hurt too much."

"You're right... some things are better left unsaid." He bent down and kissed her lightly on the cheek. At the slatted doorway, he looked back. "Call me if I can help."

"Goodbye Adam. I hope you'll talk to Ben."

She rested heavily on the cypress railing, her body drained by her confession, and watched Adam's car turn onto Willow Road. Beyond the river, the wail of an engine's whistle severed the brooding silence as the train sped through the Cimmerian darkness toward the Gulf. Knox wished, at least for a few fleeting moments, she were aboard, carried away by that night train to some faraway place.

❧

Adam thought about his visit as he drove away. He had reached two conclusions: Knox's needs, like the river beyond the levee, ran deep, and Ben's inattention created a void in their marriage. Sooner or later, Knox would fill it. He remembered the Greek axiom: "Nature abhors a vacuum." He figured that applied to relationships, to marriages. Based on what he'd heard about Brett Shelly, the filling had begun. And he suspected there would be more meetings in the forest glade, unless Ben acknowledged the problem and did something about it. Were it not for Jake, Adam could envision Ben walking into the kitchen one day soon, to a note on the counter; a simple "Goodbye."

He stopped the car at the foot of the bridge and watched the moon rise over the far embankment. Full and bright, above the shimmering face of the river, it looked almost as though the night had spawned another planetary sun. He thought of Allison and their love for each other. What made the difference? Was it chemistry? Good karma? Or the luck of the draw? Maybe it was some of each, or something more. But of this he was sure, Allison was everything he could possibly hope for. He watched the moon climb its celestial ladder and remembered Maude's words: "You're a lucky guy."

Chapter 20

Wednesday, May 24th

Adam parked across the street from Maude's downtown office. The sun had dipped below the skyline and dusk had settled serenely over the town. He could see slivers of light through the Venetian blinds and wondered why Maude was there at this late hour. He waved to Preacher half-asleep in the Packard, his chauffeur's cap slightly askew.

He knocked, then cracked the door. "It's me, Adam."

"C'mon in. I'll be right with you."

Maude sat behind a roll-top desk, in the center of which was the old Royal typewriter she used to peck out her weekly column. He flopped into the pillowed chair and surveyed the room while he waited. Fixed-pane windows were softened by white chiffon curtains. A large watercolor of a Louisiana bayou with its marsh grass and cypress trees decorated the back wall. He recognized another Drysdale. Freshly cut roses (from her garden) in a turquoise Ming vase rested on an oval table below the painting. The side walls were lined with bookshelves filled with hundreds of volumes; many of them, he had learned on other visits, were of English history and the biographies of those who shaped that country's future, from the Saxon invasion in the fifth century to the reign of George VI. And he remembered the words of Edmund Burke, a member of the House of Commons, which Maude had used so effectively in her *call-to-arms* front page editorial.

Maude pulled the paper from the Royal, crumbled it peevishly and tossed it into the wicker basket beside the desk. "I can't find the words," she said.

"Next week's editorial?"

Maude turned her chair, facing him. "I want to suggest that many people live in an existential world; for others, values are arbitrary. For the selfish and self-indulgent, expediency is the rule. No moral absolutes. But think about this: there are certitudes in the realm of science. One cannot defy the law of gravity or alter the cycles of the seasons. Likewise, there are moral equivalents, such as goodness and justice and truth…timeless and immutable; the driving force behind our crusade. Putting that concept into modern prose is not easy."

It sounded familiar. Adam thought of Al Marx's and his opening statement at the grand jury hearing. "We're really talking about *right and wrong.*"

Maude nodded. "And sometimes doing the *right thing* carries an enormous risk…even martyrdom…God forbid. But putting that in language that's clear to the reader can be a challenge."

Adam packed the bowl of his pipe and returned the pouch to his coat pocket. "I have no doubt you'll get it right."

Maude waved her hand across the roll-top. "This can wait," she said. "Any news?"

Adam lit his pipe and sent a ribbon of smoke, faintly aromatic, toward the ceiling. "I bumped into Clark Grayson this morning. He said the Hospital Board would announce their support of the petition drive within a few days."

Maude feigned surprise. "I wonder who engineered that coup."

"I suspect Clark is responsible although he gave Arthur White the credit. Our able Administrator has an uncanny way of manipulating the Board to get things done and then convinces them it was not only a good idea, but that it was *their* idea."

"I'm overjoyed that Arthur has joined us." Her eyes shone, a look of delight lingered on her weathered face.

Adam pointed a reproving finger in Maude's direction. "A man can change. Remember, I told you so."

"Nothing pleases me more. And Arthur may turn out to be our most effective ally."

"I'm sure it cost him some sleepless nights. While Ben may have been persuasive, I suspect it had more to do with Arthur's parochial schooling. And his father was a God-fearing man. 'Doing the right thing' rubbed off on Arthur and despite his indecision, he could never step out of his father's shadow."

"I feel we're gaining momentum. Or am I fooling myself?"

Adam looked at his friend, a countenance one might see in a Rockwell painting. Despite the wattle and wrinkles, her eyes, the color of cinnamon, expressed a zest for life that belied her years. While the hair was gray, pulled back in a chignon, her animated eyes were ageless.

"While I haven't talked to Hannah, I heard, second-hand, that she's ready to go," Adam said.

"No surprise. She could control a room full of rowdy teenagers."

"Hope she can meet the quota. The signings begin next month."

"I'm counting on Hannah to make it happen." Maude rubbed the knobby joints of her hands.

Adam waited. He knew she had something else on her mind.

"Heard from Markham since your pleasantries at Slim's Grill?"

Her choice of words made him laugh. "No, but he left with the hair bristling on the back of his neck. So I expect to hear from him or one of his henchmen."

"Your meeting explains our recent visitor."

Adam's face was blank. He lifted his arms...an inquiry.

"One of Caruso's boys was in town recently."

"How'd you get that scoop?"

Maude straightened up, her eyes sparkled like an exited cub reporter. She explained that every newspaper has it spies, its confidential sources. One of her informants noticed a car with a New Orleans license plate in front of the Shamrock on a Saturday morning, jotted the number down and passed it along. Because of the curious circumstances, she called Captain Wheeler at State

Patrol Headquarters in Baton Rouge. He and Ed were old fishing buddies and he still checked on her from time to time. As a favor, Wheeler called the D.M.V. and found the car registered to a Johnny Pappas, who she later learned was a trusted member of Caruso's inner circle; *Giovane D'Onore*...unusual in any Mafia family.

Maude saw the quizzical look on Adam's face. "An associate not of Italian ancestry."

Adam felt a shiver as if doused with ice water. "You mentioned the possibility of an alliance in your first editorial. The meeting with Markham seems to confirm your suspicion."

"I'm afraid so. In a matter of weeks, we've gone from the sandlot to the major leagues; no longer playing amateurs like Markham and the other tavern owners, but rather an organization that's brutal, predatory, and without conscience. It ratchets up the stakes...a mile high, along with the risks."

The images of Robin and Allison flashed before him. Maude had supplied the subtitles. The enemy had taken on a terrifying dimension. Had he jumped into the deep end of the pool...way over his head...putting his family in jeopardy? Perhaps. But the decision had been made, a commitment that could not be revoked.

Adam tapped the ashes into the wastebasket and replaced the pipe in his coat pocket. "What's next?" he asked warily.

"They'll create a climate of fear, hoping to intimidate the voters of Conway. The threat of reprisal will frighten a lot of people." Maude reached for a sheet of paper on her desk and handed it to Adam. "I suppose killing Belle was the first shot across the bow. Now this..."

"What is it?" he asked.

"A letter to the editor." Maude passed him the paper.

"I don't see a name."

"It was hand-delivered, unsigned. Slipped under the door in the dark of night. No letterhead. No postmark. But clearly a warning from an adversary."

Adam read the letter. "It's clear they plan to stop the petition drive, one way or the other," he said. "Surely the sender knows this'll never make the paper."

"Not meant to," Maude said. "Just stating the grave consequences of pursuing our objective. A warning: back off or someone will get hurt."

Adam stood up and hung over the desk. "Support for the crusade has been growing like kudzu. There's no turning back. And you can quote me," he said with a wink.

"You bet I will." She rolled a fresh sheet of paper in the Royal. "Let's give 'em hell.".

℘

Adam stood outside the office and stretched the muscles in his back. It had been a long day and the added stress of the crusade tugged at him like a heavy weight. His conversation with Maude had increased, in no small measure, his concern; a jarring reminder to raise his level of vigilance for himself and his family.

Preacher, asleep, had laid his head against the doorframe. Before crossing the street, Adam tapped on the roof of the Packard. Startled awake, Preacher strained to see the face staring through the open window.

"Oh, it's you, Doc. Kinda sceered me till I seen you."

"It's after nine. Hope you're getting paid overtime," Adam chuckled.

"Naw Doc, I use to it. Miz Maude just got more bounce then a rubber ball; frisky as a colt. I ain't never seen anyone like her." Preacher hesitated, his head drooped. "But she sho misses that cat."

Adam patted Preacher's shoulder. "Well, she'll deal with losing Belle but she depends on you and so does everyone at the church. You're a good man, Preacher."

"Thank you, Doc. I tries to do right, like the Good Book says."

Adam straightened up. "Can I drive you home? Maude is about ready to lock up."

"'preciate it but the bus runs till midnight."

Crossing the street, he thought about Preacher and his allegiance to Maude and to the church. A janitor at St. Paul's for thirty years. Maude's yardman and chauffer, longer still. Adam knew Maude could get another cat but Preacher was irreplaceable.

Chapter 21

Kenny Fluitt was ten years old and lived with his parents and older brother at the end of Karen Lane. He biked to school, passing Maude Harrington's house which sat in the center of a large corner lot.

One afternoon in late May, Kenny rounded the corner at Karen Lane heading for home. He pulled up when he saw Preacher mowing the front lawn. He leaned his bike against the curb and called out, "How ya doing, Preacher?"

The yardman pulled a rag from the back pocket of his baggy pants which hung low on his hips, mopped the sweat from his forehead and sauntered over to the street. "Ain't complaining. How 'bout you?"

Preacher's hair was sprinkled with gray; his skin, the color of ebony heartwood, was smooth and betrayed his age. With his sprightly dark eyes and generous smile, he attracted youngsters like the Pied Piper.

"I'll be glad when school's out. Just one more week."

"Yeah, time's a flying. All you kids 'round here growin' like weeds."

Kenny looked him in the eye as though he had suddenly summoned the courage to ask a forbidden question. "How old are you, Preacher?"

He flashed his white teeth and answered with good humor, "Old 'nough to know better."

"Come on Preacher, tell the truth. I'll bet you're older than my grandpa."

He stooped down to eye level. "And how old might he be?"

Kenny looked up, trying to remember. Overhead a scattering of clouds had been set adrift in a pale blue sky. Birds darted through warm currents, finding refuge among the magnolias. "At least seventy," Kenny said glumly, as if funeral arrangements were well under way.

Preacher put his hand on the boy's shoulder. "The eyes of chillun, they sees forever."

Kenny was puzzled. "Now what's that 'spose to mean?"

"Means when you is ten years old, a boy can't hear the clock ticking. But time's a passing, even when you is sleeping. Just like that river flowing into the salty waters near New Orleens." He stopped and pointed in the direction of the Ouachita which flowed past the town on its journey to the Gulf.

"Preacher, I bet you were good at dodge ball when you were a kid."

He stood up and expanded his chest with a big breath of spring air. "Guess I was right lively on my feet. Ain't bragging, but I run a pretty good race."

A savvy grin settled amid the many wrinkles as Kenny's flattery took on a whole different meaning. He wagged a crooked finger in front of the boy. "You is a pretty smart kid," he said. With that he patted the boy on the shoulder and went back to work.

The compliment made Kenny feel real good. He pulled his bike upright and pedaled away. "See ya later, Preacher."

❧

Around six o'clock, the yardman returned the hand mower and unused bags of plant food to the garage. He took pride in making Maude Harrington's lawn and garden the envy of the neighborhood. But he was weary from a long workday so he rested awhile before making the three block walk to the bus line.

Preacher lived in the Flats, a neighborhood of poor blacks south of the cemetery and just inside the city limits. The asphalt streets were rutted and most of the small clapboard houses had weathered gray and were in need of repair. The dwellings sat off the ground on brick piling to prevent damage from flooding that sometimes occurred with the heavy rains.

He rode the bus to downtown Conway, napping on the back seat. At Walgreen's, on the corner of Main and Church Streets, he transferred to a southbound bus which he rode to the end of the line, walking the rest of the way. Preacher climbed the wooden steps to a narrow porch which wore a coat of fresh paint, and pulled off his work shoes before going inside. He smelled chicken frying and followed the scent into the small kitchen where Susie, his wife for almost fifty years, was squeezing lemon juice into a pitcher of iced tea.

She was a small woman but was blessed with boundless energy, slowed only by age and an arthritic hip. Preacher moved around the small table and put a long arm around her shoulders. "Would give a day's pay for some of that tea."

"You look wore out," she said. "Sit yourself down and I'll pour you a big glass." Her small brown eyes shone with pleasure.

"Miz Maude's yard needed lots of work. The warm weather sho makes things grow, weeds and all."

"Tomorrow won't take so much outta you."

Preacher nodded. "We could get by with just my job at the church but I can't let Miz Maude down."

Darkness settled over the Flats. After dinner, Susie cleared the table and washed the dishes, traipsing barefoot around the kitchen. Preacher settled into his favorite chair. Within minutes, exhausted, he fell asleep.

After cleaning the kitchen, Susie brought her sewing basket into the sitting room and turned on the radio. A breeze came through the screen door, carrying with it the scent of menace, causing her to move uneasily on the sofa. Down the street a dog yelped, a wounded sound. Susie decided to lock the front door and finish her sewing in the bedroom. A giant moth flitted aimlessly, banging against the porch light. She turned it off and left Preacher in his chair, snoring lightly.

Around midnight, a black sedan stopped in front of Preacher's house. Two men, cloaked in darkness, climbed the porch steps and knocked on the door. One of them wore a Stetson low on his forehead with a sheriff's badge pinned to his short-sleeve shirt. The other stood well to the side and remained in the shadows when Preacher turned on the porch light and opened the front door.

"Are you Grady Henry?" The tone was civil.

"Yes sur."

"My name is Sergeant Brussard from the Sheriff's Department and I have a warrant for your arrest." With a gloved hand he held up the sheet of paper which was unreadable in the dim light.

"I ain't done nothin' wrong," Preacher said.

"You can read the charge on the way to the station." The voice was compelling. Insistent. "C'mon, let's go."

In the heat of the moment, Preacher unlatched the screen door and walked outside hoping to plead his case. He was handcuffed quietly and led to the black sedan. Earlier, Susie had fallen asleep in their bedroom and despite the disturbance at the front of the house, didn't awaken until the rooster crowed at first light.

Preacher looked out the back window of the Ford Deluxe. The front door of his house was open and the porch light grew dim as the car crept slowly through the Flats. He worried about Susie and wondered what she would do after realizing he'd disappeared. Perhaps she'd call Miz Maude or Sheriff Gilstrap.

The driver switched on his headlights as he turned left on Grand Street, away from town and the police station. They followed the levee until they reached State Highway 23, two lanes of pavement which took them due south.

"Where you'll taking me?" Preacher asked respectfully.

"Shut up nigger," the driver snapped.

Brussard removed his hat and tossed it into the front seat. "Easy, Sal. The man's entitled to ask questions."

"Thank you kindly."

Preacher closed his eyes, his cuffed hands in his lap. Trouble had found him and he searched for a reason. But he couldn't figure it out. Sure, he was a black man. Still didn't make any sense.

He glanced out the window; a foreboding darkness, only the faint reflection of the headlights.

"So, where we going? Susie gonna be worried sick."

"Just be patient. We're right on schedule."

"Sho would like to know what I done," he said, holding up his cuffed hands.

"Sometimes, Grady, an answer don't make sense."

"Still wanta know."

"Well, it's like this..." Brussard thought for a moment; looked over at Grady. "...sometimes a man is used to make a point."

Preacher shook his head. "What's that to do with me? I ain't hurt nobody."

"You were chosen, simple as that."

Preacher fell silent amid his confusion; then he began to weep, the tears trickling down his cheeks. He'd heard enough; he would never see Susie again.

The car slowed. Its headlights caught a large sign: CAPTAIN JOE'S FISHING CAMP...FIVE MILES. Sal turned right onto an unpaved road and scattered loose gravel which peppered the bottom of the black sedan.

The camp was shut down until Monday morning. A rectangle of logs and stone hugged the banks of Lake Darbonne. Boats were tied at the end of two wooden piers that jutted into the black water awaiting the first sign of daybreak. Beside the boathouse, a live oak towered into the darkness far above the building's roof line. Brussard retrieved his Stetson and stepped out of the car. He switched on a small flashlight and looked at his watch, almost one o'clock.

"Let's go, Grady."

Preacher knew he was at a dead end. There were no options other than to comply with dignity. With his hands cuffed he slid awkwardly out the door.

Sal opened the trunk and attached a silencer to a 9mm. Glock which he slipped in his coat pocket.

The three men walked down a grassy slope to the oak with it thick trunk and gnarled limbs. "Over there!" Sal ordered. "Against the tree."

Preacher stopped and turned toward Brussard. "I ain't `fraid of dyin', but I'd shore like to know what I done."

"You're a messenger."

"I jus don't understand."

He gave Preacher a shove toward the tree. "It's nothing you've done. Now leave it alone."

It was a clear night, star-strewn like diamonds on black velvet. Preacher rested his back against the sturdy trunk, inhaling the fresh air. It offered little comfort.

Sal pinned a note to Preacher's shirt and removed the handcuffs.

"Thank you, sur," Preacher mumbled, rubbing both wrists.

"Why's he thanking me?" Sal wondered. "Crazy goddamn nigger."

Brussard offered him a cigarette which Preacher politely refused. "Any last requests?" he asked.

"Sho would like to have a minute or two for prayin."

Brussard flashed the light on his watch. "Go ahead. Take your time."

Preacher closed his eyes and while his lips moved his prayer was silent. Finally, he spoke softly, "May the good Lawd have mercy on yall's soul."

Pop. Pop. A plume of gray smoke leaked from the barrel with each explosion. Preacher slid down the trunk of the tree and lay motionless in the grass. Brussard walked over and flashed the light on Preacher's lifeless body. He knelt down and with a gloved hand made sure the note, pinned to the dead man's shirt was secure: MEDDLERS BEWARE!!!

What was the meaning of the message? Brussard didn't know... or care. He had been given an assignment. No questions asked. It was the way he wanted it.

The two men walked nonchalantly back to the car. They had killed a man, all in a day's work. They tossed their gloves, flashlight and firearm into the trunk, slammed the lid shut and drove away. At Highway 23, Sal turned right, heading south.

Sal broke a long silence. "I been wondering..."

"What's there to wonder?"

"How come he wasn't scared? No begging or nothing."

"Maybe he was tired of living. Or maybe..."

Sal turned his head slightly. "Maybe what?"

Brussard replaced his Stetson and tipped it back. "He was a prayin' man. Know what I mean?"

Sal only shrugged.

"We got a long drive," Broussard reminded him. "Don't get a heavy foot 'cause we don't need no cops on our tail."

"Yeah, yeah..."

"So far, so good. Let's keep it that way. It'll make Tony happy."

Chapter 22

Sunday, may 28th

Adam glanced at the sermon title, *The Judas Syndrome,* as he passed the glass-enclosed church sign. A bit unusual, he thought, since this was Crusade Sunday and all the churches, including St. Matthews and Reverend Johnson's Assembly of God Tabernacle, were participating. They had agreed to praise the laudable goal of the coalition and announce their support for the petition drive.

The church was jammed when Adam arrived. Folding chairs had been placed along the back wall to accommodate an overflow crowd. He strolled down the center aisle, nodding to friends and slipped adroitly past a rotund Mr. Roberts, the City Comptroller, into a seat next to Allison. The Mayor's wife, who never knew the meaning of *pianissimo* was at the organ and filled the nave with a clamorous version of *Sweet Hour of Prayer.*

He gave Allison's hand a squeeze and settled into the cushioned pew. Sunlight streamed through the stained-glass windows and splashed the white stucco walls with many-splendid colors. A metallic cross rested on a mahogany table behind the chancel. To the left was an enclosed lectern draped with a tapestry of muted gold.

Adam's mind drifted during the preliminaries of the worship service. He remembered his encounter with Markham and those feral eyes. Nor could he forget the menace that emanated from the taverns and their alliance with Caruso and his ruthless organization. The acrimony was pervasive, spilling over the town's boundaries into rural Madison Parish. A dangerous confrontation was brewing like rain-laden clouds before a summer storm.

He came to attention when Hal Brady stepped up to the pulpit. Adam was anxious to hear what he had to say. The Minister stood erect and let his eyes comb the congregation into utter silence as if the church were empty.

"Through the years, the name Judas Iscariot has carried an irrevocable stigma," he began. "The bias and bitterness have become stronger with the passing of time. We have judged him egregious and condemned him to the depths of hell."

Adam stirred in his seat, surprised by the preface, but wanting to hear more.

The Reverend Brady continued: "We have shared in his condemnation like those, who with piety, took delight in pouring out their invective...like those who lifted their eyes to Heaven and prayed, 'God, let me not become another Judas'...like those who pointed fingers and cried, 'Vile...wretched... deceitful...traitor!'"

Adam gave Allison a gentle nudge. He saw the look of bemusement on her face. He shrugged as if to say, "I'm not sure where Hal's going. Judas and our crusade?"

"Centuries ago a gentle Man won the hearts of many who lived in the ancient land of Palestine. After many days of prayer and meditation, the Galilean selected a dozen men to form an intimate band of disciples. Twelve men, disparate, yet called to a common cause. Each had heard the invitation, 'Follow Me and I will make you fishers of men.' Judas signed on."

Adam stirred in his seat while Mr. Roberts sat placidly, his eyes closed, his short arms resting on his protuberant abdomen. "Get to the point before you lose your audience," Adam murmured.

"For three years Judas walked and talked with Jesus. He saw the tears of gratitude from those who touched the Master's hand. Judas looked into His compelling eyes, shared His noble dream, bore vicariously His sorrow, and invaded the secret corridors of a life that would ultimately change the course of human history.

"It was the same Judas who loved him, yet betrayed Him for thirty pieces of silver. Since that memorable night in the garden, his name has been despised, denigrated. And we continue to bury him with contempt and condemnation. No mercy. No charity. No pardon. Judas Iscariot continues to haunt those who are guilty of treachery."

Hal Brady paused while his eyes scanned the sanctuary; then a stern accusation, "In Conway, there are some who are self-serving and would betray the integrity of this town for less than thirty pieces of silver." He waited for those simple words to settle like lead weights into their collective conscience.

"Let's take another look at Judas. This much is true: he was the most patriotic of all the disciples. He loved his country; everything about it. The Jews were his people; Palestine was his world.

"He realized that the iron hand of Rome was everywhere. Roman law ruled his land and repressed her people. Burdensome taxes made them subservient to Caesar. The nation had been brought to her knees under the weight of the Tiberian monarchy. Nonetheless, Judas loved even more this land of limited freedom.

"So, it's easy to understand the reasons Judas, the fiery patriot, joined the small band of disciples and followed this Man who performed miracles, mesmerized the crowds and proclaimed the coming of a new 'nation.' Judas rejoiced."

Hal stopped and took a sip of water. "This parish is full of benevolent people who have a cause and a commitment. It may be family or a business or some charitable organization. While commendable, priorities are often misplaced, distorted by myopia. So close, we cannot see the malice that threatens our town…our homes…our children. Betrayed by blindness. Not for thirty pieces of silver, but because we cannot see clearly the evil that dwells among us.

"For three long years, Judas watched and waited; often discouraged, but never losing hope. He listened to talk of a Kingdom…but when? Meanwhile, Rome relentlessly abused her people, demeaning them with heartless demands. Disillusionment set in. So, Judas wondered if *he* could change the course of events. Perhaps challenging Him would ignite the spark of engagement and set in motion 'a new order.' So, Judas led them to Him."

Adam elbowed Mr. Roberts who had begun to snore softly. His corpulent body awakened with a jerk and his huge jowls quivered like jelly as he moved clumsily in his seat and flashed his chagrin.

"Judas forced the action. The plan failed because he placed himself above the larger interest. Rather than carry a cross, he betrayed the One who loved him the most. He died bereft, with a conscience rent by guilt.

"A final thought: Judas was passionate and energized even though he misread the epic events occurring around him. Were he here today, he would lead the parade down Main Street; the first to sign the petition. There was no place in his life for apathy or sloth. He cannot be accused of inaction. And I'm sure his advice to the people of Conway would be: 'Don't let indifference make the difference. Get out and vote.'"

Hal straightened up, his voice took on a deeper resonance. "This community is at the crossroads. We can put up with the saloons. A betrayal of indifference. We can look the other way. A betrayal of blindness. Or we can vote to make Conway a more wholesome place in which to live. Sign the petition. Talk to your friends and neighbors. For there are malevolent forces, that will defend the taverns, with violence, if necessary. Already there have been threats and acts of intimidation, but we will not be cowed or coerced; it is time to stand up with courage and be counted.

"'How can you, to whom much has been given, betray me?' he asked. The question remains relevant; we hear it clearly. How shall we respond?" Hal Brady closed his Bible, looked out over a sea of faces. "Betrayal...I hope and pray it will never happen here. Sign the petition!"

He lifted his Bible and closed his eyes. "Now may God bless you and guide you and strengthen you for the challenge ahead. Go in peace. Amen!"

The silence lingered; no sounds other than the hum of the air conditioning. Hal Brady stepped through a side door and disappeared into an adjoining vestibule.

Without instruction, the congregation arose. There was no closing hymn. No benediction. No postlude. The service had ended.

Chapter 23

Monday, May 29th
The following morning, Maude sat at the kitchen table with her cup of coffee and the Sunday edition of the *Times Picayune*. She heard the doorbell chime and wondered who it could be at this early hour. She cinched the belt of her terry cloth robe, took the last swallow of coffee, and padded down the carpeted hallway.

Through a sidelight, she recognized Randy Gilstrap, the Sheriff of Madison Parish. Maude turned the bolt lock and opened the door.

"Morning, Randy. What brings you out at the crack of dawn?"

She had known the Sheriff since he was a teenager; watched him play football at Conway High, a short and stocky fullback who loved the physical contact of the game. She made a quick assessment of him standing on the stoop: while he had gained several inches of girth, he was no taller than her memory of him in Senior High.

Randy had surfaced from his father's gene pool; a "spitting image" of Shorty Gilstrap, owner of CityWide Septic Tank Service. During the war years, CityWide had expanded parish-wide, doubling the size of the Company. Competitors came and went but Shorty was resolute, a survivor; someone had to do the dirty work. Maude had used his service years ago when suddenly a patch of emerald-green grass appeared amid a dormant lawn. She had never forgotten his one-day service, the know-how to eliminate the stench. And she smiled when she remembered her grateful neighbors.

Randy wore khaki with the Sheriff's badge fastened above the shirt pocket. He held his Stetson in one hand and greeted her with the other. "Sorry to disturb you, Miss Maude." He looked over his right shoulder, the sun creeping over the horizon. "I know it's early but I thought you'd want to know...official-like."

Maude heard a stutter in his voice. "Know what, Randy?"

The Sheriff took a deep breath, then another, as if the fresh morning air would settle his nerves. "It's Preacher..."

"What about Preacher?"

"Fisherman found his body before daybreak. He'd been shot."

Maude gasped and slumped against the doorframe; only Randy's quick reflexes kept her from falling. Tears spilled down her face as he led her to a chair in the parlor. Maude pulled a Kleenex from the pocket of her robe and wiped her eyes. "Oh, dear God, what have we done?"

Randy stooped down, his hands on the arm of the chair. "I got the call at 5:15 this morning. Lake Darbonne, near Captain Joe's fishing camp. Two shots to the head."

He waited until Maude had regained her composure. "We've cordoned off the area and called the Coroner. Two of my deputies are there and with more light we'll begin the investigation."

Maude dabbed her eyes and shook her head. "Poor Preacher, the kindest and most gentle man God ever made."

"You ought to know the gunman pinned a note to his shirt. I figured it was some sort of warning."

"Go on, Randy."

"I read it twice to make sure. 'Meddlers Beware.'"

"I know what it means," she said. "The message is perfectly clear."

Randy lifted his outstretched arms, a puzzled look on his ruddy face.

"Randy Gilstrap, listen and listen good. Forget you've cozied up to Markham. Do your job. Start with the slugs across the river. But I suspect the trail leads south to New Orleans, past high walls and security gates, to the front door of Tony Caruso in Marrero."

Randy's gimpy knees creaked when he stood up. His brow furrowed, his look uncertain. "I'll call the State Police if necessary. The State owns the Lake and the land around it. So, Preacher was gunned down on government property."

"Look at me, Randy." The demand had a cutting edge. "I'm counting on you for a through investigation. Find out who shot Preacher. If it was a gun-for-hire, keep at it until you find the one who sold the contract."

"I'll do my best," he said.

Maude was sure Randy wished he'd gone to college, then come back to Conway and joined his father's business. Had he done so, he would not be in this untenable position. He had taken money from the tavern owners "to look the other way." With a growing family, he had needed to supplement his modest salary. Now, he was in charge of a murder investigation that could incriminate his benefactors. Randy was in the middle of a tug-of-war, pulled in both directions. Already the rope was getting tighter. And with Caruso in the equation, Maude knew he must feel a sickening squeeze.

Randy put on his Stetson. "I need to be gettin' along, Miss Maude. Will you be okay?"

Maude glanced at the clock on the mantle. "Dora will be here before long." She hesitated and reached for another Kleenex. "I need some time alone."

Randy stopped at the door. "I'd rather wrestle a bear than tell Preacher's wife."

"Leave it to me. I'll call Reverend Johnson; he'll break the news to Susie."

His chest heaved with relief. "I 'preciate that." He waved and headed for his cruiser.

Maude got up slowly and steadied herself. She walked back to the kitchen and refilled her coffee cup, then moved to the screened porch and stood by the door that opened to the backyard. Preacher's signature was everywhere...the manicured lawn, the neatly trimmed hedges, the rose garden that glistened in the sun's dazzling light. She stared at the maple tree and saw Preacher dig a shallow grave and bury Belle beneath its branches. Her eyes misty; the illusion faded. A bluebird flitted about and disappeared amid the maple's dense foliage.

"Am I responsible for Preacher's death?" she murmured. Maude knew in her heart, the answer was "yes," at least in part. She figured Caruso was calling the shots. In her eyes the plan was transparent: harm those close to her; she was not a target. Her death would only inflame the entire parish and ensure the success of the petition drive. Caruso and his Organization were shrewd and street-smart, which made the conflict even more frightening. She figured that Adam too, was immune to the Mob's villainy, but not Allison or the little girl and the horrible possibilities made her shiver.

Maude knew the days ahead would be difficult, dealing with her grief. After Ed Harrington died, Preacher took on added dimensions...lawn service to caretaker to chauffeur to confidant... her "man for all seasons." Maude had known Preacher for more than thirty years; there was not a dishonest bone in his body. Patient, dependable, easy-to-smile, willing to listen...her closest friend.

She took the last swallow of coffee and felt tightness in her chest. She sat in the wicker chair and took her pulse: eighty-four and regular. No shortness of breath or light-headedness. She wondered if it was her heart or just another bout of esophageal spasm, something she had experienced in the past. Perhaps guilt was the trigger. As an activist, she had put her life on the line. Maude knew it would be a nasty fight, but she didn't intend to put Preacher or by-standers or neutral observers in jeopardy. Never in her wildest dreams, did she believe an innocent party would be kidnapped and killed. While the cause was just—Maude believed that with all her heart—she would never expunge the guilt if she lived to be a hundred.

She carried the empty cup back to the kitchen and made the phone call to Reverend Johnson. She had planned to spend the day in her office redrafting the week's editorial. However, Preacher's death changed all of that. She had something more important to say and would start over.

How'll I get to my office? she wondered. The Packard, of course. Maude had driven years ago and she could do it again. But this time, without a license. At least, until she could get one.

Chapter 24

After morning rounds, Adam removed his coat, tossed it on the passenger seat and rushed out of the doctor's lot. Running late, he foolishly ignored a stop sign and the 30 mph. speed limit. (His compulsion had cost him a traffic ticket on more than one occasion.) He turned on the a/c and pushed in a cassette...the inimitable music of Mantovani.

Summer had come early to the Deep South, fierce and sudden. The checker game on the boarding house porch moved inside; old men mopped their brows and insisted the atomic blasts that ended World War II had caused a change in the weather. Heat rose shimmering from the sidewalks and barefoot children skipped and hopped over hot cement, finding relief in the shadows of the trees or on some grassy oasis. Sounds of summer: the whir of ceiling fans and ice clinking in tall glasses floated on the heavy, humid air.

Despite the car's air conditioner, Adam's shirt was damp. He parked behind the split-level building and felt the sweat on his face as he plodded up a flight of steps.

Maggie cupped the phone as he passed her station. "Fran Shore called with apologies...again."

He shrugged and gave her a look of what he hoped was resignation.

Adam closed the office door, drawn to the window. The vista reminded him of Preacher and his senseless death more than a week ago. On the day of the funeral, he picked up Maude and drove to The Assembly of God Tabernacle. Sunshine poured through the windows as they walked down a long aisle to a front-row pew reserved for family and "special" friends. Adam remembered Susie's mournful face, her moist eyes fixed on the closed casket. He reached over, took her hand and patted it gently. Reverend Johnson spoke to an overflow crowd, reminding everyone that Grady Henry was a kind and gentle man, a loyal friend to many in attendance, someone who loved the Lord and lived by His Word. But he was a victim of Satan who would rather steal your heart than your life. And that was something Grady Henry never gave up…the goodness of his heart. After a lengthy eulogy and a chorus of *amens* and shouts of *halleluiahs*, a woman from the choir stepped forward and sang acappella that poignant Negro spiritual: *I looked over Jordan and what did I see/Coming for to carry me home/ A band of angels coming after me/ Coming for to carry me home/Swing low, sweet chariot/ Coming for to carry me home.* The voice was sweet and pure. Adam thought if he'd closed his eyes it could have been the voice of Mahalia Jackson. A hush had fallen over the auditorium and he (and others) had to wipe the tears away. It was Preacher's favorite gospel song and Adam knew that it was a *sweet chariot* and a *band of angels* that whisked him away…Heaven bound.

Maggie tapped on the door.

"Come in."

"Phone call, line two, Mr. Marx."

Adam reached for the receiver. "Hi Al, glad you called."

"A bit of good news which I'd rather give you in person. The telephone…well, you never know. So how about lunch at Buck's…say tomorrow around noon? Can you squeeze it into your schedule?"

"I'll be there."

"It's been six weeks since our last meeting…" There was a momentary lull, but he could hear Al Marx speaking in muffled tones to someone in his office. "Sorry, Fred Warren was on another line and my secretary thought it might be urgent. I'll call him later."

"I wonder how Warren feels about our putting the taverns out of business."

"He's non-committal, sitting back and watching a dangerous game, amused, since he'll win either way. But he's aware the coalition has gained momentum, increasing the prospects of success. So he wants to talk money, wonders where it's coming from?"

"That's my concern. Guess I'm banking on your contacts in Washington."

Al laughed. "I'm glad you have confidence in my capitalizing a multi-million dollar deal."

"How much?" Adam gulped.

"We'll have to wait for the appraisals. And don't expect any charitable discount from ole skinflint even though it's tax deductible." Al paused and lit a cigarette. "I heard from Washington yesterday. We'll talk more tomorrow."

"Buck's at 12:30."

"See you there."

✌

Hal Brady sat in his high-back chair wrestling with another Sunday sermon. His mind drifted, unable to summon his power of concentration. Books, file folders and a copy of *The Abington Commentary* littered the top of his desk. The yellow legal pad was clean except for a title and brief outline. He intended to write a sequel to his much discussed, *The Judas Syndrome.*

His eyes, weary from reading, wandered to the window. Dark clouds augured a summer storm. Gusts of wind bent the saplings and nandina bushes that lined the parking lot. Hal propped his feet on the ledge, leaned back in his chair and mesmerized by the steady cadence of water striking glass, dropped down into a peaceful sleep.

The rap on the door roused him. "Come in. It's open."

The knock came again, loud and impatient. Still drowsy, Hal stumbled across the room and opened the door.

The visitor, tall with broad shoulders, wore dark glasses and a Panama hat pulled down on his forehead. He stepped inside. "You the preacher?" he asked sharply.

Hal said he was. "Can I be of help?"

"You sure as hell can!" Before the words reached Hal's level of perception, the stranger swung viciously. The fist, gathering strength in its arc, caught him flush in the face and sent him reeling atop the desk. His eyes blurred and a wave of nausea rolled over him as he tasted blood flowing from his nose. The assailant moved in quickly, grabbed his shirt forcefully with his left hand and lifted him off the desk. "Listen and listen good," he said, a voice charged with malice. "Keep your fucking nose out of other people's business! Do you hear me?"

Setting him upright, the intruder swung again and sent Hal crashing over the desk into a heap below the window. Books and papers scattered in his wake and the desk lamp shattered as it hit the hardwood floor. The bedlam tilted Sallman's portrait of Christ which hung above the bookcase.

The assault was sudden, savage; a surprise which left Hal defenseless. While the will to resist survived, the body was impotent, unable to respond. Hal had always believed there was an element of cowardice in an act cloaked in anonymity, but that was small consolation as he lay dazed, against the wall, the room spinning wildly, carrying in its vortex the urge to vomit. In a matter of seconds, he fell, mercifully, off the shadowy edge of consciousness.

The dispassionate stranger assessed the results of his assignment. Annoyed that blood had splattered his white tie, he kicked Hal brutally in the side, causing his head to hit the floor. After a final survey of the office, he readjusted his glasses and pulled at the brim of his hat. He left the study unhurried, removed his gloves and stuffed them in his coat pocket. The hallway was deserted as he slipped out the side door, banging the bar with his hip, and vanished beneath the cover of a driving rain.

 formula

The lunch crowd was as loud as ever; the wailing sound from the jukebox and the clatter of dishes added a hundred decibels to the noise level. Next time, Adam grumbled, he'd suggest Renee's, a lunchroom far less noisy. While he waited, he sipped his iced tea and thought about the risk of further reprisals from the tavern owners and their Mob connection. Concern for his family had become as unshakable as his own shadow. The sighting of Johnny Pappas three weeks ago at the Shamrock supported his worst fears; a truculent adversary who played by his own rules, and with no moral compass. But Adam knew there were causes worth fighting for. Was not the country recovering from a war that took countless young lives to protect our sovereignty and precious freedoms? The cost was staggering but the cause was sacred and noble and just. Names from the past flashed before him... the apostle Paul... Thomas Becket...Joan of Arc...Simone Weil...and only a few years ago, Dietrich Bonhoeffer, stripped naked and hanged on Himmler's gallows...all martyrs for some compelling principle...a purpose greater than themselves. Adam knew with time, he could think of many others. Meanwhile, he would add Preacher's name to that list of heroes.

He watched Al weave his way through the crowded aisle. The young D.A. half-waved and slipped into the booth. Wilma arrived before either of the men could exchange a cordial greeting.

"A scorcher out there," Wilma said. "What can I get to cool you down?" She smacked her gum, her pencil and pad at the ready.

"Iced tea," Al said. "And the house salad."

"Same here," Adam added.

"Is that how you fellas stay so thin? How about the special...a tender veal cutlet with a nice pasta?" Her small blue eyes flashed with mischief.

"Go away, Wilma," Adam chuckled.

Al's expression turned grave as he leaned over the table. "I have some news of interest."

Adam waited, arms folded.

"I had a call from my friend, Chuck Wilson Monday. Senator Short's committee has informally approved the funding for your project. Of course, it depends on the success of the petition drive and city-wide referendum." Al reached in his shirt pocket for a cigarette. "Should you win the war and shut down the taverns, there will be reams of paper work, hoops to jump through, and even an invitation to appear before Short's committee. A charismatic spokesman for the coalition would re-enforce the committee's decision and put a spotlight on the Senator; a report from Douglas Edwards; a piece in the Metro papers. In D.C., nothing pleases a politician more than making the nightly news or getting a piece in the *New York Times*. Wilson implied as much."

Adam could not hide a smile. "Thanks, Al. You've made my day."

"By the way, Fred Warren's phone call was about something other than money."

"I didn't know Fred thought of anything else."

Al shook his head. "The real reason for the call was to distance himself from the tavern's owners. Warren is plenty smart and he's worried about getting entangled in a criminal investigation. He assured me he had no connection with Markham or Waters or Gambelli, other than as their landlord. In a rare moment of self-deprecating humor, he confessed, 'The only time I go out there is to collect the rent.'"

Al crushed the cigarette in an ashtray. "I'll be right back."

After a few bites, Adam pushed the salad bowl aside. He was elated by the news from Washington. He and Maude had agreed that should the coalition succeed, the buy-out would be a major hurdle. But Al had found the solution; friends in high places; their prayers had been answered.

Adam pulled a small calendar from his billfold. The petition drive would begin in two weeks, ending Sunday, the second of July. He knew that Hannah had formed a committee of dedicated helpers to work the telephones and send out reminders to every eligible voter in Conway. A banner, with the tepid approval of the Mayor, had been strung across Main Street. The message, in bold red letters on white canvas: SIGN THE PETITION... JUNE 22-JULY 2. Hannah had sent him a list of booth locations: the American Legion Hall, the Y.M.C.A., and all the protestant churches, including The Assembly of God Tabernacle. Adam sipped his tea and thought about Ben who had convinced Arthur White to support the coalition despite Arthur's grave reservations. Since the mill was outside the voting district, he had agreed for Hannah to place two "informational" booths inside the mill. Two of Hannah's most attractive committee members would man the strategic locations and hand out pamphlets in support of the petition drive. Adam remembered Maude's prescient comment: "Arthur White may be our most effective ally."

Al returned and sat back in the booth. "Where were we? Oh yeah...Fred Warren. He won't be a problem. Just a spectator; a winner either way."

Adam packed the bowl of his pipe and borrowed Al's lighter. Puffs of smoke, like an Indian war signal, floated toward the high ceiling. "No surprise. Like a lot of folks, Fred Warren will do what's best for Fred Warren; let the Devil take the hindmost."

Al looked at his watch and picked up the check.

"Before you go, I want to say... thanks! Your help has been immeasurable. I'm sure I speak for Maude and all the members of the coalition who've put themselves at risk to make Conway a better place to live." Adam relit his pipe and returned the Ronson. "I know as an elected official, you need to keep a low profile and we'll respect that."

Al waved him off. "Glad to help."

Wilma appeared like a ghost out of the smoke-filled room. "Excuse me, Doc. Phone call for you."

Adam scurried to the front. Buck, frowning, handed him the receiver.

"Doctor Swift."

"This is Nancy at St. Joe's." Her voice was tearful. "An ambulance from Nabor's just brought Reverend Brady to the E.R. He's hurt real bad; covered with blood," she sobbed.

Adam heard her crying. "Now Nancy, calm down," he said firmly. "What can you tell me?"

The nurse pinched her lips together and composed herself. "He's semi-conscious but responds to pain, Lacerations about the face. Bleeding from the nose. Pupils are equal and reactive to light. Deep tendon reflexes are 2+ and equal. Vital signs are stable." Nancy took a deep breath and continued, "I called your office and Maggie told me you were at Buck's."

"Nancy, those were good observations. Now write this down. Start an IV...5% glucose and ½ normal saline. Get a stat CBC and chemistry profile. Ask X-ray to get films of the skull and facial bones. Pack his nose with ice and I'll be there in five minutes."

He went back to the booth. Al sat on the edge of his seat, strumming the Formica top. "A problem?"

"St. Joe's E.R. Hal took a beating. Sounds like the Mafia's calling card."

Al felt the heat rise in his face. "Those bastards." He gave Adam a worried look. "Be careful, my friend. You could be their next target."

Chapter 25

Adam stopped at the doctor's lounge for coffee. After scanning his list of patients, he crossed the deserted lobby, past the portrait of Joshua White, to the bank of staff elevators. He stepped out on the top floor, greeted by a flurry of activity. It reminded him of a busy airport, holiday crowds moving in all directions. A gaggle of doctors pored over their charts in the glass-enclosed nurse's station, the fresh seven-to-three shift checked vital signs and IV lines, phlebotomists were on the prowl, a floor nurse dispensed medication amid the clatter of breakfast trays. Gurneys and wheel-chairs rolled over tile floors, scrubbed clean during the night, transporting patients to x-ray and physical therapy. The antiseptic scent lingered, pervasive. Adam knew that a hospital was unique; a complex organism, slowing its pace after midnight, replenishing itself for another busy and unpredictable day.

He pulled Hal Brady's chart from the rack and tapped a nurse's shoulder. "Morning, Dot. How's my patient?"

"Hello, Dr. Swift." She stood up deferentially, her uniform crisp, every gray hair neatly in place. "He's much better." She smiled and her genial hazel eyes twinkled. "Even complaining about the soup."

"A good sign."

"I hope so."

"Any problems?" he asked.

"We have to push hard or he won't take fluids."

"A matter of time. Meanwhile, keep his IV's going."

A speaker blared, "Dot Muller, lab report. Line 2."

"Do you need me?" she asked.

Adam shook his head. "Just take good care of our preacher-friend."

He ambled down the south wing, studying the record along the way. Adam tapped on the door of room 632 and without waiting, stepped inside.

He stood for a moment and surveyed the room. A blood-red sun had climbed over the crust of the earth and crawled through the Venetian blinds. Flowers and potted plants covered the windowsill and bedside table; news of the attack had spread like wildfire through Conway. Hal appeared to be sleeping.

Adam checked the IV and the nurses' notes hooked to the foot of the bed, then tossed the chart into the room's only chair. He put on a pair of latex gloves and rested against the side rail. "How are you?" he asked.

Hal awoke and opened one eye. (The other eye was swollen shut.) "Better than yesterday." He tried to smile, but movement of his jaw sent a volley of stabbing pain, like electrical shocks, to the top of his head.

Adam leaned closer and observed Hal's discolored and distorted face. His lips were puffy. The lacerations around his mouth and across his left cheek had been skillfully sutured. There were no signs of infection.

He pressed gently along the length of both mandibles. "Painful?"

"Hurts more to breathe," he muttered, barely opening his mouth.

"Two broken ribs." Adam touched the area lightly. "Must have kicked you in the side when you were out."

Hal extended his hands like a mendicant.

"They'll heal; just takes time."

"Whatever..." He gave his friend a one-eyed look of resignation.

"You also have a broken jaw. X-rays confirmed a fracture... about here." Adam gingerly touched the skin above the fracture site. That's why you feel those electrical shocks when you move your jaw. So, I called a Tulane classmate, Richard Toole, Associate Professor of ENT at Charity in New Orleans. He's flying up this afternoon." Adam took Hal's hand, gave a gentle squeeze. "Your jaw may need a wire, but he'll make the decision. Richard's the best in the business."

Hal nodded; he understood.

"By the way, I delayed the police investigation since you're in no condition to answer questions. But the Department is anxious to have a conversation." Adam straightened up and gripped the railing. "What about Monday? You'll be feeling better in forty-eight hours. And we'll limit their visit to twenty minutes."

"I won't help much. It happened so fast," he mumbled. "A big guy, I've never seen before."

"Off the record, Al Marx is sure you were 'set-up.'"

Hal gave him a weak, misshapen smile. "Lucky me."

"These acts of violence may backfire. Everyone in town knows Markham climbed in bed with Caruso and his mobsters from downstate. Most of the folks are incensed over your misfortune, and that can only help us succeed."

"Usually something good comes out of affliction," he whispered.

"Need anything?" Adam asked as he turned to leave.

He mimed "no" with his hands.

"Tomorrow will be better," Adam promised.

☙

Saturday, June 10th

Earlier in the day, Knox bumped into Brett at the drugstore. He was on crutches.

"What's wrong?" she asked.

He lifted his pants leg and pointed to an elastic bandage wound snugly around his swollen ankle.

"Was it really a gopher hole?" She covered a giggle with her hand.

"I wish it had been something more glamorous, like climbing the Matterhorn or riding a mean Brahma bull." He laughed remembering his misstep. "But it was a gopher hole!" (She had learned something about Brett that morning...he could laugh at himself, an ingratiating virtue.)

She promised him a slice of homemade custard pie. It was Lena's most popular desert. She would bring it over after feeding Jake his early supper. Knox realized she'd not been so bold since inviting her secret love, Billy Ray Roberts, the handsome, most-likely-to-succeed member of her graduating class, to the senior prom. (The dance was a concession by the Sisters at Christian Manor.) Other than frivolous conversation, she had spent the evening with a cup of punch, beneath a crepe-draped ceiling, streaking her mascara with hot, hurtful tears, while Billy Ray danced with all the pretty girls, including Ida Simpson who had outgrown her training bra by the fifth grade. It was an emotional trauma she had not forgotten and Billy Ray's belated apology did little to palliate the pain. Only years later, after he was arrested for embezzlement at a Metairie bank, did she feel vindicated.

At the drugstore, her offer of the custard pie appeared casual, a friendly gesture, but she knew—deep down she knew—it was an act of premeditation. During the day, when she thought about her proffer, it caused her heart to flutter and created a faint air of intrigue. Was this why she wore her favorite pink sun-dress, a trace of Channel perfume behind each ear, and a gardenia in her hair, tied back with a rose-colored ribbon?

She crossed the side yard to the front of the *garconniere*. Knox heard Brett's invitation as she passed the window. "Come on in." She pushed the front door open and found him slouched against the corner of the sofa, his swollen foot atop an apple crate, turned on end.

"How's the ankle?" she asked.

"I'm okay if I keep it off the floor."

Knox held out the dish covered with aluminum foil. "I'd better put this in the ice box."

He swung his leg from the crate to the sofa and with dark probing eyes followed her across the room, a gaze so intense, she felt the heat of his stare.

"Please sit down." He pointed to a rocker.

"That pie will go down easy with a glass of cold sweet milk."

"You're wonderful. Did anyone ever tell you that?"

Knox shook her head. She felt the color in her cheeks.

"And as beautiful as the flower in your hair."

"A girl appreciates a compliment." Her blush deepened; she averted his eyes.

Brett grabbed a crutch and hobbled a few steps. He dropped the crutch and lifted her out of the chair. He tilted her chin and spoke softly, "I can't get you out of my mind. I've tried to forget... God knows I've tried. But you've become ever-present, shadowing me wherever I go."

His unabashed confession caught her by surprise. She knew everyone thought of Brett as taciturn, a man of few words. And no one in Conway would confuse him with a poet or a lyricist of love songs. Dazed, Knox turned her head and rested it against his shoulder.

"Look at me," he said.

She raised her chin and found his eyes.

"What I'm trying to say..." He caressed her cheek and sighed deeply. "I love you, Knox. I love you very much."

In the hush that followed, her heart raced wildly. She tried to speak, but the words were stuck in her throat. The brown eyes, overwhelmed, filled with tears.

He moved his lips lightly across her face, along the bridge of her nose, then over the mouth, half-open and receptive. The kiss was gentle, tender. "Stay with me tonight," he pleaded. "I want to hold you, make love to you. Find you beside me in the morning." He kissed her again.

The raw passion Knox had felt in the forest glade welled up within her like erupting lava. Her attraction for Brett had grown almost every day since early April and this seismic disclosure only inflamed her yearning. But there were so many unanswered questions. She remembered the meeting with Adam and her confession of infidelity. And the lingering pangs of guilt.

She pulled away and walked to the window. "I can't, Brett. Jake is all alone. And Ben could leave the lake early. He's done that before."

Brett slumped on the sofa. "It's okay," he said. "But remember, I'm a very patient man."

She turned toward the door. "Guess I'd better check on Jake."

He watched her go, the graceful strides.

Know stopped at the front entrance, a long look back. "I just need time to sort things out."

Brett grimaced as he propped his injured leg on the apple crate. "I'll give you time...and space...whatever it takes."

Knox hurried back to the main house, her heart unsettled.

Chapter 26

Adam had seen his last afternoon appointment. But he had a dozen charts to dictate, chest x-rays to read, and a stack of phone messages to return; then evening rounds at the hospital. Hal Brady had been transferred to the ENT service, but Adam wanted to see him before his discharge on Saturday. With any luck, Adam hoped he would be home for a late dinner. Then he could unwind and spend time with his family; Ben was on call through the weekend.

Adam tugged at his tie and unbuttoned the collar of his shirt. As he gathered the charts, he heard a tap on the door. Maggie leaned on the frame; her shoulders sagged. Adam could read her face like a fortune teller reading a palm, and it was not something he wanted to hear.

"There's a gentleman in the waiting room who'd like to speak with you."

"Personal or professional?"

"Says he's a preacher. Name's Henry Slade. Just wants a few minutes of your time." Maggie pushed loose strands of hair behind her ears. "I told him the office was closed until Monday. But he insisted that I ask. Very polite."

157

"Okay, send him back," he said reluctantly.

While waiting, he messaged his neck and wondered if the visitor was a friend of Hal Brady. Adam thought the name, Henry Slade, was vaguely familiar but he couldn't make a connection.

Maggie made the introductions, walked out, and shut the door behind her.

"Have a seat," Adam said.

Henry Slade was a big man by anyone's standards, well over six feet tall, snow-white hair, uncommonly long, full around the ears, and in the back, curling over the collar. Captivating blue eyes looked out from beneath a prominent forehead and softened the lines in his face. A cleft chin and determined jaw which jutted a little, betrayed his intensity and a streak of stubbiness.

"I appreciate your time," Slade began. "I'm coming back in August for a tent revival at the old fairground in West Conway."

"So why the visit?" Adam asked.

"We're in the middle of some organizational and tactical sessions with the sponsoring churches. I learned early in my career that preparation and planning are the parents of success."

Adam shrugged. "I'm a little confused as to…"

Slade held up his hand and moved to the front of the chair. He took a folded sheet of paper from his inside coat pocket and slid it across the desk.

Adam unfolded the flier and read silently:

TENT REVIVAL

AUGUST 14 – 27

HENRY SLADE, EVANGELIST

PARISH FAIRGROUND

HEALING SERVICES NIGHTLY

EVERYONE WELCOME

SPONSOR: ASSEMBLY OF GOD CHURCHES

Adam, on the edge of irritation, looked up and said, "Frankly, I still don't understand why you're here."

"I wanted to get acquainted." Slade hesitated for a moment and eased back in his chair. "And invite you to our healing service."

Adam could not hide his look of incredulity. The offer, bold and unexpected, had caught him off guard. "I appreciate the invitation."

The preacher's steely blue eyes held Adam's attention. "I'm also here as an advocate. I believe in the practice of medicine as a means of healing. I respect your profession; the long hours, the emotional drain, dealing with the sick and dying. While the art of Medicine has been salutary for hundreds of years, the science has advanced at a snail's pace." He pulled his chair closer to the desk as if to share some intimate secret. "I submit there are healing forces within each of us; spiritual forces, if you will, that are elusive and ill-defined. If you tap into those sources and that enormous supply of energy is channeled into the infirmed, then miracles happen."

Slade stopped again and pointed at Adam. "We're not at cross purposes, but in fact, our roles are complimentary. I want the doctors in Madison Parish to view me with credibility, not as a charlatan or phony faith healer, but one who supports their efforts and, at the same time, believes in the rehabilitative power of prayer and in the healing elixir of God's grace and forgiveness."

Adam leaned back and observed this mountain-of-a-man sitting across from him in a white suit of worsted wool, a red carnation in the buttonhole of his lapel; probably in his mid-fifties, engaging, congenial and one who carried an aura of authenticity. He was no Elmer Gantry; so unlike the traveling evangelists of the depression years that roamed the rural South exploiting fear and ignorance and shouting their frightening message of hellfire and everlasting damnation. In their brief time together, Adam sensed in Henry Slade a deep-well of wisdom which along with his imposing physical stature gave him the dimensions of a man who *loomed larger than life.*

"I admit, we don't have all the answers," Adam said. "But the future's bright. People are living longer. The quality of life has improved. And the research programs around the country are working diligently to find solutions for many of our most daunting problems. We've climbed a long way up the learning curve."

Slade folded his hands and rested them in his lap. "I earnestly pray for your efforts and rejoice in your success."

Adam nodded.

"However, some men and women spend a lifetime with fear nipping at their heels. Others are devitalized by despair, ravaged with guilt, or immobilized by anxiety." He pointed to the window and the leaf-laden trees beyond. "Like autumn leaves, life may lose its color, its stability. The body breaks down and physical or mental illness appears. My message is simple: if a man will put himself completely in God's hands, he can find relief, the restoration of hope, the inculcation of confidence and finally, physical renewal."

Adam agreed with the premise of interaction. He had examples in his own practice in which the disease state was the physical expression of a troubled mind. Nor did he doubt that bitterness and resentment were self-destructive and if allowed to smolder, set the stage for other organic disease.

"Man is three dimensional and one segment may impact the other," Adam said. "But we need clarity, and in the meantime, provide the best medical care possible."

Slade stood and smiled agreeably. "Perhaps there was some truth in the doctor's words, spoken to a dying Lady Macbeth:

> *Foul whisperings are abroad, unnatural deeds*
> *Do breed unnatural troubles; infected minds*
> *To their deaf pillow will discharge their secrets;*
> *More needs she the Divine than the physician,*
> *God, God forgive us all.*

He stopped for a moment, pulled out a pocket watch, checked the time and replaced it with a flourish. Henry Slade looked across the desk and added his own commentary. "Shakespeare was a very wise man. Now I must go. I've taken too much of your time."

Adam circled the desk and extended his hand. "By the way, I hope we can enlist your support for our crusade."

A puzzled look crossed the preacher's face.

"There's a cluster of saloons in West Conway which contaminates our town. We have vowed to shut them down." Adam explained the several stages of the process. Should it reach phase three, a city-wide referendum would be held in late August. "That's when we could use your help."

Adam opened the bottom draw of his desk and retrieved a copy of *The Review.* He handed it to Slade. "The editorial on the front page gives you the facts. We would appreciate your support."

Henry Slade slipped the newspaper under his arm and said, "Goodbye."

Adam walked to the window and saw the preacher strolling along the sidewalk, tipping his hat to a passerby.

He wondered about this curious stranger as he watched his large frame disappear beyond the far end of the building. Where had he come from…this amicable man with the mellifluous voice? Adam liked him instinctively. A warm rapport. He had found a friend, perhaps an important ally in the inevitable showdown with the taverns.

❧

Sunday June 25
"C'mon in," Markham shouted.

Arnie Waters slipped into a folding chair near the desk. He removed his grimy baseball cap and dropped it on the floor. While checking the room, he rubbed a hand across his bald head. Nothing had changed since his last visit. The place needed a paint job.

"Where's Mario?" Frank asked.

Arnie shrugged. "Maybe he forgot."

Frank rocked back, the swivel groaned.

"The little Wop needs to write stuff down; keep a record," Arnie said.

"I just talked to him one day last week."

"He's a lazy piss ant. Nose stuck in a book half the time. Don't know how he runs his business."

Frank tapped his temple with a finger. "Smart. An I.Q. up to here," raising a hand above his head. "Don't let him fool you."

"Can't figure him out. Sorta like the spook on radio."

"Let me guess: The Whistler?"

"Naw, not him. It'll come to me…" Arnie snapped his fingers. "I got it…The Shadow."

"Yeah, imagine that, an Italian Shadow." Frank laughed at the caricature.

Arnie looked at his watch. "Hey, I ain't got all night."

Frank walked to the window and checked the dirt road that ran behind the Shamrock. No signs of Mario. He watched the growing dusk settle over the pasture. "Well, let's get stated."

Frank returned to his swivel and lit a cigarette. He took a drag and blew smoke through pursed lips. "I've got some news."

"Let's hear it."

"The petition drive started three days ago. Tex went by the American Legion Hall yesterday...late afternoon. Only thirty or so had signed. Of course, the churches probably got a thousand names this morning. But they have a helluva long way to go."

Arnie shook his head. "I don't know 'bout that. Still got more'n a week to sign and that Hannah what's-her-name's calling the shots."

"Hawkins."

"Well, the woman missed her calling. She could organize a prison riot; even put a dumb ass like Sam Gentry in the Governor's mansion."

Markham took a final drag from his cigarette and killed it in an ashtray.

"She's got Arthur White wrapped around her little finger. Same with the black preachers."

Arnie untangled his long legs and sat up. "The woman's got balls, for damn sure. Maybe the Mob should have targeted her rather than that nigger."

"By the way, I heard from Pappas."

Arnie leaned toward the desk, his face expectant. "And....?"

"Called yesterday; payphone in New Orleans." Markham shook another cigarette from the pack and lit it with his chrome lighter. "Wanted me to know that even if we lose the petition drive, they're still in the fight. And while they could pressure the Mayor and members of the City Council, the coalition would get relief from the Court, taking the Mayor out of play. That would leave the referendum; a final decision in late August, more than two months away. Meanwhile, mind our own business and leave the disruptions to Mr. Caruso and the Organization."

"Anything else?"

"Nope. Pappas delivered his message and hung up. Couldn't squeeze a question in sideways."

Arnie stretched his long arms before standing. "We'll know who signed the petition soon enough."

Markham counted with his fingers. "Just seven more days."

Arnie headed for the door. "Better tell Mario. Wouldn't use the phone. Never know who's listening."

Frank watched him drive away in his Dodge pickup. They had made a deal with Caruso, now they would follow his directions: lower their profile; no more dirty tricks; keep the taverns open; business as usual. Caruso had a plan and would provide the muscle.

Arnie was right. Frank checked the time and yawned. He would call on Mario tomorrow.

Chapter 27

On Monday morning, following a successful petition drive, Maude drove to City Hall. She had been issued her license after spending an hour with the driver's ed. instructor at Conway High. It renewed her confidence and enhanced her feeling of independence, like a fledgling leaving the nest. She had relied on Preacher for too long. Maude remembered, years ago, driving a Tin Lizzie; Ed had paid five hundred dollars for the Model T roadster. What she couldn't recall was why she handed Preacher the keys to the Packard in the first place.

City Hall was an uninspiring, red brick, two-story on Jackson Street, across from the hospital. It housed the Mayor, the city jail, a small police department and administrative offices. Boxwoods, in need of trimming, bordered all sides of the building. A few poplar trees fronted the entrance. No flowers or statuary; patches of dead grass. Maude thought the meager landscaping made the building appear austere and uninviting. And she wondered why? After all, it was the seat of city government with a steady flow of pedestrian traffic and in her opinion, deserved more aesthetic appeal. She would urge the Mayor to address her concern with a front-page editorial in *The Review*.

Maude pulled into the visitor's parking lot and dropped the keys in her purse. She followed the walkway to a pair of wooden doors, unembellished, except for brass handles and narrow sidelights. She rode the elevator to the second floor and took a seat in the Mayor's empty outer office, wondering where his secretary might be. Meanwhile, she settled into a comfortable chair and savored the success of the petition drive.

Chester Payne was near the end of his term in office and planned to run for reelection. Maude remembered the newspaper, with some reservations, had given him a lukewarm endorsement. The accompanying editorial stated the reason for its support: "While Chester Payne has no experience with governance at any level, the incumbent is feckless and the accusation of nepotism hangs over him like a storm cloud. (Three family members found jobs in City Hall during his administration.)" She was sure her endorsement provided Chester's razor-thin margin of victory.

"Good morning, Maude." Chester was breathless from rushing up the flight of stairs.

"Where's Dixie?" she asked, pointing to the secretary's desk.

"A summer virus...nothing serious." He reached down and took her hand and helped her from the chair. He affected a smile and led her into his office.

Maude noted the Mayor's bland appearance: a light-brown cotton suit, white shirt, and a nondescript bow tie; a shock of silver hair combed back, without a part, and held in place by a dab of Brylcreem. Chester's pasty skin and dull eyes reminded Maude of the mortician at Nabor's Funeral Home. Hmm...she wondered if they were related.

After three and a half years in office, Maude's paper had recently assessed the Mayor's performance. While he was neither innovative nor a visionary, he met the minimal demands of his office. He was not an arm twister or power broker; Conway's commercial landscape had not changed. On the other hand, his administration had been scandal free and restored some respect for the office.

Maude folded her hands in her lap and gave the Mayor a hard look. She knew he would vacillate when a major decision crossed his desk. (The flaw had cost Conway a poultry processing plant and a small clothing manufacturer.)

"Have you heard the good news?" Maude asked.

Chester shook his head. "Tell me. I need cheering up."

"We have over four thousand signatures. Of course, that's unofficial."

"I'm not surprised."

"The Clerk of Court received the petitions this morning. She will tally the numbers and cross-check each name with Conway's list of registered voters. Once we receive her stamp of approval, the decision rests with you and the City Council."

The Mayor frowned. "I'm not sure we're willing..."

"It's about *principle*," Maude said sharply. "Doing the right thing. Making the right choice. Ensuring a safe Conway; a better place to live and work and raise a family."

Chester shook his head. "The blue-collar worker supports the taverns and they're our most loyal voting block."

"This decision rises above politics," Maude insisted. "The integrity of our town is at stake."

The Mayor placed both elbows on his desk, his face paler than before. "Look Maude, I've read the legal guidelines. Let the final decision pass through my office, then the people of Conway can make the determination."

Maude shook her finger like a vexed school teacher. "No, no Chester. If you and your merry band reached a favorable conclusion, it would save Conway the expense of a referendum."

Perspiration speckled the Mayor's forehead and wilted the collar of his shirt. He held up both arms, a sign of surrender. "The City Council meets next week. I'll put it on the agenda."

"Remind them of their obligation to make honorable decisions. While most of their business is rather ordinary, occasionally, there are more serious matters to consider...moral choices...that profoundly impact the very heart of our town." She fashioned a greeting among the wrinkles. "I dropped one of those grenades in your lap this morning."

The Mayor turned his chair toward the window. Streamers of sunlight burnished the hardwood floor. "Maude, why are you doing this?"

She stood up and rapped on the desk. "Because it's the right thing to do."

166

The Mayor lifted himself out of his chair. "I admire your spunk. But watch your step; there are land mines scattered about."

Maude retrieved her purse and started to leave. "Remember, Chester, there's always a price to pay for taking the 'high ground'. Losing my dear friend Preacher is a daily reminder. But here's the irony, the acts of evil men reinforce our resolve."

She stopped at the office door. "Goodbye, Chester. I hope you'll see it my way."

Maude saw Chester standing at the window as she reached her car. She had hoped her visit would be persuasive. But it was only a pipe dream and she knew it.

⌘

Wednesday, July 5th

After lunch, Markham left the Shamrock, crossed Highway 23 and took the asphalt road to Gambelli's. He parked beside the tavern which rested on the highest point in the parish, giving a clear view of the picturesque river, and downstream, the bridge that fed traffic into West Conway. A wide veranda ran the length of the brick building with its slate roof; in milder weather al fresco dining was popular. A separate wing with its own entrance housed the "beer parlor" with its pool tables and jukebox, a venue for the nearby college and blue collar crowd. The main dining room offered fine wines, authentic Italian food and a pleasing ambiance. Markham knew that Mario's format was different from the Shamrock and Arnie's place; a formula that paid big dividends to Gambelli and set him apart from his competitors.

Markham stood unnoticed at the open door and scanned the office which was so unlike his own. Pale blue carpet covered the floor, a window unit hummed; a ceiling fan stirred the cool air. Mario was at his desk reading a book. Shelves, crammed with books lined one wall; on the other, a porcelain vase filled with flowers rested on an antique table. Markham figured the colorful painting above the table was the work of some dead Italian artist, but Michelangelo was the only name that came to mind. He shook his head at the handsome upholstered chairs, the uncluttered desk. Markham had wondered about Mario Gambelli since their first meeting and the well-appointed office only deepened the mystery.

Mario looked up. "Oh Frank, didn't see you standing there." He waved him to the chair nearest the desk.

"Nice place you got here."

"*Grazi,* but what brings you across the highway?"

"We missed you at our meeting. I came over last Monday but your chef said you were out of town."

After checking his desk calendar, Mario slapped his forehead. "Sorry, it slipped my mind."

"Arnie's right, you need to write things down."

"Did I miss something important?"

Markham raised his voice. "You could say that!"

Mario chose to ignore the petulance.

Markham lowered the volume. "I got a call from Johnny Pappas."

"And..."

"He wanted to assure us that Caruso is still in the fight and will handle 'our problem' before the referendum in August. Meanwhile, we're to maintain a low profile...business as usual."

Mario pointed a chiding finger at himself. "I was naïve to think that killing the cat would frighten anyone. But when the old lady and her friends got the petition signed despite the violence, well..." Mario shook his head like a metronome. "...I'm convinced their defenses are impregnable. And there's nothing Caruso can do, no matter how gruesome, that will dissuade Conway to vote down the referendum." Mario added, with a jester's smile, "To borrow one of your cliques: Our goose is cooked."

"Sounds like you're giving up."

"A realist, Frank. Just looking at the 'big picture.'"

Markham moved up in his chair. "What's that suppose to mean?"

"Look Frank, there's a good chance we'll lose the vote in August. And Sheriff Randy Gilstrap, who we've had in our back pocket, will shut us down and padlock the doors."

Markham shook his head vigorously. "Over my dead body."

"Hold on a minute and consider alternatives." Mario closed the book he'd been reading and shoved it aside. "If we lose, they pay."

"How much?"

"There'll be an appraisal to determine the value of each of the three taverns."

"What about Warren?"

"A separate appraisal of the land will set the price to indemnify Mr. Warren." Mario saw no need to disclose his own arrangement.

"Sounds like a lot of money. Think they can come up with the cash?"

Mario shrugged. "If not, we're still in business."

Markham pounded the desk with his fist. "I put my blood and sweat in the Shamrock, from pouring the foundation to topping off the roof. I'm not giving up; maybe the old biddy at the newspaper can't raise the money." He banged the desk again. "Dammit, don't sell Caruso short."

Mario fingered a small scar on his chin and locked his gaze on Markham's dark agate eyes. "It's always prudent to have an alternate plan. As a matter of fact, it's the reason I missed the meeting with you and Arnie."

"Go on," Markham urged.

"First, I did my research. If I'm shut down, where'll I go? Where is the most favorable location? The answer popped up like a jack-in-the box." He held up a folded map of the state of Louisiana.

Markham waved his fingers to hurry him along.

"Leesville."

"Leesville? Never heard of the place."

"Nice town, west of Alexandria, a bit smaller than Conway. Not a decent Italian bar and restaurant within fifty miles." Mario's brown eyes sparkled. "Leesville, the home of Fort Polk."

"I thought they closed all those military bases after the war."

"Camps Claiborne and Livingston, but the Army needed to keep Polk open. Thousands of soldiers get their basic training there. And with the crisis in Korea, the Army's ramped up the numbers. It makes this place look like small change."

"Sounds like you've made up your mind."

"I prefer to stay here. But if I'm shut down, well, I have an option." Mario described his day trip to Leesville: With some luck, he met the Mayor who welcomed all business prospects. After lunch at a local cafe, a member of the Mayor's office gave him a quick tour of Fort Polk which was bustling with activity. He had also found several desirable locations for the restaurant and an adjacent beer garden. He made it clear to the Mayor that his trip was exploratory but he would be back before Labor Day having made a final decision.

Markham stood up and turned to leave. "I'll wait and see how this plays out. But I'm planning to stay," he said pointing in the direction of the Shamrock.

Mario remained seated. "Hope you're right."

Markham stopped momentarily in front of the picture. "Just a wild guess...Michelangelo?"

"Bellini."

Markham rolled his eyes and left the room.

℘

When Markham returned to his office, he found Arnie sprawled on the sofa half-asleep. He settled in the swivel chair and opened the mail that Tex had placed on his desk. "What're you doing here?" he asked without looking up.

Arnie unwound his long legs and sat on the edge of the threadbare sofa. "Just curious about your meeting."

"I delivered the message from Johnny Pappas."

"Was that it?"

"Not quite." Markham dropped the junk mail in the trash can beside his desk. A troubled look, as he relayed Mario's plans. "Gambelli believes that despite our alliance with Caruso, we'll lose the vote. And our one slim hope is Harrington's failure to raise the cash for the buy-out. Meanwhile, he's made plans to move to Leesville if they shut us down."

"So, he's given up."

"Seems that way."

"Maybe I should have a heart to heart with the Wop," Arnie said angrily.

"Bad idea. It would only cause trouble." Markham tried to relax and clear his mind. "Besides, we don't know anything about Mario Gambelli. No family. No friends. No background. For that matter, he could be C.I.A. or working for a foreign government."

170

"C'mon Frank, you been reading too many spy novels. That little prick wouldn't know Elliott Ness from Al Capone."

Markham sighed, "Leave Mario to his own devices."

The crimson began to fade from Arnie's cheeks. "Whatever you say, Frank." He stood up and stretched his long arms. "I'm still counting on Caruso. Maybe we should go to New Orleans and have a face to face with the Boss."

"Another bad idea, Arnie. If Mr. Caruso wants to meet, we'll receive an engraved invitation. Got it?"

"Yeah, I got it," he said and headed for the door. He stopped abruptly and asked, "Where the hell is Leesville?"

"Down the road from Fort Polk, the Army's largest military training center in the country." Frank could not conceal a look of amusement. "The Italian Shadow...Fort Polk...Secret Service... Got it?"

"Yeah, I suppose," Arnie said, scratching his head. "I'm outta here."

Chapter 28

Monday, July 17th

Knox awoke early as usual, put on her robe and left Ben asleep, snoring lightly. Barefoot, she went down-stairs to the kitchen and made a pot of coffee. She took her mug to the kitchen window and watched daybreak, spilling pink and vermillion light into low-lying clouds. Her coffee, so hot it burned her tongue, reminded her to check on Jake.

Knox climbed the carpeted stairs to Jake's room. When she cracked the door she knew, intuitively, that something was wrong. She leaned over the bed, Jake's cadaver-like head with its wisps of gray hair lay peacefully on the pillow; his mouth open, sunken at the edges; hollow eyes stared at the ceiling as though startled by his own death knell. There were no signs of a struggle, no attempt to leave his bed. Knox believed the end had come quickly and quietly as it should for all men.

She caressed his face gently, the wrinkled skin already cold and stiff. Knox wondered when he had taken that final gasp. It must have been after midnight when she last checked on him and found him sleeping. She had turned off the lamp and kissed him lightly on the forehead. While it was a "good night" formality, Knox was glad she had done it.

During those first moments of discovery, she felt a profound and ill-defined sadness that seemed to transcend the short span of their relationship and encompass the loss of a father she had never seen and an infant son she would never hold.

Sometimes Ben referred to her as "the farmer's daughter." In some ways, she admitted, he was right. During the last year, Jake's increasing infirmity had drawn them closer together. When she first arrived at Hamilton House, he had been polite and amiable, the traditional respect shown by a southern gentleman. After all, she was the wife of his only heir and direct descendant. Over the ensuing years, a subtle transition had taken place. Jake's simple courtesy morphed into genuine concern, almost paternalistic. Frugal to a fault (at least that was his reputation), with Knox, he was generous; at times, even indulgent.

Until his dependence, born of age and illness, he remained stolid and undemonstrative. But Know remembered those final months; how Jake would sit with her in the garden swing and hold her hand; how sometimes the tears would flow, inexplicably, as if they had been damned up inside for years, but at last, had found release.

Knox understood Jake's Stoic façade. A show of emotion was a sign of weakness; an expression of affection was a singularly feminine virtue. His reaction was always awkward and uneasy when she brushed him with a kiss; so any show of Platonic love was reserved for Christmas and birthdays.

Nor had she heard him say to Ben or anyone else, "I love you." How sad, she mused, for Jake to have lived, by worldly standards, a successful life and yet had been unable to express without reticence simple words of endearment. Knox hoped he had at least spoken them to Martha Hamilton in the privacy of their bedroom...at some intimate moment.

&

Ben had finished shaving when Knox appeared in the open bathroom door.

"Jake's dead."

"Are you sure?"

"I'm sure."

Ben wiped his face with a towel. "I'll check. Would you call Johnny Nabor's?"

Knox stuffed the pocket of her robe with Kleenex and moved toward the door. She called back, "I'll use the kitchen phone."

Ben closed his father's eyes and pulled the sheet over him. Jake Hamilton is at peace, thought Ben, wandering out to the balcony. He felt a strange sense of exhilaration as he stood there. In fact, he enjoyed, without remorse, the resplendent dawning of a new day.

His father's death was no surprise. The small strokes had taken their toll. While he was prepared for the inevitable, there came an unexpected feeling of relief, as though some heavy weight had dropped from his shoulders. He knew a son should not revel in the loss of a father, but Jake had lived long and well. And late in life, his disease had left him demented and dependent on Knox… only the remnant of a man.

Ben was glad the end had come at night. Sleep, he thought, was the perfect way-station…a transition from this life to whatever lies beyond. No pain or anguish. No crying out or pleas for mercy. Ben thought of patients assaulted by some dreaded disease, ravaged slowly and inexorably until even the last trace of human dignity had been erased. He had heard the groans of the dying echo through the dark corridors of the hospital and watched friends and family hover helplessly over the sickbeds of loved ones like morbid spectators. Jake had been spared that added ignominy.

The sun climbed above the tallest trees and a warm breeze stirred the swirling mist that hung over the river, carrying the promise of another insufferable summer day. For reasons he did not understand, Ben felt a heightened sense of awareness; colors were brighter, sounds more acute, lines and angles more clearly defined. He wondered if Jake's death could be the reason.

Ben knew that since returning home, he'd never been comfortable in his father's house. Only the nostalgic memories of his mother; her bedtime stories by the fireplace in winter and their long talks in the summer garden, sustained him. While failing health had mellowed Jake, the old smoldering resentments continued to haunt their relationship. It was too late. The cleavage between them had become irreconcilable. Now, ironically, thought Ben, with Jake's death, there had come this euphoric feeling of release; he was free at last, not unlike the chattering sparrows flitting through the saffron sky.

Knox backed through the French doors carrying a tray which she placed on the tile-topped table.

"Coffee?"

"Thanks."

She poured two cups, handing one to him. "You're up earlier than usual."

Ben shrugged.

Knox settled into a wicker chair, and cradled the cup in her lap. Ben stood at the railing and looked at her, as the sun, slanting over his shoulder, highlighted her Madonna-like face. He felt the blood surge through his body, carnal and strong. Those passions, usually self-gratifying, contained on this glorious morning a genuine longing for *her* fulfillment. There was an urge to make love to her; to hold on to her fiercely, as if in letting go, he might lose her forever. Was this not what she had been wanting from him? But Jake's death had drained all the color from her face. Ben knew, at least for Knox, this was not the time. While restive, he would wait.

Ben, shirtless, walked slowly to the far end of the gallery, his hand stuffed in the pockets of his khaki pants. She called after him, "What are you planning to do with Jake's clothes?"

He propped against the corner post and looked toward the river still covered with the stubborn mist. "The Salvation Army," he answered indifferently.

"I went through his closet yesterday. There are some suits he must have bought twenty years ago."

"Tightfisted when it came to money." Ben moved back to the table and picked up his cup.

"I'll miss him," she said.

"You were good to him, and I guess with the exception of my mother, the only other person he loved."

"That's not true, Ben. He loved you, in his own way. Just hard for him to put it in words."

Ben shook his head as he slumped into the wicker settee. "Med school polarized our relationship. He considered it disrespectful, even defiant. Jake never conceded me the right to make my own decision."

"You're wrong. He did love you. I know he did. A while back, during our time in the garden, he turned to me and said, 'Benjamin is a good boy. Take care of him.'"

"I'd like to believe that," Ben said wistfully.

Her brown eyes flashed with conviction. "It's true. And you must believe it."

Ben took a swallow of coffee and placed his cup on the table. "I need to get going. It looks like a long day."

"Will you be home for dinner?"

"Don't think so. Hospital staff meeting tonight."

Knox was surprised when he bent down and brushed her lips with a kiss.

"Johnny Nabors will take care of Jake."

"What about funeral arrangements?"

"I'll leave that up to you and Johnny," he said disappearing through the pair of French doors.

⁊

Wednesday, July 26th

Though his ankle had healed, Brett strolled carefully through the formal gardens and across the back lawn. Miniature roses with pale, yellow petals intertwined the latticed arbor; their fragrance filled the night air like some provocative perfume. A full moon had climbed steadily above the tallest pines and splashed the arbor with its silvery light. He saw her standing in the archway. "Sorry I'm late," he said, pressing her hands between his own.

Knox walked around a fountain of Carrara marble and sat down on a wrought iron bench. "You're forgiven."

Brett knelt down and rested his back against the fountain. "I'm glad you came tonight."

"Ben's tied up at the hospital…again."

Brett sighed; he could not hide his relief.

Knox leaned forward straining to see him, shadowy in the shaft of moonlight which angled through the archway. "When you called today, you said it was urgent."

Brett stood up and walked back to the arbor's entrance. The night sky was aglow with countless stars. "It's a good omen," he said.

176

"A good omen?"

"Arcturus, brighter than I've ever seen him before."

Brett briefly disappeared, then walked back inside and placed a delicate rose in her lap.

"Thank you," she said and inhaled its sweetness.

Brett sat down beside her and took her hand. "I've made a decision to leave Conway and I want you to go with me."

"Why?"

"Why am I leaving?"

She nodded. "And me?"

"Easy. Jake's gone and he was the reason I'm here. And you, well, you're the woman I love."

Knox rested her head against his shoulder and closed her eyes. "I don't know, Brett. So much has happened during these past few months. I need time to sort things out."

"I can't promise you a big house and the security you have here. But the rodeo circuit gives you a chance to travel the West and meet a lot of nice people. Remember last spring, I confessed that I was restless? A roamer. A man with shallow roots. I've run the plantation for five years; it's time to move on."

"When?" she asked.

"I submitted my resignation to Ben yesterday with the promise to stay on until the cotton is full grown or a new foreman is hired... whichever comes first."

"Then I have time..."

"Sure, take some time. It'll probably be October before I can leave. I owe Jake that much."

"You and Jake seemed to get along; so different, yet like two peas in a pod." Knox wanted to change the subject.

"I had a lot of respect for Jake. With sweat and perseverance, he made this plantation one of the best cotton operations in the South." Brett reveled in the memory. "When we first met, he asked only one question: 'Do you think a man can get ahead by working only eight hours a day, five days a week?' I wanted the job, so I gave him the answer he was looking for: 'No, it can't be done.' Jake said, 'You're hired. Two hundred dollars a week, plus room and board.' He shook my hand and bolted out of the study. Nothing in writing. A deal had been struck."

"He was never accused of wasting words," Knox added.

Brett shook his head. "Didn't pass out compliments either. Guess he figured a man knew when he'd done a good job. But he'll be missed by a lot of folks if that crowd at his funeral means anything."

"I sure miss him. He's been the center of my life for the last few years and losing him leaves a hole right here," she said, pressing her hand over her heart. "I hate the thought of going back to the bridge club or even worse, the hospital auxiliary."

"Then come away with me," he pleaded. "You told me months ago that your marriage was in trouble. Something was missing. I believe 'unfulfilled' was the word you used."

"All of it's true," she said. "But oddly enough, since Jake's death, Ben has been more attentive."

"Think about it, that's all I ask."

"It's a promise."

Brett stood and pulled her close to him. He kissed her passionately.

She backed away, politely. "I'd better get back. We'll talk again... later."

Brett nodded. "Good night, Knox."

She turned and left the arbor. His eyes followed her slender form into the garden, and watched her disappear amid the shadows mingled with moonlight.

℞

Knox walked around the house and sat down on the front steps. She considered Brett's proposal to leave Conway and Ben and this house...forever. She knew this was one of life's hard choices; one that inalterably changes the present and profoundly shapes the future. A divided road. She had arrived at such a place.

She pressed the yellow rose against her lips. The scent stirred within her the sensual delight which she had felt three months ago in the forest glade.

A car turned off Willow Road and into the driveway. Ben was home early.

Her decision could wait and for that Knox was grateful. But it would not be easy; that she was certain.

Chapter 29

The Plantation House received high praise from Home and Garden Magazine…a five-star rating. Pappy Kemp, the affable proprietor, had spent most of 1941 at Camp Livingston tramping through the brackish bogs and mosquito-infested lowlands, enduring the blistering summer heat before being shipped overseas with the 21st Infantry Division. An Ohioan by birth, he settled in Conway after the war; divorced, highly decorated, and with one leg missing. (The result of a land mine explosion during the invasion of Salerno.)

In a matter of months, he bought and restored an antebellum home and refurbished it elegantly, including an exquisite Waterford chandelier which hung in the main dining room. Pappy lured the chef from Alfredo's in New Orleans and quickly established a popular, upscale restaurant. He was ever-present, greeting his customers cheerfully, and putting his personal touch on every phase of the operation. Pappy's formula was simple: good food of consistent quality, fine wines, and sterling service.

The Plantation House sat on high ground, its manicured lawn sloped gently to the levee below. A balustrade of swamp cypress enclosed the upstairs gallery, which extended across the front and gave a commanding view of the river and preferred seating for those who enjoyed al fresco dining. Ancient oaks surrounded the house and provided shade during the swelter of long summers. A cobblestone drive, which led to the portico, was lined by crepe myrtle, laden with flowers…clusters of flaming crimson.

ᐧᐧ

Ben stopped at valet parking and put the ticket in his coat pocket. He took Knox by the hand and led her up the three steps to the glass entrance. Pappy, tanned to a deep bronze and wearing a white dinner jacket, greeted them graciously. He was tall with an enviable waistline, genial blue eyes and a thatch of gray hair. He bowed politely and guided them, with a noticeable limp, to the desk of the maitre d' a few steps down the capacious central hallway. "It's a pleasure to have you with us tonight," Pappy said, giving Knox his most hospitable smile.

Ben glanced at his watch. "Sorry we're late."

"No problem. Your table's waiting. Buford, here, will show you the way." With a slight nudge, Ben moved Knox in the direction of a dull-eyed, young waiter, who stood with arms folded, hugging two menus and a wine list snugly against his chest.

"Let me know if you need anything." Pappy returned to the stand-up desk and drew a line through the entry: Hamilton… eight o'clock.

A table beside a front window gave them a clear view of the river, less distinct now, due to the nearness of nightfall. Knox strained to see a couple walking arm-in-arm along the levee, then down a well-worn path to the river's edge. The romantic scene was an ironic reminder of her own mind-boggling predicament. On the one hand, Ben's feeling of renewal after his father's death seemed genuine. At the same time, Brett reminded her (whenever the opportunity arose) of his true love and the invitation to leave Conway with him. Knox hoped this pleasant evening would mitigate, at least to some extent, her dire dilemma.

The waiter returned with a carafe of white wine, poured each a glass and placed the bottle in a silver-plated ice bucket beside the table. "I'll give you some time to look at the menu," he drawled, the words rolling off his lips, molasses-thick.

"Thank you Buford. We would like to relax before ordering."

After the waiter sidled away, Ben lifted his glass in a toast: "To the most beautiful woman in Madison Parish."

Knox blushed; touched the crystal lightly with her own and sipped the ambrosial wine.

Ben set his glass down and ran a finger, abstracted, around the moist rim, causing it to hum softly. "I've been thinking about us lately."

Knox straightened up and rested her elbows on the brocaded arms of the chair. "And what have you been thinking?"

"Even though Jake's gone, you haven't been getting out much. Thought we might drive to the Gulf for a long weekend...that is, if you would like that."

"Oh, Ben, I'd love that," she said. "When can you get away?"

"How about next weekend? We'll leave early Friday morning, have a couple of days of sun and surf, stuff ourselves with seafood, make love before a room-service breakfast, watch the sunset over frozen daiquiris and, after dinner, dance the night way on some moonlit veranda."

Knox was stunned, muted.

"Well, whata you say?" He held out his arms, palms up, petitioning an answer.

"No woman in her right mind would turn down an invitation like that," she said.

"Then let's drink to balmy breezes and gentle currents. And may the gods smile benevolently and bestow a generous measure of their aphrodisiac pleasures."

"I think I'm blushing," she said, feeling the heat in her cheeks.

Many times in the past, too many to count, she had longed, even prayed, for such an invitation. Why now? she wondered. His offer was as lyrical as some dreamy-eyed romantic; none of the things Ben Hamilton had ever pretended to be.

"Now that's settled, how about some food?"

They enjoyed, with little interruption, shrimp remoulade, fresh flounder stuffed with crab meat and dabbed with hollandaise sauce, homegrown wild rice, a crisp green salad with Pappy's secret dressing, and finally two demitasse and one slice of pecan pie. "Are you sure you don't want some dessert?" he asked.

"I've already had too much." She puffed out her cheeks like a swollen blowfish.

While he ate his dessert, Knox reached into her purse and pulled out a small package, neatly wrapped and festooned with scarlet ribbons. She reached across the table and placed it in front of him. "A memento of this very special occasion."

Ben laid down his folk and reached for the package. Its stark implication struck him like a searing jolt of electricity. "Our anniversary." He looked away and swallowed hard. "How could I have forgotten?"

"Ten years to the day." Though attenuated by time, Knox remembered the candlelight wedding on that sultry July evening with its Cinderella-like enchantment and golden-bright expectations.

Ben fumbled with the ribbon, finally tearing the paper away. Inside was a pair of fourteen-carat gold cuff links engraved in script with the letters, "B.H." He admired them by the light of the candle. "They're beautiful. Thanks."

"I saw you wearing a pair of Jake's, tarnished and all. Thought you might like a set of your own."

He replaced the top and put the small box into his coat pocket, crumpled up the wrapping paper, and with his finger, moved it aimlessly about the table. Finally, he broke an interminable silence. "It just slipped my mind. Can you ever forgive me?"

Knox bit hard against her lower lip. "Sure, Ben. You know I will," she said lamely.

He reached over and placed his hand gently on her arm. "Look, Knox…" Ben struggled to find the words. "…there have been times when I've failed you, occasions when I should have been more thoughtful. What else can I say…except I'm sorry?" He squeezed her arm to press his apology. "I'm truly sorry."

Tears sprang uncontrollably and ran down her cheeks. She wiped them away with her napkin. "It's okay, Ben. I know you've been busy. Guess I'm too sentimental for my own good."

"I'll make it up to you, beginning next weekend at the beach. No more broken promises." He squeezed again. "You'll see."

Before Knox could respond, Pappy approached the table. "Phone call, Dr. Hamilton. You can take it at my desk."

"I thought you had swapped call tonight."

"I'd planned to ask Adam but somehow…I guess I got sidetracked." He stood up and patted her shoulder solicitously. "Don't worry, I'll be right back."

"Can I get you something from the bar, Mrs. Hamilton?" Pappy asked.

"No thanks, Pappy. It's probably the hospital and you know what that means."

⁓

During the ride home, Knox felt the tension in her neck and shoulders. She saw the reflections of neon as they crossed the river. It was a reminder: she hoped the evening would provide clarity; instead, it had fed her confusion. She looked at Ben who drove in silence; embarrassed, she assumed, by another slight. She rested a hand on his shoulder. "It's okay Ben, you'll make it up at the beach." But Knox felt the slights, like the nicks from a knife, and she knew they did not bode well.

Chapter 30

Sunday, July 30

Adam and Allison had invited Maude for Sunday dinner. It was sunny and fiery hot when they left the morning worship service. Adam took Maude's hand and led her down the church steps to the crowded sidewalk. They spoke briefly to a few friends before heading for the parking lot beside the annex. They deposited Maude in the Packard and reminded her that Mattie would have dinner ready at one o'clock. Maude waved and assured them she would be there…and on time. Who in their right mind, she wondered, would miss out on Mattie's fried chicken and her mouth-watering blackberry cobbler?

When Adam and Allison got home, Mattie had the table set and the glass panes of the breakfront polished, sparkling with sunlight streaming through the dining-room windows. Yellow dahlias floated in a cut glass bowl, which Mattie had made the centerpiece. It was a setting for three since Robin was spending the day with Sally, her best friend and playmate.

The kitchen was warm despite the window unit that delivered cool air into the small room. Mattie lifted the lid of the cast iron pot, listened to the sizzle momentarily, then replaced the cover and turned off the eye of the stove. She unknotted the bandana from around her neck and wiped her face dry.

"Are we ready?" Allison asked, pouring herself a glass of iced tea.

"Needs to heat up the rolls."

Allison closed her eyes and savored the confluence of aromas. "You're the best, Mattie. One of these days, some ritzy restaurant in New Orleans will try to steal you away."

"Nome, Mattie's ain't goin' no place. I's born here and plan to take my last breath...right here in Madison Parish."

❦

After their meal, Mattie refilled their glasses with iced tea. "How 'bout a little more cobbler and ice cream Miz Maude?"

Maude shook her head. "Don't have room for another bite." She dabbed her lips with her napkin. "Mattie, that's the best meal I've had since ...well I can't remember when."

The compliment made Mattie smile as she shuttled back to the kitchen.

"Do you realize it's only three weeks until the referendum?" Maude asked, adept at changing the course of any conversation.

"I hope Hannah and her committee are as effective in their 'get out the vote' campaign as they were with the petition drive," Adam said.

"I talked with her earlier in the week and she plans another city-wide mailing. She's also badgered all the merchants on Main Street until most have agreed to place posters in their display windows."

"What about the banner above Main?" Allison asked.

"She got the Mayor's permission and it goes up tomorrow. It'll give the date and a simple injunction: 'Be a Good Citizen and Vote.'"

Adam suggested that Chester Payne didn't have a chance. Hannah, with that pretty face and persuasive smile, made Chester melt faster than a southern snowman. The image was a caricature: the Mayor with his top hat, scarf and corncob pipe, bewitched and slowly melting from the heat of her presence. It brought light-hearted laughter from everyone around the table.

All of them knew that Hannah was the most important cog in the coalition's wheel. Without her energy and enthusiasm, the petition drive could easily have bogged down in voter indifference. A tireless worker, she was not about to let that happen. She knew there were risks (Preacher's death had gotten Conway's attention), but she was undaunted and the threats that sifted through the town only strengthened her commitment. Maude had chosen Hannah because of her wildly successful leadership of the League of Womens Voters and her involvement in charitable fund-raining events. Maude had known her father, an activist in civic affairs and an outspoken advocate of prison reform. Like her father, Hannah had inherited his iron will and his *noblesse oblige.*

"By the way, what do you hear from Mr. District Attorney?" Maude asked in her most manly voice, a parody on the popular radio program.

Adam took a moment to consider the question. "Gosh Maude, it's been more than a month ago."

"But there's no reason to think the money won't be available?"

"In my last conversation with Al, the Senator whole-heartedly supports the park project but there'll be no committee vote until after the referendum."

Allison gave him a curious look. "You mean the Senator will call for a vote if we win the referendum?"

Adam nodded. "Al's friend, Chuck Wilson, is the Senator's right hand and our intermediary. So there's reason to believe the information is reliable."

Maude folded her napkin and placed it in the ceramic ring. "What would we have done without Al Marx?" she asked. "The paper will give him a ringing endorsement when he's up for reelection."

"Al's ambitious and has set some lofty goals. My guess is he'll run for a state-wise office."

"Attorney General?" Allison asked.

"Possible."

"Well he's got my support if he runs for dogcatcher," Maude said. "We need more people like Al Marx in charge of the people's business."

Mattie came in and cleared the table. She picked up the pitcher of tea and refilled their glasses before waddling back to the kitchen.

Maude looked at Adam with a grave expression. "Have you heard from Markham?"

"Not a word."

"Our adversaries have been strangely quiet. I keep waiting for that other shoe to drop."

"Scary." Allison shifted uneasily in her chair.

"If Caruso's still in the fight, then we can expect more trouble," Adam said.

Allison reached across the table and moved the flower bowl; just enough to catch the sunlight. "I'd hoped that the successful petition drive might take them out of the game."

"I doubt it," Adam said.

"Caruso's an evil man. Should we win the referendum, he'll remain a menace because he's angry and vindictive." Maude pushed away from the table and looked at Adam. "We agreed there were risks but some things are worth fighting for."

"Would you like to move to the living room?" Allison asked.

"Thanks, but I need to go by the office and work on this week's *Review*." Maude stood and raised her voice. "Mattie, your dinner was wonderful…good for another two pounds," she said, patting her stomach.

She gave Allison a hug, then Adam walked her to the Packard.

"I almost forgot." Propped against the car, Maude reached into her purse and dug out an envelope. "I got a letter from Mrs. LeBauer the other day." She unfolded the paper and handed it to Adam.

Dear Friends,

Thank you, belatedly, for your prayers and cards of condolence. I miss Conway, the house on Memory Lane and most of all, my friends and neighbors. Tom's River is a nice town and my daughter has been a source of great comfort. I miss Andy as much as ever and there are days when the tears still run. But time has been kind and allayed some of the heartache.

While the loss was devastating, I'm trying to forgive those responsible for the senseless death of my beloved Andy... although it is hard to do.
My best wishes to all of you.
Eve Lebauer

A note was clipped to the letter: "Mrs. Harrington, I hope you will publish my message of appreciation to the folks in Conway."

Adam refolded the letter and slipped it into Maude's purse. "I'm sure you'll honor her request."

"Next week...front page."

"A reminder of our obligation to Mrs. Lebauer...and our town."

Maude settled in the driver's seat and started the engine. "And a reminder of why we doing what we're doing...putting it all on the line." With that she eased the Packard down the driveway and into the deserted street.

Chapter 31

"You called."

"Yeah, have a seat."

Waters dragged a folding chair across the linoleum close to the desk. "Where's Mario?"

"Out of town." Markham, disgruntled, reached for the pack of cigarettes on his desk. "Probably in Leesville, negotiating his lease."

Arnie crossed his gangly legs and slouched back in his chair. "You think the Wop has run up the white flag?"

Markham shook a cigarette from the pack and lit up. His dark eyes narrowed; the look of a man who had subjugated his anger but remained visibly agitated. "Some people, like Mario, plan ahead. They have an option if things don't go their way. Others are hardheaded, stubborn as a mule." Markham pointed toward Arnie and then to himself. "And by God, I'm going to keep the Shamrock open till that weasel, Randy Gilstrap, padlocks the doors and hands me a check."

Waters was a tall raw-boned man with stolid features that resisted a smile. Markham again remembered their high school days; Arnie had the reputation of a ruffian, ruthless at times,

189

and one with a high-octane temper. While Markham knew he could take care of himself, he chose to avoid Arnie and on chance encounters gave him a nod or the wave of his hand. It wasn't fear, nor was it respect. He simply saw no gain in confronting trouble.

"I'm staying. They'll have to haul my ass out of the Ale House with a loaded gun. Besides, there's Caruso; the game ain't over yet."

"That's what I called about," Markham said

"Let's hear it."

"Pappas…a payphone as usual…well after midnight. Not much action on Monday nights, so Tex had locked the doors and turned off the outside lights. I was working at my desk when the call came."

"Dammit Frank. What did he say? I don't give a rat's ass about Tex or your fucking neon sign. What did the man say?" Water's half-shouted.

Markham dropped his cigarette, sizzling, in a half-empty beer can. He wrapped his arms behind his head. "Caruso is baling out."

"No way. No damn way! We made a deal. He can't break the contract."

"Tony Caruso's the elephant in the room; he can do whatever he damn well pleases."

The color drained from Arnie's face as he muttered another expletive beneath his breath. He jumped up with clenched fists, surveyed the bleak room as though he might find a way to vent his wrath. The girlie calendar on the side wall hung off center. He crossed the room and made the minor adjustment. Arnie stood and looked at Miss August in her skimpy bikini lounging on some pristine beach with that "come hither" look. It served to tamp down his anger.

"I pleaded our case," Markham said. "But Pappas wasn't interested."

A sullen Waters returned to his seat and banged the desktop with his hand. "Gimme a damn cigarette!"

Markham tossed the pack into his lap. "He wanted to do the talking."

Waters waited impatiently, tapping his fingers on the desk.

"Pappas made it clear that Mr. Caruso believes Conway will pass the referendum with or without his presence. While he is still interested in expanding his base of operations into North Louisiana and Central Arkansas, he is a patient man. And a fresh approach and another political cycle may be more opportunistic. Meanwhile, Conway has not heard the last from Mr. Caruso... whatever that means. As for me and you and Mario, Pappas offered no advice other than to forget the Caruso connection. We are on our own." Markham raised his arms as if to ask, "What more can I say?"

Waters hunched his narrow shoulders. "They'll be back after the dust settles. Caruso is itching to take over the tracks in Arkansas. Once he controls the horses, well, one thing leads to another. Before those dumb ass legislators wake up, he'll have slots in every convenience store from Fort Smith to Little Rock."

"Won't help us none."

"Well, I'm not ready to lie down and die," Arnie said firmly.

"It'll take a miracle."

Waters stood up and turned toward the door. "I'll think of something."

"You're wasting your time."

He put on his sweat-stained baseball cap and looked back. "Maybe, maybe not. But I'll holler good'n loud if I do.".

☙

Arnie stood beside the service road mulling over Caruso's decision. He was counting on the Mafia Boss to swing the momentum in his direction. He wasn't sure what that might be but an act so violent that supporters of the referendum feared for their personal safety and chose not to vote. But the late night phone call from Johnny Pappas had made it clear: Caruso was out of the game.

He crossed the road and found the trail that led to the Ale House through the forest of hardwood and pine. The path was seldom used and its definition almost lost, covered with weeds and wild grass. "Was there anything that could save the Ale House?" he wondered aloud, walking in the shade of the trees. Were there any possibilities? It seemed that calamity only strengthened the hand of his adversary, a fact that both annoyed and frustrated him.

Still, he refused to give up and figured it was part of who he was. The youngest of ten children, he always had to fight for position, a place at the kitchen table; those early struggles had prepared him for a rough and tumble life, sometimes at the expense of a black eye or bruised knuckles, even a broken rib or two.

He knew Gambelli was dispirited and ready to leave West Conway. Was the move to Leesville legitimate or a front for some cloak-and-dagger organization? He had never been sure what Mario was about, although Arnie doubted the slender, well-dressed Italian, was part of something sinister. The notion that Mario was an agent for the U.S. Government or even a double agent sequestered in the piney woods of a rural state was far-fetched. But where had the Wop spent the war years? When he asked, Mario answered in thickly accented English sprinkled with non sequiturs. So, it was only a guess and Arnie figured it really didn't matter. "So I'll forget the 'Italian Shadow,'" he muttered.

Beams of sunlight slipped through the overhanging limbs and Arnie felt the uncomfortable August heat. He stopped and rested against the trunk of a green ash with its broad crown and wiped his face with the bottom of his T- shirt. He could see the clearing ahead and beyond it, a distant view of the Ale House.

His meeting with Markham still flooded his mind. Mario had done the expected, but Markham was a disappointment. While he was not leaving the Shamrock, the once highly charged ex-Marine had turned into a pussy cat. Arnie found surrender unforgivable, intolerable. He was enraged that Markham chose to sit and wait when action was called for...with or without Caruso. The vote was two and a half weeks away. Something needed to be done to shift momentum and he alone had the motivation and the energy. Arnie put on his cap and headed for the clearing. He'd come up with something.

೧೨

Same day

Lena, the housekeeper, tapped on Knox's bedroom door which was slightly ajar.

"Come in, Lena." Knox lay on the bed, her head propped on two pillows.

"I thought you might like a glass of sweet tea." She placed the glass on the bedside table.

"Thank you. I can use a pick-me-up. Been on my feet all day at the hospital's gift shop. This bed feels awfully good."

"Got a pot roast cooking with all the trimmings. You gonna feel better after a good meal."

"Ben's working late, so it's just the two of us."

"I'll fix him a plate. It'll keep," she said turning to leave.

"Oh Lena," Knox called out, "I'm going for a ride. Missy needs the exercise. Keep our dinner warm until I get back."

"Sho will," she said.

Knox got up and changed her clothes. She put on her jeans, paddock boots and a frayed straw hat which she had found in Jake's closet.

The sun had fallen below the tree line by the time Knox arrived at the barn. Sam, a young black in charge of the stable, had Missy saddled and outside her stall. Knox took the reins in one hand and held a folded-up quilt in the other. With a lift from the boy, she mounted the filly. "Thanks Sam, I won't be long."

She took her usual path through the east field, a short ride to the river. Knox tethered Missy to a sapling near the water's edge, removed her riding boots, and waded through the shallows to the sun baked sandbar. She spread the quilt on the dry sand. A crescent moon had appeared even though there were still patches of blue sky overhead. Knox searched for Arcturus but she could only find the faint glow of the North Star. But she knew the heavens would be filled with star-fire once darkness settled over the river. Knox lay back, her arms for a pillow. Her thoughts turned to Ben and their weekend at the beach.

જી

They left Conway early Friday morning. The Porsche sped along the two-lane; traffic was light and a cloud cover cut the glare. Ben fiddled with the radio until he found a popular music station and the mellow sounds of Nat "King" Cole. He reached for her hand and brought it to his lips. "I'll try to make this the best weekend of your life."

His words, warm and inviting, caused her face to glow.

"For the both of us," she added.

Ben nodded. "For the both of us."

The car sped past farms and forests and open fields. The a/c droned, keeping them comfortable despite heat rising from the pavement. Knox checked the road map and made a rough calculation. "We should reach the Gulf by mid-afternoon."

"Sounds about right." He reached for her hand again, gave it a gentle tug. "I have a suggestion."

Knox gave him a curious look.

"Let's unpack, open the curtains with a view of the Gulf, and enjoy a chilled bottle of Chardonnay." Ben kept his eyes on the road; cleared his throat. "Did you know there's something magical about love in the afternoon?"

Knox's mouth dropped open; no words came out.

"Then we'll dress, and have dinner in the restaurant downstairs. It's not the Plantation House, but it's convenient. Then, in the coolest part of the day, we can take a long walk along the beach." Ben slammed a fist against the steering wheel. "Well, how do you like my plan?"

Knox felt her heart flutter. She was stunned by Ben's proposal.

"Well, do you like it or not?" he winked.

"I like your plan." She stretched across the console and kissed him on the cheek. "I like your plan a lot."

At mid-day, Ben pulled into a Stuckey's. An attendant filled the gas tank and checked the tires. Knox and Ben weaved their way around tables cluttered with gifts, souvenirs and an array of pecan candies. At the food bar, each ordered a Coke and a pimento cheese sandwich. While they waited, Ben put his arm around her and whispered in her ear, "The best weekend ever."

As they traveled south, Knox noticed the road had flattened out. She sat up, her hands on the dash. "Slow down, Ben!"

"Something wrong?"

"The Burma Shave signs up ahead."

"I love 'em."

"Just drive. I'll read: **The place to pass/On curves/You know/ Is only at/A beauty show/Burma Shave**

They both laughed.

"I've heard there are thousands of Burma Shave signs across the country," Ben said.

"I remember one jingle from years ago," pointing a finger at the speedometer, the needle at eighty. **If Daisies/Are your/Favorite flower/Keep pushing up those/Miles-per-hour/Burma Shave**

℘

Knox sat beneath a beach umbrella, her skin smeared with sunscreen. The dark green waters of the Gulf were calm. A flock of seagulls sailed over the shoreline, squawking as they passed. She reached in her bag and retrieved her sun glasses. Out of the corner of her eye, she saw Ben plodding through the sand. He ducked beneath the umbrella and handed her a tall, chilled glass of orange juice.

"Thought you might like something cool and refreshing," he said.

"Thanks. You've been reading my mind again."

He plopped down beside her and stirred his drink with a swizzle. "Would you like to hear my plans for the day?"

"Sure."

"You have the morning to swim and soak up the ambiance. I've hired a boat, half-day, for surf fishing. Mildred, at the front desk, gave me the name of a fabulous restaurant in Gulfport and she's made our reservation. Dining and dancing until your heart's content. Finally, we'll kick off our shoes and stroll the beach beneath the stars. After that...who knows?"

Know put up her hand, a stop signal. "Don't tell me more. Surprise me."

"So you approve the plan?"

"Only if we can play volley ball," she said, pointing to a net in the distance.

"Hold my glass." He jogged down the beach where a game was in progress.

Knox watched him go and wondered...he showered her with attention, but could he carry it back to Conway? Unbridled for a weekend, but would it last? He came back, flashing a smile, arms swinging like an exited teenager. A wave of guilt washed over her... for even wondering.

എ

Knox leaned on an elbow and checked on Missy. Satisfied, she looked down river; a haze of light hung over the town of Conway. Amid the stillness the questions resurfaced. Ben had kept his promise; it was one of the best weekends ever. Still, questions kept swirling in her head. Maybe she was the problem…wanting too much, like a child at Christmas, hopefully checking the tree even though all her presents had been opened and the stocking emptied.

Maybe there were limits beyond which Ben could not give. Not unlike an elastic band, which would only stretch so far…and no further, despite the effort and intentions. If that were true, she reasoned, hope dims and she was back to square one. Accept her lot or leave Conway behind.

She remembered Brett and their night in the forest glade. She felt her hands and lips tingle and sat up, resting her chin on bent knees. While Brett had honored her request to keep their relationship *respectful* until she made a final decision, his *presence* followed her, unshakable, every waking moment. And there were other vexing questions. Were they compatible in ways other than the physical attraction? After all, their meetings had been clandestine and their lines of communication untested. Could she adapt to the peripatetic life of the rodeo circuit? What if something should happen to Brett and she again found herself alone? While she was not prescient, Knox knew it was a tradeoff, either way, and there were risks involved if she chose to leave the security (and solitude) of Hamilton House. She looked at the Milky Way and found Arcturus, shining brighter than ever before.

Knox checked Missy, still contentedly nibbling the grass around the sapling. The simplicity of life, she thought. I'm envious, Missy.

"I'd better get back before Lena sends out a search party," she chuckled.

Knox gathered her boots and untied the filly, tossed the quilt over the pommel and hoisted herself into the saddle. While she rode away, her problem still unresolved, she carried back pleasant memories of this idyllic place...starlight and birdsong and the sweet bouquet of honeysuckle wafted on an evening breeze.

Chapter 32

Adam arrived a few minutes early at Renee's Tea Room. Katie Ware, the proprietress, seated him beside a window overlooking a garden of summer flowers and a view of Duval Drive, the stature of Joshua White and the entrance to Audubon Park. Adam had heard her father died, it must have been ten years ago now. He left Katie, then a school teacher, enough money to invest in this beautiful old house and convert the first floor into the Tea Room. She gave up her job to open Renee's and it was now one of Conway's most popular restaurants.

Adam stared at the statue of Joshua White shaded by an enormous white oak. He was certain Joshua would give the coalition his unequivocal stamp of approval. While he would consider the downside i.e., many agitated mill workers, unlike Arthur, he would join the crusade and become one of its most ardent activist. Adam thought of Hal and Maude and Hannah, wondering as she often did, where *their* mettle came from…was their courage and conviction a God-given gift, encoded in their genes…or the salutary influence of parents at an impressionable age…or was it simply acquired? While he was not sure, he hoped

Robin would become a young woman of conscience, true to the principles in which she believed.

Adam stirred his tea, looking back at the colorful garden of pink phlox and marigolds and snapdragons. A tap on the shoulder interrupted his reverie.

"Oh, hello Al," he said, extending his hand.

"Sorry I'm late. The Judge wanted to finish the case before adjournment. I think he wanted to go fishing this afternoon," he chuckled.

A young waitress placed two menus on the table and filled their glasses with water. "I'll give you time to decide," she said politely and crossed the room to her station.

"It's been six weeks since our last meeting," Adam said. "Maude joined us for Sunday dinner and asked about you. It was a reminder to call and see if we could meet again." Adam unfolded his napkin and laid it in his lap. "I know you prefer a low profile but you have been essential to our cause. Your office provided the legal remedy to shut down the taverns and you made the crucial contact in Washington. The coalition is grateful."

"Glad to help," Al said. "But I suspect Maude Harrington would have found a way to get it done. Any lawyer worth his salt could dig up the rulings on 'eminent domain.'"

"But the financing, in my opinion, would have been insoluble."

Al shrugged. "Sometimes it's good to know someone in Washington. But luck gets most of the credit. Had the matter dealt with Appropriations or Armed Services or some other committee, I would have been of no help at all."

"Any word from Chuck Wilson?"

"Don't expect to hear until after the referendum. But bring me up to date on Hal Brady."

"Well, the wires are out but Dr. Toole told him to take it easy; no sermons until after Labor Day. Meanwhile, A.M. Freeman, a retired minister from a church in East Texas who has a daughter living here, agreed to fill the pulpit until Hal gets the green light."

Al tucked his silk tie inside his shirt. "I've talked to law enforcement about the assault, including the State Troopers who got involved when Preacher was gunned down. There is a consensus..."

"Caruso?"

Al nodded. "But not a shred of evidence at either crime scene."

"I spent a lot of years in New Orleans; trained at Charity. I've heard the name and know he's got a Mafia connection."

"The head honcho...cunning, ruthless and unconscionable."

"Give me some background."

Al took a sip of water. "Okay, here's the short version: Tony Caruso was born in Algiers, a seedy suburb, across the river from the Big Easy. He dropped out of school as a teenager and spent a lot of time at the fruit markets on Decatur Street, a favorite hang out for hoodlums and street punks. It was there his life of crime began and it was there he made the early connections with some of the Mafia's fringe elements. Caruso's driving ambition moved him up the chain of command. His savvy business deals even caught the attention of 'big shot' Mafia bosses 'up East'. Three years ago, after the deportation of Sam Carolla, he was awarded the job that he had relentlessly pursued, the head of the Louisiana Mafia. He bought Willswood, a tavern on Highway 90, about fifteen miles west of New Orleans and made it his headquarters. He also bought six thousand acres of swampland which fanned out from the back of the commercial property."

"To dump the bodies?"

"Precisely. Anyone who crossed Caruso or got in his way took a one-way boat ride into that snake-infested swamp."

Adam felt a chill run up and down his spine.

"Caruso probably dislikes Markham more than Maude Harrington, but he'd make a deal with anyone who served his interests." Al hesitated, distracted by the irony. "He sees the taverns as routers for drugs, gambling and prostitution throughout the northern tier of the State. But what he really wants is a foothold in central Arkansas, with horse-racing in Hot Springs and the bright lights of Little Rock for his illegal activities."

Adam looked pensively at the summer garden. "Don't suppose he'd back off?"

"Not likely."

"Caruso knows the voters of Conway were not intimidated by Preacher's death or the assault on Hal Brady. He knows that whatever he does, no matter how violent, the town will still support the referendum. So, why won't he back off?"

Al shook his head. "The man is both villainous and vindictive. Even if he loses, Caruso will leave his calling card and it won't be a pretty sight."

"There's been an uneasy silence in Conway for weeks now." Adam, with a troubled look, pushed his plate away. "I keep waiting for something bad to happen."

"It will. And we don't know when or where or to whom. That's why you need to be circumspect."

A heavy silence fell over the table. Adam knew there was no way to modify the risk, but he worried about Allison and Robin, more than for himself. "How does Caruso get away with his illegal operations, putting down anyone who gets in his way? It's not as if he's cloaked in mystery, yet no one can lay a hand on him."

Al rubbed his eyes as if he himself found it hard to fathom. "For starters, he's street smart and any decision is planned in compulsive detail. Take Preacher and Hal as examples. Law enforcement knows, without a doubt, that the Mafia is culpable. But nothing to implicate Tony Caruso. And there's never an informant, never is. Caruso is a master intimidator and the proof is in the swamp behind Willswood." Al shook his head. "And he's got sheriffs, judges and a fistful of politicians on his payroll."

Adam rolled his eyes in disbelief.

"Money talks. I'm told the Organization generates close to two billion a year. It may be the biggest business in the State."

"And Caruso wants more?"

Al summoned a weak smile. "The coalition can handle Markham, Waters and Gambelli, at best, petty criminals. Beheading Maude's cat...I'm sure Caruso found that amusing. But the Mafia Boss takes the game to another level." Al pointed to the high ceiling.

Adam picked up the check and pushed his chair from the table. "You've told me more that I wanted to hear. But I guess it's better to know your opponent."

"And the dangers they pose."

Adam shrugged. "We knew there were risks, there usually are, when you disturb the status quo...in this case, shut down the taverns."

"I wish you well."

"Thanks...from Maude, too." Adam held up the check. "Lunch is on me."

೧

Adam drove to the office, his spirits dampened by Al's profile of Tony Caruso. He remembered his encounter with Frank Markham at Slim's Seafood Grill. Al was right, the coalition could handle the tavern owners but any alliance with the Mob changed the rules of engagement. He thought about Joshua White. What advice would the old man give if he were alive? He would probably tell him to stay the course, even though there may be mortal wounds when one fights for a noble cause. Adam knew history was replete with martyrs who had the courage to stand up, often alone, against the forces of evil; their sacrifice, a bright and shining light amid the darkness. But Adam found little comfort from his mind games as he turned into the parking lot.

Chapter 33

Wednesday, August 16th

Adam left his office, late as usual; dusk scattered the countryside with its incongruence of pale lights and groping shadows. He threw his coat and briefcase in the back seat, started the engine and sped away. The fairground was seven miles southwest of Conway, off parish road 191, two lanes of macadam which wound through a lush forest of oak and elm and short-leaf pine.

Crossing the bridge into West Conway, Adam could see swirls of gray smoke arising from the mill's furnaces, drifting skyward. He thought of Arthur White, who with grave trepidation lent his "name" to the coalition. It had been a welcomed surprise, since Maude and other members had counted him out. It was as if Arthur had heard the voice of his father and followed his advice.

Well past the taverns, Adam turned right onto a logging road. As he gathered speed, the car spit gravel and scattered dust, a thick contrail that obscured his retreating tracks. As Adam rounded a sweeping curve, a large bird, its coat dull in the jaded twilight, fluttered away on ebony wings, leaving behind the carrion to reek in the warm summer air. The shortcut ran diagonally through the woods to dead end at 191, just south of the fairground. Near the intersection, through the trees, Adam could see the distant lights of the revival tent.

He parked the car on a grassy berm and tramped toward the distant sounds of gospel music. This was the night Henry Slade would speak on behalf of the coalition and the impending referendum. Adam wanted to hear what the itinerant evangelist had to say.

The sawdust perimeter around the front of the tent was wet from an afternoon shower. As Adam reach the entrance with soggy shoes, he felt an odd sense of déjà vu. Since he had never attended an old-fashioned revival meeting, he reasoned there was confused recall of his last childhood visit to the Shriner's circus or of some long forgotten carnival.

He stepped inside and looked around the crowded tent. The revival meeting had attracted an eclectic crowd; farmers in freshly laundered overalls; mill workers in denim or khaki pants, white shirts open at the throat with rolled up sleeves; townsmen in their traditional Sunday best; the women in simple cotton prints, most of them waving hand fans to stir the oppressive heat inside the tent.

A wiry man with thick glasses and a beatific smile, standing at the entrance, greeted him warmly. Adam found an empty seat in the last row of folding chairs. He loosened his tie and wondered why he had not left his coat in the car. With a tilt of his head, he followed the main aisle, a trail of more sawdust, to a portable platform, draped in colorful bunting and lined by potted pink hydrangea. Behind the dais, a large white banner emblazoned with scarlet letters…JESUS SAVES…hung suspended from the canvas ceiling.

Lamar Jones, the venerable choir director of the Oak Street Baptist Church, stood center stage, waved his arms in extravagant flourishes, exhorting the audience to "let themselves go" as he led them through a spirited rendition of "Little Brown Church in the Wildwood." Lamar, bald and dour, was a mortician at Nabor's Funeral Home, but tonight in gray seersucker, he had come alive, his face shining with unlikely exuberance.

A faint scent of insecticide sprayed earlier in the day, lingered in the heavy August air, through most of it had been washed away by the rain. A mosquito flitted fitfully around Adam's face, then settled on the leathery sun-weathered neck of an old farmer in front of him who slapped at it forcefully and startled a child nearby, half-asleep in his mother's lap.

There was an atmosphere of carnival, almost irreverent, Adam thought. People stirred restlessly in their seats; a baby cried across the way. The babbling of "foreign tongues" arose occasionally, like the obscure litany of alien priests, from among a group of Pentecostals sitting near the platform. Then the hand clapping began; scattered at first, then gaining force at Lamar's urging; the pace quickened. The clamorous music, like some sensual catalyst aroused the audience with its throbbing intensity.

Suddenly Lamar raised his arms above his head and a hush fell quickly within the tent. "Let's all bow our heads in silent prayer," he intoned. "Pray for the preacher, for the miracle of healing, and if you don't have it, for personal salvation. God knows there's not a man or woman here that don't need forgiveness. Every head bowed. Every eye closed. Every heart open as you send your petition to our Heavenly Father."

The lights dimmed as the organ played softly. An abrupt and thunderous "amen" shattered the solemn silence. At the front of the stage, in an explosion of lights, stood the towering figure of Henry Slade, dressed in a white linen suit, smiling warmly, his pearly teeth gleaming, arms outstretched. "God bless you. Bless all of you. Thank you for coming on such a hot, humid night. God has great things in store for us. Miracles are waiting to happen if you only believe." Without hesitation he began to sing in a booming bass voice, *"Amazing grace, how sweet the sound that saved a wretch like me…"* The twin pianos, one on each side of the platform, joined in and picked up the rhythm. Slade gave a sweeping gesture with his arms for the audience to sing along, and soon to Adam's astonishment the tent resounded with the familiar verses of this old John Newton hymn.

Adam thought that Slade's appearance was flamboyant and effective. All eyes, including his own, were riveted on this hulk of a man and his commanding presence. It was as though he had been dropped through the canopy by some Providential Hand, rather than slipping through a flap in the back of the tent onto a darkened stage. Adam, a spectator rather than a celebrant, had observed it all with mild amusement, and grudgingly, with admiration. Slade had a flare for theatrics, he conceded; well orchestrated; perfect timing.

෨

Henry Slade, coatless, a black Bible tucked under his left arm, walked back to the center of the platform. "Friends, in a few minutes the ushers will pass among you for our nightly love offering; your visible expression of support for this ongoing ministry of healing and evangelism; for the tireless efforts of the Slade crusade throughout the South to win new converts to Jesus Christ and His Church. First, I have a special appeal for all of you…" Henry pulled a large white handkerchief from his back pocket and dabbed the sweat that trickled down his cheeks. "…it is this," he continued. "Your referendum is only six days away. If you are a resident of Conway, vote *yes* next Tuesday. Close the taverns! Why, you ask? They tarnish your town. They poison the air you breathe. They breed mischief and malice…an alliance with the Devil." Slade moved to the other side of the stage. "Cast them out," he shouted. Slade lowered his voice and continued. "I've been told that a park with playgrounds, playing fields, picnic areas, and the like will replace the taverns. What a trade-off. What a grand opportunity to put your faith to work."

Slade brushed the back of his neck with the limp handkerchief. The sweat appeared under his arms, across his back and glistened on his broad forehead like crystal beads. He took the Bible in his right hand and held it, extended. "The instructions are here," he reminded them firmly, waving the book from side to side. "Talk to your neighbor, tell your friends. Remind family members to vote. Mark Tuesday on your calendar." Slade's voice, a crescendo. "Stand up! Be counted! Vote and let your voice be heard." The preacher leaned forward and cupped his hand behind his ear. With the other hand he implored the audience to join in. The first response was timid but with Slade's encouragement the crowd grew louder. "Vote and let your voice be heard." Over and over again, the volume swelling, until it was heard well beyond the boundaries of the revival tent.

Adam was satisfied that Henry Slade had kept his promise: an effective entreaty, a persuasive ally, an unequivocal endorsement of the referendum. He could not have asked for more.

After the ushers passed the collection baskets, the healing service began. A dozen people queued up in the aisle to the left of the platform. Adam, curious, moved up in his seat as Henry Slade, standing erect, offered an invitation to anyone who sought "the healing power of God at work in his life."

He invited one respondent at a time onto the stage. "Brother, tell these folks who you are."

A gaunt, unkempt man, slightly built, stood at the top of the steps, his eyes fixed on the floor. "Willie Fowler," he mumbled, his hands stuffed into the pockets of his overalls.

Adam recognized Willie as the farmhand who had worked some years ago for Jake Hamilton. He had seen Willie professionally on at least two occasions for recurrent pain in his right shoulder. X-rays of the shoulder had demonstrated a calcium deposit and confirmed the diagnosis of subacromial bursitis. After treatment, Willie had moved to a neighboring parish and it was the last time Adam had seen him...until now.

"Tell us your trouble, Willie. And if you believe, God will heal you."

Willie spoke softly, his answer inaudible to the audience. But Slade listened intently and announced that for the past year Willie had been disabled by a "locked shoulder." And he had come seeking relief from his infirmity.

"Show the people your good arm," he commanded with authority. Willie promptly flung his left arm above his head and swung it freely back and forth.

"Now the other."

Willie looked up and grimaced as he struggled; the limb twitched but remained at his side.

Slade tilted his head back and began to pray: "God, let your healing power fill your humble servant; make him whole again. Whatever obstacle stands in his way, remove it. If there is sin, blot it out. If there is guilt, erase it with Thy grace. Let your forgiveness flow through this man and wash him whiter than snow. You have promised us miracles if we only have faith, even to move mountains, but we must believe...believe...believe..."

It was a mantra that gained strength in its repetition and reached a pitch which ricocheted off the canvas walls and filled the tent with some strange excitement that made Adam stir restlessly in his seat.

Slade stopped the prayer abruptly, lifted Willie's chin and looked directly into his dull eyes. "Do you believe?" he asked fervently.

Willie bobbed his head, then dropped it penitently against his chest.

"They didn't hear you, friend," Slade pleaded, pointing to the crowd with a sweep of his Bible.

"I believe." Willie's words were muted, hesitant.

"Speak up...louder! The Lord may not be listening. Get His attention. Shout in His ear," the preacher bellowed.

"I believe." This time Willie's voice was stronger.

"Louder, Willie, louder. Don't hold back. Let it all out. Let go! Let God heal you. Do you trust Him?"

Willie looked up, the embarrassment was gone; his body quivered with emotion as his feet move fitfully in a dance of spiritual ecstasy. He shouted, "I believe. Praise Jesus, I believe."

"Hallelujah! Now raise your arm, Willie. Lift it up," Slade exhorted persuasively. He reached over and moved the right arm about thirty degrees from Willie's side. "Move it, Willie. Lift it up and point to Heaven."

The vacant face broke into a broad smile as he continued to hop around frenetically, slinging the arm in an ever larger arc until it reached a point above his head.

The crowd reacted with a collective gasp as Willie ran across the stage, waving his arm and shrieking at the top of his voice, "Praise Jesus. He done it. Praise Jesus."

Others followed. A middle-aged widow with intractable headaches cried out as Slade petitioned for the release of demons, then crumpled to the floor, "slain in the Spirit." The procession continued as family members rolled wheelchairs up the ramp onto the platform. A young woman with multiple sclerosis sat quietly, waiting her turn. The preacher spoke to her, placed a hand on her shoulder and prayed that God's restorative power would spread through every part of her being. She smiled, replenished, but remained motionless as a friend pushed her down the ramp. The steady stream of the infirmed and enfeebled (or those who thought themselves so) lasted for an hour; in each instance Slade touched them, invoked the miracle of healing, prayed for repentance, and pleaded for God Almighty to release them from their bondage of sin and sickness. Adam watched, fascinated, and remembered the fitting line from King Lear: *"Nothing almost sees a miracle but misery."*

After the healing service, Slade launched into the sermon; the audience listened with rapt attention. What were the ingredients of Henry Slade's charisma, Adam wondered, as he watched him parade across the stage, holding the crowd spellbound with his performance as though he had sprinkled the tent with some magic potion. Was it his imposing physical presence? An appeal that transcended gender? Was he a messianic figure to some? Or was it his ability to speak of mystery, then translate the rhetoric into plain language so that even plebian minds could grasp its meaning. He used simple words, short sentences. There were dramatic inflections in his voice for effect; a mobile face and animated extremities, extolling the virtues of love and charity, exhorting them to repentance and Christian commitment. Adam admitted the performance was electric and when it was over every ampere of energy had been drained from his listeners.

During the invitation and closing hymn, Adam slipped outside and followed the sawdust trail around the tent to a small trailer parked in the rear. He leaned against the door, his coat in the angle of his arm, and watched the fireflies zigzag through the darkness, their taillights blinking. In the distance a police siren rent the silence, in striking counterpoint to the soft strains of the postlude which filtered through the canvas tent.

Adam was about to leave when he saw a shadowy figure approach the trailer. "I'm sorry to keep you waiting," Slade said as he extended his hand. "Let's go inside and have something cool to drink."

"I was fascinated, from start to finish," Adam said. He sat on the edge of the sofa bed, the coat in his lap. "You got my attention and held it for more than an hour. I'm not sure that's ever happened before, even during my most riveting lectures in med school."

The Preacher smiled graciously and handed him a tall glass of ice tea. "I'm glad you were able to join us."

"You may have missed your calling," Adam said, tongue in cheek.

"How so?"

"The theater...Broadway...Hollywood. I can see you as 'Big Daddy'; *Cat on a Hot Tin Roof,* one of my favorite movies...Better than ole Burl Ives."

Henry Slade waved his hand dismissively. "Thanks for the compliment but I've answered a higher calling."

Adam shed his tie and wiped his brow with his hand. "How do you handle the heat?"

Slade turned on a small electric fan; his broad shoulders sagged; fatigue appeared to deepen the lines of his face and the long blond hair, matted by sweat, fell limp around his collar. "I lose five or six pounds, water weight, of course, on these hot humid nights. But there's no way to cool the tent. The big fans only stir the warm air. But the folks keep coming despite the weather." Slade gulped his tea. "Maybe the heat provokes a more passionate response."

Adam shrugged. "I'm here to thank you for your endorsement of the coalition. And encouraging your audience to vote 'yes' on Tuesday. Your support will be an enormous help during these final days."

"I wish you success," Slade said as he unfolded a chair and sat down with a sigh of exhaustion.

Adam stirred the slice of lemon with his finger, ice rattled against the glass. "As you've heard the opposition is well funded and has formed a loose alliance with the Mob. We've seen their dirty tricks and expect more trouble before the Tuesday referendum."

The preacher smiled knowingly. "Any noble cause extracts a price from those who are committed and often includes, unfortunately, some casualties. Nevertheless, history is replete with worthy accomplishments because courageous men like you and Reverend Brady are willing to take the risks." He reached for his handkerchief and dabbed the back of his neck. "By the way, I'll send you a check before I leave West Conway. I'm sure you've incurred expenses; a contest of this magnitude always does, and I hope our contribution will help."

"Thanks kindly."

Slade nodded. "The revival ends Saturday night, then we'll pack up and head for our next meeting in East Texas. In the meantime, I'll keep you foremost in my prayers."

Adams stood up and placed his glass beside the whirring fan. "You're tired and I need to get home. It's been a long day for both of us." He shook Slade's hand, threw his coat over his shoulder and slipped out the screen door into a starless night.

A breeze stirred the warm air as Adam walked back to his car. Threatening clouds had rolled in belching thunder. Out of the corner of his eye, he caught the glare of headlights. Someone had pulled off the road and entered the deserted fairground. He quickened his pace. The rain would come soon.

℘

A steady drizzle had begun to fall as Adam pulled into his driveway. He stopped in the kitchen and took off his wet shoes, turned off the light and trudged up the stairs. He stopped by Robin's room; she was sleeping peacefully. His own bedroom was dark but he could hear Allison murmuring in her sleep, perhaps a dream. He tiptoed into the bathroom, undressed by a nightlight, then slipped quietly into bed.

"How was the meeting?" Allison turned over and nestled against him, her voice heavy with sleep.

"I'll tell you about it in the morning," he whispered. For a while he listened to her breathing and savored the warmth of her body against him. His mind, dog-tired from the grueling day, thought of his good fortune and the mysterious forces that had drawn them together. Finally, subdued by fatigue, Adam dropped off the edge of awareness into a shallow plane of sleep.

The dream was surreal, unpleasant. Some vague, menacing giant with large lupine eyes which burned like spotlights, pursued him through a cotton field with no place to hide. Losing ground, he stumbled and fell only to awaken, his heart racing, his face drenched with sweat. He turned and looked at the clock; he had been asleep for less than an hour.

He noticed a faint glow seeping through the Venetian blinds. Adam, curious, got out of bed and went to the window. "Allison, wake up! There's a fire across the river."

Allison struggled to her feet, grabbed her robe and followed him through the house onto the front lawn.

Beyond the bridge, the horizon was ablaze; luminous flames leaped up wildly to lick the night sky. A capricious wind, which earlier had pushed the rain-laden clouds away, had changed direction and carried on it wing the frightening roar of the conflagration. The crackling fire colored the darkness an eerie orange and scattered fiery cinders like the scintillating sparks of a *feu de joie*. Shortly, they heard the sound of a fire engine, its siren blaring, splitting the stillness that had covered the slumbering town.

"It must be the revival tent," Allison exclaimed, pointing in the direction of the fairground.

"How could it happen after all this rain?"

Allison shuddered as she watched the blaze grow in intensity. "Maybe just faulty wiring or the tent was struck by lightening."

Adam put an arm around her shoulder and held her close. "Something had to be put on a canvas tent to burn like that." He remembered the glare of headlights, leaving the trailer. Henry Slade had endorsed the park project vigorously and this was an act of retribution, but it didn't have the footprint of Tony Caruso. No, this, Adam was sure, bore the marks of Markham and Waters. "When will they learn that acts like this only strengthen our hand?" he asked rhetorically, beneath his breath.

Allison looked up, her faced filled with concern, the reflection of firelight in her eyes. She shivered again and whispered, "I'm afraid, Adam."

He stroked her cheek reassuringly. "I'd better drive out and check on Henry." As they walked back to the house, the distant rumble of thunder resounded like the groan of a despairing god across the burning night sky.

Chapter 34

Saturday, August 26ᵗʰ

The guests gathered at Hamilton House; a victory celebration. Maude and her supporters had received a majority of the votes during Tuesday's referendum. Ben had offered to host the party since the manor house was one of the few places that could accommodate the guest list. Even so, the spacious living room overflowed with coalition members and their friends, spilling into the parlor and outside, onto the gallery that wrapped around Ben's stately home.

It had been a long and treacherous journey but success was sweet and the accomplishment, while nightmarish at times, brought a euphoric sense of achievement. Congratulatory handshakes passed among the swarm of happy faces. But many remembered Preacher and Hal Brady and the burning revival tent; the win had extracted an inordinate price and tempered an otherwise splendid evening.

Knox heard the chimes over the drone of many voices. She sidled through the congested room to the entrance hall and opened the front door. Adam stood on the porch, his coat looped over his shoulder. "I'm late, as usual."

Knox took his hand and pulled him into the foyer. "We're just glad you could make it." She helped him slip on his coat. "Allison is here…somewhere. I saw her talking to Hannah," she said, pointing toward the parlor.

Adam stopped in front of the hallway mirror to straighten his tie. He brushed a hand through his hair, then reached for Knox's arm. "Before we go in…" He moved her back from the double doors leading to the living room. "…I'd like a progress report."

Knox shrugged.

"The marriage…" Adam checked the entryway to ensure their privacy. "It's been several months since we talked about…well, you know. In the meantime, I kept my promise and talked with Ben. So I'm hoping the two of you have made some headway. Tell me I'm right." Adam grimaced as if he were afraid of what she would say.

Knox did not speak nor was it necessary; he saw the answer in her eyes as the tears spilled down her cheeks. Adam searched her face but he could not find a hint of joy or hope or resolve. Had the affair with Brett Shelly damaged the marriage beyond repair? Could she not expiate her guilt? Or had she finally accepted Ben's inability to change the dynamics of the relationship? Adam wasn't sure, but when he looked at her, it was as if she were swimming hard against the current, struggling to stay afloat.

She moved close and rested her head on Adam's shoulder. "He's tried, he really has. And at times, it's better. The weekend at the beach…" She stepped back and stared at the vaulted ceiling. "I guess he forgets, and slips back into his old ways."

"Sorry," Adam said weakly.

Knox wiped her eyes with Adam's handkerchief. "I'll go rescue Allison."

⁂

Adam spotted Maude and Al Marx standing by the marble fireplace. He moved through the flock of friends and supporters until he reached the hearth. No one could miss the triumphant smile on Maude's face; even Al had dropped his guard and accepted the party invitation. Adam gave Maude a hug and greeted his friend with a handshake.

"Good turnout," Adam said, surveying the jam-packed room.

Maude retrieved her wine glass from the mantel. "Well, it was Conway's cause célèbre."

"And you were the winner," Al added, raising his glass with a flourish.

Adam remembered the party in March, standing near this very spot, and Maude lamenting the tragic accident in front of the Shamrock. Then she had broached the subject of an organized effort to close down the taverns. At first, he wasn't sure if the idea arose from conviction or whether it was frivolous party conversation. On reflection, he had decided Maude was deadly serious or why would she have invited him to stop by for coffee and explore the subject in more detail. Al Marx had handed them the legal remedy, but the five month journey had been arduous; their opponents far more redoubtable than expected. But Adam knew that beating the odds only made the victory sweeter.

"I have some news of interest," Al said.

"Hope it's all good." Maude glanced at Adam uneasily.

"The results of the referendum have reached Washington, probably by way of our Congressman. Chuck Wilson called with assurances that Senator Short is still in favor of the park project. Chuck will send the paperwork and a written reminder that two independent appraisals are needed for both the taverns and the Warren property."

"Is Chuck certain the Senator has the votes?" Adam asked.

"Apparently Short has polled his committee. The straw vote was unanimous. According to Chuck, once the forms have been completed and returned to the Senator's office, along with the certified appraisals, it's a done deal."

"I've already made arrangements for the appraisals," Maude said. "We should have the numbers in two to three weeks."

"Who will handle the paperwork?" Al asked.

Adam shrugged.

"I've talked to Hannah," Maude said. "Members of the League will be glad to oblige."

Adam's jaw dropped and the look of disbelief lingered. He turned to Al Marx. "She's amazing, always three steps ahead of us."

Maude took a sip of wine and cleared her throat. "Anticipation is the catalyst for accomplishment."

"Who said that?" Adam asked, "Ben Franklin or King Solomon?"

Maude laughed. "Moi," she said, stabbing her chest.

Adam had known Maude since the day he arrived in Conway. Preacher had parked in the driveway and she had hand-delivered a homemade pound cake and a copy of *The Review*. It was her way of saying "welcome." After becoming his patient, they became friends, often exploring topics of mutual interest. Adam assumed it was the reason he had been chosen to join Maude in a laudable but dangerous undertaking. He dug dip into memory, but he could not recall another woman with Maude's boundless energy and indomitable spirit. Anyone in Conway, who read *The Review's* editorials, knew she was as tough as shoe leather. For Maude, the referendum was more than vindication, it was about *principle,* one worth fighting for. It was simply the right thing to do.

Adam was sure Maude had shed tears privately for the loss of Preacher and the brutal attack on Hal Brady. They were shocked by the casualties, the cost of their commitment. But as the days passed, they profiled their enemy, including the blackguard, Tony Caruso, and were no longer surprised by the attempts to terrorize the voters of Conway.

He looked at his friend, her face a myriad of wrinkles, and felt only admiration for her full and noble life. He remembered the last words of George Washington and thought it was something she might say: "I die hard but I'm not afraid to go."

Maude, standing next to Al Marx, tugged his coat sleeve. "Any news on the tent fire?"

"Not a word."

"It's been ten days. Surely, there must be something..."

"Don't count on it," Al said "Our Sheriff, Randy Gilstrap, who should be cleaning out septic tanks, is leading the investigation."

"Caruso?" Adam asked, although he didn't think so and had said as much to Allison the night of the fire.

Al shook his head. "Not a chance. The Mafia would never burn down an *empty* tent."

"So we'll never know," Maude said.

"Speculation but no hard evidence."

"I just hate to see a crime go unsolved and unpunished," Maude said indignantly.

Adam spoke up. "At least Slade was not deterred. I understand he's holding his revival in Longview inside one of the large protestant churches. A new tent will be ready by the time he moves on to Tyler. I was skeptical when we first met but changed my mind after talking to him and attending one of his services. I'm convinced Henry Slade is the real deal...sincere and captivating and a master of improvisation."

Al scanned the room and offered a thin smile. "Here comes Mr. Money Bags."

Maude turned and saw Fred Warren weaving through the crowd, holding on to his Cuban cigar as if it were his lifeline. "I wonder if he ever lights the damn thing or it's just part of his Priapus Complex."

Adam grinned. "If you ask, frame the question...how should I say it... a bit more delicately? Meanwhile, I'll go find Allison."

❦

Fred Warren approached the fireplace with trepidation. He stopped long enough to fuss with his tie and button his coat. A native of Conway, he lived with his invalid mother in the ranch on Royston Road. While a man of considerable wealth, he had never moved from his boyhood home. The family had kept the house in good repair and the small yard was a veritable garden of flowers. He was a savvy business man and had made a fortune in land speculation and residential construction. Subdivisions bore his signature. During the war years, age exempt from the military, Warren headed up the local office of Civil Defense which allowed time to handle his real estate ventures and broker scalp metal to the U.S. Government.

Conway considered Fred Warren its most eligible bachelor. When asked the reason for his single-status, he replied dryly, "Work is my surrogate marriage." While he avoided most social engagements, unless there was some self-serving interest, most of Conway admired his business acumen and the devoted care of his mother.

"Congratulations, Mrs. Harrington."

Maude raised her glass of wine and smiled appreciatively.

Warren removed a small sheet of note paper from his coat pocket while looking at Al Marx. "My sources have learned that Congress will fund the buy-out...both the taverns and my three-hundred acres."

"Technically a grant from the Park Service," Al said. "It helps to have friends in high places."

Warren fidgeted with his cigar and checked his notes. "I suppose there'll be an appraisal?"

"Two...certified...both from out of town." Maude placed her empty glass on the mantel. "Don't worry, Fred, you'll get fair market value for your property."

"How long before closing?"

"Ninety to one hundred and twenty days," Al said. "The U.S. Senate moves at a snail's pace. Meanwhile, the taverns remain open, business as usual. It will give Markham and Waters and Gambelli time to make other plans. And wherever they land, we hope it's a long way from Conway."

Maude reached out and tapped Warren's arm. "By the way, while federal funds will pay for the land and buildings, there will be additional expenses to equip the park and playgrounds. A fund raiser has been scheduled next month and we hope you'll make it a charity of choice. *The Review* will chronicle those benefactors who endow the park and enrich our town." Maude closed her eyes and affected a smile. "Warren Park...that has a nice ring to it."

Al laughed. "I'm sure Mr. Warren will give it some thought after he talks with his accountant."

Warren nodded...non committal. He looked around the room as though checking the nearest exit. "Nice seeing the both of you." With that he jammed the cigar in his mouth and melted into the crowded room.

∾

"Whata you think?" Al asked.

"He'll make a modest contribution," Maude replied.

"I'm curious as to what he does with his money. He's a millionaire, several times over, yet lives modestly. Frugal to a fault. I think those Cuban cigars are his only luxury," Al chortled.

"If you don't give it away and aren't an extravagant spender and have no heirs, then it must be a security thing…like Linus' blanket." Maude picked up her wine glass and handed it to Al. "Be a gentleman. I need a refill."

While Maude waited, she looked around the room at the plethora of proud and sunny faces. Everyone at the party had played a role (if only a vote) in the success of the coalition. On reflection, she had wondered if her proposal would survive the initial phase of recruitment. When Adam signed on, it gave her hope. Shutting down the taverns was a worthy goal…of that she was certain. But there were barriers to overcome, some of them seemed insurmountable. "Good grief," Maude thought. "Who would have dreamed that Tony Caruso and his nefarious organization would ally themselves with Markham and his compatriots?"

Maude had wondered something else: why she had started this fight in the first place? Maybe she had been in the newspaper business too long, always looking for a good story; sometimes even stirring up trouble for the sake of an eye-opening editorial. But Maude knew the real reason: it was inbred. While her mother viewed a colorful world as if through a prism, her father, whom she adored, saw everything as black or white…no shades of gray. Maude admitted she had inherited his moral compass, and from his gene pool, the gift of an iron will. It explained her lifetime of "good works"… a champion of embattled causes. And most recently, her quixotic quest to expunge the blight across the river.

Chapter 35

Sunday, August 27th

The phone awakened Allison from a deep sleep. Half-awake, she squinted at the clock on the bedside table: 5:15. Earlier, Adam had received a call, and she vaguely remembered his leaving. She pulled the phone close to her and picked up the receiver.

"Hello."

"Is this Allison Swift?"

"Yes."

"This is St.Luke's hospital in Russellville, Arkansas. Your mother is quite ill and her physician felt you should be notified." It was a woman's voice, confident and professional.

Allison sat up, alarmed and fully awake. "What happened?"

"She developed abdominal pain early yesterday which worsened progressively. Dr. Engle had a neighbor bring her to the Emergency Room where she was evaluated and admitted to the medical floor."

"Does Dr. Engle have any idea what's wrong with my mother?" Allison, usually calm in a crisis, felt her eyes brim.

"The admission diagnosis is acute diverticulitis with rupture."

While Allison had no medical training, she knew enough from living with Adam to understand the potential risks. Leaking bowel content into the peritoneal cavity was a grave complication. "How is my mother doing?" she asked.

"Alert, and with medication, more comfortable. Running some fever; otherwise her vital signs are good. Last night she was started on large doses of antibiotics."

"Please tell her I'm on my way. Should be there by early afternoon."

"I'll give her the message."

Allison heard the line go dead. She replaced the receiver in its cradle and sprang out of bed. After brushing her teeth and washing her face with cold water, she sat at her writing desk, the wheels spinning in her head, and made a list of things to do before leaving Conway. She would call Ruth, Adam's mother, who lived nearby and ask her to keep Robin. Nothing made Ruth happier than to spend time with her granddaughter. Rather than try and track him down, Allison would leave Adam a note, explaining her hurried departure and a promise to call from Russellville with more information about her mother. She would underline the sentence: Robin and Charlie are with Ruth.

Allison dressed, packed an overnight bag and hurried down the steps to the kitchen. She reheated the pot of coffee which Adam had made earlier and put in the call to Ruth Swift.

"Of course, I'll keep Robin. Drop her off any time. And let us know about Emma."

"Thanks, Ruth. I should be there within the hour."

While Robin ate her bowl of cereal, Allison explained the reason she would spend a few days with Ruth. The child seemed to understand. "I hope grandma 'll be okay."

"Send her good thoughts and remember your father is here should you need him."

Allison made a fresh pot of coffee and filled a Thermos which she carried to the car along with the luggage. She left the message for Adam on the kitchen counter and a brief note for Mattie Mae who would be apoplectic if she walked into an empty house not knowing the circumstances.

⌘

It was still dark when Allison pulled into the driveway; Ruth, a shadowy figure on the front steps. Robin jumped out of the car and with Charlie at her heels, dashed to the stoop and gave Ruth a big hug. Allison followed with the small suitcase and Robin's favorite stuffed animal. She thanked Ruth again for keeping Robin and Charlie until she could assess her mother's medical status. She didn't think Adam would be of much help, working twelve to fourteen hour days, but Mattie was available if needed. She scribbled Mattie's phone number on a scrape of paper and handed it to Ruth.

Ruth took Robin's hand. "We'll be fine. Don't you worry."

After a teary goodbye, Allison drove off, stopping at Speck's Gulf station to fill up the gas tank.

"What brings you out before sunup?" Speck asked.

"Mother's at St.Luke's in Russellville. Better fill it up."

"Hope nothin' too serious."

Speck leaned on the roof of the car. "You got some mountain driving to do, so I'll see about those tires."

"Thanks Speck. That drive through the Ozarks still puts me on edge."

"You'll be fine. And the weather report looks good. A few clouds and plenty of sunshine." Speck patted the top of the car. "Pop the hood so I can check the oil."

Allison left the station and headed north for El Dorado on U.S. highway 63. The sky turned gray; gauzy ribbons of pink and lavender trimmed the eastern horizon. She hoped Speck's favorable forecast included Russellville; rain was the last thing she wanted. While a child of the mountains, the winding roads, past sandstone cliffs, plunging waterfalls and mysterious grottos, still made Allison jittery.

She flashed back to Fayetteville, where she'd grown up in the shadow of the University, her father a tenured Professor of Economics. Emma, her mother, also held an advanced degree and taught English at Highland High School. An only child, Allison had lots of friends and delighted in the familiarity of Fayetteville, snuggled in the Ozarks like a picturesque Swiss village.

The temperature soared as she crossed the state line and Allison turned up the a/c of her '48 Chevy Fleetmaster. She thought of her mother and how despite a hectic schedule, Emma always found time for Allison, helped with her homework and read to her at bedtime, a nightly ritual which made her feel loved. Allison remembered her warm, secure childhood in the small stone house on College Row.

Allison was only nineteen when her father died unexpectedly in the summer of '42. (Earlier, he had failed the Army's enlistment exam without disclosure) The loss was devastating, the tears flowed. She and her mother grieved, leaning on each other during a time of emotional crisis. The heart-wrenching loss had drawn them closer together and opened untapped lines of communication. With Allison at Sophie Newcome, they kept in touch with weekly letters and frequent phone calls.

Allison remembered the missive which came six months ago. Her mother planned to retire after twenty-five years of teaching and move to Russellville and live with her widowed sister who had developed crippling rheumatoid arthritis and needed a caretaker. And Emma would be one hundred miles closer to Conway and Robin.

Outside of Hot Springs, Allison stopped at a two-pump Texaco station. Inside, a woman with gray hair and a wizened face sat behind the counter shelling peas. She looked over her half-glasses and figured Allison was a stranger, just passing through.

"Get you somethin'?" she asked.

"Need a fill-up." Allison wanted a full tank before crossing the mountains.

The old woman stood and leaned over the counter. "Purvis, get in here," she yelled. "We got a customer."

Allison opened the ice chest and grabbed the neck of a Coke bottle. She flipped the cap and took a long swig. "What could be better on a hot day," she muttered.

Through a smudged glass window she saw a lanky teenager round the corner of the store, headed for the gas pump. The old woman spit in an empty coffee can as tobacco juice trickled down her chin. "Restrooms back yonder," she said, pointing to the rear of the building.

After settling up Allison stepped outside and spotted Purvis asleep, at least his eyes were closed, in the shade of a cottonwood tree. She wondered how he had heard the old woman call to him from inside the store. Baffled, Allison shook her head, got in the Chevy and drove away. Dark clouds had moved over the mountains. It had begun to rain. "So much for Speck's forecast," she said fretfully.

Were it not for her sense of urgency, Allison would have driven through the heart of Hot Springs. A sentimental journey. The memories of those fun-filled summer days were still acute. Her father loved to fish and Lake Hamilton was a fisherman's paradise. Emma spent her mornings at the Lamar Bath House with its steam rooms and salubrious massages. But it was the family outings she best remembered: picnics in the mountains with a splendid view of the valley below, panning the free-flowing streams for crystals, hiking the rugged mountain trails, and at night, a game of miniature golf, then strolling along the sidewalks of Central Avenue and listening to the clamorous call of the auctioneer: "Four hundred here, the lady in the pink dress; who'll give me five?" She reveled in the memories.

Allison felt the slow ascent; roads once flat were now serpentine. She had driven through the Ouachita Mountains many times and recognized some of its landmarks. (Everyone considered them a part of the Ozarks.) While the mountains peaked at only twenty-five hundred feet, the drop-offs were precipitous and frightening. Guard rails had been placed at strategic locations but Allison wondered if they would prevent an out-of-control car from plunging over the rocky ledge into a forest of oak and hickory that disguised the sides of the mountain, their limbs full, their leaves still green.

A light rain continued to fall. The payment was wet and slick. Allison, both hands on the steering wheel, slowed to a crawl on sharp curves or when passing the infrequent car or truck heading down the mountain. The palms of her hands were damp, her throat dry. She wished she'd taken another Coke from the old woman's ice chest. She turned down the a/c; the air was thinner, cooler, at the higher elevations. Allison looked at her watch; there was still a long way to go. She prayed for a break in the clouds, for sunshine and dry pavement. Instead, it had begun to rain harder and patches of fog appeared, blurring her vision. She turned on her headlights and chose not to stop at an "overlook." Allison was anxious to see her mother.

❦

Eddie and Gino had their instructions. They had been over the whole operation, every detail, a dozen times. They parked the '49 three-quarter ton Ford pick-up with a reinforced grill, in a "pull out" near the crest of the mountain. Each had a clear picture of Allison's car and the numbers on the license plate. They had followed her from Conway, always keeping their distance. The "tail" was abetted first, by the cover of darkness, later by leaden skies and a steady rain. When she made her stop outside of Hot Springs, they drove on, taking Highway 7, the most direct route through the mountains to Russellville.

Now they waited. Despite the rain that splattered the windshield, Eddie cracked his window and lit a cigarette. Gino opened the glove compartment and retrieved a chocolate candy bar.

"Is that on your diet, fatso?" Eddie laughed.

Gino, a behemoth of a man, was immune to Eddie's needle. "A pick me up," he chuckled, munching the Milky Way.

"A few more pounds and you'll have the big one," Eddie said, slapping his chest.

"I'm not worried. My ma lived to ninety-five."

"Yeah, and your ma weighed about one hundred pounds."

The conversation was cut short when Eddie caught a pair of headlights in his side view mirror. "Check it out."

"Naw, it ain't the Chevy," Gino said. "Goin' mighty slow; he may get to Russellville in time for the six o'clock news."

Eddied lowered his window further, took a long drag and tossed the cigarette onto the wet pavement. "That bitch really took the bait."

Gino pulled a sandwich from a brown paper bag and belched. "Yeah, that Delores missed her calling."

"How so?"

"Her phone call woulda fooled me. She should have been an actress."

"Being Tony's favorite playmate has it rewards."

Gino nodded. "Guess it does."

Eddie closed the window; it was raining harder. "We got lucky," he said.

"How's that?"

"If the woman had called the hospital in Russellville…"

"But Delores is so damn good…so convincing."

Eddie straightened up. He caught the lights in the mirror. The car was creeping up the steepest section of Highway 7. Despite the rain, they could see the lone female driver in the black Chevy as she passed by.

"That's it," Eddie said. He switched on the ignition and turned on his lights and wipers. He closed the distance and settled in behind the Chevy.

☙

Allison was startled, her pulse quickened. "Why would anyone drive so close, almost on my bumper?" she asked herself.

"Check the license plate," Eddie said evenly.

"She's the target," Gino confirmed.

Allison felt a surge of adrenaline and shifted into second. The wheels spun before gaining traction and accelerating up the slick road. She looked in her rearview mirror; there were only a few feet of separation. "Who could it be?" she wondered, "a drunk driver… a predator…an idiot?" The questions raced through her mind unanswered. Rhetorical. She had no enemies. It made no sense.

The truck moved closer, tapping her bumper. Allison's heart beat faster and she felt the sweat under her arms and in the small of her back "If Adam were here," she murmured.

The heavy metal grill rammed the back of the Chevy shifting it slightly sideways. Allison prayed that another car or an eighteen-wheeler would appear. Her prayer went unanswered as Eddie pounded her, pushing the Chevy across the center line.

Allison made the correction and picked up more speed. She felt she had nothing to lose. The rain and patches of fog lowered visibility and made the chase more treacherous. She knew it was almost noon but the sky was still dark and forbidding.

Beyond a large rocky outcropping, the road straightened for a short distance. The truck pulled around her and banged the side of the Chevy, pushing the right front tire off the pavement. Allison, terrified, clinched the steering wheel, trying desperately to recover. The truck was relentless; bumping and banging the side of her car, moving it off the highway and near the edge of the mountain.

Allison fought to keep a tire on the pavement. With her heart racing, she felt the futility...trapped...helpless. Tears blurred her vision. The truck's pounding moved her car closer and closer to the precipice. An image of Adam and Robin flashed before her as the Chevy plummeted over the edge, down the side of the mountain, crashing into the forest of trees.

Eddie and Gino heard the scream and its reverberating echo; it caused no reaction, no remorse. It was all in a day's work.

According to plan, they continued on to Ola, a small town south of Russellville, picked up Highway 27 S and headed home.

"Take it easy," Gino said. "We don't need no cops wondering what happened to the side of our truck."

Eddie ignored the reminder. "This time tomorrow the pickup will be dead and buried."

"Ole Tony thinks of everything." Gino looked at the dashboard clock. He hoped they would be home in time for dinner.

Chapter 36

By mid-afternoon, a stiff wind had pushed the rain beyond the mountains. Overhead, a patch of blue sky appeared and sunlight poured through breaks in the clouds. A trucker spotted the mangled car wedged between two trees. He called his boss in El Dorado, who relayed the location to the Arkansas State Patrol.

The crash site was soon crowded by a police cruiser, an ambulance from Hot Springs and a fire truck with a rescue team. The congestion created one lane of traffic which moved tortoise-like; drivers gawking, sensing an accident had occurred. A Sergeant with the State Patrol kept the cars moving, growling with impatience.

Johnny Decker, a member of rescue team rappelled down the side of the mountain, sunlight gleaming on his yellow helmet. Once on firm footing, he released the rope and stepped out of the harness. He negotiated the short distance to the tree line and with gloved hands inspected the twisted Fleetwood. Through broken glass he saw the blood-streaked face of a woman, her chest crushed against the steering wheel. Johnny looked for her purse but was unable to open the mangled doors. He felt his stomach lurch and sat down until the nausea passed.

He checked around the crash site for personal items and discovered the battered overnight bag beneath the overhang of an oak. Johnny rummaged through the bag hoping to find some identification. There was none. No name. No ID. He closed the bag and left it beneath the tree. Johnny figured the rescue team would take it out tomorrow when they air-lifted the car and its passenger.

He trudged up the slight incline and waved to Fire Chief Holloway standing on the roadside. After refitting his equipment, he extended both arms, thumbs up. A motorized reel rewound the rope and pulled Johnny up the face of the rock.

The Chief extended his hand, pulling him over the ledge. "Well done, Johnny. What did you find?"

The young fireman freed himself from the harness, removed his helmet and despite the cool afternoon, wiped the sweat from his face. He stood for a few moments and shook his head. He looked at his Chief with somber eyes. "One passenger, a woman. Hard to tell her age but I'd say late thirties. Nothing left of the car but tangled metal." He handed a scrap of paper with the license number to the Chief. "Guess I'll never get use to seeing broken bodies."

"Take a break Johnny, get some coffee. I'll handle it from here."

As the ambulance squeezed into the line of traffic toward Hot Springs, a second State Patrol Cruiser pulled in. The Captain stepped out and viewed the wreckage, wondering who was in charge.

Chief Holloway caught the Captain's eye and introduced himself. He shared what little they had learned and handed him the slip of paper with the license number. "I'm sure you can get identification from the D.M.V." The Chief rubbed his prominent jaw. "If you'll handle notification, we'll bring up the vehicle or what's left of it and the body."

The Captain pointed down the mountain. "Must be two hundred feet to the tree line. Looks like an air vac helicopter is your only option."

Holloway nodded. "Whatever it takes, we'll bring it up and turn it over to your people in Hot Springs."

"Any reason to think it was other than an accident?" he asked.

"We searched the area where she left the road and came up empty. Just car tracks, probably hers." Holloway pointed to the pavement. "It was raining earlier; the road was wet, slippery. I'd guess the young woman lost control of the car."

"Young woman, huh? Too bad." The Captain removed his Stetson and looked out absently over the valley. "Too damn bad."

෴

Late evening

Adam pulled into the asphalt lot beside the church annex. Despite long summer days, he saw a light in the preacher's study. He wondered why Hal had paged him and requested an afternoon meeting.

He looked at his watch; almost five o'clock. Running late, as usual.

Adam had called his mother before leaving the hospital and Ruth assured him Robin was fine, at present indisposed, giving Charlie a bath. But she would tell Robin her father had called.

Adam loosened his tie as he crossed the parking lot to the entrance of the annex. Despite the hour, the summer heat lingered like the sulfur-stench of Author White's paper mill on a windy day. He climbed the brick steps, the screen door was unlatched. Once inside, he stopped to catch his breath; a sudden feeling of apprehension swept over him. "Irrational," he said aloud. Adam could think of a dozen reasons for Hal's invitation. He took another deep breath and tapped on the door jam.

Hal, working at his desk, looked up; missing was the cheerful countenance. "Oh, Adam come in, have a seat."

Adam, deep inside himself, felt something was wrong, a feeling that grew stronger as he stepped across the threshold. Was it intuition or the preacher's somber demeanor? On the bookcase was a vase of flowers; some had begun to wilt. Despite the a/c, the air in the small room was oppressive. He settled uneasily in the padded chair.

Hal came around the desk and dragged a fold-up chair next to Adam. He looked into his friend's wary eyes. Even though he had spoken to many families in their time of bereavement, this encounter was somehow different, more difficult. He labored to get the words out, as if they were mired in his throat. Or was it his heart?

"There's been a terrible accident." Hal said finally.

Adam felt his hands begin to shake.

"The car went off the side of the mountain."

"Allison?"

Hal nodded. "It was raining. Slick pavement. The State Patrol believes she lost control and skidded sideways, off the pavement and over the shoulder."

"Is she alive?" he asked, a hopeful whisper.

Hal shook his head. "The car rolled down the side of the mountain, more than two hundred feet, before it crashed into the trees. I'm told the Chevy was nothing but twisted metal."

Adam covered his face with his hands. "Oh, dear God..."

Hal knew, at a time like this, words could not assuage the grief or palliate the pain of a broken heart. So he listened to the sobs of a man who had lost ineffable love. Allison, gone. Hal's own eyes were moist as he remembered her beauty, her gentle spirit. The cosmic question emerged: Why? Why Allison? Kind, devoted Allison?

Adam went to the window and stared at the nandina bushes, his tears unchecked. He wiped them with the sleeve of his shirt. "It can't be. Dammit! It just can't be," he said defiantly, banging the wall, again and again, beside the window.

Hal sat silent, respectfully. Agape. Genuine love. Such loss always evoked a spectrum of emotion: angst, anger, self-pity, grief, remorse, regrets...not necessarily in that order. Adam's pounding was no surprise.

Adam fell against the window as though his every fiber had been shredded, leaving him weak and bewildered. "Are they sure?" he asked, still staring at the bushes along the front of the parking lot.

"Wade Phillips, at State Patrol headquarters in Little Rock, whom I've known since out time in the 82nd, called and asked if I would break the news to Allison's family." The preacher gave Adam the sketchy details. "Tomorrow they will bring the car up by helicopter; the body will be sent to the M. E. in Hot Springs; the car to a police garage for forensics."

Adam turned around, rested on the window sill. "So they recovered the license plate and made the identification?"

Hal nodded.

Adam slumped in his chair his eyes red from weeping. He wiped his face with his hands and surveyed the study as if he might find the reason for his devastating loss. No answer, only the wilted flowers and the hum of the compressor outside the window. How could this have happened? Allison was a poster girl for "Driver's Ed." In bad weather, she would have slowed to a crawl. He could see her now: 25 mph, both hands on the steering wheel, eyes on the road, no diversions. Could she have been set-up? He remembered Maude's words: "The Organization is brutal, predatory and without conscience; their presence ratchets up the risk." Could it have been Caruso? The work of the Devil? A simple call to the hospital in Russellville would provide the answer.

"Would you like me to talk with Robin?" Hal's question brought Adam back to the moment.

"Thanks, but I'll find the right time; the right words. It won't be easy."

"Why don't you wait for an official identification? Wade promised to call."

Adam headed for the door, stopped short and turned around. "Allison left a note on the kitchen counter. She was on her way to Russellville. Emma, her mother, was seriously ill. I'll call the hospital and see if she's there. If not, law enforcement will have a homicide on their hands."

Hal followed him to the door. "Look, Adam, you have some tough times ahead. Questions that demand answers. Swimming in a sea of grief. Dark days. But remember, I'm here to do what I can. Just call, any time, day or night." They embraced and Hal watched Adam vanish into the growing dusk.

Chapter 37

Wednesday, August 30th

Maude parked the Packard in the back of the Madison Parish Courthouse. She stepped out into the sweltering heat and wondered if summer would ever end. Beneath the shade of the live oak, she fiddled with her wide-brimmed hat and smoothed the skirt of her gray short-sleeved dress, looped the purse strap over her shoulder and followed a concrete walkway, low heels clicking, into the three-story courthouse.

Maude checked the directory and padded down a strip of forest green carpet to the end of the hall and pushed the glass door marked Sheriff's Department.

Ginger, the receptionist looked up and offered a friendly greeting. Almost everyone in Conway knew Maude Harrington.

"Morning, Miss Maude?"

"Is Randy in?"

"Yes'um. You need to see him?"

Maude removed her hat and placed it on a side table. "Just for a few minutes."

"Go on in. He'll be glad you came."

Reclining in his chair, boots on the desk, Randy was reading *Field and Stream*. "Hi, Miss Maude. What brings you in?" he asked.

"Any news from Arkansas?"

Randy bounced out of his seat and motioned Maude to the cushioned rocker. He perched on the front edge of the desk, his short legs dangling.

"I'm hoping you've heard from the Sheriff in Hot Springs."

"Got a report late yesterday."

"Well..."

"The driver of the Chevy Fleetwood was Allison Swift. No surprises at autopsy. They're sending the body to Johnny Nabors this afternoon."

Maude could feel her heart flutter, her eyes brim.

The Sheriff reached for a sheet of paper in his outbox. "The car was a total wreck but an examiner found flecks of red embedded in what was once the door on the driver's side."

Maude wiped her eyes with a handkerchief, anxious to hear more.

"Analysis of the red flecks," Randy continued, "revealed enamel and metallic particles."

"Conclusion?"

Randy chewed his lower lip as he scanned the page. "The Arkansas State Patrol and the Medical Examiner believe another vehicle bumped her off the road and over the side of the mountain."

Maude winced; she could not hide her horror. "Anything else?"

"There was another set of tire tracks just off the pavement."

Maude waved her handkerchief, a flag of irrelevance. "There must have been other vehicles..."

"Not a match," Randy interrupted. "Big tires with a heavy tread."

"I suppose you're office is out of the loop."

Randy nodded. "But there's one other thing; the phone call to Allison Swift was a trick. Ms. Emma was in Eureka Springs visiting a friend. She's never been a patient at the local hospital."

"And Allison had no reason to think the call was a ruse."

"The guilty party was counting on that," Randy said.

The Sheriff returned to his chair and leaned on the desk. "About the loop…we're available to help if needed but law enforcement in Hot Springs has jurisdiction. Since they've declared it a homicide, I suspect they'll call in other state agencies, even the FBI."

"A waste of time; just have Mr. Hoover call me and I'll give him a name."

"Who?" Randy asked bemused.

"Tony Caruso." The words made her shiver and she spat them out like sour milk.

Randy rubbed the stubble on his chin and pondered the accusation. "Why Caruso? You won the referendum. The game's over, so what's the point?"

"We wounded Caruso in the process, a villain that's heartless, vindictive, and evil. But he's also smart or he'd never have made it to the top of the food chain. A teenage hoodlum on the streets of Algiers, a sleazy suburb of New Orleans, now heads the most powerful Mafia family in the country. So you can stop looking for the vehicle that killed Allison. It's in some junkyard, a pile of scrape metal, crushed to a pulp."

Randy squinted at the ceiling with its cedar-wood molding. "And no witnesses have come forward."

Maude shook her head. "Not likely…light traffic on a rainy Sunday."

Randy pushed the report across the desk. "I know you'll write the story. Would you like a copy?"

Maude put the folded copy in her purse and stood to leave. "Thanks, Randy."

"Wish I'd had better news." He shrugged his shoulders and pushed a hand through his thinning hair. Maude thought he looked more like Shorty every day.

Halfway down the hall, she stopped and rested against the wall. She held the braided straw hat in her hand, the purse strap over her shoulder. She thought about the very first conversation with Adam almost six months ago. At the time, it was only idle chatter, like dropping pennies in a wishing well. Don Quixote titling another windmill. But the proposal took on sinew and neurons and a warrior's heart, spawning a band of crusaders. While victory was sweet, never in her wildest dreams did she expect the loss of human life. Now, the young and beautiful Allison. Was

235

it worth the winning or was the cost, the extraordinary cost, too high? Maude knew, as in any war, there was a balance sheet and time would provide the answer.

Despite the air conditioned building, Maude could feel sweat seep into her cotton dress. She began to feel woozy, the straw hat slipped from her hand. She was relieved to see Ginger leaving the Department.

"Miss Maude, you okay?" She picked up Maude's hat.

"I'm just so upset over Allison Swift."

"Here, take my arm and we'll find a place to sit."

Ginger guided her to a chair in the lobby and brought her a glass of water. "Maybe one of the Deputies should drive you home."

Maude shook her head. "Thanks, but I feel better already."

ℨ

Maude rested awhile; then took her pulse: 82 and regular. She checked the back of her neck, her forehead. The skin was dry and she was clear-headed. Maude picked up her hat and purse, stood momentarily and felt steady on her feet. She headed out and reached her car without a misstep.

She was surprised by a man's voice as she reached for the door. "Good Morning, Mrs. Harrington. Who had the honor of your visit?" It was Al Marx with his engaging smile.

"Oh, hello Al. I wanted to see if the Sheriff had any news."

"Then you know…Allison's tragedy was no accident."

"Randy gave me the report." Maude looked plaintively at the twisted limbs of the old oak. "One doesn't need ESP to finger the responsible party, but the investigators in Arkansas, even with the resources of the FBI, will never touch him."

"Caruso?" He opened her car door.

Maude nodded and slipped into the driver's seat. She lowered her window, started the engine and turned on the a/c. "He operates in a stinking sewer and he's the only man on the planet with motive."

While Al had never met Tony Caruso, he was aware of his criminal enterprise and had told Adam as much during their lunch at Renee's. He also knew of Caruso's violent reaction to failure. And that his retribution was deadly. Al had silently vowed that should he run for State Attorney General and win the election, he would put the Organization at the top of his to-do list.

"Have you talked to Adam?"

Maude shook her head. "I'll wait until after the funeral."

Al leaned his arms on the roof of the Packard. "I spoke with him briefly. He plans to spend a few days at the beach. His mother will keep Robin and Ben will cover his practice." He looked up at the oak and heard the birds fluttering among its branches. "You can see the despair in his face. And those sagging shoulders, as if his loss is unbearable."

"No surprise. He just lost his best friend, the love of his life. Unfortunately, there's nothing we can do to ease the pain or allay the anguish. No remedy except maybe, our prayers and the passage of time."

"I suppose you're right." Al stepped back from the car. "Oh, on another matter; I received the papers from D.C. and passed them on to Mrs. Hawkins. I understand she and her League members are hard at work."

"Is there a deadline?"

"Chuck said the Senator wanted to take a vote when they returned from their August recess."

"Well, we can count on Hannah." Maude put the car in reverse and waved to Al Marx standing in the shade of the overhand, mopping his brow.

Chapter 38

Saturday, September 2nd

The funeral was over. Somehow, Adam remained functional during those heart-rending days. He handled all of the arrangements, including choosing the casket, needing to be a part of Allison's final rite of passage. He'd hoped he might find a modicum of relief from the sorrow that consumed him. But nothing, nothing at all, had changed.

During the graveside service, Adam, dry-eyed, held Robin close; surely the tears would come again. He did not remember the eulogy, but later friends told him Hal had talked of love's enduring quality which transcends this mortal life; an affirmation of faith which sustains the bereaved in their grief. Adam heard the words but could not process their meaning, his mind overwhelmed by Allison's death.

He wanted to get away and spend time at Norman Beach, listening to the waves caress the shore, walking barefoot through the sand. He and Allison had spent many of their summer vacations there. They had conceived Robin on that deserted beach; a moonless night amid the lapping sounds of an incoming tide. Days of matchless splendor.

Ruth agreed to keep Robin, something she had done many times, overnight and on weekends. Emma, while distraught, drove back to Russellville to care for her sister. Adam had agreed with her decision, since there was nothing to keep her in Conway other than her daughter's grave site and the long faces of silent strangers.

Adam left for the beach at first light. Before leaving town, he drove to the "Flats." Down the rutted road, a rooster crowed. Otherwise, it was quiet in the neighborhood of postage-stamp yards and clapboard houses, everyone still asleep. Not Mattie Mae. The kitchen light was on, her day had begun. Adam managed the uneven wooden steps and knocked on the screen door. The smell of sizzling bacon seeped between its cracks. A tall black man appeared. His voice was kind.

"Mawning, Doc."

"Good morning, Walter."

"Mattie's cookin' breakfast. Won't you jawn us?"

"No thanks, but I would like to speak with Mattie."

"Come on in and I'll fetch her."

The screen door squeaked as Adam stepped inside.

Mattie Mae handed him a cup of coffee. "Ain't you up awfully early?"

He sat the cup down and gave her a hug. "I'm going to Norman Beach for a few days...hope it will help."

"What 'bout my sweet lil girl?"

"Ruth is keeping her...and the dog." He heard a sound of relief, Mattie had not befriended Charlie. "Could you go over Monday and give Ruth a break?"

"Sho will," Mattie said. "Tell Miz Ruth to call anytime she need help."

"One other thing," Adam said, handing her the house key. "While I'm gone, get rid of Allison's things."

He saw the tears gather in her bulging eyes. "You mean her clothes and..."

"Everything, Mattie. I can't have reminders every time I turn around in that house. Pack them up in Walter's truck and take them to Goodwill." He tucked a twenty dollar bill into the pocket of her apron. "For Walter and the use of his truck."

"I'll call Lena or Susie to help. Couldn't touch Miz Allison's things...just me...in that empty house," Mattie said.

"I'm counting on you, Mattie. You've never let me down." He reached over and gave her another hug. "I'll stop by and pick up the key when I get back to Conway."

"First, they kill Preacher. Well, he just a black man. But now they kill Miz Allison. Don't make no sense."

"Look Mattie, the Devil ignores color if it suits his purpose. As Miss Maude says, 'Evil has no conscience.'"

Mattie shook her head, confused. She handed him the coffee and they walked outside, amid the silence of daybreak. A coon hound lay at the far end of the porch undisturbed. The neighborhood had begun to stir, lights appeared in windows of nearby houses. "Guess I'd better get started. It's a long drive to the Gulf."

Mattie wiped her eyes with the hem of her apron. "You be careful now."

Adam took the steps gingerly in the early light and when he reached the street he turned and waved goodbye.

જ

Adam headed east for Jackson, then state highway 49 south to Norman Beach. He didn't need a map, since he'd made the trip a dozen times. As the car sped past the parish line, the sun climbed over the rim of the earth and brushed stratus clouds with coral and crimson. At Vicksburg, he crossed the awesome Mississippi; a swirling, pearl-gray mist covered the river in a ghostly symbiosis.

The road rolled ahead interminably, leaving behind the flatlands of the river delta. The center stripe crested a hill, then dropped away like a black ribbon, undulating, almost alive. Tires thumped across asphalt stripping, creating a hypnotic cadence. A rabbit darted onto the road, stopped for a moment, then scurried, frightened, across the pavement into the safety of the brush. Dazed by despair, Adam did not remember the rabbit or even the river during the long drive to the Gulf.

He stopped at a Sinclair station in Mt. Olive for gas and a cup of coffee. A teenager pumped the gas and washed the windshield. Inside, an old timer sat behind the counter and folded his newspaper. "Anything else I can git you?"

"No thanks." Adam said. "How much do I owe?"

The old man looked over his shoulder and through the front window he could see the pumps and the traffic along highway 49. "It looks like eleven gallons @ twenty seven cents a gallon." He licked the tip of his pencil and did the math. "That'll be $2.97; the coffee's on the house."

Adam got change for a five dollar bill and dropped it in a plastic container beside the cash register, labeled, "March of Dimes."

"My grandson," he stopped and pointed to the teenager checking the tires, "had polio last summer. Thank God, it wus a mild case and he's done recovered."

Adam lifted his paper cup as if it were a celebratory toast. "I'm glad...and thanks for the coffee."

The terrain flattened out again as Adam drove south of Henderson into the marshlands. The road ran past sluggish bayous strutted with water oak and moss-laden bald cypress, their gnarled roots, like old knees, exposed here and there above the waterline. Narrow tributaries lined by swamp grass wound their way through the trees into quiet coves. Wild violets and marsh marigolds adorned the knolls, a sanctuary for the Snowy Egret and the little Blue Heron.

It was mid-afternoon when Adam pulled into the main entrance of the two-story Breeze Inn. The desk clerk, a matronly woman with a pleasant face, put aside the crossword puzzle. "Reservation?"

"No, but I'd like an ocean-side room, please."

The woman repositioned her glasses and studied the room assignment sheet. "I have one left...ocean front, second level."

A breath of relief. He was afraid the motel might be full over the holiday weekend. He paid in advance with traveler's checks and flashed his driver's license.

"So you plan to be here over Labor Day."

Adam nodded. "Until Wednesday."

"Well, if you need anything, ask for Mabel. I'm the manager and work the front desk."

"Thanks. Hope that won't be necessary."

"Now, if you'll sign the registration card, I'll get your key."

かの

Adam awoke early the following morning and made a cup of instant coffee. The room was similar to those he and Allison had shared on their summer vacations. It was not the Waldorf Astoria, but the mattress was firm, the a/c hummed and there was plenty of hot water. Clean and comfortable, all that he needed. He pulled the curtains, slipped between sliding glass doors onto a narrow balcony. He sat in a porch chair, placed the cup on a side table and savored the view: cobalt-blue skies, a white sandy beach and the dark green waters of the Gulf that seemed to stretch forever. Seagulls strutted along the shore line. He remembered how he and Allison had walked the beach and watched the birds wade the shallows looking for food.

This was their summer place. So many memories. A couple, hand in hand, strolled along the shore, their backs to the nascent sun. Adam felt a wave of nostalgia which heightened his sense of separation. He sipped his coffee and wondered if coming here was the right thing to do.

∽

Adam returned to his room after a long walk on the beach and a light lunch, feeling listless, drowsy. He opened the sliding glass doors and stretched out across the bed without turning back the counterpane. Heavy with fatigue, he slept, carried back to the beach, walking barefoot through the foamy surf. A billowing wind from the Gulf warmed his face and coated his lips with brine.

Suddenly he saw her, a distance away, but close enough to recognize her radiant face. Adam ran toward her, his heart pounding with excitement. He called, "Allison, wait…wait…wait for me!" But she moved away, illusively, like a will-o-the-wisp, his words lost in the wind. He ran faster and faster, panting for breath, but she kept retreating farther down the beach, waving at him, beckoning, finally fading into the ether like a rainbow. Adam dropped to his knees, buried his throbbing head in his hands and sobbed. Finally, he looked up with childlike expectation, only to find a desolate beach and overcast skies.

A roll of thunder awakened him. He remembered the dream, Allison, just out of reach…waving…beckoning. Had it been an illusion, born of insanity that sorrow had imposed? Perhaps a memory...luminous mist rolling in from the sea, fused with sunlight? He didn't know. Nor did it matter. Maybe he would see her again in the sweetness of his dreams.

In the drawer of his bedside table lay a spiral notebook on a Gideon Bible. He had noticed it earlier when he dropped loose change into the drawer. He opened the notebook and found three hand-written poems. Each was untitled; none were signed. He shuffled the remaining pages; all were blank. He washed his face and went back to the drawer, taking the notebook, and slipped through the sliding glass doors to the balcony.

He read the poem on the first page. A romantic, he thought. Not Tennyson or Byron or Poe, but a budding talent...perhaps.

Beside the shore, we met by chance,
Warm winds of bitter irony,
Swept in to seal our star-crossed fate,
And bind these hearts, inseparably.
So take me there, where seabirds soar,
Take me back to the sea.

Enraptured by compelling love,
Our lives entwined, enduringly,
Those blissful days, with joy replete,
Were burned into my memory.
So take me back, where sand dunes stand,
Like sentries of the sea.

Storm clouds claim the far horizon,
Torrential rains, relentlessly,
Swept o'er the shore with cruel force,
And carried you far out to sea.
Let me feel again the ocean's wind,
Blowing in from the sea;
The intoxicating scent of you
Flowing in from the sea.

The sands of time have fallen fast,
The hourglass, inexorably,
Near empty as the years have past,

Each grain a flash of memory.

So take me back to love's retreat,
My respite by the sea;
Your presence there, like a brilliant sun,
That shines above the sea. .
A shrine, 'tis true,
I've built for you,
In my heart, beside the sea.

While some might consider it doggerel, Adam found it elegiac and poignant; meter and rhyme; making him wonder if it had been inspired by the poet's own "lost love." If so, they shared something in common.

He decided to leave the notebook with Mabel. She would know who last stayed in the room and it was possible she knew to whom the notebook belonged. He scribbled a message on Breeze Inn stationary and attached it to the cover. He would take it to dinner and leave it at the front desk.

❧

The Saturday night buffet at the Breeze Inn attracted a large gathering, enough food to feed an army. But Adam was not hungry and settled for a salad and a glass of iced tea. Despite the crowd, he felt detached, alone. He saw Allison everywhere…the sheen of her hair, her violet-blue eyes. Unshakable. The small band played the Glenn Miller songs they used to dance to. Allison had become a part of him…of his identity. How he wished she were here. He signed the check and hurried from the room, passing Mabel, hostess for the buffet, on his way out.

"Doctor Swift, are you all right?"

He waved. "Just not hungry." Adam shoved the glass door open and disappeared into the lobby before she could reply.

He took the stairs to his room. From the balcony he could see the high tide roll into the shore; the foam flickered with silver like *feu follets*. He knew that solitude, like a bipolar electrode, could be either helpful or hurtful. Adam had always enjoyed brief periods of isolation; time for reading and reflection which, like the cool breath of autumn, refreshed him. He had hoped Norman Beach would be salutary as well. But instead, he felt more fragile, distanced from his pillars of support, from those who loved him and shared his profound sadness.

He kicked off his shoes and lay on the bed. He would leave in the morning and return home by way of New Orleans, that bewitching city at the maw of the Mississippi. He wanted to revisit the pediatric ward at Charity where he had first met Allison, a volunteer in a pink smock, hugging a frightened child. Despite the skeptics and cynics, it *was* love at first sight.

They had cherished their limited time together, rationed by the grueling demands of Adam's internship. Even though it had been eleven...twelve years ago, he remembered the trolley rides down St Charles Avenue with the magnolias in full bloom; boat rides at twilight on the still waters of Lake Pontchartrain; a Sunday stroll in Jackson Square, a carnival of art displays, portrait painters, jugglers, magicians and the sound of jazz from the steps of the Saint Louis Cathedral. (It was the only entertainment they could afford.) Later they would walk to Morning Call on Decatur Street for beignets and café au lait.

Adam felt traces of warmth flow through his veins for the first time. He stood up and peered over the dark waters; the faint light of a shrimp boat dragging its nets, flickered far out in the Gulf. He relished those moments of relief, clung to them like a man clutching a rope over a precipice. A matter of survival. He gulped the night air hoping it would sustain him.

By morning, the vague feeling of relief was gone and once again Adam found himself in a pool of remorse and self-pity. He skipped breakfast, tossed his bag into the trunk of his car and drove straight to New Orleans in time for coffee at Morning Call.

Chapter 39

After lunch, Hal returned to his study. He thought of his beleaguered friend and hoped that his time at the beach would help. While he shared Adam's grief, there was little he or anyone else could do to assuage his sadness. Only Adam felt the enormity of his loss and he alone must search for solace, find relief. While time attenuated the pain, Hal knew that Adam would never heal completely; the wound too deep; their love too entwined.

Hal had planned to work during the afternoon on the Sunday sermon. The preparation of fresh material was an unending, self-imposed discipline that he struggled to enforce. The temptation to pull an old sermon from the file and revise it was ever-present. But he had made a start; a homily on suffering, a subject which weighed heavily on his heart since he first heard about Allison.

He sat up and reread the introduction, written the night before while fixing a cheese omelet for supper. There was a lightning flash of inspiration and Hal wanted to bottle it before the thoughts vanished like quicksilver. He took the pen from his shirt pocket, grabbed a paper napkin from the pantry and sat at the Formica table. He began to write:

A time of travail comes to every man as surely as morning light follows the night. Bewildered, he asks the perplexing questions: "Why has this happened to me? How can a perfect Providence reconcile these imperfections within a world of His own creation?

Since primeval man, Adam and Eve, if you prefer, looked up into a star-infested sky, he has wrestled with the problem of human suffering. He observed the unalterable cycles of the suns. Florid colors erupted from flowers and fruit trees with spring's inevitable return. He watched the rhythm of the tides and the flow of rivers, always moving toward the sea. Observations were predictable. Rational. Dependable. But in pain and suffering, there was no apparent purpose. Only the random winds of fate; the caprice of a jester-God.

Our town is in mourning. The loss of Allison Swift has cast a shadow of unspeakable sadness across Conway and beyond. Benighted, like the men of old, we beat our chests and cry out against those invisible forces that we cannot control. Nor even understand.

It was a good beginning, Hal thought, as his eyes grew heavy. He laid his head on the desk just as he had done in the second grade at nap time, and dropped like a rock into a sound sleep.

There was a knock on the office door which jarred him awake. The assault in early summer was still fresh in his stash of memories. He sat up, relieved to see Adam standing in the doorway. "Come on in."

Hal circled the desk and gave Adam a bear hug. "Glad you're home," he said, motioning toward the padded chair. Hal took his seat behind the desk and looked at his friend. Adam's sports shirt was wrinkled and hung loosely about his bent shoulders. The lines of his face had deepened since the funeral...Hal was sure of that. And his eyes were dull and languid, like those of a man who had lost something of inestimable value, something irretrievable.

"How was the beach?" Hal asked.

"I thought it would help." Adam shook his head dejectedly. "It only fed my misery." He recounted the surreal dream, Allison's omnipresence at the Breeze Inn and the sentimental trip to New Orleans. "I suppose the anger cooled but there's still a big gaping hole right here," he said, fingering his chest.

"Wish I could conjure up some healing portion," Hal said. "But I'm sure of one thing..."

Adam looked up, his eyes expectant.

247

"The passage of time brings light to the dark night of the soul."

Adam, inconsolable, pushed himself out of the chair and stepped to the window. Beside the annex, two small boys had fashioned a raft from trigs and twine and transformed a shallow ditch into a make-believe river.

"Why?" Adam asked. "The question has tormented me. I drove for miles asking that question, over and over again. Why? For God's sake, why?" His voice forlorn, trailed off into soft, muted sobs and his limp frame fell back into the padded chair.

Hal shook his head. "While no one has an answer, I believe it finds an affirmation in faith. Pascal expressed it best: *The heart has its reasons, the mind cannot know.*"

Adam wiped his eyes with the heel of his hands. "Explain."

Hal searched the ceiling for a place to begin. "Everyone agrees that we live in a world which is governed by natural laws. Okay so far?"

Adam nodded.

"There are planets and stars far out in space that cannot be seen with the naked eye, even the strongest telescope. Secrets still hidden. Impervious to science or some mathematical equation. Likewise, in pain and suffering, there is a barrier which *reason* cannot penetrate.

"When tragedy strikes, there are some who put on pious faces, wring their hands, and take refuge in the shade of the Almighty. 'It's God's doing,' they say. For some reason there is a kind of contrived comfort in making Him the scapegoat. Faith, on the other hand, acknowledges adversity as a part of life; suffering is not punitive nor the result of Divine intervention, but as free agents in a free world, it occurs and reason stands helpless like a man on death row awaiting the warden's summons."

"What about this crater?" Adam again pointed to his chest.

"Remember." Hal said. "Positive currents often flow from misfortune."

"I hope you're right," Adam said weakly.

"And don't forget, you have a beautiful child. Your patients await your return. A mother who loves you dearly lives close by. And Conway is forever in your debt and will never forget the cost of your commitment."

Adam nodded, his chin drooped.

There was a long silence before Hal spoke. "May I share a personal story?"

"Sure…anything."

He hesitated, his look wistful. "When I was young I fell in love with a wonderful girl. She was everything I'd dreamed about. Our love grew and we planned to marry in late spring, before my last year in seminary. She was a councilor at a summer camp near Alexandria and on her way home, a drunk driver crossed the center lane and crashed into her '37 Ford Coupe, a fatal collision. When I heard the news, I felt my life was over, my future shattered. It was an inane act. Pointless. Completely illogical. Was man at the mercy of some frivolous deity, or worse, a God gone mad? And as you have done, I asked over and over again the only relevant question, 'Why?'"

He pulled a worn envelope from his desk drawer. "This letter is from her mother and it helped, more than anything else, to lift me out of my depression. May I read it?"

Adam straightened up. His brow furrowed with interest.

Dear Hal,

Your message, along with the other letters, has helped so much at this time. Amy loved you and spoke of you often. Her college years were a time of joyful fulfillment; each day a celebration of life. I can see clearly the smile, the sparkling blue eyes, and hear the laughter that marked her vibrant spirit. I am grateful we had her for these few short years, though now, her father and I feel so keenly that sense of separation.

However, we shall never be apart in spirit, for a love such as hers transcends time and space, and on this earth she left her love on everything she touched.

We shall try so hard to live up to the example she left, that we may, when this life is over, be united again. How glorious in anticipation is our goal.

*Thank you for all you meant to her and for the joy
you brought into her life. And through Amy, into ours.*

Gratefully

Margaret

Hal placed the faded letter into the envelope and laid it on the desk. "Those words gave me strength and consolation. If a mother spoke with such assurance abut the loss of her only child, then I figured faith must be more than a religious tranquilizer. Many months later, I found a clear direction for my life; losing Amy reinforced my decision for the ministry." Hal's eyes glowed with conviction. "Passing through that valley has allowed me to share the suffering of others, as a pastor and friend, even as a soldier at Normandy."

"And you've never married?" Adam asked, as if the letter, after some delay, had finally reached his level of perception.

Hal shook his head. "But it could happen. And you think no one can replace Allison, but time and circumstance have ways of short-circuiting that sentiment. Man was not meant to live alone. Believe me, I know."

Adam shook his head. "She owns my heart."

Hal picked up the letter again, fondled it for a moment and then replaced it in the top drawer of his desk. "Have you thought about completing your residency? I've heard you express that wish before. A change of scenery is sometimes good at a time like this."

"I don't know, Hal. It would be hard to leave Conway. I have a daughter to consider and a mother who's not getting any younger." He shook his head abjectly and added, "Then there's Ben and my patients and …oh, I don't know…guess I need to wait until the fog clears up here." He tapped his head with his finger.

Hal moved around the desk and put a hand on the shoulder of his friend. "Don't hurry a decision. As I said before, time's your friend."

Adam stood and turned to leave. "I hope you're right."

☙

The rain had stopped but a bracing September breeze caused his eyes to sting. Adam heard water running down the gutters of the building, a guzzling sound. The two small boys had deserted the drainage ditch, leaving behind a make-believe raft on their make-believe river. He stooped down, drawn by the sight of the trigs tied with twine struggling to stay afloat. He watched the small raft bob in the ditch, wondering how long it would be, before it broke apart.

Finally Adam got in his car and drove south along the levee and into the Flats. He stopped in front of Mattie's place, weather-worn, like most of the small wooden houses on her street. The only adornment was a lush crepe myrtle with red blooms in the front yard. Two of Mattie's children left their game of marbles and went squealing inside. The screen door flew open and Mattie was on the porch before Adam could cross the yard. She scrambled down the steps as fast as her fat legs would allow. "Praise the Lawd. Hallelujah! My boy done come home."

Adam wrapped her in his arms. "I'm glad to be home."

"Hope you feeling better. When you left Friday mawning you 'minded me of a whipped puppy."

Adam looked up at the blue sky, the rain clouds had passed. "My feelings?" He shook his head. "Nothing has changed. I thought the beach would help, but I was wrong. Just too many memories. So I drove to New Orleans...you remember, that's where Allison and I first met...but no comfort there. Then I thought about my family and friends here and figured it was time to come home."

She handed him the key. "Sunday, after church, I did what you ask'd, took care of Miz Allison's things. Walter wus a big help. And Dora pitched in. We put everything in the bed of his pickup and takes it to the Goodwill store." Mattie tried to hold back the tears. "I left her jewelry in the dresser drawer."

"Thanks Mattie. Everything else okay?"

Mattie nodded. "I went over yesterday and took care of my sweet lil girl. Gave Miz Ruth a chance to git out and do some shoppin'."

"How was Robin?"?"

"Some better. Miz Ruth done tucked her under her wing like a mother hen. And that lil girl won't hardly let yur mother out of her sight."

"Guess I'm lucky to have her here."

Mattie stepped back and stared at Adam. "Sho would like to fix you some supper Doc Swift. Looks like you ain't ate nothing since you left town."

"Thanks Mattie, just not hungry. I'm sure that'll change when I smell your home cooking. See you in the morning."

A lavish smile spread across Mattie's round face, white teeth gleaming like polished ivory. "I'll be there in time to fix breakfast."

He gave her hand a squeeze and waved to the boys who were watching, curiously, from the front porch.

Adam felt waves of emptiness as he turned out of the Flats and headed for the north of town. Pedestrian traffic was light as he crossed Main Street; it was the first day of the new school year.

☙

When Adam entered the house, he felt the difference. It was clean and orderly; Mattie had made sure of that. But nothing was quite the same. It was as if he had walked into the house for the first time. Adam knew the reason for this distortion and could only hope that time would work in his favor. But for now, Allison's presence was unshakable, like an attachment which followed him everywhere.

Adam left his suitcase in the bedroom and called Ruth. She assured him Robin was better and had started school. "Robin, a first-grader, can you believe it?"

"What was her reaction?"

"She was excited."

"Maybe it'll help...get her mind on other things."

"Oh, I think it will. Last night we went to Audubon Park for the fireworks. She had a wonderful time."

"I appreciate..."

"Listen, I love having her. Come over for dinner tonight, say around seven. We need to talk."

"Thanks, I'll be there."

Chapter 40

The jangling phone awakened Mario from a sound sleep. He leaned on an elbow and reached for the receiver.

"Hello."

"Sorry to call at this ungodly hour."

Mario recognized Pappas' voice. "Must be urgent."

"Meet me tonight at nine, Alfredo's." A moment of silence. "You know the place?"

"Sure, been there a dozen times." Alfredo's was a four star restaurant in the French Quarter, one of Mario's favorites.

"Don't be late. Tony's not a patient man."

"I'll be there." Mario placed the receiver in its cradle, turned over and went back to sleep.

When he awoke, light filled the small bedroom. He thought about the early morning phone call. Meeting with Tony Caruso meant it was an important assignment. Mario made the calculation: a leisurely six hour drive to New Orleans. He would leave mid-morning, arriving in time for a late lunch at Galatoires and an afternoon stroll around Jackson Square.

After a shave and shower, Mario packed an overnight bag. He unlocked the drawer of his small desk and checked the .38 Smith

253

and Wesson. Satisfied, he placed it in the canvas bag and zipped it up. He locked the door of his apartment and walked to the detached garage, behind the building.

Mario drove down Riverside and crossed the bridge into West Conway. He put on dark glasses; the river sparkled with sunlight. He turned onto asphalt, leading to Gambelli's and parked beneath the porte-cochere. The sound of a calliope greeted him; a paddle boat—in full view—steamed down river.

While the dining room was empty, the aroma of fresh baked bread filled the space. The kitchen was a beehive of activity; almost time for the lunch crowd. "Hi Joey, how's it going?"

Rizzo looked up from his chopping board. "Mario, what brings you in so early?"

"Leaving town. You're in charge."

Rizzo's arm swept the room. "Needn't worry, we'll take care of Gambelli's."

Mario mimed a coffee drinker and headed for his office. He closed the door and opened the wall safe behind the Bellini. He counted fifty hundred-dollar bills and placed them in a zipper bank-bag. Mario also included his authentic ID...driver's license and birth certificate. He would lock the bag, along with the gun, in the glove compartment of his black Camaro.

Rizzo rapped on the door.

"Come in."

The chef placed the cup of coffee on the desk. "Anything else you need?"

"Have Marty take my car and fill it up." He tossed Rizzo the keys. "I'll clean up my desk. Should be outta here in half an hour."

"Buona fortuna."

∾

Mario checked into the Howard Johnson on Airline Highway. He picked up a *Times Picayune* at the front desk and went to his room. Weary from the long drive, he sank into a cushioned chair and fell asleep, the paper in his lap. The roar of thunder awakened him and he heard a hard rain pepper the window. After washing his face, Mario decided to eschew his lunch plans and settle for a sandwich in the motel coffee shop. He figured the rain would chase the mimes and musicians from the front of the St. Louis Cathedral, the artists from Jackson Square. Standing at the window of his room, he watched the rain pelt the glass. The light from the lamp flickered. "A late summer storm," he murmured, "not the time to visit the Quarter." Mario settled in his chair and opened the newspaper.

℘

He parked (valet) at the Jung Hotel and walked to the Quarter. The storm had moved out, over the Gulf, the skies had cleared. Overhead, stars blinked in the night sky. Mario passed the police station on Chartres Street, only a block from Alfredo's.

The maitre d' bowed slightly when he heard Mario's name and looked toward the back of the dining room. "Follow me, please. Mr. Caruso and Mr. Pappas have been seated." They walked past convivial diners to the circular booths which lined the far wall. The last booth provided privacy, separated from the others by a cluster of exotic plants.

Caruso extended a hand, but remained seated. "Mario, glad you're here." He nodded to his companion. "You know Johnny?"

"Yeah, sure. We talked this morning."

Pappas poured Mario a glass of Grenache and placed the bottle in the wine cooler beside the booth.

Mario sipped the red wine, a hint of raspberry.

"First we eat, then we talk," Caruso said.

The waiter took their orders and moved away.

Mario looked at Caruso, a stump of a man, and mulled over the possibilities. What was the assignment? Since previous orders had come through a surrogate, Caruso's presence meant the job was "top priority." It piqued his curiosity but he would have to wait.

Mario pushed the food around his plate but ate little, his senses on "high alert." He noted the table nearest the booth; two men with broad shoulders and swarthy complexions, a part of the Don's entourage, the muscle necessary to ensure Caruso's personal safety.

After a meal of scallops and shrimp liguria, the waiter cleared the table and filled their cups with café au lait. Mario broke a heavy silence. "Mr. Caruso, you have an assignment?"

Caruso lit a cigarette. "You know the Dixie Mafia?"

Mario rocked his hands. He had gotten a cursory briefing at Langley.

"They're a loosely knit group of scum bags who specialize in armed robbery, safe-cracking and murder for hire."

Mario almost smiled at the irony.

"Now they're dealing drugs," Pappas added. "They've crossed the line."

Mario wondered about the connection. Why did the Mob allow a bunch of thugs to operate on the same side of the street? He figured they paid a percentage, like a license to do business.

"So why am I here?" he asked.

Pappas moved his coffee aside. "Angelo Spoto is the de facto head of the Dixie Mafia. Tomorrow that may change. But for now, he's the one we deal with."

"What's the plan?" Mario watched the two men; their eyes met...an unspoken message. He felt a stab of *unease*, but let it pass

"We contacted Angel and made a deal. Half the drug money and a promise—on his mother's grave—to stay out of Louisiana... or else."

The Greek's expression hardened; Mario knew it was more than a *deal*; Pappas had given the Dixie Mafia an ultimatum.

"You know Pelican Park?" Caruso asked.

"Sure."

"The carousel, middle of the zoo."

"I'll find it."

Pappas slid a hand-drawn map across the table. "That's the location. Angel will be there tomorrow night...ten o'clock." The Greek hesitated, modulated his voice. "Take the money, then take him out."

Mario put the slip of paper in his shirt pocket and pushed away from the table. "Got it."

"Oh, Mario, stop by Willswood Monday. A little something for a night's work."

Mario acknowledged the payment and walked out of the restaurant.

&

Mario had a late breakfast in the motel's coffee shop and devoured the Sunday edition of the *Times Picayune*. He went poolside and lay in a lounge chair, a bright sun on his face, to plan his day. While his rendezvous with Angel was hours away, he needed to canvass the park—a dry run—and locate the carousel, become familiar with landmarks and exit points. He figured the park would close early on Sunday, which meant finding the carousel in darkness; no music or squealing children to guide him. Still enough time to stroll the Quarter and enjoy the sights and sounds of Jackson Square. Maybe a stop at Preservation Hall; the sweetness of Louie's muted trumpet played with his mind. He'd make a short walk to Café Du Monde for beigets and chicory coffee; he would need the caffeine jolt. Satisfied, Mario returned to his room, showered and put on black jeans and a dark sweatshirt which covered his belt. He grabbed a drink from the Coke machine and headed for his car.

☙

At Café Du Monde, Mario sat outside and sipped his third cup of coffee. He checked his watch: 9:10. Time to go. On the drive to the park, Mario wondered about his role as an undercover agent. After two flawless assignments, he was no closer to Caruso than at the start. He knew his mission: to penetrate the Mafia's inner circle and gather information. The U. S. Senate had declared war on organized crime and he was part of the strategy. He hoped tonight's mission, if successful, would bring him into that cadre of confidantes.

He parked his car on Camp Street, a block from Pelican Park, took the gun from the glove compartment, checked the safety, his belt, the holster. Mario locked the car and stood for a moment while his eyes adjusted to the darkness. He followed Magazine to the entrance of the park, crossed the street and found the tree-lined path, leading to the carousel. The place was eerily quiet, only the whistle of a boat on the river. He looked around...nothing moved. Mario was not surprised, the park closed at seven on Sundays.

He followed the edge of the path, flashlight jostling in his back pocket. An overhang of gnarled tree limbs deepened the darkness. He was close to his target, he smelled the animals. He checked his watch again, thinking an early arrival gave him an advantage. The Live Oak, spotted during his reconnaissance, was only fifty feet from the carousel, a perfect vantage point. Mario shuffled around the tree and leaned against the trunk, a crook in low-lying limbs provided a line of sight.

He waited. Nothing stirred. Across the river, some wild thing howled at the moon. Mario grew restless; Angel was late or had copped out. He pulled the gun from his belt and moved with stealth toward the carousel. He wondered if Angel had delivered the money, but left the park, fearing a betrayal. He boarded the carousel and switched on his light. Mario moved between the animal rides, a few bench seats for adults. On one of the seats he saw the package, the size of a shoe box. He tore off the wrapping paper and lifted the lid. He flashed his light; it was full of one hundred dollar bills.

Mario tucked the box under his arm and turned to leave. He looked around and listened; not a sound. Walking back, he sensed relief. He had the money with no blood on his hands.

He passed under an archway of live oaks, their limbs dripping with moss. Mario, close to the street, failed to see the shadowy figure behind him.

"Mario!"

Startled, he turned and reached for his gun.

A muffled shot caught him in the chest. He slumped to his knees. A second shot dropped him to the ground.

Eddie knelt down and felt the pulse in his neck. There was none. He picked up the package, rolling him over with his foot.

A giant of a man appeared. "Found the black Camaro. Hot wired the car. Sittin' out front. "

The two men dragged the body to the deserted street and heaved it into the trunk of the car. "You know the plan, Gino. We'll pick you up at the airport."

Eddie patted the trunk of the car. "Adios Mario, you fucking traitor."

Chapter 41

Friday, September 15th

Maude looked at her watch. She had ample time before her appointment at the courthouse. She filled her mug with coffee and settled into a chair on the back porch. It was her favorite time of day. Maude hatched and germinated some of her best editorials from this very spot during the dawning of a new day. She took a deep breath, invigorated by the trace of autumn in the air, relieved that the torpor of long summer days would soon succumb to a more agreeable season. She looked at the red maple, which always reminded her of Belle and Preacher, and thought the leaves had begun to change their color. A thin smile of nonsense crept over her face. She knew better; mid-September was too early for the leaves to turn, even the maple. Maybe it was the slant of the sun on the tree or just her imagination...wishing it were so.

Maude sipped her coffee pensively. The thought of Allison's death cast a shadow on her reverie. The funeral two weeks ago still weighed on her heart. The hollow face of Adam, with a child clinging to his chest, sobbing softly, was a tableau Maude would never forget.

Earlier in the week, the coroner in Hot Springs had made it official...a homicide. Allison was the third causality of the crusade.

Maude got up and shuffled into the kitchen. She placed her mug in the sink. Dora would clean up.

She went to her bedroom and dressed, applied a little make-up, only lip gloss and a dab of rouge to her pallid cheeks. With her fingers, she tucked a lock of gray hair into place. Satisfied, she grabbed her purse and headed for the garage.

The handsome Madison County courthouse sat in the center of freshly mown fescue, overlooking South Grand and the river. Maude parked in the back and admired the holly shrubs and colorful flowers. They jogged her memory; she had planned to write an editorial, needling the Mayor; a mortifying reminder, to upgrade the seedy grounds at City Hall.

Maude stood for a short time beneath the oak's broad canopy and dropped the keys in her purse. It had been only two weeks since she was here for the meeting with Randy Gilstrap and her chance encounter with Al Marx.

She followed the tree-lined walkway into the courthouse and took the elevator to the third floor. The D.A.'s suite was at the end of the south corridor, past judicial offices and an empty courtroom. Maude checked her watch as she entered through a pair of paneled mahogany doors. Della, the receptionist ushered Maude into the D. A.'s office.

Al Marx stood, looking dapper as usual in his blue blazer and paisley tie. "Morning, Maude." He waved a hand toward the wingback chair near the desk. "Please."

"Al, you are a busy man, so I'll get right to the point. I want to thank you, in person, for your invaluable help in our efforts to close the taverns. Without your assistance, our mission would have failed."

"I'm not so sure, Maude. You put together a formidable coalition." He unbuttoned his coat and folded his arms on the desk. "But you could have called, saved yourself a trip across town."

"Your role was so essential, the message had to be delivered in person."

"Glad I could help."

"I should have thanked you sooner but..."

"No apologies, please."

Maude had known Al since he was a boy and had followed his career with a maternal interest. He had finished L.S.U. Law School with honors, editor of the Law Review. During the war years, he served stateside in the Judge Advocate General's office, under Major General Thomas Green, returned to Conway in 1948 and ran for District Attorney. He won overwhelmingly, a six year term; the youngest D.A. in the state of Louisiana. Maude believed Al Marx was an honest and honorable man. *The Review* had supported his candidacy without reservation.

"Another compliment…" she tilted toward the desk. "Should you run for a state-wide office, and I hope you will, you'll again have my full support." Maude winked playfully. "You still have four years to serve and at my age there are no guarantees."

Al laughed. "I predict you'll be around still publishing *The Review.*"

Maude rearranged herself in the chair, the wrinkles that lined her face deepened. "Any news from Washington since we last spoke?"

Al retrieved a legal pad from the credenza behind his desk. "Chuck called two days ago. The full Senate has approved the appropriation bill. Short expects passage in the House sometime next week. Chuck reminded me that the wheels of Congress move at a snail's pace. But funds should begin to flow by late October; funneled through the city of Conway, then to the account of the Civic Improvement Coalition (CIC) at the Central Bank." Al looked down at his notes. "The funds can only be used to buy out the owners and restricts the use of the land to "parks and recreation.""

"So the CIC is the fiduciary and will handle all transactions based on the earlier appraisals?"

Al nodded. "The trust department at the bank provides oversight. And if all goes according to Chuck's timeline, closure will occur by the end of November."

Maude could not suppress a look of satisfaction. "We'll move promptly into phase II."

Al gave her a quizzical look.

"Fund raising," she said. "We have the architect's drawings, a plan for the park. Remember, I broached the subject with Fred Warren at Ben's party." Maude stifled a sneeze. "We need money for landscaping, tennis courts, a picnic area, softball courts, a marina on the river…well you get the idea."

"How much?"

"Two million…just a rough estimate."

"Put Hannah Hawkins in charge. She'll wring donations from old 'Skinflint' Warren and she has Author White wrapped around her little finger."

"I plan to use the paper and put pressure on the Mayor. I believe Chester Payne can find some discretionary funds in his supplementary budget. After all, a generous contribution and an agreement to operate the park would allow the Mayor to consider it a city project."

Al laughed. "Let me know when and where to send my check."

Maude picked up her purse and wiggled out of the chair. She stood for a moment, one hand on the desk. She gave Al a look of frustration. "Like an infant, I have to stand before I walk. Otherwise I'll end up on my backside. It's hell to get old." She dabbed her nose with a Kleenex. "But I don't like the alternative."

When Maude reached the door she stopped and turned around. "Have you talked to Adam?"

"I called a couple of days ago. He's back at work, full time, but it's not been easy."

"I do wish we could help." Maude shook her head disconsolately. "He loved her so much."

"He has lots of support which should lift his spirits."

"Oh, by the way, I've asked Mason Smith, the architect, to draw up a memorial to Allison, a center piece for the park. Something eye-catching, like Chicago's Buckingham fountain, encircled by her favorite flowers."

Al stood, nodding his approval.

"It may be controversial, but I'm putting a bronze stature of Grady Henry in some propitious location."

"It's an appropriate gesture and you have my backing."

Maude waved goodbye and closed the door behind her.

"She's amazing," he said to an empty room.

രു

Fred Warren parked his new Lincoln Continental, with its eight cylinder engine beneath Gambelli's porte-cochere. It was two o'clock in the afternoon and the Friday lunch crowd had come and gone. He stopped long enough to absorb the scenic view of the river and wondered why he had not added that amenity to Mario's lease agreement. He crossed the wide veranda and entered the restaurant.

Unlike the other taverns, it had been built to Mario's specifications by Warren Construction in exchange for a long-term lease. The south wing of the building had its own entrance and served only snacks and beer. A jukebox pumped out country music. But the spacious room was soundproof; Mario wanted to keep the "Beer Parlor" separate from the more formal dining room. Warren felt the coalition, unfairly, had dumped Gambelli's in with the other taverns.

Fred, slightly stooped, wore casual attire…a sports shirt that hung outside his khaki pants and brown loafers without socks. He stopped at the front desk and lit his cigar, the opal in his signet ring catching the light from his Zippo.

The dining room was empty but he heard the clatter of dishes and the sound of voices coming from the kitchen. While there was a bar at the back of the room, Fred Warren considered Gambelli's a well-appointed restaurant, not a tavern. The tablecloths were of white cotton and shiny silverware rested on linen napkins. The walls were graced with Antonio Gravina originals. Warren had visited each of the venues from time to time, a kind of on-site inspection, and Gambelli's was a different brand. If it were New Orleans, Warren thought, he could make a comparison: Antoine's or Brennan's in contrast to some boisterous and rowdy joint on Bourbon Street.

"Oh, hello, Mr. Warren. What brings you across the river?"

Tony Rizzo, short and stout, was the chef at Gambelli's. Warren knew that Tony also managed the place. What he didn't know was the connection between the two men. A relative? An old friend from the past? An obligation? It didn't matter so Warren never asked.

"Is Mario around?"

"Haven't seen him in a week."

"Where can I reach him?"

Tony shrugged.

"He's two weeks late with the rent."

"Mr. Warren, you know Mario! He's away a lot." He let slip a modest smile. "He knows that the restaurant is in good hands."

"Not even a phone call?"

Tony shook his head. "He'll show up...when he's ready."

Warren puffed his cigar and sent spirals of smoke toward the high ceiling. "I know he plans on moving to Leesville. Heard he found a place, a strip mall, between town and Camp Polk." Warren, perplexed, fished a handkerchief from his back pocket and wiped his wide forehead.

"Don't worry, Mr. Warren, he'll turn up..."

"But I do worry, Tony. This is the first time he's been delinquent. Not like Mario."

Tony hunched his shoulders. "Slipped his mind. It happens."

Warren was still curious. "I hear he was last seen a week ago."

"Look, Mr. Warren, he'll be back. In the meantime, come for dinner tonight. A real Italian meal. And it's on the house."

"I'll see...not much for dining out. But if Mario shows, gimme a call."

Fred Warren had an uneasy feeling as he drove back to his office. While no one in Conway knew much about Mario Gambelli, a few facts were indisputable. He ran an upscale restaurant with the best Italian food in Madison Parish. He had hired a gourmet chef who managed the place and the two seemed to have shared secrets. But Fred Warren was most troubled by Mario's failure to pay the rent, something that had never happened before. While there was much he didn't know about his tenant, he knew first hand, Mario was meticulous, compulsive and responsible. Suddenly, the pattern had changed. As he crossed the bridge, Fred Warren wondered if he would see Mario Gambelli again.

∾

When Fred got back to his office he put in a call to Maude Harrington.

"Hello, Mr. Warren. A surprise hearing from you."

"I just got back from Gambelli's and wanted to make a suggestion."

"I'm willing to listen," Maude said.

264

"You probably know that I own Mario's building and the adjoining acreage."

"And you will be paid a fair price."

There was a long silence; Warren wondered if Maude was still on the line.

"During my afternoon visit at Gambelli's, I realized it would be a crime to demolish that building."

"Our plan is to lock the doors. Later, we'll figure something out."

"Why not reconfigure the building, take out the south wing, and make appropriate renovations. You need a restaurant for park visitors who would like to enjoy a good meal." Warren paused and tapped the ashes of his cigar into an ashtray. "It's my understanding the park and all the amenities will be on the south side of the highway. Gambelli's with its sweeping vista of the river would be an ideal location for a fine restaurant and when weather permits, dining on the veranda."

Maude wondered about Warren's proposal. Was there an ulterior motive? She could only think of one; he had built Gambelli's and it would pain him if it were neglected or defaced.

"Are you still there?" he asked.

"I'm thinking."

"Talk to your friends in the coalition."

"Who'll pay for this project?" Maude asked. "It's not covered by the grant."

"Warren Construction will do the work pro bono. Consider it my contribution to your fund-raising efforts."

Nonplussed, Maude took a few seconds to find her voice. "That's very generous Mr. Warren. I'll take it under advisement. Thanks for calling." Maude set the phone in its cradle and nibbled on her lower lip. Warren's proposal had its appeal. She would talk with Hal and Hannah; poor Adam had more important things on his mind.

Fred Warren leaned back in his chair and fingered his cigar. His conversation was a reminder that Mario was missing. Despite Tony Rizzo's cavalier answer, he felt something was wrong. He would turn the matter over to Randy Gilstrap if Mario failed to show.

Chapter 42

Tuesday, September 19ᵗʰ

Brett Shelly stopped at John Deere to pick up parts for a faulty tractor. When he got into the Ford pickup, he thought of Knox as he did so often. But this time there was an urgent need to see her. The hospital was less than a mile away and he remembered she managed the gift shop on Tuesdays. While their separation was painful, he had kept his word and maintained an arms-length relationship until she could decide to stay or to go. He had made the final decision to leave Conway and she needed to know. Time was running out. Brett knew his visit was inopportune since Knox had been emotionally distraught by Allison's death which further blurred the lines of her dilemma. But he loved her and hoped that despite the distractions she would choose to leave Conway... with him.

He lowered the window of the cab, a fine morning, not a cloud in the sky; the perfect backdrop for the arrival of autumn. He crossed Main and passed Buck's Cafe where an early lunch crowd had gathered, and headed down tree-lined Church Street and St. Paul's on the corner, into the gated visitor's lot of Saint Joseph's hospital. As he made his way to the portico, Brett tried to collect and organize his thoughts. He hoped to be persuasive; the showdown was only ten days away.

He felt unsettled as he entered through heavy glass doors. A hospital always made him feel uncomfortable. He wondered why? Was it a phobia? Was it simply an unfounded fear? He knew the feeling was irrational, since he had been an in-patient only once... as a child...a tonsillectomy. Maybe something untoward happened at the time that planted the seed of apprehension. If true, he was too young to remember what it might have been. And he knew the reason for his reaction was too obtuse to unravel. So why waste time thinking about it?

Brett crossed the lobby to the information desk. A woman with rheumy eyes fashioned a smile among the wrinkles. "May I help you?" she asked.

"I'm looking for the gift shop."

"Down the hall," she said, flipping a thumb over her bony shoulder.

The gift shop was a small congested room just off the lobby. Brett stood at the front window and watched Knox ring up a sale, marveling at the amount of merchandise in such limited space. There was no one else in the shop...at least no one he could see. He waited for the customer to leave before stepping inside.

Knox could not disguise her surprise. "Oh hi, Brett." She felt her heart skip a beat. "What brings you to town?"

Brett looked toward the back of the shop.

"There's no one here. Gloria's gone to lunch."

He leaned over the counter. "I have some news..."

She placed two fingers on his lips. "Shhh. Not here."

"But it's important," he insisted.

"The sandbar, at five o'clock."

Bret agreed, reluctantly. "I'll be there."

On the drive to the Plantation, Brett thought about Knox and the hard choice she faced, a defining moment in her life. Which path to take? He hoped with all his heart she would follow him. But should she decide to stay, he knew the reasons. Ben Hamilton was a decent man; he gave Knox security and treated her with respect. Yet, Brett knew Ben would never fulfill her deepest longings. He hoped the meeting at the sandbar would work in his favor. At least,

Knox had to choose; the clock was ticking. In ten days he would head west, joining the rodeo circuit in El Paso.

そ

Afternoon, same day

It had been five days since Fred Warren last talked with Joey Rizzo, so he went back to the restaurant. The lunch crowd was gone; the dining room empty. Fred went through the swinging door into the kitchen. The Chef, working at a small desk, stood up and extended his hand. "*Buon Pomeriggi*, Mr. Warren."

With the formalities out of the way, Warren got right to the point. "Have you seen or heard from Mario?"

Joey shook his head. "But he'll turn up...maybe tomorrow... maybe next week."

"How can you be sure?"

Joey shrugged. "It's happened before."

"Any idea where he might be?"

Joey turned his hands, palms up. "Mario is a very private person. He never tells us where he's going or for how long. When he left two weeks ago, he simply said 'goodbye.'" His arm arced across the kitchen where three other young helpers were preparing the evening's menu. "He knows we will take care of Gambelli's."

"Hope you're right but why all the secrecy?"

"As I said, Mario keeps everything inside. We only talk about the restaurant. Beyond these four walls, nothing."

"Thanks, anyway." Warren, confounded, turned to leave.

"Mr. Warren," called Joey. "Don't forget you've got a gourmet Italian meal on the house."

The words failed to register. Warren's mind was on other things.

Fred Warren climbed into his Lincoln and drove out of Gambelli's onto Highway 23. He crossed the bridge and turned right on South Grand, heading for the courthouse. He planned to report a "missing person" and drop it on the desk of Randy Gilstrap. The Sheriff may be impotent, Warren reasoned, but he had the authority to contact the Louisiana Bureau of Investigation and under certain circumstances, the FBI.

Warren parked in the back close to the enormous live oak. He sat for a few minutes wondering why he was doing this. It was not about the rent money (although that was a minor consideration). After all, he owned Gambelli's; Mario only leased the place. And once the grant money made its slow, winding way through bureaucratic channels from Washington to Conway, the coalition would buy Gambelli's and the adjacent property from him...not Mario. So why the concern, despite Tony Rizzo's assurances? Was it Mario's air of mystery? His frequent disappearances? Or rumors of some connection with clandestine government agencies? Warren shook his head, he wasn't sure. But if any of this were true, Mario might be in trouble...big-time trouble. The thought made Warren uneasy. He would report Mario as missing, something any responsible citizen would do.

✑

Brett dismounted close to the tree line. He watched her from a distance, the tender craving welled up within him. He knew it was real, he had never felt this way before...for anyone. Oh, there had been other women in his life, but those relationships were shallow and stunted, destined to fail. "Why is Knox different?" he asked himself. Brett shook his head; he didn't know. Words could not explain it. He figured, as he'd done before, it was simply a matter of the heart.

Knox had spread the quilt on a patch of dry sand and sat with both arms wrapped around her legs. The slant of the sun caused the water to sparkle, picking up highlights in her hair. She seemed pensive, looking downriver, lost in her own thoughts.

Brett tethered his horse to a sweet gum and followed a narrow, beaten-down path to the river. As he drew near, he removed his wide-brimmed rodeo hat and waved. When he got no response, he called out. "Hey there. You're early."

"Hi Brett, come on over."

Without removing his boots, he wadded the shallows to reach the sandbar. He dropped down on the quilt beside her.

"Come here often?" he asked.

"On occasion."

269

Brett looked in all directions. "It's like a grand cathedral without walls...peaceful."

"A place to sort out my problems."

Overhead, a Red-tail Hawk sailed by, graceful as a Prima ballerina. Brett followed the hawk until it disappeared beyond the bend of the river. He looked back at Knox and saw in her face, the beauty and symmetry of a bird in flight. He wanted to reach out and hold her. These past few months of separation had only stoked his fierce love for her.

Brett sat up and placed a hand on her knee as though he needed some physical connection.

Knox broke a long silence. "What's so important that it brought you into town?"

"I have news that affects us...you and me."

She looked at him; a worried look. "Well...?"

"I talked to Ben yesterday. He hired Guy Roberts, foreman of the Reynolds Plantation in Alabama. Mr. Reynolds, the family patriarch, is not well and plans to sell the place. Roberts, who thought he was out of a job, jumped at the opportunity. He'll be here Friday."

"But you won't leave until he's ready to take over...right?"

"Roberts spent ten years running Reynolds. Shouldn't be more than a week to acquaint him with the way we operate."

"That means you'll be leaving soon."

"The end of the month. That's what...ten days?"

"I can't stand the thought of you going away." Knox could not hide the disappointment, her eyes betrayed her.

"Look Knox, I love you with all my heart. I've asked before and I'll ask again: come with me. There's an exciting world out there," he said, letting an arm sweep the western skyline. "And we can be a part of it...together."

Knox looked away, across the water, a faraway look.

"I'll not ask again. The thought of leaving you haunts me, but I need to move on. Please come with me."

Brett grabbed his hat and stood up. He reached down and caressed her shoulder before walking away. There was nothing else to say. After mounting his horse, he looked toward the river, her solitary figure silhouetted against a glorious sunset.

He knew she was anxious, tormented by her indecision and emotionally drained. But he wasn't sure, even now, as he rode away, which road she would take. Whom would she choose? He could only hope and pray.

Chapter 43

It was almost dark when Ben left the boathouse on Black Bayou. Before leaving, he cleaned a stringer of fish and packed them in ice. He could see the look of delight on Lena's face; fried fish was soul food. Since the smell of fish made Knox's stomach lurch, Ben always released his catch, only saving enough for Lena and her family. It was a gift which cemented her loyalty. No one could pry Lena Jones away from Hamilton House, no matter how hard they tried.

Ben checked the clock on the dashboard: 6:30. The Sunday evening traffic was light; he should be home in two hours. During the drive, a pang of guilt ripped through his heart. Months ago, he had made Knox a promise: to be more attentive, to spend more time with her. But he knew he'd been inconsistent, old habits were hard to break. Ben could justify, at least to himself, the weekend spent on Black Bayou. It was his last fishing trip until spring. When he told Knox, she only turned and walked away, but he remembered that split-second look in her eyes. Her silence shouted louder than any expletive-laced rant. Now he must find a way to appease her; to let her know that he loved her and never wanted to lose her.

Ben was surprised when he turned into the long driveway. Hamilton House was half-hidden by an ink-black night. The porch was dark, no light from the windows. He stopped at the front of the house and hurried up the steps to the veranda; he would unload the car later. Ben unlocked the front door, stepped inside and turned on the lights. He called out; no one answered. He called again, louder; only an echo. He wondered if Knox was upstairs asleep. He took the steps two at a time until he reached the landing. He stopped and listened but heard nothing but his own heavy breathing. He turned on a table lamp and walked to the end of the hall. The door to the master bedroom was cracked. He pushed it open and called her name. Only silence. Ben crossed the master to the bathroom and hit the light switch. The bed was made, nothing had been disturbed. It was as if Lena had just cleaned the room. Where could she be? Worry rattled his brain. Ben canvassed the house. No overturned furniture or open drawers. The windows in each of the rooms were secure and all the doors were bolted. There were no signs of a forced entry.

Ben looked at his watch, almost nine o'clock. Had she gone for a walk or taken Missy for a ride, she would have left the house lights burning. Maybe she spent the night with a friend, but Ben knew that was unlikely. Could she have become ill and gone to the ER? Adam would know since he worked the weekend. While Ben had never felt "at home" in Hamilton House, tonight there was something more; an eerie feeling that caused him to shiver. He went down the stairs and into the kitchen. He poured himself a glass of milk and tried to decide on a course of action. Who should he call? What should he do?

He sat at the kitchen table and considered his options. When he placed his glass down, he saw the folded sheet of paper. A premonition caused his hand to tremble. He unfolded the note and held it up to the light.

Dear Ben,
I know you have tried to make our marriage work. Perhaps I am to blame...asking too much...more than you can give. Whatever the reason, I feel lonely and dissatisfied. Brett is leaving today and I am going with him. I have taken nothing

other than a few clothes. Your mother's diamond pendant and my engagement ring are in the top drawer of your dresser.

Take whatever legal steps are necessary and regain your freedom. I'll not be back even if I've made the wrong choice.

Please don't try to find me. I made the decision after months of deliberation. I believe it is best for the both of us. Move on with you life; those things that bring you pleasure and fulfillment. And find someone who will love you without limits.

You are a good man, Ben Hamilton; You gave me security and treated me with respect. For that I shall be forever grateful.

Fondly,

Knox

Ben stared at the note as if he had misread it. He sat silently and absorbed the full meaning of her message. He wiped his eyes; it was the first time he had cried since the day his mother died. He put the note in his pocket and flicked the switch on his way outside. On the veranda, a Luna moth danced fitfully around an overhead globe of light. Ben pressed against the cypress railing and looked ruefully into the moonless night. "What will I do without her?" he asked himself, half aloud. He'd never loved another woman other than Martha Hamilton. While many in Conway had made Knox uncomfortable from the day she arrived, Ben took pride in her presence and remained faithful beyond reproach. His heart ached; he wanted to talk with someone about this devastating loss. Maybe Hal Brady. Meanwhile, he had to unload the car, putting the chest in the garage's freezer. He wondered if Lena had an inkling or would she also be shocked and surprised? He would find out tomorrow.

Chapter 44

Saturday, October 7th

Maude awoke early and as usual had her coffee on the back porch. It was a pleasant morning; no need to turn on the ceiling fan. A cool breeze from across the bayou stirred the privacy hedge along the back of the lot. The sound of chattering birds among the trees, the unfolding of a new day. She sipped her coffee and focused on the red maple. This time Maude was sure the leaves had begun to turn; she saw clusters of burgundy and ocher and orange. But the serenity of early morning had been spoiled by the tragic events of the past few months. Now the unfathomable; Knox's decision to leave Ben and her unequivocal note of finality. It saddened Maude that the marriage failed; more so since once it seemed full of possibilities. Rather than dwell on things she could not change, Maude decided to dress and drive the Packard to her office. She needed to work on next week's edition of *The Review* and hoped it would move her thoughts out of the melancholy past and into a more constructive frame of mind.

Maude sat in front of her roll-top desk and stared at a blank sheet of paper in her old Royal typewriter. She wanted to pay tribute to those who made the coalition's victory possible. And especially to Grady Henry and Allison Swift, who like the martyrs of history, gave their most precious gift. But she couldn't find the words to express her heartfelt sentiments. Maude knew there were times when, inexplicably, she labored to craft a coherent sentence. "One of those days," she mumbled to the Royal. "I'll try again tomorrow."

Maude heard a knock at the door, relieved by the diversion. She looked through the sidelight and unlatched the bolt. Randy Gilstrap, in uniform, stood stoop-shouldered on the sidewalk.

"Randy, what are you doing here?"

"Morning, Miss Maude."

"C'mon in." She motioned toward the pillowed chair. "Coffee?"

"No thanks, I've had my quota." He put his Stetson on his knee as if it were a hat rack.

Maude sat across from him. "What brings you out so early?"

The Sheriff lowered his head. "I'm real sorry 'bout Ms. Swift. No one seems to know for sure who's responsible."

"Tony Caruso," Maude said as if it were an indisputable fact.

Randy looked up. "Ma'am?"

"Caruso, the Mafia Boss. It's really no mystery."

Maude spoke with an assuredness that surprised the Sheriff.

"Common sense, Randy. Caruso doesn't like the taste of defeat. First it was Preacher, gunned down at Captain Joe's fishing camp on Lake Darbonne. Then Allison was set up and run off the mountain; a well-executed act of pure evil." Maude removed her glasses and wiped them with a Kleenex. "You know, Randy, the feds are gearing up for an all out war with the Mafia. Even the U.S. Senate is sticking its nose into the Mob's dirty laundry. But of all the families, Tony Caruso, will be the toughest to bring down. He is well-organized, with politicians in his pocket and policemen on the payroll, including Frank "King" Clancy, the corrupt sheriff of Jefferson Parish."

"Yeah, that parish is a hotbed of gambling," Randy added.

Maude nodded. "While Caruso has little formal education, he is the sharpest knife in the drawer; brighter than Lucky Luciano, Frank Costello, Meyer Lansky...the list goes on and on."

Randy looked at his watch. "Guess that's a reminder...why I stopped by."

Maude replaced the glasses on her nose, hoping it might be newsworthy.

"A couple of weeks ago, Mr. Warren came by my office and filed a missing persons report."

It was Maude's turn to show surprise. "Who in the world...?"

"Mario Gambelli."

"I heard he was moving to Leesville and opening a restaurant and beer garden."

"Yes'um, your right. He signed his lease on September 7th; last seen at his restaurant two days later."

"'Know your enemy'. The coalition took that war-time slogan to heart and we learned all we could about Markham, Waters... and Gambelli. But I was always curious about Mario, the way he disappeared for weeks at a time. He left his chef in charge and the restaurant never missed a beat."

Randy pulled a telegram from his back pocket and passed it to Maude. "After Mr. Warren's visit, I called Captain Mark Simpson at the State Bureau of Investigation and asked him to check it out." The Sheriff retrieved his hat and fidgeted with the brim. "Before I turned around, the FBI and CIA were in the mix." He straightened up, a toothy smile bent his lips. "Sure glad I punted."

"What's this got to do with me?"

"It will be a great story for *The Review*. A headliner. Double your circulation." With his small stubby hands, Randy urged her on. "Go ahead, read it."

Maude held the telegram to catch the light from the window. She read aloud, softly:

Sheriff Randy Gilstrap,

I was at my desk in the Bureau's office in Baton Rouge, when I received a call from airport security in Alexandria. The complaint of a foul odor led them to a black '48 Camaro in the back of the parking lot. Security discovered a body in the trunk of the car. They cordoned off the area and notified the police. The body, badly decomposed, went directly to the city morgue and later identified by dental records as that of Mario Gambelli. There were two entry wounds in the chest. No fingerprints; the car was clean. Awaiting a full autopsy. Thanks for giving us jurisdiction. But the State Bureau has been told to step aside. The Feds have usurped the Investigation. Thought you'd like to know. Regards, Capt. Mark Simpson

Maude folded the telegram and handed it to Randy. "I think even Markham and Waters wondered about Mario. Where did he come from? What about his family? Was there a woman in his life? And those periods in which he disappeared...where did he go?" Maude gave Randy a puzzled look. "Think the Feds have made a connection?"

"Caruso?"

"Possible."

"Mario was Italian, maybe Sicilian."

Maude conceded the possibility. But there were others. Could it have been personal: an argument out of control, a jealous lover, a case of mistaken identity, or simply wrong place, wrong time? She quickly dismissed her list when she reminded herself that federal authorities were involved. No plausible reason for their presence unless Mario worked for one of the Agencies or was a subject of interest.

Randy thought he could hear the wheels spinning in her head. "Well, what's your best guess?"

"I like your take."

"Caruso?"

Maude nodded. "But for a different reason."

Randy could not wipe the puzzled look from his face. He rearranged himself in the chair and replaced the Stetson on his knee. "So you don't believe Mario worked for the Mob?"

"I'll bet a hundred bucks that Gambelli worked undercover for the good guys, probably the FBI. The Kefauver Committee began its investigation of the Mafia in May. It makes sense that the government could obtain valuable information by infiltrating Caruso's inner circle. Mario was Italian and had the additional cover, along with Markham and Waters, of providing a base for Caruso's expansion into North Louisiana and Central Arkansas. In addition, the take-down had all the marking of the Mafia...

body stashed in the trunk of Mario's car and left in the airport parking lot, more than a hundred miles as the crow flies, from New Orleans. No fingerprints; no witnesses; no evidence. In my opinion, that's Tony Caruso's signature."

"Miss Maude, you shoulda been a cop."

"Wrong gender."

The Sheriff seemed bemused.

"I don't think J. Edgar's fond of women. It'll be a cold day in hell before a pretty face will carry the badge."

"Well, you'd get my vote, Miss Maude." The Sheriff stood and turned to leave.

"Thanks for the vote of confidence, Randy...and for the story."

He put on his Stetson and tipped it back. "By the way, I've submitted my resignation to the Police Jury effective year end. Billy Ray King, one of my Deputies can handle the job until the next election."

Maude knew the answer before asking the question. "So what's next?"

"Shorty needs some help. The business is growing and he's not getting any younger." Randy dropped his chin, looked at the floor. "I'm not real proud of my record as Sheriff, but I plan to bust my butt and make City Wide Septic Tank Service bigger and better than ever."

Maude stood at the window and watched him cross the street and get into the cruiser. She was sure he'd made the right decision. His dishonorable dealings with Markham and Waters tainted his reputation and seriously jeopardized any chance of reelection. And Maude knew his public apology would not assuage the guilt that besieged him. Perhaps he could find restitution in his father's business and commitment to some charitable cause. Usually, others will forgive those whose mea culpa are sincere, then take steps to fulfill the promise. Randy had a good heart and she believed he would be successful at City Wide.

Traffic had picked up. Conway was awake and beginning to stir. Maude made a pot of coffee, filled her cup and returned to the roll-top desk. Reenergized, she started to type.

Chapter 45

Maude had made a good start on the tribute to Grady Henry and Allison Swift, along with the other heroes and heroines that made the crusade a success. After Randy's visit, it was as if the dam broke and the words spilled out. Maude felt those names should be engraved in Georgia marble or on a bronze plaque and placed in the park near the dedicated fountain. It was important for future generations to know of those whose sacrifice had made Conway a better and safer place to live and work and raise its children. It was a costly battle; the legacy should not be forgotten.

Some might say it was a Pyrrhic victory but Maude knew otherwise. Costly, yes, but the goodness that will flow from it was beyond measure. It had sweetened the air like spring flowers and softened the heart of a town. For Maude, *uplifting* was the word that best described the successful campaign.

She turned her chair around and surveyed the book shelves that filled two walls of the office. Maude had been a student of history from a very young age; a child of the Reconstruction which stoked her love of the past.

While there were many lessons to be learned, one observation was fundamental: there have been good and evil forces in the

281

world since man first appeared on life's inchoate stage. The duality has always been a part of the human condition. A vignette had just played out in the small town of Conway. And as in the past, doing *the right thing* carried a huge price tag; higher than she had ever considered. That's what Maude wanted to print in next week's *Review.*

The gangster-style murder of Mario Gambelli would make an eye-popping headline, but it had to wait until she could verify Randy's account and get additional facts from her "sources." She would call her friend, Captain Wheeler at the State Patrol office in Baton Rouge. She preferred to delay and print an accurate, compelling news story rather than release an account with sketchy details and unnamed informants. Nor did she want a sensational "cloak and dagger" expose to overshadow her editorial. Maude had never resorted to "yellow journalism" and would not start now. She had no interest in emulating the style and substance of a tabloid like the *Inquirer* or the *New York Daily News.*

Maude stood and stretched. Steady on her feet, she walked to the kitchenette at the back of the office, poured herself a cup of coffee and tried to refocus on next week's editorial. But a loud voice from the front caused her to flinch. She had failed to lock the door after Randy left the office.

"Hello! Anybody home?"

She peeked down the short hall, relieved to see a familiar face. "Oh, Adam. I'll be there in a minute." She filled a second mug and carried it to her office.

She handed Adam his coffee and gave him a peck on the cheek. "I don't like to drink alone," she chuckled.

"Hope I didn't frighten you."

"No, I'm fine. Glad you came by."

"Just left the hospital and caught the light in your window. A little surprised, Saturday and all. I figured it was you, so I stopped by with some news."

Maude placed her coffee next to the Royal and sat down, a cushion at her back. "I hope it's good news for a change."

Adam plopped in the pillowed chair and cupped his mug with both hands. "It's personal, a decision I've made."

It had been six weeks since Caruso's thugs pushed Allison off the mountain. Maude was pleased that Adam appeared brighter, more animated. She was sure the inexorable hands of time had helped. Maude sipped her coffee, anxious to hear Adam's disclosure.

Adam eased forward, his eyes on Maude's wintry face. "I'm leaving Conway."

"You can't be serious," she said.

"I've talked with Dr. Lawrence Kyle, chief of medicine at Tulane, about a two-year fellowship. When I was there, almost a decade ago, I applied for a research grant which never materialized. It's a dream I'd like to pursue."

"So you think moving to New Orleans will be salutary?"

Adam waved at the street beyond the window. "Allison shadows me everywhere, as if she has become my guardian angel. At home, I see her ghost-like face in every room and at times, I even hear her voice." Adam stopped and held up a hand. "I know...I know it sounds loony, but the house is full of memories...too many reminders. Even Hal Brady, whom I've clung to like a drowning man, thought a change of scenery was a good idea."

Maude's eyes lost their luster. The thought of losing Adam made her heart ache. "What about Robin?"

"She'll stay with Ruth until school is out. Then they'll join me in New Orleans."

Maude had formed a deep and abiding relationship with Adam. His leaving filled her with an inexpressible sadness. She wiped her eyes with a Kleenex and moved uneasily in her chair. "Will you be here Christmas?"

"My timing is terrible but I'll stay until we recruit my replacement. Ben has already made some inquiries."

"How is Ben?" she asked.

"Devastated. But you know Ben...he puts up a good front."

Maude shook her head, baffled. "Why in the world would Knox leave so much behind for an uncertain future with Brett Shelly? I don't get it."

"Ben was good to her but he couldn't provide the things she needed most."

"Which were...?"

"More of his time and affection. I'm sure Ben loves her, but like his father, couldn't express his feelings. Knox felt isolated in that big house, Jake's caretaker, while Ben spent most of his free weekends fishing or camouflaged in a deer stand. For Ben it was a diversion from the stress of a busy practice, but he excluded Knox from a huge part of his life."

"I had no idea," Maude confessed.

"Allison told me months ago that the marriage was in trouble. When I challenged her, she said it was just a woman's intuition."

"I can't believe we've lost both of them." A long silence hung over the room like a morning fog.

"I have other news of interest," Adam said.

Maude held a hand to her ear. "I'm curious, of course."

"Ben plans to sell the plantation and move into town."

Maude was aware of the rift that had occurred between father and son, one that the years could not repair. She also knew that Ben surrendered any affection for the plantation the day that Martha Hamilton died. (The sycamore tree may have been an exception.) So the rationale for his decision was easy to understand. Ben was never comfortable in the big house nor did he want to be a 'gentleman farmer.' "I'm not surprised," Maude said. "He would have made the decision a long time ago had it not been for Jake. While their relationship was strained, even abrasive at times, I'm sure he stayed out of respect and a feeling of fealty."

"I think if Knox were here, Ben would have kept the house," Adam added. "He knew Shelly was leaving and had hired a new foreman. But he wrong-headedly believed the plantation gave Knox security and bolstered her self-esteem, perhaps paring his failure to meet her deeper needs." Adam uncrossed his legs and shifted his position in the pillowed chair. "Ben never understood that Knox had no filial attachment to Hamilton House; something she made clear, to his shock and dismay, the night he found the note on the kitchen table."

"I was fond of Knox," Maude said. "Her leaving without a goodbye...well, it makes me sad. And I'd bet the ranch, she won't be back."

Adam looked out the window. "Nor will Allison."

Maude sat quietly, wondering whether Knox would ever find happiness. Could Brett succeed where Ben had failed? While Maude had no idea of their whereabouts, she silently wished them well. Knox was gone and if the avatar of resolve wrote that note, she would not be back. It was irony Maude thought, how often separation brings closure to a relationship.

Adam sprang to his feet and placed his cup on the desktop. "Need to get moving."

"What's the hurry?"

"I promised Ruth I'd join them for lunch."

"By the way, you're a lucky guy to have a mother who has taken Robin under her roof."

Adam shook his head abstractly. "What would I have done without her?"

Maude managed to lift herself from the chair and threw her arms around him, a grandmotherly hug. "You'll be missed but I understand your leaving. Just don't forget we're here; we want to stay connected. And you must see Allison's fountain, the centerpiece of the park."

"Don't worry. Conway will always have a special place in my heart. And who knows...after my fellowship, I may come back... that is, if Ben will have me."

"Don't wait too long. My clock is ticking," she said with a glint in her eyes.

Adam stopped at the door and looked back. "As your physician, I know you inside and out and you're good for a hundred."

"I hope you're right. Someone's got to run this damn newspaper."

Chapter 46

Sunday, October 8th

Frank Markham had the Shamrock all to himself. He stood at the office window, a deer scampered across the pasture and into the woods. The skies had turned sullen and gray, thunder rumbled in the distance. Gusts of wind caused dust to swirl like tiny twisters off the service road. Frank thought the gloomy afternoon and the prospect of an impending storm were the perfect backdrop for the tavern's demise and his unsettled future.

He lit a cigarette and retuned to the swivel behind his desk. Frank had seen the appraisals. He knew the amount of the check which he would soon receive. But where would he go? Maybe a trip to Leesville. The "Italian Shadow", stuffed in the trunk of a car, gunshots to the chest, was no longer interested. Markham thought he might take advantage of Mario's misfortune; a new lease waited to be signed.

Leesville…a possibility? Maybe, maybe not. Mario had failed to mention that central Louisiana is hotter'n hell; the summers are suffocating. Frank let his mind run free, consider the possibilities. Why not take a trip to a Florida beach, soak up some sun, guzzle a few cold beers and enjoy the bikini-clad scenery? Or Alaska, the new frontier; he had read the story in National Geographic.

Hunting moose and caribou had its appeal. But the thought made Markham shiver; snow and ice, colder than the freezer in old man Duffy's Butcher Shop. He dismissed the option summarily. Money was not an issue; he could go anywhere he chose; relax and plan his future.

A Florida vacation reminded him of his mother whom he had not seen for fifteen years. He felt a pang of remorse for his neglect. He remembered her letter from Boynton Beach earlier in the year. Should he make the trip to Florida? Visit the pale green house with the pink flamingos? The Reverend Hardeman might be a problem. Frank had never forgiven him; the draconian rules and his stuff-it-down-your-throat religious ranting. Frank had wondered how his mother had survived, living in the same house and sharing the same bed, with that holier-than-thou prick. For her sake, he would try and avoid a confrontation. But he would enjoy nothing more than to kick Hardeman's sorry ass across South Ocean Blvd. into the Atlantic.

He pulled the swivel close to the desk and ran a total on last night's receivables. Business was booming, a raucous Saturday crowd jammed the tavern. Markham could only look at the numbers and shake his head. The thought of closing the Shamrock made the hairs on his neck bristle. He slammed his fist hard against the desk, papers flying, the girlie calendar jarred askew. "Self-righteous bastards," he shouted to an empty office. Markham massaged his forehead vigorously and let the anger simmer down. He quickly regained his composure. Despite the fiery outburst, he had accepted with mortification the final verdict. The voters of Conway had spoken and there was not a goddamn thing he could do about it.

He put the money in a cigar box and locked it in a desk drawer. Tomorrow he would make a deposit at the Central Bank. As he reached for the pack of cigarettes, he saw the bald head of Ernie Waters pass the office window. "C'mon in, it's open!"

Ernie dragged the folding chair close to the desk and sat down with his long legs extended, his arms folded. "A storm's brewing."

"I appreciate the weather report." Frank said facetiously. He pointed toward the window; rain had begun to splatter the glass.

Ernie shrugged. "You pissed at somebody?"

"Yeah, the do-gooders that shut us down." He lit his cigarette and tossed the pack across the desk.

"Caruso copped out. Otherwise, it woulda been a different story."

Frank shook his head dubiously. "I'm not sure that even Caruso could have changed the scorecard."

"Well, it's time to make other plans. I figure six more weeks before they lock the doors."

Ernie had finally accepted the inevitable. (Something Markham had done after the Pappas' phone call.) He had organized the miscreants that burned the revival tent; a final (and feeble) attempt to frighten the voters of Conway. He felt helpless, his hands tied, unable to make a difference. Despite his own molten anger, he needed to consider life after the Ale House. He fingered a cigarette from the pack and snapped his lighter.

"I'm thinking a vacation in South Florida. You know…plenty of sunshine and sandy beaches." Frank let the image hang for a moment before his mind's eye. "What better way to spend the winter?"

"Sounds sweet, if you've got the dough."

Frank flashed his teeth yellow. "Perfect place to make a long-term plan, sipping a cold beer in the shade of a beach umbrella while bikini babes lather their skin with lotion and promenade across the beach as if it were the runway of a Christian Dior fashion show."

"Don't know the name," Ernie said.

Frank waved him off. "So why the visit?"

Ernie leaned forward, sharp elbows on his knees. "I've made a decision."

"Let's hear it."

Ernie lowered his voice as if it were some well-kept secret. "I'm moving to Dossier City and open up a bar and grill with pool tables upfront and slots in the back room."

Frank was not surprised. He knew that Ernie had owned and operated a pool hall in Conway, a very profitable business during the war, until the Defense Department closed the air base. In a matter of months, he'd sold the pool hall, signed a lease with Fred Warren and started construction in West Conway on the Ale House.

"Smart move. You've been there before. And I understand Dossier is wide open."

"The slots may be a little risky, but if you know the right people..."

"Under the table?" Frank interrupted.

"Something like that." Ernie's face morphed into a frown. "I hope the Mafia don't get a whiff of the deal. Caruso might change his time table."

Frank shook his hand as if he were erasing a blackboard. "Don't matter who's running the slots, when Caruso's ready he'll cut a deal or more likely, muscle his way in and take control."

"Only talked to a 'runner'. Coupla layers between him and the real operators."

Ernie moved to the window. The rain fell in torrents; the pasture was barely visible. He leaned on the frame and wondered if he'd made the right decision. The bar and pool room were a given; he could run them blindfolded. But the slots were the *gravy*. A downside? Absolutely. The resolve of a few lawmakers in Baton Rouge to enforce anti-gambling laws; more likely, the intrusion of Caruso and his cut-throat capos.

Frank moved up in the swivel and lit another Camel, sending a cloud of smoke across the desk. He noticed Ernie staring out the window, speechless.

"Too bad about Mario," Frank said, finally.

"Yeah, he must've pissed off somebody...big time."

"It's all rumor, but I heard he was undercover...CIA."

Ernie's eyes widened. "The little Wop worked for the Feds?"

"The tavern was only a cover."

"You kiddin' me?" Ernie shook his head. While he had his own doubts about Mario, it was still hard to fathom.

"The federal government has decided to clean up organized crime. Mario's job, as I understand it, was to infiltrate Caruso's inner circle and feed information to the Feds. Musta made a mistake; ended up in the trunk of his car, shot in the chest."

Ernie stared out the window at the driving rain; a look of incredulity on his unshaven face. It took him a few minutes to process the information. "I'll be damned; so Caruso got him?"

"Probably...but they'll never prove it." Frank crushed the cigarette on the inside of the metal wastebasket.

Ernie came back and slumped in his chair. "Maybe you and me got lucky. If we'd done business with Caruso…well, cross him once and end up in the trunk of your car or in that swamp on Highway 90 with the snakes and alligators."

Frank thought about Mario and his nagging suspicion that Gambelli was something other than he appeared to be. A man about whom he knew nothing: the Bellini paintings, his nose in a book, strange disappearances …not the profile of a hard working, butt-busting tavern owner. Now the picture was clear and explained Mario's bizarre behavior.

"At the time it sounded like a damn good idea…I mean working with Caruso." Ernie rubbed the bump of cartilage in his long neck. "Guess I'm glad he bailed out."

"Well, we hoped he'd frighten the voters of Conway. But I'm convinced the referendum would've passed even with Caruso in the game."

Ernie bounced out of his chair. "Gotta go."

Markham coughed violently. He searched for the pack of cigarettes hidden beneath the scatter of papers.

Ernie looked at the window as lightning bolted through gunmetal skies. "How 'bout a ride?"

"Sorry, got work to do." He waved an arm across his cluttered desk.

"Man, it's a fucking deluge." He pulled the grimy baseball hat from the back pocket of his rumpled khakis.

"You won't drown. Besides you need the exercise."

"C'mon, Frank. Do me a favor."

"The last time I checked, I don't owe you no favor."

Ernie felt the heat rise in his neck, his cheeks color. He grabbed the folding chair and sent it skimming across linoleum, banging into the far wall. He glared at Markham with belligerent eyes, darted for the door and threw it open. "Thanks, for nothing, asshole," he screamed and disappeared into the rain.

Frank closed the door, mopped up the water with a couple of old towels and moved to the window. He caught a glimpse of Ernie Waters, shoulders bent, cap low on his head, heading for the woods and the path that led to the Ale House. He remembered their high school days. Ernie had always had a short fuse. He was a trouble maker. Nothing had changed. It was a miracle the two of them had avoided a nasty confrontation. But once again, Frank had shown restraint.

He checked the service road, but the heavy rain obscured his view. Markham could not suppress his pleasure, thinking of Waters trundling through the woods, soaked to the bone. Since Dossier City was not in his plans, he would never see Waters and that bald head or bobbing Adam's apple again. It was a pleasant thought, the best he's had all day.

Chapter 47

Six months later

Adam's small office on the fourth floor of the Research Building overlooked a parking lot and a tree-lined side street. He opened the casement window and welcomed the arrival of spring. The air was fresh, invigorating. At the entrance of the asphalt lot, forsythia intertwined their golden strands around the wooden gate.

He remembered the day he arrived two months ago. It was raining and a frigid wind swept off Lake Pontchartrain. Pedestrians, chilled to the bone, dashed into stores and restaurants to escape the bitter cold. Visitors chose the Gray Line Tour rather than walking the narrow streets of the French Quarter with the wind whistling in their ears. No mimes or musicians in front of the Saint Louis Cathedral; no artists peddling their wares around Jackson Square. Beyond the levee, the mighty Mississippi, defied the weather; cargo-laden barges moving upriver, freighters and cruise ships steaming out to the Gulf.

Adam's groaned when he entered his apartment in the Garden District with its faulty heating system. It was a nostalgic reminder of hearth and home: Allison stoking the fireplace, the familiar smell of wood-smoke and the crackle of burning logs. He had taken the St. Charles Avenue trolley from the medical center but the icy drafts had finalized his decision to abandon the trolley and wait for warmer weather. As a last resort, he would go to Maison Blanche on Canal Street and buy a London Fog overcoat with fur lining. Brrrr... he was sure New Orleans had experienced the coldest winter on record.

Adam returned to his desk and opened a spiral notebook. He reread the log from the previous week and jotted down his schedule for the day. He placed a star beside the two o'clock appointment, the time to meet Tony Caruso unannounced. Adam sipped his coffee and wondered if he should cancel the plan. He had called Alex Cleary at the local FBI office and apprised him of his intention. Adam remembered the agent's advice: "Reconsider. Caruso is volatile and dangerous. Only a fool or a madman would meet him on his own turf." But Adam felt compelled to confront Caruso...face to face.

A knock on the door jam interrupted his train of thought. "Hello, Adam. Could I bum a cup of coffee."

"Oh, hi Ben. Come in."

Ben dropped into a chair beside the desk.

"What brings you to New Orleans?" Adam asked.

"A seminar...infectious diseases...at the Monteleone."

"Nice hotel." Adam rolled his chair to a hotplate which rested on a small table. He poured coffee into a Styrofoam cup. "Still take it black?"

Ben nodded. "How're you doing?"

"A little better. The memories are there, but getting away has helped."

"I noticed a 'for sale' sign in front of your mother's house."

Adam explained that Ruth and Robin would join him at the end of the school year. And he'd bought a modest, three-bedroom ranch in Metairie; ample room for the three of them. There was little news since he had only been in New Orleans a short time. Other than the galactic weather, he had no other complaints.

Ben put his cup on the desk and moved to the edge of his chair. "All the folks in Conway hope to see you again, once you're finished here."

"I do miss my friends." He unzipped the tobacco pouch and filled the bowl of his pipe. "Have you heard from Knox?"

"Not a word. But she said as much in the note; the one I found on the kitchen table." Ben looked dispirited at the floor. "I want her back. There is so much I have to say. Maybe a miracle…"

"Perhaps it's better to accept your lot and move on with your life." Adam paused and lit his pipe. "That's what I'm trying to do."

Ben brought his eyes back to his friend. "You know, sometimes I think that recovery from divorce is more difficult than…say, a loss by illness or accident. Does that surprise you?"

Adam only shrugged.

"There is finality and dignity in death which permits closure, allows one to grieve; buoyed by the consolation of friends and family, then to begin again. But my wound is forever open by wishing and waiting. I look for her at every turn, hoping she'll come home."

"I don't know, Ben. No one can measure the magnitude of another man's loss or the depth of his despair."

Ben's neck sagged, chin against chest. "I have so many regrets…" His voice faded, letting the sentence hang.

With a start, Ben stood and looked at his watch. "I'd better go. Don't wanta miss the lecture on exotic parasites?"

"Yeah, you never know when you may run into a tape worm."

"It'll be the first time." Their laughter broke the somber mood.

"When you're home, please give Maude and the gang my regards."

"You bet…and don't forget…your office is vacant."

಄

Same Day

Adam's interview with Grace Henderson had been a formality. He found her attractive, in her late-twenties, a master's degree in microbiology. Grace had accepted Dr. Kyle's request to work with Adam during his tenure at Tulane. After the first few weeks, Adam gave her high marks; she was bright, congenial and committed to the research protocol. He sent a note of appreciation to Dr. Kyle's office.

Adam and Grace had lunch in the cafeteria and chose a table in the far corner of the room. Adam took a few bites of his salad before putting his folk down and pushing his tray aside.

"Something wrong?" Grace asked.

Adam shook his head. "But I need a favor."

"Sure. Anything."

"I have a meeting this afternoon…"

"A meeting?"

"Nothing to do with the medical center and I'd rather not go into specifics. The less you know…"

"Sounds awfully secretive." She gave him a curious look.

"Believe me, it's better that way."

Grace demurred. "Okay, you mentioned a favor."

Adam retrieved a piece of paper from his shirt pocket and passed it across the table. "If I'm not back by five o'clock, call that number. Alex Cleary is with the local office of the FBI."

He saw the apprehension in her eyes. "I plan to be back; just an insurance policy."

"It's none of my business, Dr. Swift, but I wish you'd tell me what's going on." Her voice carried a nervous edge.

"When I get back, I'll tell you the whole story."

She put the slip of paper in the pocket of her lab coat. "It sounds scary…"

Adam drained his cup of coffee, pushed back from the table. "I've spoken with Mr. Cleary and he knows about my meeting."

Grace reached across her tray and placed a hand on his. "Please be careful." There was concern in her engaging blue eyes.

For the first time in six months, Adam felt something stir inside; maybe the feeling was a good thing.

Epilogue

Same Day.

A little after two o'clock Adam turned right on Highway 90. He hoped bright sunshine and blue skies were good omens. As he drove out of the city, Adam felt his pulse quicken, his heartbeat more forceful. He crossed the river on the Huey P. Long Bridge into Jefferson Parish. He knew the mission carried some risk; Alex Cleary had said as much. Foolhardy, perhaps, but an inner voice, maybe his conscience, enabled him.

Adam had no trouble spotting the freshly painted Willswood Tavern. He turned into the paved drive and parked near the main entrance. There were no other cars in the front, not unusual for the time of day. He assumed Caruso and his minions parked their Lincoln's with tinted windows behind the tavern.

Adam stood beside the open door of his car and looked around. The swamp was closer to the property than he had imagined. He had heard stories; it was the place Caruso's goons dropped the bodies. A weathered dock extended into the slimy water; a fishing boat with an outboard motor was tethered to a piling. The backyard of Bermuda grass was emerald green and spring flowers grew in profusion. Adam marveled at the juxtaposition: a verdant lawn with its colorful gardens and the dark, forbidding swamp. He thought Hal Brady would find the perfect metaphor for a Sunday sermon were he standing here.

Adam felt a rush of adrenaline as he opened the front door and stepped inside. A flash of memory: the sixth grade, a bundle of nerves, waiting to fight Harry Profit, the school bully. He remembered his bloody nose; this time he hoped for a happier ending.

The dining room was empty; tables were set for the evening diners. Behind the bar, a hunk of a man put down the towel and hung over the railing. "Whata you want? We're closed till five," he said sharply.

Adam had not expected a hospitable reception, but he had a message to deliver and hoped to do it with impunity. He took a deep breath and marched up to the bar.

The name tag of this bear-of-a man was pinned to his black vest. Adam looked him straight in the eye and said, "Gino, my name is Adam Swift, glad to meet you." He extended his hand which the bartender ignored.

"Whata you want?" Gino had turned up the volume.

"I'd like to speak with Mr. Caruso." Adam pointed to the back of the room. "I hear voices so I assume he's in his office."

"He don't like uninvited visitors." Gino pulled a .38 from his belt and placed it in front of him. "Understand what I'm saying? Outta here!"

Adam stood perfectly still, both hands on the railing, in clear view. "Please ask Mr. Caruso to speak with me. I'll only take a few minutes of his time. I have a message I'm sure he wants to hear?"

Gino picked up the gun. "Get the hell outta here," he shouted, loud enough to rattle the glasses. Adam raised his hands in surrender and stepped away from the bar.

A door in the back opened. "What's the problem, Gino?"

"This crazy fool just wandered in. Wants to talk with the Boss."

While vetting Tony Caruso and his Organization, Adam learned that the Don had two sons; Joey, the youngest, was a neurosurgical resident at Duke. Adam thought a telephone conversation with Joey Caruso might serve as an entrée to the father. He had constructed a story, a fictional third party, which captured Joey's interest and served Adam's purpose.

"I'm a doctor at the Medical Center. And I have news of Joey."

Johnny Pappas gave Gino a withering look. "Put that thing away."

The Greek asked Adam to stand and remove his coat. He patted him down and removed his wallet. He checked his driver's license, then returned the wallet. "I apologize, but we can't be too careful." Johnny smiled at the memory: "Ole Huey was shot by a doctor...in the State Capitol...broad daylight."

"I understand," Adam said calmly.

"Care for a drink?"

"No thanks."

"Follow me."

"Smart ass. Thinks he runs this place," Gino growled out of earshot.

❧

Johnny Pappas led Adam to the Don's office. "Stay here until I speak with Mr. Caruso." He stepped inside and closed the door.

Adam glanced over his shoulder, Gino staring "daggers" at his back. If looks could kill… oh well, he figured he'd cleared the first hurdle.

Pappas kept him waiting. Adam hoped he had called the Medical Center. Kyle's office would verify his position as a research fellow attached to the Department of Medicine. He thought that would satisfy any misgivings that Pappas might have. And he knew the mention of Joey's name would get Caruso's attention.

The door swung open and Pappas motioned him inside. Tony Caruso sat behind a large mahogany desk smoking a cigar. Since no one offered a chair, Adam stood in front of the desk. He saw dark eyes and thick black hair, neatly trimmed, but the swarthy face was inscrutable. Short and stocky, this stub of a man had more influence and power than Earl Long, a two-term Governor of Louisiana. And of course, Adam had heard of the enormous cash flow generated by Caruso's illegal activities, whose tentacles reached beyond state lines, into East Texas and along the Gulf coast of Mississippi.

Adam folded his arms to hide the tremor and with effort, straightened his shoulders. He looked at Johnny Pappas, leaning beside the window; the Greek nodded.

"Mr. Caruso, I have two messages and the first is from Joey."

"You talked to Joey?" Adam *had* his attention.

"A few nights ago."

Caruso put the cigar aside, elbows on the desk, wanting to hear more.

"Before we ended our conversation, he asked me to give you and his mother, Anna, his love and best wishes."

Caruso cast his eyes on the sun-splashed window, a wistful look. "I'm afraid I've lost my son."

Adam could see Caruso, though he ran a violent business, cared for his family; a splinter of light in a dungeon of darkness. "You may have heard that he'll complete his residence in two years and already he's being heavily recruited."

"Yeah, I guess everyone should have a doctor in the family," he said without inflection.

"I met Joey by chance, while attending a meeting at Duke. He is wildly popular and highly regarded by his associates and that should make you proud."

Caruso waved his hand; a signal to close the subject. He relit his cigar and rocked back in his chair. "What else? Make it quick," he snapped.

Adam knew the mention of Joey afforded some protection and while the story had softened him for the moment, the image was fleeting. In front of him now, he saw a baleful Tony Caruso who would drop you deep in the swamp at the first sign of intrusion or betrayal or duplicity...inside or outside the Organization.

Adam cleared his throat and dropped his arms to his side. "Mr. Caruso, does the name Allison Swift mean anything to you?" He saw Pappas stir out of the corner of his eye.

The Don swatted the air with his hand as if the question was an annoyance. "You're time is up. Now get the hell out of here before Gino takes you for a boat ride."

Adam felt the chill but stood firm. "I need to leave the rest of the message."

Caruso half-stood, pitched forward on the desk. "I'm not interested in your stupid message." His angry invective rocked the room. He turned to Pappas and roared, "Throw him outta here!"

Adam flinched. But before anyone moved, Adam held up his hand, a stop signal. "Mr. Caruso, do you know the name...Alex Cleary?"

Caruso dropped back in his chair but offered no answer.

"I believe you've met Mr. Cleary. Well, he knows I'm here and he's expecting me back by four o'clock." Adam noticed that Johnny Pappas had stepped back toward the window. Caruso stroked his chin, factoring the information.

"I am here to clear my conscience, Mr. Caruso. Allison Swift was my wife. Law enforcement believes you are responsible for her death. While you'll never be charged, you need to know that I know and wonder why? Like Joey, she was young and attractive and loved her family. So what was the point?"

Caruso motioned vigorously to Johnny Pappas. "Get this liar outta here," he screamed.

. "I'm leaving, Mr. Caruso." Adam pulled a slip of paper from his shirt pocket and placed it on the desk. "A gift, for you." He waved to Johnny Pappas and left the office.

Caruso looked at the note; one word, in large block letters: *FORGIVENESS*. He wadded the note heatedly and tossed it into the wastebasket.

When Adam passed the bar, Gino gave him a menacing look. He ignored the threat and hurried out of the Willswood Tavern into the bright sunshine. Mission accomplished.

On the drive back to New Orleans, Adam reviewed his meeting with Tony Caruso. He felt the confrontation with the Mafia Boss brought closure, at least to the degree possible. He knew that he could not carry a vendetta. Nor could Arkansas Law Enforcement bring criminal charges, since there were no witnesses and the truck that pushed Allison over the edge of the mountain had been crushed and buried in some out-of-the-way junk yard. He wondered if his note would create a scintilla of remorse but Adam knew that was wishful thinking. *Forgiveness* was a meaningless word to a man without conscience or compunction. But the note was necessary for his own healing; Adam knew the failure to forgive could leave one bitter and cynical and spiteful.

A few clouds scudded overhead and wild flowers adorned the roadside. It reminded him of Maude's editorial: *The redolence of spring with its promise of renewal…shouts its affirmation. But evil is all around us and rears its blighted head, a reminder of man's failure and futility…and the voice of the Turtle Dove is heard throughout the land… God, dear god, help us all.*

After crossing the bridge, Adam caught a glimpse of the city's skyline. He relished the thought of Ruth and Robin joining him for the remainder of his tenure at Tulane. And he was excited about his research, convinced that he could prove his premise: that certain viruses damage the heart, then demonstrate the mechanism by which that occurred. Nor would he forget Frank Markham at Slim's Seafood Grill or Tony Caruso and his evil empire; the staggering price of victory that meant a finer, safer Conway. And, of course, Allison…dear, sweet Allison would never be forgotten; tucked safely away in his bank of memories.

With the sun at an angle, glare bounced off the pavement and caused him to squint. He reached into the console and retrieved his dark glasses. A cloud passed over the sun causing the windshield to shadow. In that fleeting moment, he caught a reflection, an arresting face. Was it his imagination…or something more?

"Could it have been Grace?" he wondered.

Something stirred inside; that feeling again.

And he remembered his promise, to tell her the whole story.

CPSIA information can be obtained at www.ICGtesting.com
224749LV00003B/20/P

9 781450 281126